Also by Marie Harte

Smooth Moves

MARIE HARTE

sourcebooks
casablanca

Published by Sourcebooks Casablanca, an imprint of Sourcebooks
P.O. Box 4410, Naperville, Illinois 60567-4410
(630) 961-3900
sourcebooks.com

Printed and bound in the United States of America.
OPM 10 9 8 7 6 5 4 3 2 1

To DT and RC.
And to Marines everywhere.
Thank you.

Chapter 1

LATE JUNE IN SEATTLE SOMETIMES DELIVERED THE HEAT. Cash Griffith looked up. Just his luck—thick, dark gray clouds converged overhead, heavy with the promise of rain.

He rubbed the back of his neck, his nerves stretched thin on this particular moving job.

From hell.

He forced himself back inside the large Miller house, now marked with a FOR SALE sign out front. The place would no doubt sell for big money, a posh spread like this in Madison Park just a few blocks from Lake Washington. Cash could maybe afford to *rent* a house a quarter of this size, and certainly not in this area. It gave him the jitters being around money and class. Both of which he had in little abundance.

And he was just fine with that.

Getting back to work, he did his best to avoid the problem areas in the home—namely, anyone connected to the name Miller.

"Yo, you ready?" he asked Hector, who stood at the other end of a heavy-ass curio cabinet that had to have cost a fortune. They carefully walked it out of the dining room and through the kitchen to the mudroom and then maneuvered it down the ramp they'd placed over the steps leading into the attached garage. They'd have to find a spot in there to regroup, where they could wrap the curio in blankets. Then they'd only have to take a few steps outside, leading up the ramp into the moving truck, which they'd backed in the Millers' long, wide driveway. At least this way they didn't have far to go when loading. The only plus Cash had seen thus far on the job.

Screams and laughter came from somewhere behind him, making him think of the telltale theme from *Jaws* as it grew nearer, signaling the return of a monster.

"Hurry up," Hector warned as they paused inside the garage. "I think the kids are coming back."

"Put it here." Heidi waved them over before walking back outside to catalog the boxes and other items already on the lawn.

They moved the curio to where Heidi had indicated and set it down gently.

Hector bent over, panting. "Jesus, is this thing made of iron or wood?" Considering Hector had considerable strength, on par with Cash's even, the mass of the cabinet was truly astounding.

Cash grunted and flexed his hands. "More like gold, considering what Judy Miller said it would cost to replace." And she hadn't been the least bit subtle about how important her dead mother's things were to her.

Cash wished he could relate, but the only things his recently deceased mother had left him were nightmares and a house that caused tension between him and his brother.

A shrieking demon raced into the garage, circled around Hector twice, then ran away after shooting Cash between the eyes with a squirt gun. *Damn it*.

Hector laughed as Cash wiped his face. "Aw, ain't that cute? Demon Spawn number 1 likes you."

They'd taken to calling the kid that after hearing his own mother yell the same thing when said spawn destroyed an expensive vase on a tear through the house, trying to track down his bratty twin.

Something inside crashed, and he heard Jordan yell at the boy to slow down before he hurt himself. More power to her. If anyone could get that kid to slow down, it was the sexy ex-Army MP.

He frowned at himself, mentally removed the word *sexy*, and tried to focus on the job and not his recollection of the way Jordan filled out a pair of shorts.

He and Hector wrapped the curio and a few large dressers and chairs in blankets then brought a few more of the Millers' more expensive pieces into the garage before Heidi rejoined them. Once satisfied the items had been properly protected, she started directing them into the moving truck.

Vets on the Go! employed military veterans and provided the citizens of Seattle exceptional service for their local moving needs. Business was booming, and in order to keep it thriving, Cash had been ordered to keep his big mouth shut and let his muscles do his talking for him. Difficult, but he'd been adapting.

Though Cash was the oldest, his younger brother, Reid, had taken their company from small and barely managing to a real success. So Cash did his best to keep his opinions to himself and packed, lifted, and moved.

He took a step back and nearly fell on his ass when a skateboard slid out from underneath him. From the direction of the house he heard snickering. *Those freakin' kids*. Cash swore, wishing Mrs. Miller had listened the first three times Hector, Heidi, and Jordan had politely asked her to keep her twins safely out of the way and pen up the damn dog. He'd have said something too, but it wouldn't have been polite or pleasant, so he'd let the others say it for him.

Something licked his leg.

Cash grimaced and glanced down at an adorable yellow lab that didn't understand the word *no*. "Crap. Not you again." Helpless to stop himself, he leaned down to give the canine a pat behind the ears. The dog huffed and flopped to his back, exposing a fuzzy belly.

"Sucker." Hector tried not to smile.

"Please. I've seen you wrestling with this little guy twice today."

"Well, he's loveable. And I have a heart."

Cash straightened and managed to avoid an unpleasant canine nip. He looked down at Hector, and a petty part of him liked looming over the guy. By a few inches, but still. "You're saying I *don't* have a heart?"

"What you don't have is a concept of time," came the husky grouse from behind him. "Look, Cash, play with the dog later," Jordan ordered. "It's going to rain any minute now, and Judy Miller wants this stuff out of here today. She refuses to let us come back in the morning, when it's supposed to be sunny, to finish. I think being here is hard for her."

"It's hard for me," he muttered and nearly tripped over the skateboard again, which at least sent the dog racing away.

Jordan placed her hands on her hips and scowled at him. "Yeah? Suck it up, princess. And quit playing around." She glanced at the skateboard and sniffed.

He heard Hector snicker but couldn't take his

attention from Jordan. "*Playing around?* I nearly killed myself on that thing."

"All the more reason to keep moving so we can get out of here in one piece." She cringed when the dog barked and peals of creepy childhood laughter echoed inside. "Poor Judy keeps breaking down in tears." She lowered her voice. "And you assholes keep sticking me with her. I feel for the woman, but her husband should really be the one here helping her. I feel like I'm making everything worse every time I tell her things will get better."

Yet Jordan would do whatever she could to help Judy because Jordan was like that. Caring and concerned yet hard as nails when it came to dealing with him and the guys.

A more detailed study revealed feminine curves under her shapeless Vets on the Go! T-shirt. Something he shouldn't notice of a coworker.

And besides, she clearly wasn't his type. Jordan didn't have blond hair and huge breasts. Wasn't too tall and didn't act all breathy, batting her eyelashes at him and making him believe he was a god. Which, in the sack, he sure the hell was.

Still, something about her had been on his last goddamn nerve from day one. A sizzle of attraction. A spark whenever they accidentally touched. And she made him laugh with that huge attitude stuffed in a tiny, appealing package.

He stared at her from under his lashes, pretending to be focused on the small but heavy butcher-block island he'd just wrapped while subtly cataloging Jordan Fleming's finer assets. Five and a half feet tall, if that. Athletic, toned, with shaggy, shoulder-length black hair loosely tied back in a ponytail. The ex-Army soldier acted like everyone's buddy and tolerated Cash more than most without getting her panties in a twist.

He glanced up from her tanned, muscular legs showing under her knee-length shorts and saw more annoyance. He bit back a sigh.

"Take a picture next time," she growled. "It'll last longer."

Hector snickered.

Cash blinked, pretending innocence. "I'm sorry, what?"

"Jordan?" Judy Miller called, interrupting. She appeared in the doorway of the mudroom and smiled with relief. "Oh, there you are. Would you help me with Mom's jewelry?"

Jordan pasted on a smile. "Sure thing. Just making sure we're almost ready to add more to the truck."

"Oh, lovely. We really need to—" With a mother's instinct, Judy hurried back inside, yelling, "Alex, stop that right now! Put your brother down before you hurt someone."

Jordan turned, took several steps toward him, and poked Cash in the chest.

"Ow." He rubbed the spot, impressed by the strength in that small finger.

"Hurry. Up," she said between gritted teeth, but he saw the smile she tried to hide. She pointed to Hector. "And you too, sailor boy. Or I'll tell the twins about *your* twin. And gee, wouldn't you just love to hang around with the boys while the rest of us finish this job?"

"Oh, uh, no problem. We're moving." Hector rushed past her into the house.

"You're good." Cash grinned at Jordan.

"I know. Now please, for the love of God, hurry up so we can get the hell out of here." She left him to help Judy.

Cash needed to get past this—whatever *this* was—for the woman.

Firmly placing Jordan in the back of his mind, he worked with Hector to stage more furniture and boxes on the lawn, narrowly avoiding the demon twins and the dog time and time again. Cash liked to think of himself as a simple guy. He'd more than once been labeled nothing more than walking muscle.

At six four and built like a tank, he used his body daily, either working out or at the day job. Many found him considerably less refined—some said less intelligent—than Reid. Again, Cash didn't mind, pleased to leave the running of the business to those better suited to it. He hated the thought of a desk job, preferring to get his hands dirty in their family-owned local moving company. Life in the Marine Corps had been all he'd wanted. Until the end, of course. Dicked over by some screwed-up shit he'd had the gall to report to the authorities.

The past two years in the civilian world had been... challenging. But now he had work he actually liked. A job he'd held onto for more than a year. And he had yet to strangle any of his coworkers or clients.

The dog nipped at his calf, finding flesh, and darted away.

Cash added under his breath, "Or dogs. I haven't strangled any of them yet." Cute and furry was one thing, but those teeth stung.

Next to him, Hector frowned. "You say something?"

Heidi walked by, muttering about the unwise decision to stage things on the lawn. He agreed.

"So Heidi," Cash asked as he picked up a heavy box to load into the truck. "Did you see what Latoya did to Michele last night? Shoved her nearly off the catwalk." A love of reality television had bonded them. That, and a love for the Marine Corps, since Heidi had done her time in both the Navy and the USMC.

Heidi grew animated. He could tell because she actually said more than two words at one go. "Yes. I watched that and the aftershow," the tall blond said with enthusiasm, her German accent thick. "I can't believe Roger lets her get away with that nonsense."

Hector watched them with a grimace.

"What?"

"How do you watch that crap?" he asked Cash. "And more, why do you admit it?"

Cash shrugged. "I'm not embarrassed to watch only the most amazing show on television."

Hector smirked. "*The Real Housewives of Seattle*?"

Heidi frowned. "There is such a show? Because Cash is talking about—"

"What, are they arguing the merits of organic over GMO quinoa?" Hector was on a roll. "Next Level Burger over Mickey D's?"

From what Cash knew, the vegan "burgers" were pretty damn tasty. Not real meat, but they'd fooled Reid a few times. "Well, actually, I like—"

"Did you see a fistfight over a line at Whole Foods? Oh, wait. I know. Had to be a brutal disagreement between a Starbucks lover and some indie coffee shop junkie. Oh, the drama." He started laughing but quickly moved out of the way as Jordan returned.

She handed Cash a box. "This is full of jewelry, so

put this with the other things Judy's taking home in her car tonight."

They'd sectioned off a corner of the garage for those kinds of items.

Cash gave her a salute since she just loved bossing him around.

Jordan smirked at him. "Nice to see you can take orders." He waited for it. "For a Marine."

Heidi snorted. "For a man, you mean." She left the garage as thunder rumbled, signaling the coming rain.

"Aren't you two hilarious?" Cash could deal with less trash talk about his Corps, but Jordan had already turned to leave. And he sure did like watching her walk away.

"No, Cash." Hector shook his head. "Just…no."

He'd been hearing that from Reid for a while too. Cash shrugged. "What? I'm not doing anything. Just looking, man. Just looking." He and Hector started walking the heavier items into the truck. Thank God for that ramp. "So do you want to hear about Charlene and Tara or not?"

Hector shook his head, saw that they were alone, and leaned in to murmur, "Okay, tell me. I don't really care though. I'm just humoring you."

Cash smirked. "Sure you are."

—◆◆◆—

Jordan left Cash and Hector, wondering how the pair had managed to keep their cool for as long as they had. Judy Miller was a nice enough woman, and Jordan felt for her, dealing with the passing of both her parents in the span of a few months. But the woman's six-year-olds were terrible. They didn't listen, backtalked, and had nearly injured themselves several times. Only by sheer luck had they managed to avoid broken bones.

Jordan had tried, unsuccessfully, to get Judy to take her boys home or to her sister's house. But Judy remained adamant they stay with her to say goodbye to Nana.

Jordan found Judy sobbing in her mother's bedroom.

"Oh, Judy, it will be oka—"

Alex—or was that Jacob?—smacked Jordan in the back of the leg with a sword. The twins had fashioned a weapon out of their grandfather's bamboo cane. She swallowed a snarl because it *hurt* and yanked the cane out of his hands. As close as she'd come to thumping both boys on the behind, she'd refrained. Judy didn't need more drama on top of her grief. Then there was the fact that Jordan could do without an assault charge for disciplining someone else's kids.

"Come on, guys," Jordan tried. "Why don't you go get Buster and play outside and get messy? I think it's going to rain."

Their eyes lit up. "Okay," one of them said and ran away, followed closely by his twin.

Judy blew her nose and ignored the situation with her children. "It was just so sudden. Mom was fine one day then gone the next." A frail woman with soft, smooth hands that had likely never seen a day of hard labor, Judy possessed an air of gentility that made Jordan want to protect her. From what Judy had said, she'd grown up fairly well-to-do, married her attorney husband Gerald, and lived happily ever after since, caring for her family.

"I can't believe little Edith will grow up not knowing her grandma." Judy patted her flat tummy.

"Oh, when are you due?" Great. Jordan hadn't

realized the woman might be even more emotional due to pregnancy. Man, now she felt even worse for her uncharitable thoughts about Judy's mothering skills.

Overhead, thunder boomed.

"In January," Judy murmured. "Oh no. The rain's here, isn't it?"

Which is what we tried to tell you before you insisted on us laying out your mother's prized possessions on the front lawn. "Yes."

"We'd better hurry to get everything in the garage!" Judy had been adamant she'd wanted to organize the move, and to do so she'd wanted to see everything lined up together before the truck was loaded. Since the only way to do that was to move it all outside, the crew had accommodated her. Even though they'd all mentioned, more than once, the threat of rain.

Judy and Jordan hurried outside to see the skies open up. Heidi, Hector, and Cash double-timed through the drenching rain to protect everything with tarps while simultaneously bringing in boxes and furniture into the crowded garage. They'd already moved at least half of the large items into the truck, so they'd have space in the garage to fit the rest. Jordan hoped.

In the front yard, away from the mess, the boys and their dog played. Thank God at least the kids stayed away, frolicking in the growing wet.

Cash swore and slicked his hair back, and Jordan tried really hard not to ogle the man. But the rain made it difficult to ignore the crew's fine physiques—at least, that was her excuse.

Hell, even grieving Judy gave the gang a second glance. Heidi had an attractive if cool exterior, a tall

Nordic blond with a bodybuilder's tone and striking bright-blue eyes. Hector was stunning, his dark skin defining his heavy muscle, his laughing eyes and wide smile a draw no matter where he went. His charming, open personality provided a nice counterbalance to Heidi's brisk, no-nonsense approach.

And then there was Cash. Part owner of the company, yet he worked alongside the guys as if just another employee. All too easily she imagined former Gunnery Sergeant Cash Griffith in uniform. Sadly, she'd noticed everything about the man from day one. Cash exuded leadership. Though what normally came out of his mouth was either crass, obnoxious, or rude, he made people laugh and somehow *want* to follow him. Hell, he annoyed her to no end, but she could see his natural fit for command.

He had legs like tree trunks, a broad chest, and thickly muscled arms she'd dreamed of holding her more than once. His short, dark hair spoke of time in the military, kept trim but not buzzed short. And that stubborn jaw had tempted her more than once to punch it then kiss it better.

Cash's bright-green eyes seemed to be constantly on her, filling her with heat.

As they were now.

She pretended she hadn't been staring at him so hard, and he snorted. The big, bad man who intimidated most others didn't frighten her in the slightest. Because Cash was a protector at heart. He might swear, act gruff, and loom over everyone with that condescending smirk, but he was always the first in line to offer to help.

And he hadn't lashed out at the kids all day, when he'd had plenty of opportunity to do so. Especially now. She groaned. "Judy, am I seeing things, or did the boys just go inside the truck?"

Judy frowned. "They were told not to do that."

Several times today. "Hey, Cash. The boys are—"

"I see them," he snarled. Apparently, he'd reached his limit. He stalked inside the truck, and she heard, "That's it! You two, out, now. And take your dog with you. This is no place for kids."

Silence reigned for a moment.

"You can get hurt if—"

Something crashed, the dog bolted, and the boys screamed. Not a *we're-having-fun* yell but the scared kind.

Everyone rushed to the truck, and Hector, closest to the ramp, hurried inside first.

"My babies!" Judy cried, but Heidi held her back from entering.

Jordan gasped. Inside, Cash looked like Atlas, crouched and holding the weight of a large grandfather clock on his broad shoulders and upper back while one of the boys lay under him, frozen in fear.

The other twin stood on a couch behind the overturned furniture, staring in shock.

Hector rushed to pull the boys out while Jordan helped a visibly straining Cash edge the clock off his shoulder.

"Why did the kids have to tip this thing over? Why not the lamp that weighs ten pounds? Oh my God. This is heavy." She couldn't believe he'd been holding it, crouched as he was, off the boy.

"No shit, Sherlock," he said through gritted teeth.

Her own shoulders ached as she laughed. "Okay, okay. Don't be so dramatic." She paused then added the ultimate insult, "Nancy."

He laughed. "You're such a pain in my ass."

"Ditto."

Then Hector and Heidi were there, easing the furniture and a few other skewed pieces back into place.

Once everyone had exited the truck back into the shelter of the garage, Heidi glared at the twins, her accent growing thicker the madder she became. "I *told you* not to play in there. Nothing is strapped down yet. You could have been hurt."

The boys looked a lot more sulky than sorry, reminding Jordan of her own brother. *Rafi*, who'd taken money from her wallet. *Rafi*, who'd involved himself with a questionable bunch of teens. *Rafi*, who seemed to be on the verge of throwing his entire future away. *Rafi*, who needed a firm kick in his teenage ass.

Sorry, Judy. This has to be done. Jordan stepped forward and grabbed each boy by the neck of his T-shirt, yanking him forward. She glared into their beady little eyes. "That. Is. *It!* If Cash hadn't been there, one of you might have been seriously hurt. Or crushed."

"Or dead," Cash said bluntly. "That clock weighs a ton, enough to crush a tiny little skull for sure. You ever seen brains leak out of your head, kid? It's gross."

"*Ja*. And messy," Heidi added, her face stiff.

Hector pinched the bridge of his nose, and Jordan felt for him, sensing her own headache coming on.

The twins flinched. *Finally*.

She dragged them closer. "You will now thank Cash for saving your sorry little asses."

They stared at her with wide eyes. Judy blinked at her through tears.

"And you will apologize to your mother for worrying her. She just lost your nana. She doesn't want to lose you too. *Look at her.*" She shook them, not hard but enough to get their attention. "She's worried about you."

Judy had been silently crying.

The boys lowered their heads in shame. Jordan heard sniffles. If only it were that easy to get her brother in line.

"We're sorry, Mom."

"Yeah. We're sorry."

Jordan nudged them toward Judy. "Now you go give her a hug. Then you stay with her. Because if you don't, Cash is going to paddle your butts until you can't sit for a week. And your mom won't even mind."

Cash flexed his huge hands, and Jordan saw the boys' fright. Heck, she wouldn't want to be spanked by a hand that large either.

Well…No. No I wouldn't.

"We have a job to do. Judy, please go on inside and get dry. Watch some TV or play a game and try to relax. I'll come get you when we're ready for you."

"But—"

"*Now,* Judy." Jordan wore her military police face, the one that said *I'm tired of fucking around.*

Judy swallowed. "Okay." Before she went inside, she crossed to Cash and gave him a quick hug.

He froze.

"Thank you for saving Alex."

He mumbled something but didn't move.

She left with her boys and the crazy dog in tow.

Jordan turned to see everyone staring at her. "What?"

Cash, instead of seeming grateful, looked agitated. "Why the hell didn't you do that at the start of our day?" He stomped out to the lawn, moving more items into the garage and continuing to swear.

"Don't mind him." Hector held out his hand for a high five that Jordan slapped. "He's just embarrassed we saw him being a good guy."

Heidi nodded then gave a sly smile. "I shall go and tell him how wonderful he is."

"Oh, good idea. Me too." Hector laughed. "Thanks, Jordan. You really made my day."

She stared at the backs of her teammates and heard Cash swear at their many compliments. "I'm working with a bunch of wackos for sure." But she laughed as she moved to help them.

Jordan tried not to stare at Cash and his tight, wet clothes for the rest of the day.

And failed miserably.

Chapter 2

THE NEXT DAY PASSED MUCH THE WAY TUESDAY HAD, THEIR stay extended at the Millers' thanks to the rain. To Cash's relief, the kids and the dog stayed well away from the property. They finished the job and split the team to cover more moves. For some reason, Reid had paired Jordan up with the new guy—Smith Ramsey, asshole extraordinaire.

At the day's end, Cash found his brother in the office. He had to bite back what he'd planned to say when he saw Reid was not alone. Instead, he took a seat opposite his brother, watching as a leggy redhead leaned against Reid's desk. She sparkled with a vibrant personality and killer smile.

He muttered, "Oh, it's you."

Naomi Starr had been laughing at something Reid said and turned to regard Cash with a raised brow. "And hello to you too."

Cash gave her a weak wave, fuming as he stared at Reid. Normally he'd go off on the guy, but he didn't want to throw any kinks in the works between Reid and his new girlfriend. They'd had a rocky patch a few weeks back, and Cash liked his brother actually having a life despite Reid being such a dick lately.

Reid smiled back at Naomi, and Cash felt a pang at seeing how well the pair fit. Both smart and driven, dedicated to their work and to each other. Cash had a sinking feeling they'd end up getting married. He'd met a few of Reid's old girlfriends, and none of them came anywhere close to Naomi Starr in looks, character, or that smokin'-hot body.

"Anytime you want to stop leering," she said, sounding coldly amused.

Reid frowned. "Not *any*time. Quit eye-fuc—ah, eye-balling her *now*."

Cash held up his hands in surrender, watching the lovesick pair.

Naomi chuckled. "Nice catch, Reid." She leaned down to kiss him, and Cash quickly glanced away, weird about catching a glimpse of her fine ass since she belonged to his brother.

At the thought of a fine ass, Jordan immediately came to mind.

No, no. Jordan isn't attractive. She's an employee. A moving buddy. Just some chick who works with me.

More like *for* him, but Cash made a distinction with everyone. Working alongside the guys on a daily basis, he deferred to Reid on most business decisions, preferring to get his hands dirty as just another employee—one who owned a piece of the company pie, but a small piece.

Naomi left the office, answering a call on her phone.

Reid regarded him with a quizzical expression, younger by two years yet always acting so much more mature.

"What?"

"I've said your name twice already. You high or something?"

Cash flushed. "Ass. You know I don't do drugs." The occasional beer, but that was as hard as Cash hit anything addictive. He prized being in control of himself. Growing up the way he had, he needed control to feel sane.

Which brought to mind a conversation they needed to have, but one he'd been putting off. Fucking family drama. Even dead and gone, his mother continued to annoy him. "Ah, I, well… I need to talk to you about something."

Reid shook his head. "Let me stop you before you get started. Jordan and Smith work well together. Like you, he has a tendency to alienate others. Yet he's worked well with her before."

"What?" Not the conversation Cash had expected.

"We need everyone working this week. We're tapped on time and jobs, and Bro, we are seeing a real *profit*." Reid perked up, his gray eyes bright with excitement. Like Cash, he had dark hair and the Griffith good looks. But he didn't have the breadth of muscle and height Cash had. No one would ever confuse them for twins, but they for sure looked enough alike to pass as siblings.

"Yeah, that's great." Cash paused, rationalizing his need to avoid the uncomfortable topic of their mother with the more important here and now—the job. "But I thought the teams were my responsibility. I had them all planned out."

"They were. Until you kept pairing yourself with Hector or Jordan on the smaller jobs. We need our experienced movers with the newbies, just to make sure we can trust them. That way in the future we know they're doing what they need to do when not supervised." A good point. Then Reid ruined it by sounding dictatorial. "Spread the love, man. The only guys I agree should stick tight are Martin and Tim. I don't know how they do it, but they're our most effective unit."

"That's because Martin talks for them both and Tim's a workhorse. Bastard can probably lift as much as me."

"High praise," Reid agreed.

They grinned, then Cash remembered to be annoyed. "Look, I appreciate you doing all the office paperwork crap—"

"Because you refuse to do it, and Evan hasn't quite cut the cord with his job yet."

"—but you know the people side of Vets on the Go! is mine." At Reid's raised brow, he amended, "The people side as in who I work with, not the annoying customers."

Reid's lips quirked, but he didn't quite smile. "Speaking of annoying, maybe you and Smith should go out and get to know each other better."

"Now who's high? I'll kill the asshole if I'm near him for more than two seconds."

"Jordan doesn't mind him."

Cash glared, not liking the reminder. "Jordan's too nice for her own good." Something he'd never thought he'd say. "Look, if we're so busy that we all need to be out in pairs, you know it makes sense to pair me with someone I work well with."

Reid checked his notes. "How about Finley?"

Finley, an ex-Navy Master at Arms, what the Navy called its military police, had a decent sense of humor and an affinity for magic tricks. Weird and mostly harmless. But he sure didn't fill out a pair of shorts like Jordan. "Fine. I'll go out with Finley, but if he tries pulling a quarter out of his ass, I'm done with him."

Reid chuckled. "Better his ass than yours."

"Which is what I told him the first time he tried to impress me."

Reid kept laughing until Cash pointed out that the stack of invoices on Reid's desk hadn't gone down any since the day before.

"Yeah, well…" Reid studied the papers and groaned. "What else is new? Oh, and so you know, I'll be at Naomi's tonight."

Nothing Cash hadn't already anticipated. Squelching the idea he was starting to lose his brother, he nodded and left. He jumped in his car, having the perfect excuse now to get things done. Cash would go to their mother's, and Reid wouldn't be reminded of the old house and the issues that came with it, leaving Cash to clear out all of their mother's things.

At the thought, Cash drifted back to that dark place in his mind, hating the feeling but unable to make it go away. *Worthless. A waste of space. Should never have had you, you damn sorry prick. You're nothing more than a mistake.* His father's voice and his mother's avoidance never failed to leave their impact, especially at thoughts of going home. Something he thought he'd never do again.

Yet following the death of their mother a month ago, he'd learned the shocking, disturbing truth: their mother had left her property and everything that came with it to *him,* the same child she'd ignored for the past twenty-plus years.

He and Reid still didn't understand it. Even their cousin Evan, the decidedly brightest Griffith of the bunch, had no idea why she'd done it.

For the first seven years of his life, Cash had been loved by Angela and Charles Griffith. He and Reid had shared an idyllic boyhood. Until something happened that to this day he still didn't understand. He could remember the sun shining, a hint of lavender in the air, and the sound of a favorite cartoon in the background. Then the hatred in his father's eyes and the immediate reversal of everything good in his life, including the gradual decline of Angela as she ignored the family more and more until Cash might as well have ceased to exist.

Angela even ignored Reid, the golden child, lost in her soap operas, books, and television. The woman preferred fantasy over reality, and the shell of the mother she used to be literally hurt to remember.

He and Reid had speculated about what might have caused the huge rift, though, come to think of it, Angela had never been too firmly planted in the here and now even before that traumatic day.

Had it been a massive fight about finances? Secret debt? A secret baby? Unfaithfulness? That Cash and Reid had different fathers would make sense. Except they looked too much alike, and Charles had never thrown the question of Cash's parentage in his face. His old man had called him every name under the sun. He'd been verbally abusive, at times physically abusive, and had never held back from telling Cash how little he mattered. Yet the old man hadn't mentioned infidelity.

As Cash pulled onto the cracked driveway of his mother's house—*his* house now—he wondered how much it was worth, located as it was in West Woodland. The woman had lived in it for more than forty years until she'd needed assistance with the day to day, unable to care for herself. With no friends, her husband deceased, and her sons away in the Marine Corps, she'd checked herself into a care facility where she'd lived until just recently.

From what Cash and Reid knew, their Aunt Jane had visited her a few times over the years, though the women, sisters-in-law, weren't close. In addition to seeing her boys once a month the past two years, Angela had apparently possessed one friend, a mystery woman who'd helped her take care of legal matters. Something they'd only recently found out when their mother died.

From the lawyer's reading of the will, they'd learned their mother had given some money away to charity, the rest to pay her bills, and a small bit to take care of her property. But the majority of her "wealth" lay in the real estate Cash, not Reid, now owned.

He knew it had shaken his brother to be cut off so unexpectedly, especially because Angela had always seemed to favor her younger son. She'd been distant but affectionate…when she knew who he was. Reid had truly loved the woman no matter what. A good son, Cash thought. Not like the older loser with attitude.

With Cash, Angela had been there and not there. Never mean but cruel all the same in her neglect.

He knew his younger self must have done something to push her over the edge. Because try as he might, he couldn't dismiss the reality that he *was* the loser his father had always accused him of being. He just liked to pretend to the world, and himself, that he could be so much more.

Since Angela's funeral, he'd only been by once to test the keys, but he hadn't been able to stomach being in the home that held so many bad memories. He knew he needed to clear the place out. Maybe then he and Reid could turn the house around and sell it for a profit.

If not for the fact an old Marine Corps buddy was

renting them their current house for cheap, things might have been tough. Instead, they lived comfortably. Although...now with Angela's place paid off and the title theirs, they had another option—to move in and live rent free.

Cash stared at the cracked front door and felt like an idiot for procrastinating. He let himself into the house he dreaded entering.

It smelled musty. Old. Dust and cobwebs had accumulated. He opened windows and the back door to let in some fresh air.

A glance around showed worn furniture, ugly wood paneling, faded green walls, and a tacky, rose-floral wallpaper that used to mesmerize him as a kid. Cash would sit in the corner and count the mini pink roses on lime-green vines that ran up and down the walls while being punished for one infraction or another. Truth be told, he'd preferred the silent treatment of the corner to his father's verbal assaults. Only once had his father left major bruises, when Cash had been in high school. But before that, the threat of a slap or punch to the gut had scared him all the same.

He studied the tears in the wallpaper and the listing framed posters of old movies and soap opera stars and cringed. Cash, who had little in the way of taste, knew the house needed help. A few coats of paint, new flooring, some decluttering, and it just might be livable.

As he toured through the place, he found Angela's bedroom as it had been back when he'd left more than a decade ago, chockful of VCR tapes, two old TVs— the kind with the cathode-ray tubes, making them super bulky—and rows upon rows of books, tchotchkes, and creepy dolls. Not the collectible kind but the one-plastic-eye-is-half-open kind.

With his parents deceased, the house felt both empty and tainted by the haunting notes of apathy. The shadow of neglect continued to cling to the present, a testament that as much as he tried, he hadn't yet outrun the past.

He continued through the hallway beyond his mother's bedroom. To his surprise, Reid's room retained his stamp, filled with trophies, old jerseys, and clear containers of his old toys. As if his brother had never left. Yet a door down, Cash's room had been wiped clean of his presence and stuffed full of Angela's fantasy life in fictional media—piled high with more books, videotapes, and boxes.

A pang of anger then grief filled him, having been erased from this house filled with bitter memories. Then he drew a deep breath and let it out. Time instead to focus on the present and, hopefully, the future.

He headed to the garage and found a bunch of cardboard boxes and a roll of heavy-duty trash bags. The garage itself remained, to his surprise, fairly empty except for an expected buildup of dust and dirt.

He returned to his old room and started packing. Because that room still belonged to him, deep down, and he reserved the right to do whatever the hell he wanted in *his room*.

"Hell. Day or night, I'm on the job," he mused. But this time he missed having a partner. If he'd had his choice, he'd have chosen the mouthy ex-Army soldier to help him pack. Jordan had a gift for making things fit. Her nimble hands tucked away treasures into containers with both respect and skill. That, and she made him laugh with that sarcastic sense of humor that always lightened his mood.

She'd have made this chore easier. And harder because being near her caused his heart to race for no good reason. She distracted him with that light floral scent that caused other parts of him to get as excited.

He sighed, knowing his life had to pale in comparison to hers. No doubt she was hanging with a bunch of friends or sharing a meal with her family while he packed away his dead mother's most prized possessions.

Well, at least one of them would enjoy some peace before the workday began again in the morning.

––––––

Jordan glared at her younger brother, wishing her parents had done a little more to stick it out and help their youngest child instead of giving up at the first sign of trouble. Okay, not exactly fair. Rafi had been a major pain for months, but still. Maria and Carl Younger had a tendency to give up when the going got tough. Though she loved her mother and stepfather, sometimes she didn't like them very much. And her sister... Jordan refused to think about Leanne at the moment, sure her head would explode if she did.

She glared at the sulky teenager, glad the handsome punk hadn't yet gotten in trouble with girls. At this point, she could barely handle bad grades and an attitude, let alone the scare of teen pregnancy. "Really, Rafi? An F? You're so much smarter than that!"

Her fifteen-year-old brother shrugged. "Simpson is a dick who doesn't care if we learn or not."

"The comments on your quiz show you didn't do your homework to prepare. How is that him not caring?"

Rafi glared. "What the hell do you know about it? You're not there."

"No, because I'm a grown woman who did her time in school already," she said slowly, praying she could manage to keep her hands from encircling his skinny neck.

Like Jordan, Rafi took after their mother, dark-haired and with a skin tone that always looked tan. When Jordan and Leanne's father had died twenty years before, their mother had remarried a lovely man in Carl Younger. Carl, like Jordan and Leanne's father, had Norwegian ancestry. Carl and Leanne looked more alike than the rest of them. Which might have accounted for the reason her parents treated Leanne as if she could do no wrong and Jordan and Rafi like problem children.

Jordan had been a typical teenager. Not a trouble-maker, not really. But not exactly agreeable either. Jordan liked to ask questions, to disagree, to argue with things that didn't make sense. So did Rafi. But her idiot brother took it a step further. He'd been hanging with a few boys of questionable reputation, getting in trouble at school, and not doing his work.

After blowing up a toilet in the boys' bathroom months ago, he'd been suspended from school for a week. His grades, already teetering below average, had plummeted. By the end of the school year, he hadn't managed to bring up his grades. Hence his stint in summer school to hopefully make up for his poor performance in his sophomore year. It was either that or the military academy her parents had researched. While

Jordan thought the military might help her brother, she thought it should be his choice, not a mandate.

Thus she'd stepped in (because Princess Leanne certainly hadn't). "Look, Rafi. You know the score. You either do well this summer at school or you go to that military academy. Mom and Dad aren't playing." She blew out a frustrated breath. "I'm trying to help you, sweetie."

He glared, but she saw a suspicious shine in his eyes. "Yeah? Because I heard you on the phone. Oh sure, I know how much you're helping. How much you *don't want me here!*"

"That's not true." Well, it wasn't true when he acted like the baby brother who'd once hugged and kissed his bigger sister. This hormonal, angry teenager she didn't know anymore. "I was arguing with Mom about you because you need more help than I can give you." And more money, but her parents weren't budging on that. If she wanted to help her brother, it was all on her, financially and emotionally, because they wanted him to get outside help, away from those who might "coddle him." After only four weeks, she'd felt the strain. "I love you, Rafi, but—"

"Rafael. Not Rafi," he corrected.

She took a deep breath and refused to be baited into a fight. "*Rafael.* Sorry. I love you and want what's best for you. You don't see it now because summer school sucks and you just want to party all day."

He scoffed. "Party? Yeah, right. I just want to do what I'm good at."

"Your art? You refused to take lessons." Her brother had real artistic talent. Ever since he'd been little, he'd been able to recreate any image with a pencil and paper.

His portraits were on par with those she'd seen in art exhibits, but when she tried to guide him toward embracing his talents, he shrugged them off as a silly hobby.

"Not that." He snorted. "That's just for fun."

She groaned. "Not that stupid video game."

"It's not stupid. People make money live-streaming! My friend Daniel said he makes serious cash doing it."

"Oh, right. Daniel, the kid who lives in a regular house in Fremont? The kid who does nothing but play video games all day long when his sister isn't nagging him to stop? Even you said he was a hopeless nerd with no social skills."

He flushed. "Well, yeah, but he's making bank." At her raised brow, he amended, "Well, he knows people who make bank. Besides, I don't need a diploma to get a job."

"Rafi, you're smart. You know as well as I do that the majority of online gamers make nothing. We aren't rich. You don't have millionaire parents who are going to buy you a gaming system or a Porsche or pay for you to go to Stanford when the time comes."

"Daniel doesn't have any of that. And Stanford is a nerd school," he muttered.

"Those nerds get high-paying jobs. Hello? Dad went to Stanford."

"Um, Dad's a nerd."

"An employed, financially comfortable nerd," she fumed. *Idiot.*

"Hate to break it to you, Jordan. But we aren't rich."

She clenched her fists. "That's not the point—and what I just said! You have to work for what you earn in this life. I did. Mom did. Carl did. Leanne…" She paused. Bad example, which he quickly pointed out.

"Ha! Leanne does shit and gets whatever she wants."

Sadly, that was true. "Watch your language." She paused to regroup. "Leanne graduated high school and college with honors. No one gave her those grades." Actually, her old PE teacher might have fudged a few because Leanne had been "sick" for a lot of those gym classes back in the day. "She has a great job and independence because—"

"Mom and Dad love her best," he said quietly. "Yeah, I know. They're always comparing us both to her. Just because she's blond and pretty and has a rich fiancé, they think she shits rainbows."

"Rafi!" She had to bite her lip to keep from agreeing because the kid was spot-on.

"It's not fair. I try. I hate math! I hate science. It's confusing. I just want to do other stuff, but they harp on everything I do that's wrong."

"They wouldn't bug you about school if you weren't getting in trouble so much, and you know it." She noticed he didn't argue that point. Her brother might be a pain in the ass, but he had intelligence and a smart sense of humor. Heck, he'd been reading at a college level since the sixth grade. If she could get him through this rough patch, she knew he'd turn out all right. She prayed... "Come on, Rafi—Rafael," she corrected herself before he could. "Isn't the tutoring making things easier?"

Another reason she had to work so hard. Tutoring didn't come cheap.

He didn't answer, but he seemed to be listening.

"Look. Get through summer school. You have to. I'm your last hope, buddy." She drew him in for a hug. At first he resisted, but when she kissed his cheek, he relented, sagging in her arms. It continued to surprise her that her "little" brother now stood a few inches taller than her five-six frame. "I loved the military, but it's not for everyone. If you want to do it, it should be on your terms. But honey, if you don't get through summer school, what happens to you is out of my hands."

He stiffened and pulled back, still holding tears at bay in dark eyes so like hers. Such a handsome young man. Smart yet rebellious. God, she wanted to shake him and hug him and protect him all at once.

"If they try sending me, I'll run away."

"Rafi, stop."

"It's *Rafael*," he said, swore, then stormed out of the tiny apartment.

Jordan felt awful, failing with her brother yet again. Tempted as she was to call her parents or her older sister, she knew they'd simply tell her to let him pass or fail on his own. To an extent, she agreed. But adolescents rarely made good choices if left to their own devices.

She wished Rafi had a better role model than Carl. Bless him, but Carl could out-stubborn a mule. He'd made up his mind about this tough love approach to parenting Rafi and refused to change it.

Which for some reason made her think of Cash Griffith. Cash would hold his ground under heavy artillery for sure. But unlike Carl, he at least had the sense to back off; she'd seen it. When dealing with Reid, Cash often argued, listened to Reid make sense, and at some point became reasonable. Or at least his version of reasonable. From the stories she'd heard Reid tell, Cash had been much less than an angelic youth.

Maybe Cash could help her with Rafi. She'd thought

of asking him, but pride kept her from reaching out. That and the remembrance that she'd been burned before by trusting those she shouldn't have. She'd learned that lesson the hard way. Ten years in the Army down the drain.

She scowled as she made her way into the kitchen, only to see Rafi had left an empty milk carton in the fridge and the bread and jars of peanut butter and jelly open on the counter. And near those was a crumpled-up printout of a science quiz with a D at the top of it. She crunched it tight and tossed it into the trash can.

Damn it all, she hadn't planned on getting out of the service only to babysit her brother. But if Jordan didn't help him, no one would. Her parents had given her the same ultimatum years ago, but she'd at least gotten herself through high school before enduring threats of reform school. Joining the military had been a decision she'd never regretted. She hadn't been ready for college or living on her own back then. In the Army, she'd matured under the watchful eye of Big Brother.

Given health care, an allowance for quarters and food in addition to her paycheck, and structure, she'd been taken care of by a much sterner parent in the guise of her drill instructors and NCOs. She'd worked her ass off to earn her stripes, and she'd been proud of her commitment to duty and honor. Until it had ended, showing her a side of the command she'd wished to God she could unsee.

But Jordan refused to allow that situation to poison her against the military. What had happened to her best friend there could happen to anyone in the civilian sector as well. Dicks were dicks the world over.

Problem was she'd also seen the unhappiness that came from being forced into a lifestyle not of one's choosing, met plenty of guys who hadn't joined the service because they'd wanted to but because they'd had to for one reason or another.

To save her brother from a potentially damaging future, she'd do whatever she could.

And if it took sucking up to Cash Griffith to further that end, she'd play nice. She'd heard a way to a man's heart was through his stomach. Cash seemed to eat a lot. Maybe she could make him dinner? Or if not, there had to be *something* she could bargain the sexy jerk with in return for some guy guidance, right?

And kisses are off the table.

Sad she had to keep telling herself that.

Chapter 3

WORKING WITH SMITH HAD ITS MOMENTS, JORDAN thought. Thursday afternoon, after they finished moving a woman from Queen Anne to Kirkland, which had taken all day thanks to traffic and a mother of a haul, Jordan sat with the taciturn man as he drove them back to the office.

"You don't talk much." She studied him.

He looked a lot like Cash. Had she not known better, she'd have thought them related. Big, strong, and obnoxious when he did deign to speak, he resembled Cash in mannerisms too. Probably why she got along with him so well.

Hector and his twin, Lafayette, didn't mind him, but they got along with everyone. Heidi didn't seem to care for him, nor did the others. But Jordan thought of Smith as a surly younger Cash, and to her befuddlement, he made her feel safe, like one of the guys. Finley liked to flirt, and she knew had she given him the slightest encouragement, he'd have been after her for a date. Hector had given off a playful vibe as well, and she knew he'd welcome a chance to get to know her better. As much as she genuinely liked him, she didn't feel anything but friendship toward him.

Not the way she felt for Cash, which still confused her. She felt attracted, annoyed, and disturbed that she thought about him at all, especially since he was her boss. Smith, her coworker, had the same rugged good looks, an amazing body, and an attitude that amused more than aggravated her. But she didn't feel that same spark she felt for Gunnery Sergeant Annoying.

"Why are you staring at me?" Smith growled.

"Just wondering what crawled up your ass and died." He smirked. She grinned.

"I like doing my job. Didn't know I needed to talk about it."

"You don't. But it wouldn't hurt you to say more than 'on your left' when you pass by. You could say, 'Gee, Jordan. You're super efficient. Mind if I watch and learn?' See, that would be nice. Or you could just grunt hello and goodbye instead of disappearing like a ghost."

"You want me. I knew it." He sighed.

She blinked. "What?"

"Women get chatty when they want some of me. I can't help being this fine. But, honey, I'm too much for a sweet thing like you to handle."

That was more than Smith had said at once in all the time she'd known him. Had she wanted him to be more chatty?

"You know what? Don't talk."

He grunted.

She turned up the music, and they listened to alternative rock on the drive back.

It surprised her when Smith spoke again. "You like Cash, don't you?"

"He's okay for a boss."

Smith sneered. "He's an asshole playing at being 'one of the guys.' How can you stand him?"

She'd wondered at the hostility she'd sensed from

Smith toward Cash and sometimes Reid. But he'd never said anything about either one of them before. "If you hate Cash so much, why work for him?" To be honest, Cash insisted they worked *for* Reid and Evan. The movers worked *with* Cash, as far as Cash was concerned.

She didn't know why he continued to make the distinction, but it seemed important to him that everyone agree. And since he never acted superior, just led by example, she humored him.

"I need the job," Smith said and went back to being quiet. After another quarter hour in standstill traffic, he asked, "What about Reid? He's a douche, but not as bad, right?"

She blew out a breath. "Look, Smith. I like working for Vets on the Go! It's not something I'll do forever, but it's a job I can honestly be proud of. I enjoy my coworkers—usually." She glared at him, uncaring that he glared back. "If you're just going to bitch, keep it to yourself or quit. It's exhausting enough working all day moving heavy crap. Having to listen to you complain about the job is torture. Shut up, move on, or deal with Cash and Reid on your issues, okay?"

He shut up until they'd parked the van in the warehouse. "Anyone ever tell you you're kind of direct?"

"What clued you in?"

"I like that." He actually smiled at her, and wow, did a smile on his face make a huge difference. "Okay, no more comments about our fuckhead bosses."

She rolled her eyes.

"Want to grab a beer?"

A surprising invitation. She almost took him up on it, wanting to know a little more about Smith Ramsey. But she spotted Cash going up the stairs. "Raincheck?"

"Sure." He nodded and left to finish with the paper-work and hang up the keys.

Jordan darted up the stairs after Cash. The moving office consisted of a large warehouse to accommodate their moving vans, a gigantic space they shared with a neighboring bakery's trucks, and an upstairs office. The second floor of the building was home to a clothing store, watch repair shop, computer repair shop, and, at the end of the hall, Vets on the Go!

She followed the sound of Cash's low rumble midway down the hall on the left, where the lady who worked at the vintage clothing store stood talking to him by her door. Jordan had been interested to see what Miriam's Modiste offered, but the shop kept weird hours, and she'd never managed to catch the place when open.

The lady talking to Cash wore a long, clingy dress, making her look taller than what couldn't have been more than five feet, and that was in heels. A middle-aged woman with dark hair and thick black glasses, she had a lush frame. Cash, to his credit, hadn't looked below her chin, though he did seem a little tense.

Jordan neared to overhear the woman asking, "Are you sure? I can pay you. You'd be more than stimulating for my clients."

Cash noticed Jordan, and a look of relief washed over his face. "I really can't, Miriam. Jordan wouldn't like it."

"She's not very enlightened then, is she?" Miriam turned to study Jordan's approach.

Curious, Jordan stopped by Cash's side and smiled. "Hello. I'm Jordan. I work for Vets on the Go! So, you're Miriam. Is this your store? I've been dying to check it out."

"I am, and it is." Miriam beamed, her bright blue eyes sharp behind her lenses. "We're not only a vintage clothing store. We offer classes on female empowerment to assert the feminine perspective in a world largely dominated by men."

Jordan didn't know what to say, but she had a feeling she should say something. "Interesting." Next to her, Cash took a step back, but Jordan latched onto his wrist to prevent his escape. "Hold on, Cash. I need to talk to you."

He sighed. Loudly. But he stayed put. The sly look he gave her warned her to beware as he said, "You know, Miriam, even though Jordan probably wouldn't like me involving myself in your classes, I bet she'd get a lot out of them."

"Hmm." Miriam looked her over, and Jordan was dying to know what the classes involved. Something weird because Cash had a suspicious gleam in his eye.

"What exactly do you teach?" Jordan asked.

Miriam puffed up. "I instruct women in truly embracing and accepting what it means to be a woman. We reach for our full potential by expressing ourselves intellectually and emotionally through physicality. I call it a stimulation of the senses in their entirety."

Sounded like more of Seattle's alternative thought processes that frankly gave Jordan a headache. But she liked the idea of embracing her own inner power. How often had she been talked down to, working in a male-dominated environment like the Army? Maybe she'd give it a shot. "When are your classes?"

"We have one later tonight."

"Oh, I can't tonight. I have to get home."

"We also offer weekend sessions. Would you like to come this Saturday? We have a new rotation starting. It's an advanced class, but it would give you an idea of what we do. You could try our first class for free to see if you like it."

Cash stood way too still, his expression one of guarded amusement.

She didn't care. She'd take the unspoken dare and come out on top. After giving him a look, she answered, "Sure. I'd like that."

"Great. Nine o'clock Saturday morning, right here." Miriam shook Jordan's hand. "A pleasure to meet you, dear."

"You too." After Miriam went back into her store, Jordan turned to Cash. "Why won't you help with her class? Female empowerment sounds positive. Don't tell me it insults your over-the-top manliness?" She felt left out of the joke when he laughed.

"Oh God. Please let me watch Saturday morning."

"Sounded like a woman-only kind of thing." She frowned. "And why bring up my name to get out of helping her? What do I have to do with it?"

Cash shrugged. "Hell. I'll admit it. I panicked. I might have let her have the impression you and I are involved and that you wouldn't want me helping out."

"What? Why?"

"Never mind." He turned and walked away.

"Hold on." She had to chase him down the hall, the way he ate up the corridor with those long legs. "You lied, used my name to get out of work. You owe me."

He stopped so suddenly she barreled into his broad back. "I owe you?"

"Yes. And it just so happens I need your help."

He turned and raised a brow, appearing uncannily like Smith at that moment, even more so than he looked like Reid. "Oh?"

She started to reply but stopped when Smith joined them.

"Slumming?" he asked her, giving Cash a dismissive once-over.

"Smith," she warned.

Cash gritted his teeth, and Smith chuckled, then asked, "Is Reid in?"

"How the hell would I know?" Cash answered at the same time Jordan said, "He's supposed to be."

Smith left them, and Cash glared at Smith's back until he disappeared into the office. "I hate that guy."

"I think the feeling is mutual." She wondered why.

"Has he been bothering you?" The look in Cash's dark-green eyes warned her the man spoiled for a fight.

"Nope. He's easy to get along with."

Cash seemed disappointed. "Oh."

"And he rarely talks. We got the Jasper job done in one day. Would have been back sooner, but traffic sucked."

He let out a long sigh. "So what's this favor I 'owe you'?"

"I need you to talk to my brother." The admission she couldn't handle her own family felt easier while looking at his chest.

"Your brother?"

She glanced up, saw his interest, the way it lit up his face, and did her best not to stare at his firm, kissable lips. *Damn it*. She needed to focus on the man's irritability, not his sex appeal.

Jordan swallowed. "How about I tell you about it over

dinner tonight? And before you get any weird ideas, this is in no way a date. I do *not* want to have sex with you. I am *not* flirting or leading you on in any way. This is strictly to help my brother."

He just stared at her. Unfortunately, behind him, Reid and Smith stared at her as well.

She felt her cheeks heat and wished she could sink through the floor.

"Man, I heard *that*," Smith just had to say. "She in no way, shape, or form wants you, Cash. Not fucking at all." Smith laughed as he walked away. His shouted "*Rejected*," followed by more laughter, boomed down the corridor.

"Please tell me I can hit him," he said to Reid.

"No. But I'm curious to hear why Jordan thinks she has to have this conversation with you," Reid said. Jordan privately thought of him as Cash-Light. He had the same good looks but not as concentrated. Reid had a more slender build than his bulky older brother, and he had gray eyes. Not the mysterious, deep green of Cash's. The debonair Griffith as opposed to Cash's raw, wild bad boy.

"I'm not harassing her. Jesus, Reid." Cash ran a hand through his hair, which caused his massive biceps to bulge. "Tell him, Jordan."

A sucker for a pretty body more than a pretty face, every time Jordan looked at Cash she felt as if she'd been hit by a two-by-four because he possessed both. She nodded, distracted, wondering how much he could really bench-press.

"He *is* harassing you?" Reid asked, frowning.

"What? *No*, not at all." She felt like a moron and

forced herself to meet Reid's concerned gaze. "Sorry. I meant I agreed with Cash. He's fine. I just wanted to make sure my offer of dinner wasn't confusing." She wryly added, "You know your brother does better when things are laid out on the table."

"True. Subtle he is not."

"I'm right here," Cash growled.

They both ignored him. "So you're good then?" Reid asked her.

"Dandy."

"Great. I'll see you tomorrow. Cash, I'll be—"

"At Naomi's. Shocker." Cash shrugged, but Jordan had a sense his brother's new relationship bothered him.

Reid didn't seem to notice. "Have a good night, you two." He started down the corridor. "Oh, and Cash, close up for me, would you?" Reid didn't wait for his answer as he disappeared into the stairway.

"Why not? Not like I have a life or anything," Cash muttered as he walked into the office. "Well? You coming?"

Jordan hurried after him and helped him turn everything off and lock up. They walked down the stairs and exited the building to the parking lot. She took a moment to watch the sun hide behind some purple clouds. Orange rays penetrated the sky-blue horizon and dotted through indigo and pink clouds, painting a picture. She wished she could bask in the moment, letting go of the worries dragging her down.

But Rafi hadn't been around for breakfast this morning, and she knew he'd avoided her on purpose. Between yesterday's conversation and the call she'd earlier received from his school advisor, she'd come to the end of her rope. And the timing couldn't have been better, with her brother spending the next few days at their parents' for a change.

Cash stopped at his car and turned to her. "Your place for dinner?"

"Yes. Follow me. It's a ten-minute drive. I'll text you the address in case you get lost." She sent it to him before getting into her car.

He followed without too much of a hassle since the hour had passed six. Once at her place, she parked and waited for him. The apartment complex didn't look like much on the outside, but she had a furnished, one-bedroom unit for under a thousand in rent, and the landlord seemed like a nice lady. Since Jordan was ex-military, the woman had foregone the $200 nonrefundable cleaning fee and full rental deposit.

After letting them both in, Jordan took a glance around. The addition of Rafi to her tiny apartment made life cramped, but Jordan had lived under worse conditions. The place was clean, fitted out, and, if not to her taste, at least nothing to be embarrassed about. Yet she felt a case of nerves as Cash shadowed her, his large presence impossible to ignore.

At least she didn't have to worry about Rafi tonight. Four more days of peace before the turmoil that was her brother returned.

She shut and locked the door then removed her shoes.

"Take 'em off," she said to him when he watched her.

He grunted but didn't argue. As he struggled with his laces, she walked past the entrance to the living room and turned into the small kitchen. Bordered on three sides by cabinets, a refrigerator, and oven, the open concept layout included the living area, where a small table marked the dining space. She'd put leaves in it, allowing for more room.

With Cash's size, he'd appreciate the space.

She took the casserole she'd prepared earlier that morning from the fridge.

Cash entered, making her kitchen feel ten times smaller. "What's for dinner?"

"Ham and cheese noodle casserole."

"Sounds awesome." He glanced around, seeing her pine cabinets, tan Formica countertop, and mismatched white and black appliances. She found everything to be functional, so she couldn't complain. The oversized furniture had been in fashion in the early nineties, but it seemed clean and smelled nice. A good place to start until she figured out what she wanted to be when she grew up.

The notion she neared thirty and still needed direction irritated the hardcore soldier still within her.

"You're tidy." Cash nodded. "I knew you'd be."

"Yep."

Rafi's things no longer littered the living space, the items now tucked away in the corner in the duffel bag containing his clothes. He'd taken his laptop, she noticed, and hoped he'd use the time with their parents to catch up on some schoolwork.

Yeah, right.

She shook her head at her delusions and put the casserole in the oven, allowing a little extra time for the oven to preheat. "Want something to drink?"

Cash tucked his hands in his pockets and leaned against the wall, watching her. "What do you have?"

She opened the refrigerator. "Beer, water, an energy drink, and milk."

"Beer. But only if it's not some bullshit light beer."

She flipped him off and handed him a local IPA.

He grinned and accepted it. Unfortunately their fingers touched, and she hurriedly dragged her hand back, ignoring the spark of heat that followed the slight contact.

His grin faded, but he made no mention of the exchange. Probably didn't feel it the way she had, but whatever. She needed his help, not his unwanted attention. *Unwanted? Liar.*

She grabbed a beer for herself, opened it, and took a long drag. When she finished, she saw him staring at her. "What?"

He looked flushed, which was weird, and took a sip of his own. "Nothing."

She nodded to the table, and they sat across from each other. With Rafi, the table seemed plenty large with the leaf in it. With Cash, she felt too close to the man. *Time to stop dwelling on his looks and get to the point.* "I need your help."

He held up a hand. "Before you start, this 'I owe you a favor' bullshit isn't working for me. You want my help? You gotta give me something back."

"I'm giving you dinner right now." She eyed him with suspicion, and he laughed. "What's so funny?"

"The look on your face." He took another sip of beer, looking full-out relaxed. "The dinner's a start, but it's not what I need. Now hold on. I'm not after your virginity, sweetcakes." He chuckled at the second finger she shot him. "I need your help packing up my mom's place."

She knew his mother had passed away not long ago. "Oh, sure." That had to be tough.

He frowned.

"Now what?"

"That was awfully easy. What exactly do you want me to do with your brother?"

Jordan sighed. "I need your help getting him to see his mistakes, and I can't think of who else to ask."

His expression grew serious. "What do you need?"

She'd expected a few wisecracks, some dig about her being unable to handle the male mind. But he didn't do either.

"Rafi's become a real—"

"Wait. Rafi? He's your brother?"

She didn't understand. "Who else am I talking about? I only have one brother."

Cash relaxed even more. "Sorry. Go on."

She explained about the teenager's recent failure at school, his rebellious attitude, and him falling in with the wrong crowd. And about her parents dumping everything in her lap. "I know he's young. Hell, I went through the same things at his age. Though to be honest, I at least knew to get through high school. Rafi's a lot more aggressive than I was back then. Must be all that testosterone going through his pubescent body." Just thinking that made her ill. Puberty. What a crappy time of life.

"He hasn't hurt you, has he?" Cash asked, his voice quiet.

"What? Hurt me? Hell no. He'd wouldn't even *think* about hitting me." She paused, smirking. "Not that I'd ever let him—or anyone—try."

"Good." Cash finished off his beer. When she stood to get him another one, he waved her to sit.

"I'll get it." When he rejoined her, he asked, "So what do you want me to do?"

God, he looked good. No, no. She had to stop staring at the strong line of his throat and square jaw, to ignore the overwhelming masculinity in that body. Jordan had never been bowled over by a man before. But something about Cash called to her.

"I, um…" She coughed to gather her thoughts and sound halfway intelligent. Cash had women falling all over themselves for him at any given time. She'd be damned if she'd be one of them. "I've heard you and Reid talk about what a pain you were growing up." She continued over his scowl, "And I thought you could help Rafi, talk to him man-to-man about getting through the teenage years. I don't know if he's ignoring me because I'm a girl or because I'm his sister, but I'm really worried about him."

"Is the crowd he's hanging with all that bad?"

"I don't know. They seem mostly harmless, though there's one kid who's not that great. Juan something. It's nothing terrible, really. Mostly minor, rebellious things. Bad grades, talking back. Though the prank putting firecrackers in the boys' bathroom was inspired," she said drily. "I don't think he'd have done it on his own, but he refused to rat anyone out, taking the full blame himself."

"Good kid."

She'd thought so too, even if being silent hadn't helped him. Jordan praised loyalty, but Rafi should know better than to damage school property. "He seems to have no drive, just a need to lose himself in video games. He needs a hobby. Real friends. Something."

"High school is hard. I never got on well with my parents. And I was on a real road to self-destruction."

"What made you change direction?" Curiosity drove her to know more about Cash. She told herself it was just for her brother, but Jordan knew it was more than that.

"Reid needed me. That helped. Plus, I just wanted to escape. It seems like your parents care enough to try going the tough love route. And he's got you."

"Yeah. We all care. But I seem to be the only one who cares about making *his* life better, not just improving my own by sending him away."

After a moment, Cash smiled. The look he gave her softened somehow. "You're a good big sister."

"I don't know."

"Yeah, you are. You're taking care of his sorry ass whether he wants it or not. You could just dump him back on your parents."

"Then they'll just put him in that academy for screw-ups." *Let's call it what it is.* "And my sister is no help, so intent on her upcoming wedding and her own life she's never seen the rest of the world as anything but something to serve her." Jordan heard the bitterness but couldn't censor it in time.

"Whoa. Now those are some family problems." Cash leaned forward. "Tell me more."

She had to laugh. "What is with you and drama? Between you and Heidi—oh, and Hector, don't think I haven't seen him egging you on for episode recaps—those train-wreck shows on TV take up a lot of talk at work."

He shrugged. "Maybe it's because it's not my life that's so fucked up. I don't know. I guess I get a kick out of watching other people act stupid. It's funny. Plus I don't think even half of it is real."

"That makes sense. Probably why people are so into

reality TV and the old soaps. It lets you escape from life, you know?"

A shadow seemed to pass over his face. But he smiled, and she wondered if she'd imagined it.

He studied her. "You never seem up-to-date on quality TV."

"No, I have you and Heidi for that."

"What do you do for fun, Jordan? Besides moving other people's stuff and watching your brother? Oh, and aggravating me. I forgot that."

Hearing her name on his lips made her feel tingly inside, and she hated the moment of feminine awareness. She couldn't wait to take Miriam's empowerment class on Saturday. Time to own her insanity and stop yearning for something Cash would likely not have in him to give.

She pasted a smile on her face. "Aggravating you does make life worth living." She had to laugh at the face he made. "Oh, I have a life. I just like to keep it separate from work."

"Yeah? What's so special you keep it a secret?" Cash paused, his gaze intent. "Some guy you're afraid to tell me about?"

She just stared, confused, because Cash sounded almost…jealous. But that couldn't be.

Could it?

Chapter 4

CASH WANTED TO TAKE BACK THE WORDS AS SOON AS HE said them because he didn't want to know about Jordan's love life. He especially didn't want to know that she had a significant other. For some reason, knowing she might share some part of herself with someone other than him grated.

She frowned at him. "My relationship status is none of your business."

Man, when she grew agitated, her brown eyes burned with fire. He'd swear they lightened, and he had a powerful urge to watch them cloud with lust while he—

He cleared his throat. "Well, now. It might be. What if this guy you're seeing is messing with Rafi's head? Kids, especially young men, can be defensive about the women in their lives."

She huffed at him. "Please. Rafi's not like that."

"Did you or did you not come to me for help?" He finished his second beer and decided to shift to water. The last thing he needed was to cloud his mind with alcohol and let loose the impulse to drag Jordan off to her bedroom and test out her mattress.

"For God's sake. There is no man in my life. Happy now?"

Yes. "Hey, it's not about making me happy. Although...you want to make me happy? Give me some of that mouthwatering thing cooking in the oven. Because it smells damn good."

She grinned. "It is. I can cook, you know."

"I can't."

"Why am I not surprised?"

Cash watched her fiddle in the kitchen. She returned with a plate of cheese and crackers, olives, and a bowl of pretzels. He looked at her.

"Beer food. Figured the cheese and crackers might be too fancy and throw you off."

"Brat." He shook his head and dug in, famished. Jordan watched him before joining in, shoving his fingers out of the way when he took *her* olive. Damn, but she made him laugh. She didn't mind getting her hands dirty, at work or at home, apparently.

As they snacked, they talked about work and Reid and Naomi, speculated about what Heidi did in her spare time—bench-press Humvees was his guess—and discussed Lafayette's new boyfriend.

"Hector likes him." Jordan nibbled some cheese, and it took work to stop thinking of her nibbling on him. "I haven't met him yet. Have you?"

"Not yet. I think Lafayette is afraid I might scare the guy." Cash smiled, glad that Lafayette and Hector had signed on with Vets on the Go! He considered the guys true friends, and he didn't have many of those. "That, or he's afraid I'll steal him away with my amazing looks." He pumped his arm, teasing, and saw Jordan give his muscles a thorough inspection.

Did she like his looks? He hoped so. Not that he worked out to impress women, but it never seemed to hurt. And considering he didn't have all that much else going for him, he had to play to his strengths. Jordan, though, didn't react to him the way other women did. Perhaps that was what attracted him to her. That inability to predict her reactions.

"So what about you?" she asked him after they'd spent a few quiet moments stuffing their faces. She had great taste in cheese. "Am I getting you in trouble with your girlfriend for being at my place unsupervised?"

He swallowed down a big piece before laughing. "Hell, no. I answer to no woman."

"That's mighty progressive of you, Conan."

He really liked the little smartass. Problem was, it would be easier to deal with Jordan as nothing more than a coworker if she didn't sport such an amazing body. She had a streamlined, athletic build. All muscle and soft skin, but she was a grown woman with the right curves to have him sitting up and taking notice.

As usual, just being around her heated his blood. The woman wore long jean shorts and her work tee, and he still wanted to bend her over and do her until neither one of them could walk.

"What is *that* look?" She leaned closer, and he saw golden-brown striations mixing with the mahogany of her irises. Her pert nose and full lips made her both cute and sexy. And the creamy tan of her skin tantalized him to touch.

He blinked, horrified to feel an erection pressing against the fly of his jeans. As he did his best to think about something else, the oven beeped, drawing her attention.

Thank you, Jesus.

She moved away to get their dinner, giving him a minute to calm himself down and come up with some lame excuse for staring at her like a lovesick asshole. "Sorry if I was staring. I'm just not used to being around you when you're pleasant."

"Funny. You do know I can poison your food and you won't know it until it's too late?"

"A risk I'm willing to take." His mouth watered as he watched her bring him a heaping plate of her casserole. Proud of himself for not falling on it and devouring his dinner before she'd had a chance to sit down, he waited until she sat and took a bite herself. Then he bit into the most decadent macaroni he'd ever had. The meat was almost an afterthought, and Cash had always been a huge meat guy.

"You like it?" She watched him.

He nodded and swallowed a heavenly mouthful. "Oh my God. This is best thing I've ever had." He didn't wait to see if she liked his compliment before falling on his food with complete abandon. He didn't come up for air until he'd scraped his plate clean and licked his fork.

When he did glance up, he saw her staring at him. Embarrassed, he apologized. "Sorry. I missed lunch today, and I haven't had anything this good in forever. Reid can't cook either, and the few meals Naomi has made were good but nowhere near this."

He saw her pleasure, and it warmed him to know he'd earned that shy smile.

Shy? *Jordan?* He blinked, stunned to see another side to the mouthy woman who didn't take any of his crap.

"I like to cook, but I haven't had anyone to cook for but Rafi since I got out four months ago. And before that it had been a good year since I'd been dating."

He didn't believe it. "No husband, fiancé, boyfriend?"

"Nope. And no lasting boyfriends during my time in the Army. You know how it is. It's hard." She shrugged and ate with manners, reminding him to do the same.

Still, something didn't seem right. Jordan was fucking awesome. How could she still be single? And why did that matter so much? He focused on his plate. "You mind if I get more?"

She moved to stand, and he waved her back. "I'll get it. You eat. You're too tiny as it is." He ignored her glare and got himself another huge helping. If she'd fixed dessert, he might have to break down and marry her.

A joke, but something about that thought stunned him enough to have him freeze his fork by his mouth.

"Cash?"

He shrugged the foolishness away and ate at a much slower, more mannerly pace. "If you'd have fed me first then asked for my help with your brother, there's no way I could have said no."

"You didn't say no."

"But I did ask you to help me at my mom's." He sighed. "I won't take it back, but damn, girl, I'm willing to trade you anything if you'll cook for me again."

She laughed. "You really are easy to please. Who knew?"

"That's classified. You can never tell."

Jordan snorted. "Who'd believe me if I did?"

"Have I called you a brat lately?"

"I believe you did."

"Trust me, sweetcakes. It fits." He loved how red her cheeks got when he called her pet names. Such an adorable bundle of rage.

"You know what else I bet fits? Your head up your ass. Keep it up and we'll see before the night's over."

He choked on laughter and had to drink his water to breathe again. But it was worth it, especially when Jordan broke out a homemade cherry pie.

—◦◦◦—

Jordan dared him to be mouthy again, holding a slice of pie in front of him. Cash had fallen on her food as if the Russians were coming, and nothing could have pleased her more. Call her old-fashioned, but Jordan liked cooking for more than just herself. Especially for someone who appreciated it. She was an independent woman who'd made her place in the world all by herself. She was single by choice, and she had no problem indulging in casual sex when the mood struck.

So it had always surprised her to find she took after her mother when it came to relationships. Maria Younger liked to coddle Carl, the same way she'd taken care of Jordan's father. Jordan took pleasure in cooking for, cleaning up after, and generally sharing herself with her boyfriends.

She'd dated some nice guys, but timing and her work in the Army had made commitments tough to keep. Had she found someone who truly clicked with her, she'd have changed a few of her decisions. But no one had pressed all her buttons, not like…not like the man she did *not* consider anything more than a friend and coworker.

Yes, she'd made her best dish to persuade Cash to help her brother. And, yes, she'd made a cherry pie for dessert because she knew it was his favorite but also to seal the deal concerning Rafi.

If only she could stop thinking about Cash in any non-platonic kind of way. She had intelligence, yet lately she seemed to be thinking with her ovaries and not her brain.

"Seriously. I have no idea why you're not married right now. You're cute, and you can cook." Cash finished his slice of pie and sat back, patting his washboard of a stomach. "Oh, that's right. You're mouthy. Forgot about that." His eyes sparkled, as if he enjoyed their verbal sparring as much as she did.

Quietly, and just to screw with him, she said, "Maybe I was married and my husband cheated on me. Maybe he took my kids away from me. Maybe he wasn't the man I thought he was."

Cash looked suddenly angry. "Are you kidding me?"

Fascinated that his moods vacillated from happy to angry in the span of a heartbeat, she kicked back and put her hands behind her head. "Yes, I am kidding you. As if I'd let some asshole steal my kids…when I have any." She huffed. "And just maybe, jackass, I don't want to get married. This is why you should never assume."

He paused, started to say something, then broke out in laughter. He laughed so hard he cried, and she couldn't help grinning with him.

"Fuck. No wonder I like you so much. You're worse than I am when it comes to getting under somebody's skin."

"Thanks a lot." Not exactly flattered, she stood to clear their plates then started to run the water.

Cash suddenly stood behind her in her tiny kitchen. He turned her around, too close for comfort. "Hey, now." He wiped his eyes, but a hand remained on her shoulder, burning through the cotton of her T-shirt. "I'm kidding. Lighten up, Fleming."

She looked from his hand on her shoulder up to his darkening eyes.

His gaze changed, the focus no longer on her face but somehow on her mouth. His breathing quickened. So did hers.

"S-so you'll help me with Rafi, and I'll help you pack." Great. Now *she* couldn't look away from *his* mouth. Such firm lips, so full and pretty yet masculine. Weird.

To her consternation, her nipples hardened.

"Yeah, sure," he agreed absently. Then the sexy jerk rubbed a thick, callused finger over her lips.

She sucked in a breath.

"Shit. Okay, we're just gonna do this once because I can't fucking wait another minute wondering."

She licked her lips, and his eyes narrowed. "Wondering what?" she asked, sounding weak, feeling like a limp noodle under his strong hands.

"What you taste like." He lowered his face slowly, taking his time and giving her every chance to pull away.

"Damn it, you're taking too long," she groused and yanked him down to her.

The first taste of him knocked her world off its axis. He tasted sweet, a mixture of cherries and man and sex combining to send her heart into a race it might not finish.

He groaned and lifted her in his arms, their mouths still melded, the full-body hug turning her on like a drug. He settled her on the counter, his hands clasped on either side of her hips, and angled himself between her legs.

For the life of her she couldn't think about anything

but how well Cash fit there, as if he'd been made just for her. The breadth of him overwhelmed her, and she clung to his shoulders, dizzy and wanting and afraid to fall off one helluva ride.

He moaned her name and deepened the kiss. Starved for oxygen, she pushed at his chest, and he backed away, giving her the space to stare up at him.

She froze at the look of carnal need on his face; she'd never seen such a beautiful man in her life. Then Cash was kissing her again, gripping her hips and twisting her shorts under those big hands.

She wanted more, to feel him closer. But try as she might, tugging at his shoulders, he refused to budge. All that strength and power... She shivered under the onslaught of desire.

He slipped his tongue into her mouth, and the sly press of his tongue reminded her body of where he'd do even more good. She felt weak and strong and needier than she knew how to handle, aching between her legs with a ferocity that startled her.

Cash ripped his mouth away and stared down at her in shock, panting. "*Fuck*. You're a menace." Then he stormed out of the kitchen.

She landed on the floor with wobbly legs and tried to follow him but made it no farther than the wall in the hallway. After an embarrassing moment, she steadied herself and saw him halfway out the front door before he stopped, realizing he had forgotten his shoes.

"Motherfucker." He shoved his big feet into them then glared at her. "That's it. Never again. And stop looking at me like that, or I'll fuck you right here in your goddamn living room."

Jordan could only stare at him, not sure what to say to that. *Please? No? How many times do you think you're good for?*

Cash swore again then walked right up to her and took her face in his hands. His touch was gentle, so at odds with the fierceness in his gaze. He kissed her, the touch light, wrought with an emotion that made no sense.

This time she pulled back, so confused…and freakin' on fire to have him. "Wh-what?"

"Yeah. That's what I'm sayin'." He blew out a breath and let her go, taking a step back. "We never do this again."

She nodded, knowing the rightness of what he said if quietly regretting the necessity. "Never happened."

"Right."

"We work together. Friends."

"Work. Yes. Friends." He seemed to have trouble taking his gaze from her eyes, staring holes through her.

"I'm still going to help you pack your mom's place."

"And I'll still help you with your brother." He paused. "Might be a good thing to take a break from working together tomorrow, just for a breather."

"Um, yeah." She breathed deeply, searching for calm and not finding it. "So, get out. I have stuff to do."

He shoved his hands in his pockets, drawing her attention there, and she made the mistake of looking at the massive bulge straining his fly. She swallowed audibly.

"Cut it out." He groaned. "I can't help it. I have to go."

Before he got through the door, she grabbed his arm. He froze, and she said, "Is Saturday okay? To help you pack stuff?" And to get this debt repaid, the quicker the better.

"Um. Yeah." He coughed, didn't turn around. "I'm

off this weekend. And we can figure out what you want me to say to your brother and when."

Reluctantly, she let him go, knowing it was for the best but regretting the fact she'd assuaged her curiosity and kissed the man. "Right. See you later."

He took a step and paused then looked over his shoulder at her with a huge grin that did something funny to her insides. Not just her girl parts. Her heart started hammering even harder. "Why don't we meet Sunday morning instead? Because, you know, you have an appointment Saturday morning with Miriam."

She frowned. "What do you know about this that I don't?"

He shrugged, but she didn't buy it. "How could I know anything? I'm a guy. I'm too 'empowered' as it is."

"Shut up." She couldn't hide a grin.

His smile left him. Cash scowled, took one step closer, and paused. "Nope. Can't do it. Can I—? No." Then he turned and left.

Jordan shut and locked the door behind him then plastered her back to it and slid to the floor.

Her entire body still throbbed, needy, aching for a man. But not any man. Aching for Cash Fucking Griffith.

She groaned and covered her eyes with a hand, astounded at having made the mother of all bad choices. *He's my boss. I'm attracted to my boss, and the man is part Neanderthal. What the hell is wrong with me?*

———— ⁓⁓⁓ ————

The next day, Friday, was the end of Jordan's workweek and passed smoothly enough. She worked alongside Smith again, and as usual, he didn't say much. They spent all day moving a client's belongings from a storage locker in Green Lake to a storage locker in Renton, an easy day since they hadn't been hired to do more than move things from point A to point B.

It turned out a bunch of the guys planned to hang out after work at Ringo's Bar, a short drive away. It also happened to be closer to home for her, so she joined them. Cash and Reid were noticeably absent, but she didn't mind. Cash had been right; she needed the break.

Her dreams had been filled with naughty images of Cash doing even naughtier things to her body. For some reason, his head had figured prominently between her thighs in most of her fantasies, and it had taken her a bit of time in the shower to cool off.

"You've been quiet today," Smith was saying as she sat with him, Hector, Lafayette, Finley, and Funny Rob, one of the new guys. For some reason, the gang considered her an old-timer, and she'd only been with the group for a month and a half, though it felt like a lot longer.

Funny Rob, oddly enough, wasn't that funny. A tall Asian man with a dry sense of humor who'd been a mechanic in the Air Force, his full name was Robert Tung. She liked him, though she didn't know much more about him than that he preferred country music and ate a hot dog for lunch every day. Odd facts to know about a coworker, but he had an easygoing temperament.

Since she'd been with Vets on the Go!, she'd only had an issue with one employee—now an ex-employee since he'd been fired then arrested for trying to steal from one of Reid and Cash's friends while pretending to work for the moving company. Talk about a headache.

She tuned back in to Smith's comment. "What exactly are you complaining about? You like it when I'm quiet."

"Ah, there she is." Smith took a large swig of beer then left to get another pitcher.

"He's in a good mood. Strange." Hector grinned. Too handsome for his own good, the stocky, muscular ex-Navy sailor had several women giving him the eye. Jordan liked working with him, and she liked hanging out with him even more. He set her at ease, almost like a protective older brother. And she'd never had anyone to look after her except the Army, not since leaving home at eighteen.

"It's a strange kind of day," she agreed.

"I heard that." Lafayette, Hector's identical twin, nodded. And by identical, Jordan meant the *exact same*. Same shade of brown skin, same laughing eyes, same big muscles. She could only tell them apart when they told her who was who.

"Lafayette, can Simon tell you two apart?" she asked of his new boyfriend, looking from him to Hector.

"As a matter of fact, he can." Lafayette grinned wide. "That was also a huge factor in Hector giving my new man a glowing rating."

"Rating?" Funny Rob dipped into his nachos. "Like on Yelp? Did you try him out first, Hector? Or are you just browsing?"

"Funny Rob, you're really not that funny," Hector muttered.

Lafayette laughed. "I don't know. I like his sense of humor."

"When do we get to meet Simon?" Jordan wanted to know. "I'll tell you if he's good enough for you. I have an eye for these things."

"You do, do you?" Hector sized her up. "Why don't we double date and see, Lafayette?" he asked his brother while flirting with Jordan.

Considering what a terrible thing she'd done by kissing Cash, Jordan decided a different good-looking man for a night might be just the thing she needed. "You know what? I'm in. But only as friends," she emphasized when Hector lit up.

"Friends, sure. I'm down with that." He lifted her hand and kissed the back of it. "Friend."

Smith arrived with a new pitcher and made a face. "Keep it in your pants, Romeo. Don't you know you never fuck around at work? Makes things awkward."

Funny Rob blinked. "'Fucking around' has a lot of connotations, but you're meaning that literally, huh?"

Smith frowned, and it felt as if a thundercloud darkened the area above his head.

Jordan was impressed. "You do menacing pretty well."

Smith shrugged. "It's a gift."

"Speaking of menacing, where's Cash?" Hector asked her, of all people.

"How should I know? I'm not his keeper." She sounded defensive, even to herself. She got a few raised brows and groaned. "If you tell me I sound like him, I might just shoot you."

Hector smothered a grin. "Another beer?"

She shook her head. "I can't. Got an early appointment with Miriam tomorrow."

The others froze.

"Okay, what did I say that's got you all spooked?" Now more than ever she knew she didn't have all the information about Miriam's Modiste.

Lafayette put his beer down. "Say again? You have an appointment?"

Jordan nodded. "She's giving a new session of empowerment classes. First one's free, so I thought I'd check it out."

Everyone leaned closer.

Hector's and Smith's wide grins looked feral.

Jordan scowled. "What's wrong with Miriam?"

Hector laughed. "Nothing at all. But…promise you'll tell us all about your 'empowerment' session on Monday."

Lafayette leaned close to whisper something to Funny Rob, who broke out laughing while staring at Jordan.

"Oh, you have to go," Rob said.

She frowned at the guys. "Okay," she said slowly and watched her friends try to stop laughing and grinning. And failing. Heck, Hector kept choking on his beer while trying to pretend to be serious. "I swear I'm going to kill the lot of you if the class is as bad as you're pretending it will be."

Smith winked at her. "I hear it's not bad at all. Heidi went once, and she loved it."

He'd winked. It took Jordan a moment to process Smith acting like a human. "Heidi went?"

Hector, now able to breathe on his own, nodded. "Yep. Swear to God, she did." He sounded strangled. "She's going again. Hell, she might be there tomorrow."

That put a different spin on things. Except Heidi wasn't exactly, ah, normal. Then again, none of Jordan's wacky veteran buddies were. She sighed and held out her glass. "Fill me up, Smith. I have a feeling I'm going to need it to deal with tomorrow."

Which started the group on another round of laughter.

Great. Between Miriam and dealing with Cash on Sunday, she wondered which task would give her the biggest headache.

Chapter 5

CASH WOULDN'T HAVE THOUGHT IT, BUT HE'D MISSED Jordan the minute he'd left her apartment. And after last night, the pretense that she was just a coworker and meant nothing to him was more difficult to maintain. He had no idea how he could feel simultaneously comfortable and aroused by a woman at the same time.

At least at work, Finley hadn't annoyed him too much. Knowing Jordan had again been paired with Smith bothered the crap out of him, but he'd never admit as much to Reid, so he let things lie. When several of the gang decided to meet at Ringo's that night after work, he took a pass, complaining of a headache.

As he'd said to Jordan, he needed a break.

Because as God was his witness, he'd never felt so out of control in lust before. Combining that with genuinely liking the woman, his libido was off the charts. His hands on her hips, holding on tight, had been the only thing stopping him from doing her right there in her tiny kitchen last night.

So he understood her looking both sexy and confused after they'd kissed each other senseless. Or at least, *he'd* felt muddled. Maybe she'd been confused about something else. Had she felt the same tsunami of desire he had? Man. He hated not being sure.

The smart move would be to stop working alongside her altogether and keep things professional. No more dinners. No helping him pack up his mom's place. No talking to her brother. No personal relationship, period.

But that would be akin to cutting off his arm. He *wanted* to be around her. Even to joke around, all platonic-like.

Did she still think about that kiss? He did. Hell, he'd beaten off to it this morning. Twice.

He groaned, glad that at least he had the weekend to think about how to deal with the mouthy beauty.

Later that evening while the gang met at Ringo's, Cash sat beside Evan at his cousin's place, sharing a pizza.

Evan frowned at him. "You okay? You've been groaning a lot lately."

Cash shrugged. "Life." He reached for another piece of extra cheese and finished off their first pie. "Good thinking, getting a few boxes."

Evan grinned. A lot like Reid but more easygoing, Evan Griffith had also done his time in the Marine Corps. Unlike Reid and Cash, Evan had become an officer. A logistician, and from what Cash knew, the guy had been on his way to making real grade. But Evan had left the service as a captain, become a CPA, and made enough money that he'd been able to afford investing heavily in Vets on the Go! He was the other, more silent, partner in the business.

"So when are you gonna quit your job and work with us full-time?" Cash asked, having heard his cousin complain about his beautiful, brainy, domineering boss one too many times.

"Pretty soon, I think." Evan started on his fourth piece, no slouch at putting down food. "I've been redoing my five- and ten-year plans. With what I have put aside, some investments, and some ideas, I think I might be able to take a break for a while."

"A break? As in not work?"

"Why not? I've earned it."

"Well, I guess." Cash couldn't imagine doing nothing. Oh, for a day or two, he could focus on the gym, petty chores, watching his dramas or seasonal sports on TV. But too much time gave him too much potential to get into trouble.

Evan snorted. "We're not all obsessive type A's like you and Reid."

Cash huffed. "Please, Evan. You're worse than Reid is. I work because otherwise I get myself into trouble. That and I like to eat." He started on another piece of pizza. "Being able to afford food is a pretty decent motivator to keeping a job."

"Yeah. Especially with as much as you put away."

"You're no slouch." Cash stared at his cousin's now-empty plate. "I'll open the other box."

"Do that." Evan sighed and sank back in the couch. "Yeah, my time at McNulty & Campbell is at an end. I just don't want so many hours. Vanessa's a workaholic yet still has time for her husband and little girl. I have no idea how she does it." He sighed. "I feel tired all the time."

"You look like shit."

"Thanks so much." Evan rolled his eyes. "I know you think I'll become this huge sloth, but I just need a week or two off to relax. Then I'm thinking of working part-time, doing people's books. The rest of the time I'll help grow Vets on the Go! Thanks to Reid and Naomi, we have a decent start." He paused, saw

Cash's annoyance, and added, "Oh, and you too. You are the one who beat up that burglar on TV. Way to save Gotham, Batman."

Cash could do without the sarcasm. "First of all, I was stopping some lowlifes from knifing a kid. I didn't know anyone was filming it. Second, that they happened to be robbing the neighbors made hitting them feel damn good. I felt like I should have been paying them for the privilege." Cash shrugged. "So suck it if you don't like my skills."

"Whatever. Still, that heroic act got us the attention that's made a real difference. Remember where we started? With just you and Reid doing all the lifting?"

"More like me lifting while Reid bitched about it," Cash murmured.

"Right. But now we have, what, ten employees?"

Cash did the math and nodded. "Not counting me, Reid, and Dan." Retired Gunnery Sergeant Dan Thompson, their elderly office manager they couldn't do without.

"Right. Even with all the overhead, employees, trucks, and maintenance, we're making money. That's *huge*. We need to keep capitalizing on Naomi's PR strategies."

"You know, that's great. But could we not talk about work for a while? I'm beat."

"Sorry," Evan said. "I'm just excited to be getting out of my job. My brain hurts at the end of every day."

"Yeah? If you don't want to think too much, come move stuff for a living. I'm not too proud to admit I'd die if I had to work behind a desk. I want to get out and do shit." He filled his plate with more food, famished despite having devoured more than half a large pizza.

The food satisfied but was nowhere near as tasty as Jordan's meal had been.

And that easily, he was thinking of her again.

"Evan, man, how come you're not married?"

Evan choked. After he'd caught his breath, he glared at Cash. "You too? My mother on my ass is bad enough."

Cash felt for the guy. Aunt Jane had given birth to Evan at an older age, making her feel more like a grandmother than an aunt to him and Reid. She'd always been sweet to them though, and the fact she hadn't cared much for Cash's mom was another point in her favor.

"You can't blame her. You're single and rich." At Evan's expression, he corrected, "I mean, comfortable. That's the word, right?"

"Yeah, yeah."

"Buddy, you got a mom who loves you. She wants grandkids because she wants little mini-me's of *you*. Make her happy and get married. Settle down."

Evan studied him, a bemused look on his face. "Did you give this same speech to Reid?"

Not that Cash needed to. His little brother had already fallen hard for Naomi. Cash saw it in the way Reid looked when talking about her. And to see Reid get all dopey around the chick… "Didn't need the speech. He's already a goner."

Evan nodded. "He and Naomi are good. I like her."

"I do too." *And I don't because she's stealing Reid.*

"Too bad you haven't given that speech to Reid. I'd love to see his face when you tell him about making little mini-me's." Evan grinned. "Better yet, tell that to Naomi."

"Hell, no. I don't tell that woman what to do. I don't have a death wish." His brother's redhead had a temper.

"Well, what about you? You're the oldest of us. You're, what, thirty-eight?"

"Thirty-six, dickweed."

"I'm only thirty-one. Still a baby, really."

Cash scoffed.

"I have plenty of time to fall in love, have kids, get divorced, start all over, get married and divorced again, then become a raging alcoholic because my life is a mess. You're not getting any younger."

Cash shook his head. "You really went there, huh?"

Evan laughed. "Hey, I watch all the same shows you do, Drama Queen. I've also been to several weddings in the past ten years, and only about a third of those couples are still married."

"Yeah, but your mom and dad loved each other."

Evan smiled. "That's true. Dad passing about broke Mom's heart." He sighed. "And now I'm feeling guilty for ignoring her. But she nags me about dating every friggin' time we're together."

They sat in silence for a moment then resumed eating.

The next time Cash spoke, he asked the question he'd always wondered about his cousin. "Hey, I've gotta know. Is it weird that your parents were always so much older? I mean, people used to ask if you were with your grandma, not your mom."

Evan made a face. "Yes and no. When I was little, I didn't care. But as a teenager, it was a little embarrassing. And then I'd feel bad for being embarrassed. Now Mom is realizing she's getting up there in age. That's the reason she's all over me to settle down. So she can handle a grandkid before…before she can't."

Aunt Jane had just celebrated her seventy-first. "I get

you. But at least your mom loves you. Mine was too spaced out to do more than blink for most of my life."

"That's true. Your growing up wasn't so good." Evan didn't need to say more than that.

Cash shrugged, so tired of having nothing good to look back on except for Reid. "Maybe that's why I don't see myself ever getting married. Chicks are a lot of work." Jordan wasn't. "Women expect too much."

"No, they don't."

Cash sat up to study Evan, who watched him with compassion. Not pity but empathy. Cash didn't like it, but he could handle it.

"A good woman can make you feel like Superman," Evan said. "It's the ones who want nothing but money or your dick who aren't worth the effort. Mariah wasn't worth it, Cash. You know that."

"I don't like to talk about her."

"Suck it up. I don't like to think about Rita. But she existed. Ignoring her doesn't make her go away."

"Doesn't get you married any faster either," Cash muttered then wished he could unsay the words.

Evan had paled, and the last thing Cash had wanted was to come down on his cousin, who'd been nothing but nice.

"Shit. I didn't mean it."

Evan sat back and propped his feet on the coffee table. "Doesn't mean it's not true. Yep. I avoid getting serious with a woman because I don't want to risk getting hurt again. You avoid women because Mariah was a bitch and you think you'll never be good enough. Your father was a tool."

The blunt truth, coming from laidback Evan, shocked

Cash into a laugh. "Harsh but true." He drank to soothe his parched throat. "I appreciate it, but I'd rather not talk about my asshole dad and cheating ex, thanks."

Evan groaned. "See? This is the real reason I don't date. I used to be good with people. Especially women. Now I say all the wrong things. Friday night isn't for lamentation, it's for enjoying our time off."

"Lamentation? Been reading again, eh?"

Evan snorted. "You should try it. Broadening your vocabulary impresses people." He paused then added with a sly smile, "Especially pretty Army vets who have too many men circling them as it is."

—⁓—

Evan knew he shouldn't have badgered his cousin, but he and Reid had talked, and Evan shared Reid's concerns about Cash. Though Evan hadn't been around the Vets on the Go! crew much due to work, he'd seen the way Cash responded to Jordan.

From what Evan knew of the woman, she seemed smart, did her job well, and could handle Cash. Something many people couldn't.

Evan's oldest cousin had always been someone he'd respected. Cash was big, strong, and bold. When thrown out of the house by his parents—really his father, since Aunt Angela had been clueless about everything—Cash hadn't broken down. He'd thrived, working on his own, doing well despite all the challenges he'd faced.

Secretly, Evan had been envious of his cousins, wishing he'd had a close brother instead of being an only child.

Despite Cash being older and away from his home,

he'd waited for Reid to graduate so they could join the Marine Corps together. There he'd earned accolades and awards for bravery in the face of danger several times over. Cash led people because he was real. He did his best to help others, not to make himself look good but because he cared.

Buried deep down beneath all the bluster and machismo, Cash liked protecting those he cared about. He'd been built to defend the little guy. Probably conditioned into it by having to protect himself and anyone Charles Griffith deemed unworthy.

Mariah cheating on him then stealing from him had been a blow. Especially coming on the heels of a mother who hadn't loved her sons equally or well.

Yet nothing stopped Cash—except the man himself. He had a big mouth, and Evan doubted he knew the meaning of the word *compromise*. But he loved well and deep. If someday he did find a woman worthy of him, Evan knew that woman would never want for anything.

Maybe Jordan could be for Cash what Rita had once been for Evan. If the big doofus would stop irritating her enough to find out.

"You don't know what you're talking about with Jordan." Cash flushed but did his best to appear stern.

"Yeah, right. I don't work there. I'm barely around you two. But the few times I've seen you guys together, the sparks fly."

"We don't get along."

"Well, she is kind of mouthy."

"But smart," Cash said, immediately backing her up. "Funny in an obnoxious kind of way."

"Personally, I find her charming. Pretty too." Evan

watched his cousin, noting the telltale clenching of his jaw. "You know, you make a good point."

Cash blinked. "I do?"

"Yeah. You two don't get along too well. But she seemed to like me, and you're right, I should start dating seriously again. Do you think she'd mind if I—"

"She's busy with her brother. Doesn't want to date for a long time."

Evan stared at him.

Cash glared. "What?"

"So lame."

Cash glared a moment more then covered his face with his hands. "I know."

"Are you even a little embarrassed you're so obviously into this woman?"

"Yes. Fuck, Evan. I work with her. I'm technically her boss."

"That's true. You really need to ease away from the situation." But he knew Cash wouldn't.

"So do you."

"Oh, so that's how you want to play it? We're both her bosses, so we can't date her?"

"Exactly."

Evan studied his cousin, noticing his wan features. "Are you losing weight?"

"No. Maybe. Been working hard."

And stressed from Aunt Angela dying. Or was his cousin lovesick? "Okay. So maybe we shouldn't date her. But Hector or Finley certainly could."

"No fraternization at work. That's our policy."

Evan wondered if Cash heard himself sounding so possessive. Poor, poor Jordan. He grinned.

Cash scowled. "I mean it."

Evan held up his hands in surrender. "Hey, I'm fine with that policy. But that's not going to stop men who don't work for Vets on the Go! asking her out. She's pretty, smart, and funny. Lethal combo there."

"I know." Cash swore. Then swore again and said something under his breath.

"What?"

Cash looked miserable. "We accidentally made out last night."

"Accidentally?" Evan raised a brow. "What, did you trip into her lips?"

Cash growled. "Tell Reid and I'll bend you into a pretzel."

Evan decided to shut up. Fast.

"I'm trying to pull back. But I really like her. And the kiss…" Cash swallowed. "It was…good. Really, really good."

Evan had hope for the knucklehead. "I would remind you that you are a minority partner. In fact, you've been pretty clear that you just work with the guys, drawing a paycheck the same as them."

"I'm still her boss." Weaker.

"Not really, but kind of. You know, we could say only Reid and I can hire and fire. We're majority share-holders. We just talked about this last week."

"Oh. We did, huh?" The pathetic hope on Cash's face was embarrassing.

"You really need to stop sleeping through our meet-ings. But that kiss—technically you didn't do anything wrong. You know damn well you guys don't have a no fraternization policy at work. I do agree that her boss should steer clear. But like I said, you're not her boss." He paused. "And after that accidental meeting of the mouths, was Jordan upset?"

"No. I don't think so." Cash stared at his hands. "She didn't say much, but if she'd been mad, she'd totally have let me know. Jordan doesn't hold back."

"Well then. There you have it. You two kissed, you got that spark out of your systems, and you're done. No harm, no foul. You can still be friends and coworkers." Evan didn't believe a word he was saying.

"Sure, sure." Cash ate more pizza, like a man starving, a glint of purpose in his eye.

Cash would go after Jordan like a heat-seeking missile on target. Had Evan had any worries about Jordan coming to harm, he'd have subtly crushed Cash's hope. But he had a feeling about the pair.

And it would be nice to see Cash happy for a change. At least until he annoyed Jordan by being stupid and insensitive about something. But, hell, from what Cash had said, Jordan could hold her own. Maybe the pair had a chance at something more.

Just because Evan despaired of ever easing his loneliness didn't mean all the Griffiths were doomed to failure. Look at Reid and Naomi. So good together, so in love...

He cleared his throat, erasing memories of Rita. "Now how about we stop talking about girls for two seconds and watch *Drama Island*? I hear Valerie is trying to overthrow Celia as Island Queen."

Cash sat straighter and leaned toward the TV. "Seriously? As if that's gonna happen."

Evan shook his head. His cousin was a goner. He just

hoped Cash would remember that most of the things Charles Griffith had said in the past were lies and should stay buried. Like the man himself.

Chapter 6

HE HAD NO REASON TO BE NERVOUS. NONE AT ALL.

Yet Sunday afternoon, Cash had to work to keep from appearing agitated as he waited for Jordan to arrive. He sat in one of his favorite diners near the house, Rusty's Rest, a hip kind of greasy spoon that had affordable and mouthwatering food.

The diner had a fifties feel, with shiny red vinyl booths, white-and-black-checkerboard flooring, and a jukebox filled with Elvis, Jerry Lee Lewis, and Chubby Checker. Stuff his Aunt Jane still listened to when he made the odd visit over.

And speaking of which, he needed to drag Reid with him as payment for Evan's pizza. Aunt Jane needed the company, and they liked her. Reid could keep it in his pants for one night and spend a few hours apart from Naomi, couldn't he?

Surly and hating that he felt at all jealous, he didn't notice Jordan until she stood over him with a smirk.

"Well, well. That's a pretty big frown. I guess you didn't go to church and rid your soul of evil this morning." She grinned down at him, looking way too cute in shorts and a Lynyrd Skynyrd shirt.

"Yo, fellow sinner. Have a seat." He glanced at the clock on the wall and couldn't resist. "You're late."

"I knew you'd say something." She sighed and plunked down across from him. "You're lucky I'm here at all."

"Oh?" Had something bad happened?

She frowned at him. "Yeah, *oh*. I went to Miriam's class yesterday morning. Asshole. Thanks for the warning." That he hadn't given.

At thoughts of Jordan attending Miriam's empowerment class, he started laughing. And he grew hard, but he focused on the humor of the situation.

"You know what? Get whatever the hell you want. It's on me."

"I'd already figured that."

"But you *have* to tell me what happened yesterday."

She just looked at him.

"Coffee on me all this week too."

She grunted. "Fine. So, yesterday... For starters, all of my classmates wore robes...with *nothing underneath*," she added in a hiss.

Which sent him into more gales of laughter. His favorite waitress, a sweet, middle-aged woman by the name of Irene, wandered over with a pot of coffee, knowing him all too well. Cash didn't ask, just turned over Jordan's cup. "Just black for both of us, Irene."

Jordan continued to glare at him as she sipped. They took a quick moment to scan the menu then ordered.

"Breakfast for ya both. Got it." The older woman sailed away to refill more coffee cups as the place continued to crowd.

"This is the best breakfast joint in all Seattle," he told her. "Rusty's Rest even beats Biscuit Bitch and Krispy Kreme. Straight up." He visited at least once a week and tried to sit in Irene's section. She always gave him extra everything at no charge.

Jordan drank more coffee then sat back and crossed

her arms over her chest. It never failed to surprise Cash to see those arms full of muscle. Jordan had a stream-lined build, ropy arms and thighs, but not like a body-builder. More like a sleek roller derby girl. Two sides of sexy mixed with whoopass. Her breasts weren't too big or small but just right. He wondered what she'd be like in bed, especially after that kiss…

"Hello? Eyes up here." She pointed to her face, her cheeks flushed.

He slowly raised his gaze to her face and tried to appear innocent. "Sorry. I was trying to read your shirt."

"Right." She blew out a breath and groaned. "How could you not have told me what those classes were about?" She slapped her hands on the table and leaned close. After glancing around to see they were alone, she whispered angrily, "Those chicks got naked and started touching themselves!"

"Oh God." He tried not to laugh again. But her angry embarrassment made him want to lean close and kiss her.

"Yeah, they were saying a lot of that too." She huffed, but he saw her lips quirk, as if trying to hold back the laughter. "I knew something was up from the way the guys were teasing me Friday night. The same way you did. But I thought it would be some kind of weird woman woo-woo thing. Not a group masturbation session!"

The waitress stood at the table, blinking down at them. Jordan turned tomato-red. Cash bust out laughing.

"Ah, I just wanted to confirm." Irene cleared her throat and asked Jordan, "Eggs Benedict for you, right? I meant to ask if you wanted the crab Benedict or the classic?"

Jordan blew out a breath. "Classic, please."

"Anything else I can get you? That's on the menu, I mean?" Irene shot a stern look at Jordan. "We run a family establishment, hon. So I can't get you anything more than that. No group...specials."

Jordan looked as if she wanted to sink through the floor.

Irene winked. "Kidding. Sounds like you had a great weekend. I'll be back with your food soon." She laughed. "Ah, to be young again." She waved at Cash, and he promised himself to tip her heavily.

"I cannot *believe* you threw me to the wolves like that," Jordan muttered.

Cash finally stopped laughing and drained his water glass, his mood better than it had been in a long time. "Come on, details."

"For details, I'd better be getting a to-go box of donuts on the way out," she grumbled. "I earned it."

"I bet you did." He felt like his smile had taken over his face, it was so wide.

"You're such an ass." Yet her reluctant grin said otherwise.

"And you wouldn't have set me up on something similar?"

"You know I would have—and will if I get the chance." She paused. "Hold on. Didn't Miriam try to get you to help her class out?" Her eyes widened. "Doing what?"

"Let me ask you this. How exactly did everyone get, ah, in the mood?"

"You don't want to know."

"I do. I *so* do."

She let out a loud, dramatic sigh. "It started out okay." Jordan paused when Irene brought their plates and refilled their coffee. After the waitress left, she continued. "Miriam had a dozen of us in the back room. Her place is a lot bigger than it looks from the outside. Once you get past all the vintage clothes and doodads on sale, she's got space. So I joined a bunch of normal-looking women in the back."

"Normal-looking?"

"A few around my age, some older, maybe two or three younger. The back room had pallets, like yoga mats but softer. And they had been arranged in a ring around Miriam at the center. Incense burned, smelling like roses and lavender. It was relaxing. At first."

"At first!" Once his laughter wound down, he apologized and waited for her to continue.

"Dick." They paused while they began devouring some delicious down-home cooking.

A busty blond woman slowed as she passed by and winked at him. He didn't respond so she kept walking. He said nothing, not wanting the distraction. He used to consider it a point of pride that women liked him enough to be so bold. But he didn't want it anymore, too used to the superficial attractions that never went anywhere once his admirers looked deeper.

So he made no mention of the woman, and Jordan didn't either. She swallowed down a forkful of her breakfast and pointed at his plate. "I don't know how you're going to finish all that. What's in there?"

"Biscuits, eggs, sausage gravy, sausage, cheese, potatoes, and something else. It's amazing." He'd thought about getting a double serving but didn't want to look too piggish in front of Jordan.

"Wow." Without asking, she dug into his food and took a huge bite. "Oh, that is good."

"Help yourself," he said with no small dose of sarcasm.

"I did." She beamed, naughty and sexy and so damn pretty.

He let out a quiet breath then drank more coffee to distract himself. "Waiting on those details…"

"Of course you are. Right. So everyone is looking comfy in their robes, lying around Miriam's 'Modiste.' Miriam hands me a robe, and I just put it on over my clothes. I had no idea everyone else was naked until later." She frowned. "Still not sure about where you'd fit into her class."

"It'll come to you." No pun intended. "What happened next?"

"Some interesting talk, actually. About taking control of ourselves, to stop apologizing for being women. To feel free to reject a man's advances and feel good about it. Not as if we owe him anything."

"Why are you giving me that look?"

"You're a man, aren't you?"

He glanced down at his hard-on, fortunately hidden by the tabletop. "Pretty sure that's a yes."

She glared. "A man who threw me *under the bus*. All that girl-power talk went on for an hour. And we shared, and I actually liked that part. Everyone talked about how they'd been screwed over by a guy at some point. Or a girl. We had a few lesbians in there too. Don't get me wrong. It wasn't a man-hating session. Just a place where we all shared experiences of not feeling in charge of ourselves at some point in our lives.

"It was a nice group. Like, no one cared about where you came from, only that we were all women together. It felt good."

He waggled his brows up and down. "How good?"

Her groan turned into a pained laugh. "Up until the part where the women disrobed and showed themselves in all their glory—led by Miriam's naked splendor. So the nude bit threw me, but then I thought, hey, be okay with a woman's body. Like, they got really into being okay with themselves."

"I so wish I could've been there." He had to stifle more laughter.

"Yeah, then Miriam starts, ah..." She glanced around, her gaze focused on Irene across the diner. "Well, Miriam started doing it right there."

"I'm sorry. Doing *it*?"

"Don't be a jackass," she snapped. "You know." In a lower voice, she added, "Touching herself."

"Where?" He couldn't help prodding her.

"I hate you."

"Hate is just the flipside of love, you know."

She blinked. "What?"

"Something I once heard Miriam say." He laughed at her blush. "You can't leave me hanging. What happened next?"

"God. This is so embarrassing."

"I know. I love it."

She flipped him off. "So then the other ladies start doing it. Fondling themselves. I'm sitting there frozen, not sure what the hell's going on. And the moans and groans are just awful. Before I can move, Miriam's shouting 'Oh yes, oh yes.'" Jordan rubbed her eyes and cringed.

"Getting her happy on?"

She looked miserable and took a swig of coffee. "Exactly that. I had to leave. Except I tripped on my way out and ended up sprawled on someone in the throes, if you know what I mean. It was awkward."

"*Awkward?*" Cash just stared at her, imaging the scene. Then he laughed so hard he cried until he wheezed, having trouble breathing. God. The image. He kept laughing and wheezing.

Jordan stared as if not sure what to make of him.

He finally stopped, told Irene he was okay, and accepted her offer of coffee refills. Once she left, he asked, his voice hoarse, "I have to know. How did Miriam get herself started? I mean, was she just talking herself through the *oohs* and *ahhs*?"

Jordan shook her head, as if to blunt the memory. "God, my ears. But yes. Mostly."

"Mostly?"

"You never did tell me. Why did she want your help with the class?" After a pregnant pause, Jordan's eyes widened and she gaped at him. "No."

―――ᴟᴟ―――

Which set him off again, laughing himself hoarse. Jordan had a feeling she knew the answer. She wouldn't have shared the details of that insane class, except it *was* funny, and she knew Cash would get a kick out of it. Oh, she planned on getting her revenge. But she couldn't fault him for getting one over on her big-time.

"Miriam"―he paused to wipe his eyes―"wanted me to inspire her class by getting off."

"Oh my God. No."

"Oh my God. Yes." He grinned. "Had I known you'd be going Saturday, I'd have volunteered my services instead of declining."

"Liar. You used me to get out of saying yes."

"I did." He nodded, his green eyes bright. "I thought about it the first time she asked me, but Reid said no. Then I realized that might make things awkward. You know, Miriam sees how hung and amazing I am, and then she'll be hooked. Her students would be so gaga over me they'd start clogging the hallways." She rolled her eyes, but that didn't stop him. "Passing by them all every day while they pined after me would get weird."

Jordan felt her cheeks heat, remembering his impressive size from Thursday night—a night that refused to leave her thoughts no matter how hard she tried. "I can't believe she wanted you to…perform… for her class."

"Oh yeah. We're not talking standing there looking pretty. She wanted to see some action. Like taking myself in hand and—"

"I get it." She did, too well. "So that was my Saturday. After tripping over a woman having an orgasm, I dropped the robe and took off. I don't know how I'm going to go by her store on a daily basis." She cringed. "And you're telling me Heidi takes those classes?"

He nodded. "She finished her sessions already, but she said something about taking the next level after she's done training for her upcoming race." He pushed aside his empty plate and sipped his coffee. "I wonder if they do other sex stuff, or if it's some kind of sexual meditation? Do they bring in partners?"

"Please stop talking."

He shot her a wicked grin. "Can I tell you how happy I am you took that class?"

"Asshole." She fumed, trying to disguise her amusement with anger. "You're gonna owe me a bazillion donuts for that."

"All I can say is it was worth it."

An hour later, they stood in his mother's—*in Cash's*—house, eating donuts. Though Cash had bought them for her, he'd already eaten three of them. The man had an appetite, but it sure didn't hurt his physique any.

He looked like a Greek god come to life in worn jeans and a faded blue T-shirt. Make that a sad god. His expression as he stared around him seemed lost, and Jordan empathized. How terrible to have to pack up his dead mother's belongings.

She swallowed a bite of Boston Cream donut and sighed with pleasure, hoping to perk him up a little. "God, I love sweets."

"There's a joke in there somewhere, but damned if I can find it," he said around a mouthful of sugared dough. After he'd finished and dusted his hands, he waved around him. "Well, this is the place. Most of the shit is my mother's, but there are a few things of Reid's still around."

"Not yours or your dad's?"

"She must have taken care of the old man's stuff a while ago because I haven't seen anything of his except for some tools in the garage." He grimaced. "Me? I might as well not exist. I'm still not sure why I inherited the house."

"Just you?" She'd heard one of the guys at work mentioning something to that effect, but she hadn't realized Reid had been cut out of the will.

"Yep, just me. Quick background—my family sucked. My father was an asshole who hated me, and my mother barely knew I existed. Which is to say I was kicked out of the house when I was sixteen and never came back. Not until now."

"Wow. That's terrible."

"Yep." He gave her a pathetic look. "Does that make you want to cuddle me? Offer comfort? Maybe hug me tight, to make me feel better?" His sly grin made her belly do somersaults.

This man she could handle. "I would, but I have a firm policy against not hugging dickbags."

"Lets me off then." He grinned, comfortable with her razzing.

She wondered if her ability to withstand his buried charm and amazing looks made her more of a challenge. The guy had women looking at him all the time. She saw it whenever they went out. Case in point, that woman who'd had the nerve to wink at him while Jordan had sat right there, across the table from him. At least he'd ignored her.

But Cash was like that. A weird combination of obnoxious blowhard and gentleman. At work, he kept things professional with clients, ignoring any come-ons from interested parties. Sure, he'd talk a good game behind their backs, but he never followed through on it—that she'd seen. And it wasn't every time. He wasn't a sex magnet per se. Yet it happened often enough that Funny Rob had started calling him Gunny Gigolo behind his back, which was kind of funny except she had a feeling it would bother him to know.

Not that she could blame any of them. Cash's big

mouth rarely made him less attractive to his many admirers.

Not Jordan though. She worked with her *friend*. That kiss they'd shared had meant nothing. Had to get it out of the way so they could focus on…focus on… His lips kept moving, but she didn't hear him.

"Hey, you having a sugar rush or what?" He frowned. "Hello? Earth to Jordan?"

She ignored the heat in her cheeks. "Sorry, I'm still digesting that big breakfast. Sue me for not moving faster."

"Try moving at all." He shrugged. "Fine. Keep digesting that fat pill, and follow me on the tour."

He showed her the many boxes he'd already packed up and moved to the side of the living room. A ton of romance books, videotapes, and even a few DVDs mixed with collectibles and plain junk were stacked nearby. The sheer number of books astounded her.

"Wow. It's like a library in here." She stared in awe. Though his mother had clearly had a problem collecting things, she'd kept the place fairly neat. They had plenty of room to move around through the expected dust and occasional cobweb from a house that hadn't been disturbed until recently. "Your mom has all the classics. Is that a VHS tape of *Casablanca*?"

He shrugged. "Probably. Too bad they didn't have streaming back then. Would have saved on a lot of space."

The tour through the hallway into the back bedrooms showed a heck of a lot of movies. "Do they even make VHS players anymore?"

"I think so." He scrubbed the back of his close-cropped hair. "There's so much here. I swear I packed up half a room last week. And it doesn't feel like I did anything."

"What are you going to do with it all?" she asked him.

"Dump it."

"What? No." Jordan saw the anger in his expression and sought to ease some of it. "Think of all the people who could use some fun in their lives."

He snorted. "Fun? Try escape. Why help someone else ignore their kids or husbands? This shit needs to go."

"Not everyone goes to the same extremes your mom did, Cash." She moved closer to him and put a hand on his forearm, feeling his tension. Understanding it. "Hey, my parents didn't understand me at all. And sometimes I still don't like them all that much. But my mom used to read romance books and didn't ignore me or my family because of it." No, she'd ignored Jordan anytime Jordan did something she didn't like. But that had nothing to do with avoiding her family in favor of entertainment. "I know a lot of people who enjoy TV in a healthy way. Sometimes when your life sucks, that kind of fun takes you away from your misery."

"I guess." He looked around and sighed. "So you think I should try to sell it all?" He didn't sound enthused.

"You could, but it'll be a hassle. I think you should donate it. Give it to Goodwill, a woman's shelter, or some place that could use it for their own fundraiser."

"Not a bad idea." He planted his hands on his hips and stared around him. "I'll be honest. I want this shit gone so much I hadn't thought about where to take it. Just boxing it up and dumping it sounded like a plan." A moment of silence as he took in everything. "Um, would you mind helping me out with the donations? Maybe see who needs or wants this stuff?" In the corner, he knelt and picked up a tattered child's book, one that had obviously seen its share of wear and tear. He didn't say anything as he stood, clenching it in his hand.

Jordan felt for him. "Sure. I can help with the donations. Let me make a few calls then I'll help you pack."

He looked up and met her gaze. It was as if she saw the real Cash, the hurt little boy inside the man needing reassurance. In a blink, the expression vanished, but she knew what she'd seen.

She pretended not to notice the suspicious shine in his eyes and left the room to find something to write with. After she'd made a few calls and found places to donate, she rejoined Cash in his mother's bedroom.

More of the room had been packed up, his mother's clothing bagged and tagged, the way they did it for Vets on the Go!

"Hey, you're actually not bad at this."

He turned to see her and forced a smile that hurt her to see. "Yeah, how about that? I got some skills."

"You mean, more than just making women faint from the sight of you?" she added in a dry tone, pleased beyond measure when he gave her a real smile.

"Well, there is that." He leered at her. "You feeling the magic, sweetness?" He flexed a huge bicep her way, and she had to fight to pretend disinterest. "How about now?"

"Ohh. Please. I want you," she said with no inflection whatsoever. "So, so bad."

Cash chuckled. "Man, you are such a ballbuster. No wonder I like you."

"You like it when people bust your balls?"

"Yeah. You're real. I can work with real."

She couldn't read the look he shot her, but it felt intimate. Something more than a friendly glance. Simultaneously relieved to see him happy and nervous to be at the center of his attention, she didn't know what to say next.

"All right, Fleming. Enough. Quit slacking." *Thank you, Cash, for smoothing over that suspended moment of awkwardness.* "I paid for your time with a baker's dozen of health-hazardous sugar crap—even let you get those frilly pink frosted donuts that are, frankly, embarrassing. Now get to work."

"Such an asshat," she muttered, heard him laugh, and packed with a smile on her face.

Chapter 7

CASH AND JORDAN GOT A SURPRISING AMOUNT OF WORK done. He wouldn't have thought they could do so much in so little time, but with her help, a few hours saw them clear out a good sixth of the house.

They'd stacked the donations along one wall. On the other, trash. To his bemusement, something good would come out of Angela's shit. They'd use her belongings to help others. He knew Reid would agree, might even be proud of him for acting so mature about things. All thanks to Jordan.

The memories he'd tried to bury as he'd sifted through Angela's possessions—those things that had been so much more important to her than him—hadn't hurt as much as he'd imagined they would. What did that mean?

"Good job." Jordan smacked him on the shoulder, her version of an attaboy that was supposed to hurt more than it did, most likely.

"Thanks. I mean, *ow.*" He rubbed his arm and pretended it hurt.

She rolled her eyes. "Those boxes over there can be donated too. But that last one has stuff you probably need to look through. I'll be back."

"Back? Where are you going?" She wasn't leaving already, was she?

"To the john. That okay with you?" She turned on a huff and left him.

"Prickly little thing." He moved the boxes then found the one she'd pointed out. He took it to the kitchen table, sat, and opened it.

Only to find it full of old photographs.

Back then, his mother had been keen on family. She'd documented everything, filling old photo albums with a zeal to capture every memory.

Shock held him immobile as he stared at a picture of him, Reid, and his parents, all smiling and happy. He had to be five or six years old, so little, and so proud of that stupid football he'd received as a present from his father. He turned it over and saw the date. Christ. That picture was from his sixth birthday party. He remembered his mother kissing his cheeks and laughing. His father tossing the pigskin and smiling, praising Cash for being such a natural. Then Reid begging to play too, and the four of them enjoying the sunny spring weather before Cash's friends arrived for his big birthday celebration.

It all seemed so normal, a long-ago life belonging to someone else.

So strange to remember that time as if it were yesterday, a clear and present echo of better days.

Because just a year later his life had changed, and everything he'd once thought about himself had gone out the window. He hadn't been a good boy at all; he'd been bad. The worst son a parent could have. Shitty and worthless, except in Reid's eyes.

His brother used to look at him as if Cash could do no wrong, no matter what their father said. Until Cash had fucked up one too many times in high school and been kicked out of the house. Fourteen years later, he'd been booted out of the USMC. Fired from one job to the next until Reid had created Vets on the Go! to help Cash.

Reid had fixed everything, the way he'd been trying to fix everything throughout their childhood. What kind of life was that for a young boy who'd never put a foot wrong?

Standing here, in the place where Charles Griffith had made it his mission to teach Cash how useless he was, brought it all back.

He sifted through more photos, all of him and the family in the "golden" years, that time before life had turned upside down.

Footsteps neared. "Wow. Is that you?" Jordan lifted a picture from the table to study it closely. "You were so cute," she teased. "What happened?"

He shrugged and started stuffing the old photos back into the box. "Good question." After a moment of silence, he glanced up and saw her watching him.

She handed him back the photo, her gaze soft. "I was just kidding."

"I know." He stuffed it back in and closed the box. "Put this with the throwaways."

"Do you think Reid might want some?"

Cash glowered. "Who the hell knows?" Though the plan had been to go through everything and give Reid a chance to look through some things, Cash didn't want to remind Reid of a time that had never been real, or of Cash's youth, back when he'd first shown signs of being such a fuckup.

I've grown since then, done a few good things with my life. Hell, I even saved a few guys from enemy fire.

The thought of having done some good meant shit because here, in this house, he was nothing but a loser who hadn't amounted to anything.

"I'll take care of this," he said to Jordan, unable to face her, sure she'd see the truth he always tried so desperately to hide.

He grabbed the box and stacked it in the disposable section.

He didn't know what to say to her. How to feel. Because it made no sense to be feeling depression and grief for a family that had never really existed, for a boy who'd been nothing but worthless his whole life. *Shake it off, man. Let it go*, he could hear Reid telling him. *They're gone.*

Almost three decades had passed since that stupid picture had been taken, and Cash knew better than to expect happy thoughts from this hellhole.

He cleared his throat and announced, "We're almost done, Jordan. Let's wrap up soon." *Reid should be here doing this with me, damn it.* Then he went back to the bathroom to clear out the cabinets and cupboards.

It was as he was cleaning out the linen closet that he found himself suddenly unable to process it all. Tucked between some dusty towels on the highest shelf in the closet, a small ceramic lion with uneven legs, a too-large brown mane, and googly eyes stared up at him.

A project he'd been assigned to make in elementary school. Silly Cash had thought to make his mother something special for Mother's Day. But when he'd given it to her, she'd pushed it aside to make room for the new radio his father had purchased. His father had tossed the lion, breaking off its tail.

Cash stared at the thing, confused, because he could have sworn Angela had dumped it in the trash. Instead, the lion and its raggedy, glued-on tail sat protected. And next to it, the elephant Reid had made for her two years later.

He sat in the hallway, staring at the things, wanting to throw them against the wall and watch them shatter. Wanting to know why. Why had everything changed so suddenly?

He felt Jordan's hand on his shoulder, but he couldn't speak. His eyes felt dry, his throat scratchy. Yet he was frozen, so unworthy and so unlovable.

So why had Angela kept his lion?

———～～～———

Jordan felt for Cash. She kept piecing things together from what he'd told her and what she'd witnessed in this house.

How awful to have parents who hated you or, worse, who didn't care.

Granted, she knew her family clearly favored those who gave them no trouble—namely, Leanne. Yet she couldn't fault them completely; Jordan had tried her best to earn their displeasure. Still, that her parents favored Leanne wasn't fair. Should she ever have children, she'd love them all unconditionally, equally. Like Rafi, who merited a second and third chance. He was her brother—family.

Watching Cash stare at creations only a child could have made, looking so lost and hurt, pained her deep inside.

She sat next to him, saying nothing, wanting just to be there for him. They sat in silence for some time until she carefully took the ceramic figure from him and placed it in the box he'd wanted to get rid of, the one she'd tucked away so Reid and Cash might have something from their childhood to remember.

Yeah, it wasn't her place to interfere, but screw it. Cash deserved some decent memories.

She returned to see him lying in the hallway, staring up at the ceiling. His big body took up a lot of room, and she had to carefully ease around him.

"I hate popcorn ceilings," he said in the sudden stillness. "They really date a house, you know?"

Shocked he'd even know what a popcorn ceiling was, she sat perpendicular to him, her back propped against the wall. Then she made a bold move and lifted his head to rest in her lap.

He didn't resist her, but he did tense. "What are you doing?"

"Shut up." She didn't look down, instead stared at the walls, studying some fugly wallpaper as she stroked his hair. "I hate lime green."

That startled a chuckle out of him. "Me too. I used to stare at that nasty wallpaper for hours when they sat me in the corner. Fucking lime-green vines and ass-pink roses."

She blinked. "Ass-pink, huh?"

"Well, I had a few other words for it, but *ass* is the nicest one I could come up with in mixed company."

She chuckled and continued to stroke his hair, taken with the softness on a man with such an unbending will. She heard him sigh and, out of her periphery, saw him close his eyes. Touching him felt right, as did the notion she'd brought him some comfort in a place made up of painful memories.

She couldn't have said how much time had passed, but he shifted beneath her. She glanced down, saw him staring at her, and stared back.

"Why did you do that?" he asked, only the sound of a clock's ticking heard between them. As if they both held their breaths, anticipating her answer.

"Because I can?" A stupid answer, but it was light enough that Cash didn't bolt. He smiled.

So damn pretty was all she could think. Then she leaned down and kissed him with a tenderness that surprised them both. She drew back and caressed his hair one final time. "Time for me to go."

He nodded, lifted his hand to her cheek, and stroked her with a callused finger. "Yep. Time to go."

By mutual agreement, neither spoke about what had happened. Cash locked up behind him and headed to his car, blocked by hers in the drive. He leaned against the driver's-side door. "So, your brother?"

She nodded, not wanting to deal with Rafi but needing to stop ignoring the situation. "Can you come over tomorrow night? We'll do a mini-intervention. Fair warning though. He's a smartass and won't appreciate your time."

He snorted. "Like his sister."

"Hey."

But Cash ignored her pique. "No problem. I remember being an asshole when I was younger."

"Remember being one?" she said, not quite under her breath.

"Be nice or I won't give you the leftover donuts." He held out the box and didn't appear surprised when she darted close to nab it.

Before she could go, he grabbed her by the shoulder. Then he shocked her by kissing her on the forehead. "Thanks, Jordan."

She blushed. "Um, sure. But consider yourself repaid. Between these donuts and Rafi, we'll be even."

"Nah. I figure I'll still owe you."

She couldn't read the look he shot her, but the warmth in his gaze was impossible to miss.

Flustered and not sure why, she hurried into her car and left. "Must stop thinking about that man. He's just a friend. Nothing more."

So why then could she still feel his soft hair under her fingers? And why was she reliving that kiss over and over, feeling his lips against hers as if he'd just touched her?

———∿∿∿———

"For the last time, I'm not telling you about Saturday morning. Yeah, you'll just have to imagine it." Jordan glared at the guys during lunch. A major move Monday morning had five of them working together. They only had two days to get everything packed and shifted to the big truck for a four-bedroom house. But the owners were also hurrying to help, so they might just make it before the Fourth of July.

Outside, dining on top of the hood of Lafayette's old truck, Heidi, Jordan, Lafayette, Finley, and Cash hurried to eat.

"It was a mind-opening experience," Heidi offered, her voice soft and, to Jordan's ear, amused.

"I can't believe you went back for more," Jordan muttered.

Cash remained silent, but the wide grin he wore said what words didn't.

Heidi tilted her head as if in thought. "I found it... instructional."

The guys laughed. "You're cruel for holding out on us, Jordan." Finley wiped an imaginary tear. "I can only imagine you and Miriam and the other ladies getting... instruction."

"And Miriam wanted me to provide inspiration," Cash had to add. "Can you imagine how awestruck Jordan would have been to have seen me *inspiring* the crowd?"

Finley perked up. "I wonder if she's still looking for help."

Jordan and Heidi shared a grimace, and Heidi said, "Ah, no thanks."

Finley shook his head. "Oh, not for you, Heidi. We know you dig chicks. I mean for poor, sad little women like Jordan who have no life and might not remember what the male form looks like."

Lafayette grinned. "You know, Finley, I bet there's a *male* empowerment class we could get you into. I'd be willing to take it. You know, in this light, you look a little like my cutie, Simon."

Finley turned bright red, and Jordan laughed and bumped fists with Lafayette.

Finley raised a brow. "You think I won't do it?"

"Oh God. I can't handle the thought," Heidi groaned.

"Me neither," Jordan agreed but winked at Finley to salve his ego.

Cash saw and raised a brow, but she ignored him.

"Come, let's finish. I have a race to train for," Heidi reminded them. Meaning she would be off for most of the next month while she geared up for a summer mara-thon she intended to win. "We have Wednesday off and two more moves scheduled for you guys for Thursday without me to help."

"Good point." Cash nodded. "We only have Heidi today and tomorrow. Let's get this house done."

The group broke up and headed back inside.

Cash always acted like a seamless addition to the team. Jordan watched him when he wasn't aware, notic-ing how he fit in. He pulled his own weight, joked with the guys, and kept gossiping with Heidi about wacky housewives and reality TV.

As much as he'd hated all the drama his mother had indulged herself in, he didn't seem to see the irony of his own interests. She had no intention of mentioning the comparison, but she wondered about his passion for chaos.

He seemed like an orderly type of guy. His handwrit-ing was always legible and tidy. He kept his spaces at work neat, his locker too. She had no idea what it would be like at his home though. Thoughts like that had her heart racing, wondering if he kept his bed tidy and made. Or messed because he'd gotten some exercise between the sheets...

Someone cleared his throat by her, and she jumped, bobbling a box of linens.

"Easy, Scrappy Doo. It's just me."

She blinked at the sexy bane of her existence. "Excuse me? Scrappy Doo? More like Daphne, I'd say." She looked him over. "I'd peg you as Scooby Dum."

"Huh. I thought for sure you'd make me Old Man Smithers or something."

"More like Miner49er." She grinned, bemused that Cash knew about Scooby Doo of all things. She'd loved the canine detective and his friends as a kid, a passion that had never waned. Sometimes when her brother wasn't around, she secretly streamed the old animated episodes, getting a kick out of them, especially as an adult.

"Hey, you two, quit flirting. We have work to do," Lafayette reminded them as he passed by, carrying two boxes.

"No one's flirting, Romeo," Jordan hit back. In a low murmur to Cash, she said, "Quit flirting. I'm busy."

"Please. You want me. It's a curse being this fine."

She tried to hide a smile. "Whatever." She whispered, "Seven o'clock tonight. My place—for Rafi."

He lost his smile and nodded. "Don't worry. I'll be there." He paused. "You cooking?"

"Yes. Now shut up and get back to work."

He moved back and in a loud voice said, "Yes, boss. No need to crack the whip on me."

Finley snickered and made whip-cracking sounds. Which got everyone talking about who was really in charge of the team.

"I'm not getting any younger," Heidi informed the team. "Hurry up. I have ten miles to run later today."

Today, they all agreed.

Heidi was in charge.

—◦◦◦—

Cash felt nervous as he approached Jordan's door later that night. He had no idea why. It wasn't a date. He hadn't needed to go home and shower and change before meeting at her place for dinner. Bringing her a box of the chocolates he'd overheard her mention to Heidi was probably a stupid move too. But he figured she could use the boost.

No one knew better than Cash how family could cause you to lose it.

Reid, big surprise, was once again spending the night with Naomi. It didn't bother Cash as much tonight though, because he had other plans. Like helping his friend and coworker handle a family problem.

He knocked and waited.

And knocked again.

"Hold on," a young male snarled from behind the door.

He heard arguing between the male and Jordan. Then the door opened and a male version of Jordan gaped up at him.

"*Shit*. Bigfoot has arrived."

"Rafi," Jordan admonished from behind him. "Be nice. Hi, Cash. Rafi, this is my friend from work, Cash Griffith. Cash, come on in. This is Rafi, my brother."

Cash stepped inside, handed off the chocolates to Jordan, and stared down at an almost pretty young man. Thick lashes covered dark-brown eyes that snapped with impatience. Rafi stood a few inches taller than Jordan but a head less than Cash. Whip-lean and strong, no doubt from carrying around so much attitude.

"Yo." He nodded to the kid.

"Hey." Rafi gave him a wary nod.

Jordan tugged Cash further into her apartment. "Thanks for the chocolates." She shoved Rafi out of the way since he hadn't budged, staring at Cash.

"Nice, Jordan," Rafi sneered.

"Move next time, knucklehead." She crossed her

eyes at Cash, who grinned. "Kid is fifteen going on forty. Want something to drink?"

"Shouldn't we be sober for an intervention?"

The kid stared back and forth between them. At the word *intervention*, he'd stiffened. "What's he talking about?"

Cash had thought about how to handle the situation, wondering how he'd have responded to some random guy when he'd been fifteen.

Jordan glared at Cash, and he shrugged. "Hey, I'm not your guy for subtlety. I'm a straight shooter." He ignored her mutterings. "Rafi, I—"

"It's actually *Rafael*," the boy said, stiffly.

"Rafael," Cash emphasized, "your sister tells me you need help. It's pass summer school or you go to some shitty military academy. And your attitude ain't helping."

"Please. What does some ex-military asshole like you have to say to help me? Be all you can be?"

Cash wanted to laugh at that, but Jordan's tight-lipped expression told him not to.

"Nah. That's Army, kid. You don't want to go there."

Rafael blinked. "No?"

Jordan placed her hands on her hips. "Why not? What's wrong with the Army?"

"Please. What's *not* wrong with the Army?"

She gasped. "You're such an asshole."

Rafael looked from her to Cash and let himself grin. "You know, I think this guy's not so bad after all."

"Buddy, I was Marine Corps. All the way. It's a great institution, well, minus the shitheads and politically correct bullshit everyone's peddling nowadays."

Rafael just stared at him, so Cash moved deeper into

the living room and took a seat on the couch. His casual attitude had Rafael following him while Jordan shot daggers his way.

"What? So I should join the Marines?"

Cash agreed with the kid's skepticism. "Hell no. Not now. Your mouth would get your head ripped off and shoved right up your ass."

"Cash, language," Jordan growled.

"Sorry. But it's true. Look, Rafael. I'm not here to sell you on the Marines." He added under his breath, "The only good service, you want my opinion." In a louder voice, he said, "I'm just here to talk to you about being a man."

Rafael stared up at the ceiling and groaned. "God, not the safe sex talk."

Jordan moved a chair from the dining table closer to the couch and sat. "No, it's not the safe sex talk, you moron." She nodded for Rafael to sit on the ottoman by the coffee table.

Cash was surprised when the kid obeyed.

"So if it's not a safe sex talk, why are you here?"

The word *sex* made him think of Jordan, so Cash ignored her, needing to focus on the boy. "Look. I'm just here to help. I remember what it was like to be an obnoxious teenager always getting into trouble. Fact is you're gonna do what you're gonna do. It's the truth, Jordan," he said to forestall her. "But, kid, I can tell you that blowing off school won't help. You just have to get through the next two years, right?"

Rafael shrugged.

"I take that as a yes. So why is it so hard to shut the fuck up and do your work without aggravating the world?"

Jordan groaned. "Language."

"Please," her brother scoffed. "I'm grown, Jordan. A *fuck* here and there isn't going to corrupt me." Rafael was full of that famous Fleming sarcasm.

Cash nodded. Looking directly at her, he raised his eyebrows. "Jordan, why don't I take Rafi out to grab some ice cream?"

"Oh, I can do that," she said, getting the hint. "You guys stay here." She hurried to grab her keys.

Rafael agreed to some private time, surprising him. "Yeah, Jordan. Pick up some Rocky Road while I talk to your boyfriend."

"I told you before. He's not my boyfriend." Jordan glared at Cash.

"What the hell did *I* do?"

"He's someone who knows what it's like to be you," she said to her brother.

"I highly doubt that." Rafael glanced at Cash's body, specifically at his arms.

"Hey, I grew into these. At your age, I was a smartass with tiny fists. A lot like you and your sister."

That got a grin out of the kid and a scowl from Jordan.

"Hey Jordan. I'm a fan of Rocky Road too." He hurried to hand her a twenty before she left, then sat back on the couch, hoping she was on board with his little plan. "Would you mind grabbing us dessert while we have a man-to-man talk? He'll pretend he's listened to get you off his ass. Then we'll eat, and I'll go home." He turned to Rafael. "If you go to bed early, I promise not to bone your sister with you right next door."

Rafael nodded. "Thanks, man. I appreciate that."

"Oh!" Jordan literally stomped her foot. "You are *not*

my boyfriend. He's not," she said to her brother. "He's a huge asshole!"

"Jordan, language," Rafael said with a wicked grin.

"I'll be back in fifteen minutes," she snarled.

Cash coughed to muffle his amusement, and they both watched her slam out the door.

Rafael dropped his smile, looked Cash in the eye, and said, "Now tell me the truth. What are you trying to do with my sister? And why do you think talking to me like you care is going to get you there?"

Chapter 8

RAFAEL DIDN'T KNOW WHAT THE HECK HIS SISTER WAS thinking by inviting Conan the Barbarian to join them for dinner. First of all, it was obvious the dude was into Jordan. Second, no matter how much time had passed between her Army days and sporadic visits home, Rafael knew his sister. She liked this big idiot.

Since she'd started working for Vets on the Go!, she'd mentioned little things about her "boss." Like how much Cash annoyed her, how he bragged too much, and how that didn't seem to matter because so many women rubbernecked at the douche's muscles and good looks. Then she'd mention how hard he worked alongside them, that he was a decent if irritating coworker who refused to act like her superior.

But seeing how flustered she got around the dude, Rafael knew she *liked* the guy.

He didn't know how to feel about that. Especially since she'd dragged the monster's sorry ass into a family issue Cash had no business being a part of.

"Look, Rafi—"

"Rafael," he said through gritted teeth, even though he actually preferred Rafi. But *Rafael* made him sound older. More like he could be a part of his friend Juan's crew than just some teenage flunky at summer school.

"Sorry. *Rafael.* Your sister loves you, and she's not

sure what else she can do for you. She told me you flunked hard on a bunch of classes. High school is no joke. They actually care what kind of grades you get if you want to get to college. She also said you're really smart." The look Cash shot him told Rafael that the guy didn't exactly agree with that assessment.

Rafael swallowed the *fuck you* because the guy was huge and Jordan wasn't around to step in if things got rough. "I am smart. Smart enough to know high school sucks and I'm not learning anything. A, D, F, what does it matter? Most people nowadays don't even go to school and make money."

"Yeah? What do they do for a job then?"

"Did you get good grades?"

Cash snorted. The man had a square jaw, a body similar to those on the covers of fitness magazines, and a short haircut that might as well have spelled out ex-military. And his hands. Jeez, he had big hands with bruises on his knuckles. Not a guy who posed as a badass but the real deal.

Though Jordan had never brought her dates home, having spent so much time overseas and in other parts of the country, Rafael had seen pictures of her with boyfriends. None of them had seemed so hard-core.

"Did *I* get good grades?" Cash asked. "Fuck no. I joined the Marines. Did a lot of stuff I can't talk about." Cash shot him a hard smile, and Rafael did his best to look casual and not alarmed. "Shot guns and shit. Then made the mistake of trying to do the right thing and got my ass tossed out of the service."

"You got a dishonorable discharge?" Rafael gaped. His sister would never be with some guy who had been thrown out of the military. She was all for rules, discipline, and order.

"Nope. I've got honorable discharge on my paperwork, so don't even think of trying to rat me out to your sister on a lie."

"I'm no narc," Rafael said.

"Only good thing you've got going for you at this point."

"Fuck you" slipped out in Rafael's anger.

"Gee, that hurts." Cash snorted. "Look, kid. Your sister is worried about you. She's a good person. A hard worker. And she's smart. She doesn't take anyone's shit, least of all mine."

Rafael tensed when Cash stood because the guy was huge. Rafael stood as well, hoping to look not so small.

"But she loves you, enough that she's taking on a teenager and working her tail off to help you out. So what's the real problem? You don't like school."

"I don't."

"Right. But it's not a forever deal. Just get decent grades until you're done. Enough to pass, then your life is your own." Cash ran a hand over his hair, and his biceps strained his T-shirt.

"Jesus. Are you on steroids or what?"

"Nah. I just lift a lot. At work and for fun. It's a great stress reliever. You should try it. I can take you to my gym if you want."

Sadly, Rafael felt like a ten-pound weakling next to Cash. No way he wanted to stand next to the guy in a gym. "Listen, I don't need a big brother. I don't even know why my sister asked you to talk to me." *Man, Jordan must really be freaked to ask Mr. Marine over.*

"Look. You talked. I listened." He ignored Cash's snort. "Can we let this go?"

Cash studied him. "I can tell you're smart. Well, a smartass at least. But your grades suck, and you're hanging with questionable kids, according to your sister. So what's the real problem?"

"Why the hell should I tell you?" Rafael didn't like this guy poking into his private life. "It's not your business. And I don't give a shit if you are fucking my sister. You don't—"

He gasped because suddenly Cash loomed over him, and the look on the guy's face was anything but pleasant. "You've got issues. I get it. You're an angsty teen with bigger balls than brains. But your sister is one of the best people I know. You will *not* disrespect her. Not around me."

Rafael swallowed, hating that he felt so much fear. From this guy, from his life, from his inability to understand so many things. Fury overwhelmed him, and he struck out as hard as he could.

He made contact with Cash's flat belly. Either the guy had expected the hit and tensed to brace himself or, worse, he always felt like concrete. Rafael didn't know, and now his hand hurt. He didn't plan to hang around for the repercussions.

He tried to run and found himself jacked against the wall, Cash's mighty forearm against his chest, the big guy not even winded. Rafael flailed a little more and got nowhere.

"Not bad. You done?"

He felt a second wind coming. "Don't you touch me," he shouted and tried to break free.

Cash sighed. "Kid, if I 'touched' you, you'd know it. I don't hit teenagers. And I sure the hell don't let anyone talk bad about Jordan."

Rafael's heart rate started to settle.

"*That's* why you're up against this wall, and you know you deserve it."

Rafael started to sag, embarrassed it took someone not family to defend the only person who genuinely cared about him. His eyes burned.

Cash slowly eased back and stuck his hands in his pockets, no doubt seeing the tears Rafael didn't want to shed. "Look, Rafael. Jordan loves you. If I'd had a sister that great when I was your age, someone who took care of me and wanted the best for me no matter what, I might have turned out a better guy. You've got that. Don't blow it. I don't know what your shit is. I do know you have it in you to be a better person. And that's not about grades or school or joining the *Army*." He sneered the word, and Rafael wanted to both laugh and cry. "But don't get your ass arrested because it'll fuck up your life before you can get started."

He paused, still watching Rafael so carefully. "You're not the only one dealing with crap in your life. Everyone has it. It's what you do about it that counts. So you suck at school. So what? I can't spell worth a damn, and I don't care. I'm amazing. Just look at this." Cash flexed his biceps and grinned. "I focus on the things I can do right. I'm big. Might be dumb as a rock, but I know how to protect the people I care about. And, yeah, I move shit for a living, something anyone can do. But when I'm doing it, I'm the best damn mover you've ever seen."

Rafael wanted to say something mean, but what

could he say? Cash laid it out, called himself stupid and awesome in the same breath. "I...I hate school."

Cash said nothing.

"My life is my business. Not yours."

Still nothing.

"But I won't drag Jordan down."

Now the big guy nodded.

"I didn't mean to before. It's just that I get so frustrated. School sucks so much. It's summertime, and I'm having to deal with learning stuff."

Cash sighed. "I feel for you. I hated classrooms. And it doesn't stop after high school. There's always something you gotta learn. But stripping an M-16 was fun. So was learning offensive tactics and blowing crap up. So maybe you find something you like, and you can focus on that." He paused. "I'm not gonna Big Brother you. I know you're a man and can handle yourself. But a man takes care of his family first." Cash frowned. "Just between you and me, your folks are sorry-ass people."

On that Rafael agreed. Though he loved his parents, he didn't understand why they wanted to throw him away.

"I mean, why aren't they helping you? Why does your sister, who just got out of the service and is still adjusting to civilian life, have to deal with your problems? Not saying she shouldn't because she's that kind of person. She's got heart. But, man, your parents have money and time Jordan doesn't have."

And that made Rafael feel even worse about everything. He was so stupid, always making mistakes because his brain didn't work right. Bad enough he'd sunk himself. Now he'd brought Jordan down into his mess.

Cash kept talking about life choices, that new tutor

Jordan wanted him to use, and how high school didn't really matter in the end so long as he got through it. Rafael heard the words but couldn't make sense of them, too trapped in misery. He wanted space to think, time to figure out what he needed to do to make things right.

Jordan came through the door carrying a container of ice cream, and her obvious concern tore him up. Handling all his shit on top of her own issues. Because, yeah, he'd seen her looking at different college applications for herself, at trade schools, other jobs she might want. Stuff she couldn't do while helping him deal.

"Everything okay—Rafi!" She was fast and grabbed him by the tail of his shirt before he could bolt.

Afraid to cry in front of her and Cash, he tugged away and waved over his shoulder as he rushed past her. "I'm good. Just going to grab something and give you two lovebirds some space. I'll be at Daniel's, I swear. I'll text you." Then he hurried to freedom…well, as much as he could get on his limited bus fare budget.

———

Cash didn't know what the hell had gone through Rafael's head, but he'd thought the kid had heard him on all the finer points. He seemed a decent enough boy, if a little sarcastic. But didn't everything merit rebellion at that age?

"What did you do?"

Uh oh. Jordan looked angry, a momma bear protecting her young. He held up his hands. "Whoa. Don't look at me. I tried the heart-to-heart with the kid. He hates school, is frustrated with life, and doesn't understand what the hell I'm here for."

She kept frowning but deflated a bit. She left to put the ice cream away then returned with a question. "Why did he take off?"

"I don't know. Maybe so you wouldn't see him crying?"

"You made him *cry*?" She stormed over to him and poked him in the chest. "What *exactly* did you say?"

Woman had a bony finger. He rubbed his chest and tried to back away but found himself blocked by the wall. "Hey, now. Easy, killer." She didn't seem amused. "Look, I tried to tell him to just deal with the next few years, then live his own life. I told him how lucky he was to have you batting for him." He didn't think he should mention the part about Rafael hitting him or about the kid speculating on who Jordan might be fucking. And that whole conversation about shitty parents probably wouldn't go over well either. "You didn't see any bruises on him when he left, did you?"

She continued to glare at him. "I better not ever see one on him from you. Ever."

"Got it." Was it wrong that he loved how protective she was about her brother? God, could the woman do something to annoy him out of this stupid crush he had on her? "So, um, dinner?"

She took a step back and frowned. Before she said anything, her phone jingled. She reached into her back pocket, read the screen, and sighed. "Rafi's hanging with Daniel, who's not a bad kid. A nerdy gamer, but he's decent enough, with a nice mom. Rafi said he's fine and that you—Conan—didn't do anything to make him leave."

"Okay then." Out of that doghouse at least. Good to know the kid really wasn't a narc. "So you were going to tell me about dinner?"

"You and food." Jordan shook her head. "Has anyone ever come between you two?" she joked. "Because I can see you marrying a lasagna, but nothing else long term."

Mariah came to mind, and he shut the thought down fast, though he felt grateful for the intrusion. Yeah, he'd once put himself out there. And look at how that had turned out. This fascination for Jordan meant nothing. Just a hot chick with a core of honor whom he happened to work with. It was natural he'd be attracted to qualities he'd once hoped he might possess.

"Nope." He forced a grin. "Nothing beats a decent mac 'n' cheese."

She shook her head. "It was a casserole, not a simple mac 'n' cheese."

"I don't care what you call it. What's for dinner tonight?"

She sighed. "Come on. You can help me peel the sweet potatoes and chop up the onions."

"Wait. Those are vegetables."

"So smart. You sure you were a Marine?"

He glared at her, saw her smile, and felt his palms sweat. "I can't believe I have to work for my meal. And let me tell you something, Jordan. You keep rolling your eyes like that, and one day they won't roll back normal."

She laughed. "Whatever. Now grab a peeler and stop giving me shit." She pointed that steel finger at him.

"Fine, fine. No need for violence. Just tell me what to do."

Over an hour later, he felt more than satisfied. The baked chicken, noodles, and veggie mash had gone down smoothly. He'd forced himself to only take two helpings, still hungry, but sadly not for food. He wished he didn't remember how she tasted or how right she'd felt when he'd lifted her onto the kitchen counter and settled between her legs.

He hustled her out of the kitchen when she tried to do the dishes. "Go sit and look pretty. Knit. Whatever you women do when you're not working."

"Knit?"

He filled a large pan with soapy water and, unable to help himself, tossed over his shoulder, "Or, you know, provide some inspiration and 'empower' me."

"You just had to bring that up, didn't you?"

Sadly, his comment and, damn, her very presence had already brought him "up." He braced himself against the sink, trying to get rid of the hard-on that wouldn't quit. And what the hell had he been thinking to bring a condom with him? It was like he wanted to die, smothered in the flames of his dirty mind and her hot body.

"Promises, promises," she taunted.

"Oh please." *Damn it, woman, I'm doing my best to keep it together*. "As if you could handle me."

"I think I handled you pretty well the other night."

He glanced at her, seeing her so smug and sexy. So annoyingly unfazed by their shared connection. "You just had to go there."

She grinned. "You did it first. Deal. Now get busy and do my dishes, sugar chop. I'm going to sit here and watch a pretty man working in my kitchen, you know, while I'm thinking of knitting patterns." She snickered.

Fed up with her for being so damn cute and too much to resist, he left the sink with soapy hands and dared approach her.

She narrowed her eyes on him. "Don't even think about getting me wet."

He paused. She blinked then turned a wonderful shade of pink.

His smile grew. "Aw, are you saying you're already wet for me? Don't need any help to get there?"

She glared. "You wish." Her gaze trailed down to his fly, and she swallowed audibly, not helping the situation. "You, um—"

"Yep. I'm rock-hard for you, sugar plum." Cash was only human. A guy could only take so much. "You know, I haven't had my dessert. I think I'm due." He pounced.

She stopped him with hands on his shoulders.

They stared at each other, and he saw the same hunger he felt in her deep-brown gaze.

"This means you're going to eat me. For dessert, right?"

He hadn't realized how much he'd be affected by frank words. But he should have realized Jordan wouldn't mess around. "Yep. Gonna lick you until you come." Just thinking about it hurt because he felt ready to split his pants.

"Oh, ah, okay." She licked her lips, and he groaned. "But what about sex?"

"What about it?" he asked, his voice deep, obviously aroused.

"Are we going to have it?"

"Yeah." He blew out a breath. "For some stupid reason, I brought a condom with me."

Her surprise turned into a naughty grin. "Oh. Interesting." The damn woman licked her lips again. "So it'll be safe sex."

"Safe for you, maybe. I'm about to explode," he confessed. "I'm clean, huge, and ready to fuck. I want you.

Any more questions? Is this a damn debate club, or can we get busy?"

She frowned. "You don't have to get testy about it." Then she grinned and stared between his legs. "Testy. Get it? Like, your testes? Should I spell that for you so you get the joke?"

"You're a brat needing a good fuck, I think."

"Don't brats need spankings?" She yelped when he lifted her up and over his shoulder in one smooth move, holding her in a fireman's carry.

He'd smacked her ass twice by the time he'd made his way into her bedroom. Once inside, he closed and locked the door behind him, should her brother for some reason return earlier than he thought the kid might.

Cash saw a room filled with shades of blue and lavender but held off on the inspection. Not now, when he had a warm, willing woman to plunder.

Feeling decidedly piratical, he tossed her onto her bed and followed her down.

She huffed, but before she could say anything, he pinned her to the mattress, conscious of how much larger, and harder, he was. "You sure about this? I need to know." He couldn't help grinding against her when she shifted, her legs spread and cradling him in the best way.

"We do this, it's not weird after. I mean it." At his fervent nod, she dragged his head down to her. "About time. Now inspire me, Cash. Because I'm feeling a little less than empowered right now."

He groaned and kissed her, and his world settled on nothing but Jordan Fleming. She smelled like some kind of flower. Her skin smooth, her lips like the best-crafted beer, rich and full and so damn tasty.

She moaned into his mouth, and he squeezed her breast, not sure when he'd put his hand there. He had to touch skin and quickly moved under her shirt then palmed her, reveling in the taut nipple under the silk of her bra. He pinched her, and she shot up off the bed into him.

He pulled back to see her dark gaze cloudy, her lips ripe and red, swollen from his kiss.

"Now. In me," she demanded and pushed him up to give her some space.

He stared in awe as she shimmied out of her T-shirt and bra then waited, impatient.

"I haven't got all day, you know."

He laughed, surprised he could feel anything but all-consuming lust. "Still such a smartass." He stared at her, astounded someone could look so perfect. "But such a sexy smartass." He caressed her, watching her face contort with pleasure and needing to be inside her in the worst way. But Cash didn't want to rush this, not when he finally had her in his arms.

He bent down to take her nipple into his mouth and wanted to shout with delight when she clenched her hands in his hair, urging him for more. He sucked and teased while molding her other breast and realized he'd been thrusting against her.

"Need you," he managed when he could think to release her.

"Take off your clothes," she ordered.

He pulled back and left the bed to disrobe, watching her do the same. They stood there, naked, just taking in the moment before reaching for each other. Cash felt her hot little hands on him, and he nearly lost it.

"Wait, wait." He slid her hands from his cock to his chest and tried to breathe through the out-of-control lust.

"Oh, you're sexy. No wonder everyone wants you," she teased.

"Stop it, woman. You're killing me. I'm trying to last."

"Only good for one round then? Not living up to the hype, Griffith."

"You are so asking for it." He shoved her back, not so gently, to the bed, only to hear her laugh. He left her there, on the hunt for his jeans to grab the condom. He finally had it in hand before stubborn Jordan darted off the bed to grab him again. On her knees on the floor, she reached for his erection and fondled him.

He shook, so close to climax. Then she let him go, and he let out a breath, only to stare down at her nearing him with parted lips.

"Fuck. Jordan, you put that mouth on me, and I'll come down your throat. I'm too close."

"Promise?" She paused. "You did say you're clean."

"I… Shit. Of course I'm clean. No, wait." He closed his eyes at the feel of her hot breath over his dick. "What are you doing to me?" he rasped, overcome with feeling.

Jordan palmed his balls as she drew his cock into her mouth. The feeling was indescribable, as if she surrounded him with everlasting warmth. She bobbed over him once, twice, and he came so hard he saw stars.

He heard himself moaning, felt the release fill her mouth, and couldn't stop from pumping between her lips.

After he could think again, he withdrew, still semi-hard and catching his breath, gripping her shoulder so as not to fall over.

He watched her wipe her lips, first with her tongue

then her finger. She stared up at him as she dragged that wet finger down her chin to her breasts, circling her nipples before continuing lower.

Fed up with letting her lead him by the balls—because, Christ, she had—he lifted her in his arms and kissed her until she moaned his name.

Then he placed her on the bed and spread her thighs wide, kneeling between them.

"Go on, sweet thing. Inspire me." Her eyes bright, her lips shiny, and her body taut, she slowly slid that hand between her legs.

"That's right. It's your turn," he purred, prepared to show the little brat just how much pleasure he could give her before she lost all control. "And get it right. Time you followed a few orders from your superior." He smirked then lost all sense of humor as her fingers got busy.

Oh, hell yeah.

Chapter 9

JORDAN HAD NEVER BEEN SO TURNED ON BEFORE. TAKING the lead with Cash was a dream come true. Seeing his pleasure, knowing she'd given it to him, had been hotter than she'd imagined sex with him could be.

She, Jordan Fleming, had made Cash Griffith tremble. *Go me*. But now, with Cash ordering her around? Wanting to watch her pleasure herself?

"Oh, yes," she moaned, loving the intensity with which he stared. She stroked herself, so wet and hungry for him that she didn't have to work to build her arousal.

The scent and feel of him did as much to pleasure her as her fingers did. He leaned over her and kissed her, his tongue in her mouth, invading, retreating, then coming back. Bringing her closer to her own climax.

He played with her breasts, and she got the feeling he loved them, because he didn't stop. His kisses moved from her mouth to her neck and then her nipples. He kissed and teethed, causing her to lose her damn mind, especially when he withdrew her hand from between her legs and took her fingers in his mouth.

"So fuckin' sexy," he paused to mutter before drawing them back in.

His mouth over her fingers could be felt all over her body, the pull of his thick erection once again dragged over her belly. Then the stubborn man trailed down her stomach to rest his head between her legs.

He inhaled and sighed. "You smell so sweet."

"Cash…oh God."

He kissed her clit, making love to it with his mouth. Sucking and licking, then using his thick fingers to stroke her folds before easing them inside her.

The sensation of fullness made her light-headed, especially when he started fucking her with his finger while feasting on her at the same time. She couldn't help being washed away by a tidal orgasm, shivering while he continued to lick.

Her sensitivity grew, but he pushed past it, easing her into a deeper, fuller feeling of desire. She rocked against his face, needing more as much as she needed him to relent.

But he didn't stop, and she neared a second climax too soon.

He finally pulled away and donned the condom as she watched intently. "See how big you make me, baby? This is going inside you."

Spreading her legs wider, sitting on his heels as he knelt between them, he drew her up to him and positioned himself at her entrance. "Watch me," he growled, then slowly eased his huge shaft inside her.

They stared at the sight of his sheathed cock penetrating until he was balls deep.

The fullness was incredible, his snug fit locking him inside.

"*Fuck*, that's good," he rasped, staring down at them. Then he rubbed her clit and started pumping, the cords of his abdomen in stark relief with each push and pull.

She exploded and screamed, so lost she didn't sense

him until he blanketed her body, pounding harder and faster, until he seized and groaned, pouring his release.

Exhausted yet exhilarated, she stroked his arms, feeling him shake as he continued to jet into the condom. Such a big man with such a huge orgasm.

She shifted under him and sighed, feeling another jolt of pleasure as he remained thick and firm inside her.

"Cash, just…wow."

"Yeah," he said on a breath, leaning over her. His eyes appeared darker, the green barely discernable around the wide pupils. "You sucked all the life out of me, you little witch." He moaned and leaned down to kiss her, the connection still tight.

She kissed him back, stunned and starting to realize just what she'd allowed to happen.

But too well pleasured, she couldn't worry about it. Recriminations would come later, she was sure. For now, she'd bask in her incredible lover, wondering if he could go for round three.

Well, just as soon as she got the energy to move again.

"Right now, breathing is about all I'm good for," he admitted, as if reading her mind.

"Um."

"I'll take that as an agreement." He closed his eyes and blew out a breath. "Fuck, you're tight. I don't want to move, but I think I need to."

It didn't feel as if he'd lessened any, but when he withdrew, she could tell he'd started to soften. "Man, that's a lot of come," he said and left her to dispose of it in the bathroom.

She belatedly hoped her brother hadn't come back because she thought she might have screamed.

Cash returned, rubbing his groin with a hand towel. "Sorry. Thought this would work best and be less obvious it was used." He shocked her by rubbing the damp cloth between her legs, earning a hiss as the terrycloth rubbed against her clit. He frowned. "You hurt?"

"Sensitive." She moaned because he moved the towel and kissed her there. "Stop that."

"Why?" He stroked her with his tongue, tenderly, yet her body knew nothing but that it needed to rev up again.

"Don't you ever stop?"

He pulled up and grinned. "You want me to?"

"I, ah…" She wasn't stupid. "Since you're down there anyway, you might as well finish."

He chuckled against her folds then set about kissing her into a lather. She hadn't realized her sex drive had been so empty that in just one night with Cash she'd light up so damn many times. But before she knew it, she crested on the edge of another climax.

She felt him lean up, knew he watched her, and couldn't help sighing into an almost peaceful release.

Cash kissed her once more and stood, his cock thick, ready. "I'd better go before I forget I only brought one condom. I'm too tired to come again. I think." He stared down at himself, as if puzzled. "You spice up that dinner with Viagra or something? Damn, girl. You have me hard again."

She smiled and stretched, tingling from her head to her toes. "Well, if anyone had something magical, it was you. Maybe that extra protein I swallowed tonight was the secret."

He swore. "Would you stop? I'm afraid it's gonna fall off from overuse." He took a step toward her and

froze. "No. I get near you, I'll want to fuck you again."
He glared at her. "The more I think about it, the more I
want you. No."

Seemed like he had to convince himself of that
more than her. Knowing he was right, she got up and
somehow managed to put her clothes back on while he
watched her and did the same.

"Wait for me out there, would you?" she asked as she
headed to the bathroom.

He nodded, his stare full of heat and not the distance
she'd have expected.

After cleaning up, she joined him in the living room.
Fortunately, Rafi hadn't returned. She had time to recu-
perate. She found Cash pacing in her living room, looking so handsome and gruff she wanted to drag him back
into the bedroom and cuddle for hours.

Cuddling. With Cash Griffith.

Yep, sex had surely made her deluded. "Okay, you
have to go."

He blinked. "Wait. You just had your way with me, and
now you're kicking me out? Damn, Jordan. That's cold."

She flushed but saw him grinning. "Stop. My brother
will be back soon. I don't want him to think we did
anything."

"You mean, you don't want him to know you blew
me, swallowed me, then had me return the favor? Or
that I came so hard inside you I nearly blacked out into
a coma?"

"Yeah, all that," she said wryly. "I don't need a recap,
genius. I was there."

"Yes, you were." He grinned, his smile so bright
and infectious she had to laugh with him. "Fine. I'm

leaving." Cash made no move toward the door. "But this, us, isn't the end."

"No, it's not." Surprised she meant it, she added, "Because I'm not done with you."

He cocked his head, looked as if he might argue, then nodded. "Fair enough. But at work, we keep it the way it's been. I can't handle you getting all possessive and jealous. Would bring morale down, you know." His fat head seemed to get bigger with each word. And that smirk had to go.

She just watched him, crossing her arms over her chest. "You done?"

"I think so." He shoved his hands in his pockets, outlining that monster between his legs. Did it ever go down?

"Sounds good to me. Oh, and don't be all dog-in-the-manger when I go out with Hector this week. We're doubling with Lafayette and Simon."

Cash glowered. "You're fucking *Hector?*"

"No, you moron. I had a standing date with *my friend, Hector,* before you and I did the horizontal grab. It was great. And you know I'm the best you've ever had, but don't let it get to your head."

He looked as if ready to go to war and moved into her personal space. "You are not fucking Hector."

"I'm not...now."

He leaned down, and she could see lighter green striations in his eyes. "Not. Ever."

"Hmm. Now who's acting all possessive and weird?"

He clenched his hands into big old fists, yet she had no urge to step back or fear he'd harm her. Hector, on the other hand, might not fare so well.

"Oh, relax, Conan." Her brother hadn't been far off the mark. "Hector and I are friends. I'm not someone who sleeps around." She gave him a look.

"Hey, neither am I. It's not my fault ladies like me." At her raised brow, he added, "I'm with one woman at a time. And until I'm done with you, that means we're it. No other people during this fuckfest." Cash at his most romantic. "What are you smiling at?" he growled. "And why aren't you agreeing with me about this?"

She found his aggression to cover his vulnerability oddly appealing. "Hey, I was fine calling it the beginning of a sexual thing between us. You said 'fuckfest.'"

He eased back. "Well, around you I just want to fuck. You're kind of addictive." As if having said too much, he turned bright red and headed for the door. "Enjoy the chocolates, and I'll see you tomorrow."

"At work," she agreed. "Where you and I continue as *coworkers and friends*."

"Yeah, yeah. Isn't that what I said?" He'd opened the door and started to leave, then turned around and hauled her into his arms for a kiss that left her breathless. "Christ. You broke my dick. Around you, it's always hard. Damn it." Then he stormed off and slammed the door behind him.

The moment he left, she realized what she'd done. She'd had sex with Cash Griffith. Several times. And she had a feeling had Rafi not been coming back, they could have spent the night screwing and not gotten it out of their systems. And he'd called *her* addicting?

Floundering, she looked around at the dishes in the sink, knew she needed to air out her room and adjust the bedding, and contemplated jumping in the shower to wash his scent off her skin, to erase the memories of how good he'd felt inside her.

Instead, she grabbed the box of chocolates and dug in, needing the sustenance, so that by the time Rafi returned, she had the house neat, herself in pajamas, ready for bed, and no hint that her entire world had turned upside down.

⎯∿⎯

Cash told everyone to have a great Fourth by the end of the workday Tuesday. He still didn't understand the dynamic between himself and Jordan, but damned if they hadn't fallen right back into their routine on the job. He teased her and tried to tell her what to do. She told him to kiss off and teased him right back.

They acted exactly the same with each other, except for a few stolen glances when no one was looking.

He'd never had that kind of rapport with a woman, and he didn't know how he could possibly have it with Jordan. She was smart, funny, and sexy. Exactly the type of woman who normally saw through bullshit and ended nonsense before it could begin. Yet she'd already agreed to come to his place Friday night so they could discuss Rafi and Cash could make *her* dinner.

He didn't understand why she wanted to be with him outside the sex part. Because that he did exceedingly well.

"Hey, my eyes are up here," Hector teased, and Cash realized he'd been staring at Hector's broad chest while holding a large box.

"Funny." He scrambled for an excuse for his absentmindedness. "I just can't figure out what to do about

Smith. Everyone's got assignments for next week except him. And me."

Hector slapped him on the back. "And there's your answer. It's your turn to take one for the team. You and Smith really need to get to know each other better."

"Fuck you."

Hector chuckled. Jordan happened to walk by and overheard. "Stimulating conversation with Cash Griffith, as always, eh?"

Cash felt out of sorts, so he fell back on what he knew. "Sorry, Jordan, but no. When I said fuck you, I was talking to Hector. That wasn't an invitation, but hey, you're cute. Someone out there will make a nice Mr. Fleming."

Hector guffawed.

Her eyes narrowed. "Is that right? Sugar nuts, you couldn't handle me if you tried." Then she turned to a laughing Hector and gave him a sweet smile. "I'll see you later tonight at Simon's."

Hector blew her a kiss and kept laughing, this time at Cash's expression. "Relax, man. We're hanging so I can pretend I'm not checking out Lafayette's new man."

"I'm relaxed." He forced himself to laugh. "That woman is a viper." He knew it came out complimentary.

"She is indeed. Hey Little Army, wait up," Hector said as he went to help her move a few items.

Cash shook his head. They'd been trading barbs all day, and it felt natural. Except to know she was going out with Hector. That bothered Cash because in Hector he saw a guy worthy of Jordan. A decent man, one who knew how to treat a woman, who was selfless, dedicated, and smart.

Someone who'd make a much better fit for the hot

little woman who'd somehow wormed her way into his head and heart when he hadn't been looking.

He shook his head. "Women."

Near him, Heidi shook her head. "*Ja*. Women suck."

Agreeing wholeheartedly with the sentiment, he helped her finish the job. As he drove the truck back to the office, she mentioned she was going to spend a little time with her sister in Whidbey Island. He learned she had family there as well as back in Germany. Each day with Heidi he found out something new. And the more he got to know her, the more he liked her.

Reid had been right about what he'd said weeks ago. The team felt more like family, and Cash should know better than to screw up a good thing.

Guilt hit him, that he'd done what he'd promised not to do and seduced Jordan. Though, to be honest, hadn't she seduced him right back? Hell. She'd started it. What kind of woman asked for sex then blew a guy *and* swallowed?

Feeling the start of yet another erection, he growled all the way up to the office and sat in front of Reid's desk, staring at a mound of paperwork.

The light flicked on, and Reid entered, surprised to see him. "What are you doing here?"

"We just got back." And Jordan would be going home to get ready for her big date-that-wasn't-a-date with Hector.

Cash wanted to pound something.

"You want to grab dinner?"

Cash blinked at his brother. "You're not out with Naomi tonight?"

Reid smiled. "We're not joined at the hip."

"More like joined at other places."

Reid laughed. "Come on, Bro. Let's hit the town and hang out. It's been a while."

It had been. "Yeah, okay." Cash followed Reid outside. They drove home in separate cars.

Their rental fit Reid perfectly, located between Green Lake and Ballard. A snooty, highbrow area full of corporate types and soccer moms. Cash snorted. Not like *his* class of people, more comfortable shooting pool or working up a sweat in a gym that smelled like a gym, not a perfume dispensary where the female gymgoers circled like sharks in fancy tights and makeup.

Once home, Cash headed for the shower. After they'd both cleaned up, they headed to one of the more popular sports bars in Northwest Seattle, forgoing Ringo's for once. Cash was just as glad. He didn't feel in the mood to deal with anyone from work because work reminded him of Jordan.

"You okay?" Reid asked after placing an order of appetizers and a pitcher of beer.

"Fine. What about you? You going to marry the redhead or what?"

Reid frowned. "The redhead has a name."

Cash rolled his eyes. "Okay, Mr. Sensitive. Na-o-mi. The sexy chick with legs to here." He held a hand up to his forehead. "You going to get serious about her or what?"

"I'm already serious about her."

Cash's stomach sank, and he hated the jealousy that had no place between him and Reid. "Yeah? Like I couldn't tell."

Reid studied him.

"What?"

"You seem, I don't know, different."

"Probably just not used to seeing me when I'm off my workouts and tense. We've been so busy lately I haven't been by the gym, and it's making me jittery." As good an excuse as any.

"Yeah, that's probably it." Yet Reid kept watching him. "Work is going well. Everything good with the guys? With Jordan?" Reid smiled. "I heard she went to Miriam's last Saturday. Man, what I wouldn't have given to see that."

Cash laughed with him. "She won't tell us what happened, but we can all imagine. Heidi's going back for another session of classes though. When she's done her training."

"Heidi cracks me up." Reid accepted the pitcher and glasses from the waitress and poured them both a beer. "I'll bet you she wins her marathon."

"I won't take that bet because the woman has the constitution of a marathoner and pro-wrestler all in one. I went to the gym with her a few weeks ago, and I think she nearly outlifted me." He wondered if Jordan liked to work out, if they had that in common too.

Too? What else did they—

"Hey, Bro. What's going on? It's me."

Shit. "I'm distracted because I'm tired."

"No, it's something else."

In an effort to not talk about Jordan, because he had no idea what he thought he was doing with her, Cash brought up the topic sure to make Reid uncomfortable. Unfortunate, but hey, maybe it was time they had this conversation. "I'm not a talker. I'm a doer. And I'm the only one cleaning out Angela's stuff."

Reid's face froze. "It's your house."

"Oh, bullshit. The woman didn't acknowledge me for twenty-seven damn years. Then she loses her mind, dies, and leaves *me* the house? Whatever. You know it's yours too."

"Maybe." Reid drank, his entire body stiff.

"She loved you forever. I know it hurts, but fuck, get over it." Cash hated all the talky-talky crap. "I bet Naomi has told you to deal."

Reid frowned. "We haven't talked about it."

"Liar. I know that woman, and anything that bothers you bothers her."

"That's true." Reid toyed with his napkin. "But I don't like talking about Mom."

"That. See? You call her Mom. I think of her as that crap mother Angela. You know, the one more interested in fantasy than her own kids."

Reid choked. "Cash."

"What? She hated me. Charles hated me. You think I want her shit? I don't. But someone has to box it up and get rid of it. The house is livable, man. If not, we could sell it and make some serious cash." He paused. "I know you put up most of the money for the business. You should get it back."

"I am getting it back," Reid said, earnest. "Because the business is booming. It's really taking off, Cash. The money's starting to pour in, for all of us." He paused. "Listen, I want you to have the house."

"What? Why?" He hated the panic in his voice, but he had a bad feeling he knew where this was going. The things that had made sense for the past year and a half were changing.

"Because Naomi and I have been talking about moving in together."

The bottom dropped out, though he'd been expecting such news. "So you want me to move out?"

"No, dumbass. I'll move in with Naomi. But that'll mean you have to pay for our rental yourself unless you get a roommate. And we both know you hate everyone."

He grunted his agreement.

"So you're free to stay and pay both rents. *Or* we can both move out. I'll move in with Naomi, and you can move into Mom's—your—new place."

"I hadn't made up my mind yet on whether to keep it." Cash glared, unable to understand how Reid could just cut all ties to their mother. "The house is *ours*, Reid. We've talked about this. Stop being such a pussy and help me clean it out. You know a lot of the stuff there is yours."

Reid sighed. "I know. And you can say what you want. But she left it to you, not me. In a way, it's a relief. Mom had problems. Now she's gone. Dad's gone. We're free to live our lives, man."

"Hate to break it to you, but we were free before."

"Were we?" Reid asked quietly. "We both know you have issues with the way we grew up. Hell, I do too, and they were nice to me."

"I don't want to talk about this. I just want you to come help me." Why the hell was Reid being so stubborn about all this? Was it his way of cutting ties with Cash a little at a time so it wasn't so obvious he was leaving?

"I will."

"Will what?"

Reid frowned. "Come help you clean out Mom's."

Cash let out a relieved breath.

"But not yet. I need time to process. I still don't understand everything that's happened. Then there's Naomi in my life. I'm trying to adjust."

And leaving me far behind. "Yeah, sure."

Reid groaned. "I knew you were going to take this the wrong way."

"What's the right way to take it? You want space, and I'm obviously in the way. So go. Move in with Naomi. I don't need you to babysit me, Reid."

Reid frowned. "Naomi has nothing to do with us, you and me."

"Please. I'm not stupid." *Not about things that matter.* "I'm not standing in your way. Go be with your hot chick. I have plans tonight anyway." He stood and dragged a few bills from his wallet. After tossing them on the table, he stepped away.

"Damn it. Don't be like this."

Cash shrugged. "I'm giving you what you want. I'm not your problem." *And I never should have been.* What kind of big brother needed his younger sibling to watch over him? A loser, that's who. "Go hang with Naomi. Later."

He left with Reid calling after him, determined to do nothing that would necessitate his brother bailing him out. No getting drunk. No getting into a fight. No trouble he couldn't handle by himself. What better place to work out his frustration, safely and legally, than at the gym among fellow Marines?

Chapter 10

JORDAN HADN'T EXPECTED TO HAVE SO MUCH FUN WITH Hector and Lafayette, but she had. Simon, Lafayette's new boyfriend, was adorable. Quiet, shy, and sweet. And of course, sexy as all get out. Figured Lafayette couldn't just settle for a normal guy.

The date wound down two hours later than she'd expected, the four of them having a blast playing silly board games while the Jackson twins tried to outspell and outwit each other. Cash would surely have hated it.

Damn it. Could she just for one night not think of the man?

After Jordan and Hector said goodbye to the cute couple, he walked her out to her car, laughing about something Simon had said. "So what did you think?" he asked as she unlocked her door.

"I like him. And even better, Lafayette likes him."

Hector shoved his hands in his jean pockets and leaned against her front panel. "Did you see the way Simon was looking at my brother? Like, he's way into Lafayette. But did you think he was playing up since we were there?"

"No." She frowned. "Why so concerned?"

Hector sighed. "My brother has a habit of trying to rescue people. His last boyfriend weaseled three months' worth of rent money out of him. The guy before that was using Lafayette as a standby while he worked out issues with his ex." Hector blew out a breath. "Lafayette met

Simon while helping Simon fix a flat tire on the side of the road. Once again, Lafayette to the rescue. It pisses me off that he never considers that they might be using him. He says it's all some stupid journey and he likes being helpful."

Surprised to hear a tinge of bitterness in his voice, she paid Hector more attention.

"Don't get me wrong. I want my brother to be happy. He likes taking care of people. But just once, I'd like someone to take care of him."

She nodded. "You two are a lot alike. If it makes you feel any better, I got the sense Simon really likes Lafayette. And in case you didn't notice, we had a gourmet dinner at Simon's house, and Simon cooked it."

"Yeah, that's true." Hector studied her.

"What? Do I have food between my teeth or something?" She ran her tongue over her teeth but couldn't find anything.

He shook his head and grinned. "You sure do make me laugh, Jordan. Thanks for coming over tonight."

"That's what friends are for." She socked him in the gut, hard enough to get his attention but not hard enough to hurt. "Even though you know you did me wrong by not telling me about Miriam's."

He rubbed his flat stomach, and she wished she could be as toned as the guys she worked with. Hector looked like a model and had twelve-pack abs. When he took his shirt off, his body was clearly defined. And yeah, she'd looked.

He was smart, nice, and handsome.

"Okay, now you're staring at me. Do *I* have food in my teeth or something?" he asked, humor in his voice.

"Kiss me, Hector."

He blinked but stepped closer without hesitation. "You sure about this?"

"Let's think of it as an experiment." If Jordan should like anyone, it should be a man like Hector. Someone who had his act together and treated people with kindness. He didn't bury a big heart under anything. No, Hector wore his intentions on his sleeves for all to see.

"Try not to faint when it's over," he warned.

"Ha ha." She waited.

Hector slowly reached for her, his large hands on her shoulders, bringing her closer. He lowered his head, and the kiss, when it came, felt soft, dry, and…nice.

Not exciting, not panty-dropping or insanely hot. For a woman who didn't like to deal with drama, he would be the ideal mate.

And he'd bore her to tears in weeks. A safe bet, like her exes.

She pulled back and forced a smile. "Thanks, Hector."

"Well?" Hmm. He didn't seem to be breathing too hard either.

"You tell me." She crossed her arms over her chest, waiting.

"It was good."

"Yes, it was *nice*."

He groaned. "Nice. That's the kiss of death. Literally."

She chuckled. "Look, you're sexy, and you know it. But you're not exactly throwing me to the ground to get it on."

He perked up. "You want that? I'm your man."

"No, and stop. You felt no spark. It is what it is." She shrugged. "But we're still friends."

"Of course." He sounded surprised to think they'd be otherwise. And that's why she loved the guy. "But so you know, I'd throw you down and do you anytime, anywhere. All you have to do is say the word."

"Aw, you're so sweet." She patted him on the cheek. "So...nice."

"Jordan." He gave her a sad face.

She laughed at him. "Yep. So cute. Okay, muscle man. Go home and think about why your brother and Simon are good for each other. And only part of that equation is that they can't keep their hands off each other."

He frowned. "You know, I could have done without hearing that."

"Yeah, but you know you like Simon wanting your brother. A relationship should be all in, right? Love and respect. And great sex."

He grimaced. "Please, Jordan. I just ate. I really don't want to think of my brother and some guy."

"Not just some guy—Simon." She gave him a considering look. "You know, he's really hot. Your brother has good taste."

"Okay, you're done. Go home." Hector watched her get in the car, but before he shut the door, he smirked at her. "Or are you going somewhere else? Maybe to Cash's house to tuck him in for the night? You know, he was frothing at the mouth earlier, knowing we were going out."

"He's just protective of me because I work for him."

"Yeah? Because he's not making sure Heidi's okay all the time. And what about me? I work for him. I don't see him having a hissy because I went out last week with the guys. And he doesn't care if I flirt with other people."

"I don't flirt."

"No, you don't. With anyone. Do you even have a life?"

"I have a teenage boy living with me. What does that tell you?"

He winced. "Ah. Right. How's your brother doing?" Bingo. Subject changed.

She'd talked to Hector a little bit about her brother's struggles. But Cash had been the person she'd immediately wanted to help her with Rafi. Because he'd work on her brother until the kid came around. Or tried to knife him. Either way, Cash's persistence and ability to get the job done were skills she respected.

Realizing Hector was waiting for her to answer, she said, "Rafi's okay. He just needs time and some space. I remember being fifteen, and it wasn't all that fun for me."

"Yeah. Everyone putting pressure on you to grow up then yelling at you for being too grown and not listening to the adults talking." Hector snorted. "And then there are the smells, the acne, the never-ending hunger because you can't stop growing."

"Puberty is not for the weak," she agreed. "So, that kiss we just shared. What's it worth? And don't lie to me. I know the people I work with." No doubt bets had been placed on the night's outcome.

He grinned. "Funny Rob and Smith each owe me ten bucks."

"Gimme a piece of that action, and I'll swear you gave me tongue."

He laughed. "Sure. Just don't tell Cash, or he'll eviscerate me."

"He will not."

"Jordan, open your eyes. He's possessive. He growls

around you like a freakin' dog." She did her best not to laugh. "He looks at your ass when you're not looking." Pause. "Same as you look at his when you think no one is watching." *Oh, hell*.

"Hector!"

"Hey, don't shoot the messenger. Or should I say witness?"

"Oh, shush." She ignored his laughter, hoping he was the only one who'd picked up on her attraction, and waved out the window as she drove away, pleasantly tired.

Not two miles from her house, her phone rang. Since she didn't have fancy Bluetooth in her car and didn't want to be pulled over for talking on her cell while driving, she waited until she arrived at her apartment building and parked before returning the call. Someone picked up.

"Hello? Who is this?" she asked, not recognizing the number.

"It's me. Cash."

The man simply would not give her a break. Either in reality or her fantasies, he kept appearing. The fatigue she'd been feeling after the date disappeared in a blink. "What's up?"

"I need a favor."

"How big?"

"Huge. I need you to come pick me up. I supposedly can't drive." In the background she heard someone say, *You can't, idiot*. "And you can't tell Reid."

"Family drama. Color me intrigued. So what do I get out of the deal?"

He sighed. "How about an 'I told you so'?"

"Done."

When Cash saw Jordan, alone, not with Hector, he relaxed. Thank God he hadn't interrupted anything. Or had he?

She pulled up in her crappy little car and got out, bustling to his side, her eyes narrowed on the ice pack he held against his aching head. "What the hell did you do?"

Next to him, Gavin Donnigan, his friend, his trainer, and a fellow Marine, laughed. "She called it." Gavin gave her a bright-white smile, and only the knowledge the guy was totally in love with his girlfriend saved him from being shoved on his ass for standing too close to Jordan.

"Hi." Gavin held out a hand to her. "I'm Gavin. Best damn trainer Jameson's Gym has."

"I don't know if I'd say best," Cash commented and was ignored.

"With those arms, I'll bet. I'm Jordan." Jordan smiled—at another man while Cash sat injured in front of her.

He glared.

She glared back at him then smiled again at stupid Donnigan. "So what happened?"

Before he could answer, the instigator of all the trouble walked out and joined them. "I'll tell you what happened. Cash Griffith is my hero! He saved me from some troublemakers in the parking lot."

"They weren't just some troublemakers, Elliot," Cash spoke quietly, doing his best not to aggravate his growing headache. One of the combatants had nailed him in the side of the head with a barbell and rang his clock. "Some assholes who were kicked out of the gym a while ago for being dicks—"

"And not the good kind. The bigoted, violent kind," Elliot said with a wink at Cash. "But you tell the story, my hero."

Cash flushed and ignored Elliot in look-at-me mode. He'd befriended the guy a few weeks ago, understanding his popularity since he'd clearly charmed Cash—who disliked most people. Elliot had a sincerity under the glossy charm of good looks and innuendo, and for some reason Cash liked the guy's quirky sense of humor. Seeing Elliot the center of a gang beatdown hadn't sat well at all.

Unfortunately, Jordan's wide grin told him she'd caught Elliot's flirting. God, he'd never hear the end of this.

"So, anyway, I was leaving when I saw three guys jump Elliot—and not in a good way," he said before Elliot could expand on that. Elliot grinned and winced, and the bruises on his face aggravated the shit out of Cash, that he'd almost been too late to prevent serious injury. "Yeah, three on one, and all three of those pussies are as big as me."

Gavin nodded to Jordan. "Ahem. Language."

"Little Army's heard it all before." Cash raised a brow at her. "Right, Jordan?"

"You call me 'Little Army' again, and I'll shove that bruised head up your ass," she muttered.

"Oh, I like her." Gavin chuckled.

"Me too." Elliot smiled. "Jordan, I'm Elliot Liberato, owner of Sofa's Bakery. Come in and get cookies and coffee on the house anytime."

"You're on." She shook Elliot's hand, studying him closely. "I've seen you before."

"Probably on TV. We do a big Halloween at the bakery each year, and last year *The Stranger* did a huge story on us."

Jordan brightened. "Oh, yeah. Sofa's. My brother loves your croissants. And I think I saw a rerun of *Best Of*s on TV the other day, and you were on the Halloween special."

"Yep. That's all me," Elliot said with no hint of modesty.

"All *us*, you mean. He doesn't run that place by himself," Gavin added. "His sisters are partners. I'm telling Sadie you're taking all the credit again. You're in so much trouble."

Cash cleared his throat. "I'm so glad you're all getting along. But you know, *I* wouldn't mind free coffee and cookies, Elliot. Hello. Icepack? Head? Concussion? I saved your life!"

"I don't know that I'd call it saving a life," Gavin interjected.

"My face is my life. Thanks, Cash. But I thought that was a given. You're welcome in the shop anytime for my *freebies*." He waggled his brows.

Gavin chuckled. Jordan grinned, and Cash groaned. "You're not helping my headache, Elliot."

Jordan took charge. "Okay, so the hero saved the day, somehow got his head bashed in—"

"The little guy had a hand weight," Cash growled. "I made him drop it, and sadly it sailed through Mac's car window."

"Mac?" Jordan asked.

"The gym's owner," Gavin answered. "Who is not

going to be happy about this at all. I might have to sit on him so he doesn't give Brashear more bruises to cover the ones Cash already gave him."

"And by little guy," Elliot said drily, "Cash means the one who weighed two-forty. I probably could have handled one but not all three. I really do appreciate it, Cash."

Cash stood and clutched the ice pack to his head. "I think it's a stretch to say you could have handled any of those pricks, but you keep thinking that. And it was no problem. I haven't had a fight in a while. I think I was due."

"A while? It's been a few weeks since I personally saw you brawl," Gavin said, and not under his breath. When Jordan shot him a curious look, he told her, "A long story. I'm the one who told Cash he couldn't leave unless he had someone to look out for him. I wouldn't be surprised if he has a concussion, but he refuses to go to the hospital and get checked out."

"It's not a concussion."

"How would you know?" Jordan asked.

Gavin sighed. "Look, Cash. Go home. Get some rest. Mac will go after these guys—legally—for damage done to his car. And Elliot's pressing charges too. You'll need to make a statement to the cops."

"Hell. It was just a fight. We don't need cops and lawyers."

"I'm making a statement?" At Gavin's nod, Elliot sighed. "You're right. I am. They deserve it. I just didn't want the hassle. But if they targeted me because I'm gay, that's got to stop."

"I think they went after you because of your smart mouth," Cash said.

"And because they're homophobes—I know these guys," Gavin added. "They weren't happy when Mac kicked them out or when you basically told them to kiss your ass on their way out the door."

Elliot frowned. "Oh yeah. I did, didn't I?"

Cash would have rolled his eyes if it wouldn't have made his headache even worse.

Gavin said in a dry tone, "Yeah, you did. You also made an easy target out here by yourself in the back parking lot. So it was probably a combination of them hating you, hating Mac, and hating gays. So, yes, you need to put the screws to them."

"Okay."

Cash was done standing around talking. He had a splitting headache and wanted to go…not home, because Reid would be there and somehow turn this into Cash needing help again. The reason he'd told Gavin to call Jordan in the first place.

The side of his head throbbed, just above his ear, and the ice pack started to warm. He closed his eyes and took a deep breath. When he let it out and opened his eyes, he saw Jordan watching him with a frown.

"Can we go now?"

She nodded. "Come with me." She told the others goodbye. Cash left with a grunt in their direction after grabbing his duffel bag.

In her tiny car, he extended the seat back as far as it would go and leaned the uninjured side of his head against the headrest, tossing the duffel in the back.

After a few minutes, Jordan spoke, sounding amused. "Should I be flattered you called me?"

"I'm not sensing any sympathy, Jordan."

"Fighting again? How often do you get banged up?"

"Come on. I took one to the head trying to save a guy. I could have internal bleeding. This could be my last night alive." He saw her concern and went in for the kill. "Show me some skin, sugar lips. Let me see those beautiful breasts once more before I die."

"Yep. Taking you to the hospital." She started to turn the car around.

He grabbed her arm to steady her. "I was kidding."

"I'm not. Cash, you could be really hurt."

He hated hospitals. Considering the last time he'd been in one had been four weeks ago, watching his mother take her last breath, he had no desire to go back. "I'm sore but fine. I know what a concussion feels like."

"Do you?" The stubborn woman made him recite his phone number, address, and the alphabet. Then she had him recite the alphabet backward.

"...E, D, C, B, A. I'm done. And if you try making me walk a straight line or straighten out my arm then bring it in to touch my nose, I'll hurt you," he growled, though they both knew he didn't mean it.

"Well, your faculties, such as they are, seem to be intact." Then she asked him the question he'd been hoping she'd put off as she pulled into her apartment parking lot. "Now why can't you go home to Reid?"

He groaned. "Can we talk about this later? My head hurts."

"Nice try. Get out."

There was no getting around this woman. He followed her inside and saw Rafi lying on the couch watching TV. At the sight of Cash, he froze, then hurried to sit up straight.

"Relax, Rafael," Cash drawled. "I'm not here to shake you down. I'll wait until the commandant is done interrogating me before screwing with you."

The kid sneered. "Very funny." Rafi looked him over and whistled. "What happened to you? Try to roll a kid for her lunch money and fail?"

"He is *so* your brother," Cash said and sat next to Rafi.

Instead of scurrying from the couch to get as far away from him as possible, the boy looked him over with the same scrutiny Jordan had. "Is that blood?"

Cash frowned. "Shh." Jordan had gone to get him a towel. "I thought it had dried."

"You should go to the hospital."

"What are you, her parrot?"

"I'm just sayin'."

"Saying what?" Jordan asked as she returned with a towel and ice in a baggie.

"He should go to the hospital."

"I'm fine." Cash's head hurt, but other than that he felt okay. And yeah, he knew it was stupid. But if he was going to bleed out and die from internal injuries, he'd rather do it here than in some antiseptic death trap.

Jordan sighed. "You're not being smart about this. If I had my head caved in by a dumbbell, you'd tell me to get help."

"Yeah, but you're little."

Her mouth flattened. "Try again."

"I mean, he didn't hit me that hard."

"He's bleed—"

Cash talked over her brother. "It hurts, but I've been hit plenty of times before."

"That I can believe," her brother muttered.

"And I know what a real head wound feels like."

Jordan just stared at him. "It's official. You're a moron."

"Hey!" Too loud. "I mean, hey. I'm hurt, not stupid."

"Seriously? I don't know what I was thinking listening to you." Her eyes widened when she saw the blood he'd been trying to hide. "No, no, no. Cash, get in the fucking car."

He'd never heard her sound so…mean. And he was in no mood to argue, so he grumbled as he got to his feet and followed her out to her vehicle.

Rafi had come with them, but she turned and stopped him. "Rafi, please stay here. I'll be back when I can."

"I'm good. If you're not back before school tomorrow, I'll get myself up and going." The boy nodded at Cash. "He looks like walking death. Go on. I'm good."

"I'm fine, I said," Cash grumbled, but no one seemed to be listening to him.

She looked torn, and Cash felt like a heel for making her leave her brother alone. It wasn't that late yet, but Jordan had a life. One that didn't have to be constantly fucked up by Cash if he could help it.

He swallowed his pride, needing his brother after all. "Hell. Jordan, just take me home, okay? I swear I'll get medical help. Reid can take me."

She stared at him, and he didn't know what she saw. But she seemed to make a decision. He just hoped she wasn't considering putting him down, like a dog.

When he suggested she might, she swore at him and helped him into the car then walked her brother back to the apartment complex. Once behind the wheel, she drove him…not toward his house but to an emergency clinic.

"What are you doing?"

"Shut up. You have insurance, yeah?"

He shrugged. "Probably in my wallet."

"Get it."

He reached back, slowly, for his gym bag and grabbed it. She took it from him then helped him out of the car at the clinic.

"You've done this before."

"I was an MP in the Army, so yeah. Lots of drunk and disorderlies." She grinned at him. "You're certainly disorderly."

He stopped them at the doorway to the clinic, alarmed at how nice it felt to be cared for. "Seriously, you don't have to do this. I don't want to take you away from Rafi." He swallowed, the knot of feeling for this woman growing. "Thanks for getting me here."

She pointed at the door. "Oh, we're not done. Let's go."

"I'll get help. I'm here, I might as well."

"How will you get home?"

"I'll call a cab."

"I'm already here with you. Come on." She pushed them through the door and wormed her way under his arm, by his side, as if her small frame helped him balance.

He leaned on her all the same, not too much but to validate the connection. And damn but she fit like she belonged there. "I, um, I didn't take you away from your date with Hector, did I?"

"It was already over. And it wasn't a date." She chuckled. "Though I did make a few bucks on it."

"Huh?"

She blushed. "Never mind. Oh good. You're next." She pushed him none too gently toward the front counter. "He's got a head wound."

The lady behind the window frowned. "Let's get you in, fella. You don't look so good."

Chapter 11

AN HOUR AND A HALF LATER, JORDAN FELT TORN. SHE SAT in Cash's living room, waiting while he cleaned up and changed into something comfortable. As she'd suspected, the doctor at the clinic had determined he had a concussion. Since he seemed coherent and hadn't slurred any words or acted in any way incapacitated, they'd sent him home on the condition someone look after him.

He'd filled her in on the confrontation with the bullies at the gym. Once again, Cash had taken care to protect someone and gotten hurt because of it. How could she fault him for doing the right thing?

She couldn't. Truthfully, she felt so proud of him. Which was stupid. He wasn't hers, yet she wanted to hug him and take care of him all the same.

And thinking of hers… She called her brother to check in. "Sorry it's late. I'll be home in a little bit. I took Cash to the clinic, and like we suspected, he has a concussion. I'll stay with him until his brother gets back. You good?"

"I'm not a baby." Rafael didn't sound surly tonight. Thank God. Just his usual snarky self. "Glad Cash isn't going to get any more stupid than he already is. Big guy needs all those brain cells."

"Rafi." She laughed. "Not nice."

He chuckled. "He's not so bad for a Marine, I guess. I think he likes you."

"We're just friends."

"Whatever. You're taking care of him at eleven on a weeknight. At his house. That's not exactly in your job description, is it?"

"Shut up."

A snicker. "Just don't do too much 'overtime,' if you get my meaning."

"Rafael Younger, you're not too big to spank."

He laughed some more. "I'm going to bed. Don't wake me when you get in. *If* you get in." He hung up. The punk.

She smiled, relieved that he seemed to be acting like the old Rafael again. They could come and go, his moods. But at least tonight he sounded upbeat. Probably because they had the day off tomorrow and would be going to their parents' for a Fourth of July picnic. With any luck, her folks would do their best to make it a nice day and not jump on her brother's case. Of course, if Leanne came, Jordan would be the one struggling to deal with an attitude.

But that was for tomorrow. Tonight she had a cranky Marine to deal with. A glance around his house showed he had nice taste, a surprise she'd attribute to Reid. She just couldn't see Cash picking colored throw pillows and accented floral prints on the walls. The furniture was comfortable, a brown-leather couch and matching side chairs centered around an oak table, all facing a large-screen TV mounted to the wall over a stone fireplace. A side table and mirror stood sentry in the hallway just inside the entrance. Farther in, a large space had been designated the dining area with a Craftsman-style table and four chairs.

The place was homey, comfy, and tastefully

decorated with cream-colored walls, honey-blond built-ins on either side of the fireplace, and a darker hardwood floor. The kitchen, newly renovated with stainless-steel appliances and a black-quartz counter that also covered the center kitchen island, had invited her to take a closer look—which she'd done while he was dressing. The cabinets had the same light-colored finish as the built-ins in the living room.

Overall, the house had a polished finish she envied. It also didn't seem to fit Cash at all. Reid, sure. But not the hulking Marine addicted to reality TV, beer, and "chicks who dig muscle."

Shuffling drew her attention to the lumbering slab of injured male entering the living area. She turned her head to say something smart and gaped instead. Cash wore a pair of loose gray jersey pants and carried a T-shirt with him. He yawned and put it on as he neared, but the sight of his half-naked body stole her ability to think. That he didn't appear to be trying to impress her made it worse. God, the man was *Built*. With a capital B.

"Thanks again, Jordan." His gruff, deep voice had her taking a second look. A stubbled jaw and tousled hair added to his tired appearance but didn't detract a bit from his sex appeal. If anything, it made it worse because he looked as if he'd just rolled out of bed. *Good Lord, stop thinking about his bed!*

"How's the head?" she asked when she could form words again.

With care, he touched the side where he'd been hit. "Sore but otherwise fine. It was a superficial cut that bled a lot. Like I said, he rang my bell. But I'll be okay. You should go home to Rafi."

She nodded and rose from the couch, stepping toward him. "I will. First, sit down and let me look at you."

He sat on a stool in the kitchen, and she approached him, now at eye level with the man. She looked at his head and saw a still-oozing cut on his scalp under his hair. "They put a sealer on it?"

"Yeah. The cut wasn't deep enough for major stitches."

So close, she felt his body heat surround her. She stroked the hair around the cut, taken by his softness. "Good. I bet it hurts though." She spoke in a soft voice, petting him, offering what little comfort she could.

"Yeah," he responded in a tone as quiet. "Feels better now."

"You took some ibuprofen?" He'd mentioned he had some at home and hadn't needed any medication from the clinic. Not that she could blame him at ten bucks a bottle.

"Yeah. But I feel better because of you. You help just by being here." A whisper of a confession.

He wouldn't look at her, and in that moment, he just seemed so alone. Reid obviously wasn't at home, not that Cash had wanted her to call him. Cash had no one to take care of him.

Jordan did what felt right. She took a step closer and hugged him. At first he tensed, but then he eased into her hold and sighed, resting his head on her shoulder. She stroked his arms and his back and massaged his neck, smiling when he gave a soft groan.

Cash didn't make any sarcastic comments or try to turn the embrace into a sexual hold. He was off his game, and not having a familiar, sarcastic Cash to deal with bothered her. She didn't like him hurt because his pain felt personal. That level of attachment to the man should have bothered her more than it did. Instead, she felt it her responsibility to get him on the mend. To care for him.

"How about some tea or something to drink?"

He shrugged but didn't move away from her. "Tea would be good, I guess. We have some in the cabinet." He paused. "Reid got it for Naomi."

She reluctantly pulled away and saw him watching her. But she didn't have a clue what he was thinking.

He pointed her to a cabinet, and she grabbed the tea then turned on an electric kettle. "Nice place. How long have you lived here?"

"A year now. A buddy of ours from the Corps owns it and rents it for cheap. But with Reid moving out, I'll probably end up leaving too." He sighed. "Too bad, really. Because all the nice furniture stays with the house."

"But you inherited your mom's place. You could move in there." In an ideal location, his mother's house wasn't too far from this one. "It might take a little work to get it livable, but the house has good bones."

He sighed again. "I guess."

She fixed him tea and grabbed a cup for herself. "You want anything in it?"

He nodded. "I like it sweet."

"Me too. Milk and honey okay?"

"Perfect."

She smiled.

His smile, when it came, stole her breath. Because she saw Cash unguarded, simply taking joy in the act of sharing the moment.

They drank their tea at the kitchen island, staring at each other, until she broke the silence. "So, tell me. What's with you and Reid?"

His eyes narrowed, shuttering his expression, and she regretted the loss of his earlier joy. "It's a family thing."

"Uh-huh. I don't care. Tell me what's going on. You can talk to me, you know. I'm no narc."

He gave a ghost of a grin. "That's what your brother said about himself."

"Well, we Flemings—and Youngers—are good like that."

"Youngers?"

"Rafi's technically my half-brother. My sister and I are from my mom's marriage to my dad, Jeff Fleming. My dad died when I was little. Car accident. Mom remarried Carl Younger, my stepdad. He's Rafi's father, but we all call him Dad. He's a good man." She wished she knew why he thought distancing himself from his son was the right thing to do. "It's just, he and my mother, they—No. We're not talking about me. We're talking about you and Reid."

Cash scowled. "Are we?"

"Yes." She moved around the island to sit next to him. "What's going on between you guys? Why didn't you call Reid for help? Or Evan? You're tight with your cousin, aren't you?"

"Huh. Hadn't even thought about Evan." He cupped his huge hands around the tea, and the mug disappeared. "You sure you want to hear this? I don't want to lay all my crap on you."

She put a hand over his, taken with the strength that could pummel a bully or caress her with such gentleness.

"Sometimes laying it out makes you feel better. And, hey, you listened to me about my brother."

"I guess." He turned to face her, and she did the same, their knees brushing. "Reid and me, we've always been close. Even after I moved out of the house at sixteen, I waited for him before joining the Corps."

"You joined together. Did you serve together too?"

"Some. But, you know, you get assigned a duty station, you have to go. The little shit went and got a different MOS, was in a different unit for a while. Radio Recon is okay, I guess." He grinned, pride in his eyes. From what she knew about Radio Recon, the guys were pretty high-speed. "He's hell on wheels and knows it. Anyway, we've always been tight. But he's constantly bailing me out of trouble, which is ridiculous. I'm older. I should look out for him."

Yet she could understand, knowing the two men. Reid, the levelheaded, responsible one, always there to lend a hand to the brash but brave brother who leaped before looking.

"So what? He looks out for you because he's your brother and he loves you."

"I guess." He glanced at his knees. "I don't do well without focus. It's no big secret that I have a tendency to find trouble. Not my fault, it just happens."

"Like the burglars you stopped over a month ago and the fight in the parking lot tonight."

He nodded. "I don't go looking for it. But I deal with shit when it comes at me."

"Right."

"I did pretty good in the Marine Corps. Would have stayed in to retire too, but I didn't like the way some stuff went down overseas. Some assholes in our company were stealing and selling U.S. gear. Weapons too, but no one believed me on that one 'cause they covered their tracks in time. I called them on it, but they had contacts higher up." If he ever saw Jim Sanders again, he'd give the guy a beating he wouldn't walk away from. "One of them had a dad who was a general. So it got hushed up, but I wasn't having it. Somehow a fight started. I, ah, well, I punched a few officers. In self-defense, but who would take my word for it? I would have been court-martialed, except they knew I'd tell everyone the truth in court about what I saw. So it was either get out with an honorable discharge and keep my mouth shut or rot in the brig and serve out the rest of my time on shit duty. I got out."

"That sucks." She could totally see it all going down, his situation similar to the way hers had happened. "They suckered you into a fight, and you took the bait. Then they used it against you."

"Yeah." He took a sip of tea. "Reid wouldn't have fallen for it. He'd have been smart and quiet and gotten word to someone higher up about what was happening. I saw something wrong and tried to fix it—my way. My way never seems to work for me."

A big old pity party for Cash, but she felt for the guy. And after the beating he'd taken tonight, he'd earned some compassion. "So how does this relate to you and Reid not getting along?"

Cash sat glumly regarding his mug. He glanced back up at her, his frustration evident. "He and Naomi are a total couple. I saw it happening, but then it was just there. The two of them together all the time. I'm glad for him." She saw that, but she saw something else as well. "But I miss my brother sometimes. He's *always* with her. I feel like a loser for not being happier for him, but, shit, we never hang out anymore."

"That's gotta be hard."

He nodded. "It is. I'm trying to be mature"—he glared at the half-cough/chuckle she couldn't keep inside— "about it, but I can't help feeling like she's stealing him. Happy now?"

"Hey." She put a hand on his knee, and his gaze shot to hers. "I get it. It's totally understandable. You're not a loser for feeling jealous."

"I'm not jealous exactly. I'm… Hell. I'm jealous."

"I've gone through what you're feeling."

He blinked. "You have?"

"With some friends when I was in the Army. You have a tight group, then someone hooks up, and suddenly you never see them again. But none of them were my sister."

"Yeah, you have a sister too, don't you? Are you guys close?" He put a hand over hers then lifted it from his knee and just held it.

"No. I used to wish we were, but we have a funny family dynamic." She stopped herself from spilling her guts.

"We have a lot in common, don't we?"

She nodded. "It's weird. The way you left the Marines? That's kind of what happened to me. A friend of mine was assaulted by her CO. She didn't want to report it, because it always ends up falling back on the woman. As if she should be blamed for that asshole forcing himself on her." Poor Sharon. That prick captain had been a jerk from the beginning of their deployment. The one and only time he'd tried to get closer to Jordan than he should have, Jordan had "accidentally" kneed him in the balls. He'd never come near her again. Sharon had been a lot cuter and nicer. Unfortunately, he'd also gone after her.

Cash squeezed her hand, and she looked up into his eyes, not surprised at his anger. He let loose a string of colorful swear words. "I hate scumbags who do that. We had our share of female Marines. Not in the infantry so much but the support staff. You could always tell the assholes by the way they treated the WMs." WMs—Women Marines.

She nodded. "No one much liked Bowers, but he was in charge. Problem was we didn't have any decent staff NCOs in our unit once Staff Sergeant Keen left. Sharon got raped—because, yeah, that's what it was—by Captain Dickhead, who couldn't keep it in his pants. She told me about it, in tears, and I reported it."

He stroked her fingers in his large hand. "I bet that went over well," he said with derision.

"Oh yeah. I got so much shit from everyone. It surprised me how few of my friends stuck by me. Even Sharon bitched me out because she hadn't wanted me to tell. Then a few other females came forward to corroborate what had happened. My so-called friends gradually apologized, but it was too little too late for not believing in me. Almost everyone disliked the guy, but as soon as one woman said he was a no-good rapist, it was as if I'd targeted all of them. A big old man-hater hose attached to my mouth." She huffed. "The worst thing is they shipped him home. Quietly. I heard he got assigned a crappy duty station, suffered a slap on the wrist. Fucker is still in the Army."

"Man. Want me to go kick his ass? Or better yet, hold him down while you tag him?"

She grinned, her anger fading at Cash's enthusiasm for violence. "I wish. I'm a firm believer in karma. You get what you give." She looked down at their joined hands. "I was all set to have a career in the Army, you know. I was good at it. When I was a kid, I was like Rafi. I had no idea what I wanted to do or be. The Army saved me." Her eyes burned, and she held tears back with sheer grit. She would *not* cry in front of Cash. "Now I'm starting over. And I have no clue what I'm supposed to do with my life." She forced a laugh and met his gaze. "But so far so good. Without me organizing Vets on the Go!, you all would be hopeless."

"You got that right. But you think you have it bad—"

"What, is this a contest?"

"Yes, it is, so shut up." He stood and pulled her into his arms. "I got out of the only thing I was good at. Couldn't hold a civilian job for more than a few weeks at most. Kept arguing with my bosses, getting in fights. I was so mad all the time."

She loved looking up at him, feeling all that strength so close.

He continued, "Once again, Reid saved the day. He started Vets on the Go! for me. Hell, he was fine working in some fancy office, making big money. Instead he quit, went in with Evan and the five bucks I could scrounge up."

"Five bucks? That's all?" Her breath hitched when he brought her hand to his mouth and kissed her palm.

"Yeah. But it's the best five bucks I ever invested." He leaned down and whispered a kiss over her lips. "I've kept my job for over a year and a half. We're finally no longer broke as hell. Now we're muddling through."

"M-me too."

He kissed her again, lingering this time. "And I get to work with the best people." He drew her in to his body, letting her feel all of him. Such heat, such *firm,* glorious strength. "Now if I have a problem, I know this certain snarky Army chick will have my back. And she's so fuckin' hot. I was lucky enough to slide inside her sexy little body the other night."

"Lucky, hmm?"

He kissed her again, and she turned into a molten mess.

"Yeah. So lucky. She could have anyone she wanted." He squeezed her waist. "And if she ever thinks Hector might be able to satisfy her huge, roaring sex addiction, I'll bend the guy in half."

"Roaring sex addiction?" She wanted to laugh, charmed by his possessive tone, which was so unlike her.

"She addicted me for sure." He squeezed her waist again, this time in warning. "But she better not seduce anyone else."

"Oh, how scary. I bet she's too intimidated to say no to you."

"Yeah?" He cracked a laugh. "Because I think this chick would kick me in the balls and lay me out flat if I so much as looked at her wrong. She's kind of obnoxious too. But for some reason, she gets me so hard."

"Even now?" With him leaning down, she could thread her fingers through his hair, taking care not to brush against his injury. "I mean, you have a concussion...you sexy idiot."

He chuckled. "Well, she'd have to be very gentle with me. But right now, I can't think too much about anything more than the pounding between my legs. I'm hard as a rock, Jordan. For you."

She loved hearing that but tried not to let it mean too much. "It's just because we're new."

He snorted. "Sugar Soldier, I've been hard since you first walked into the office with that smart mouth and those sexy arms."

"Sugar Soldier?" She laughed. "That's awful. But I agree on the sexy arms." She flexed to intimidate him, light-headed at the thought of how much she was coming to care for the big, gruff troublemaker.

"It's just weird that you're so sexy and toned. And so tiny." Then he flexed, and all the blood rushed from her brain.

Arousal took her over completely. "Now you're gonna get it." She pulled away from him, grabbed him by the hand, and tugged him with her down the hall. "Which way?"

He pointed past her to the room on the left and followed with a meekness she didn't believe for a second.

She shut the door behind them and locked it then turned to see him slowly easing his shirt off.

That made her pause, realizing he still hurt. But not so much that his erection faded. Goodness, but his tented pants showed off every aspect of her larger-than-life lover. He continued to take off the rest of his clothes until he stood naked, watching her. So handsome, so damn hung…and so injured.

"You are not okay to do this, buddy. So I'm going to tuck you in instead." The room was just like him.

Everything put away, out of sight. A lot like Cash and the real emotions he masked with bravado and tough talk.

His gentleness and buried kindness continued to soften her toward him.

His eyes narrowed. "I'd have to be dead not to be okay with this."

She shook her head. "I know you think you're okay, but you still have a headache, don't you? And what do you think an orgasm will do for you? It'll just make your head pound even harder."

He groaned and held himself. "You'd waste this?"

"In a heartbeat if it meant I'd get to use it later, you know, while you're still alive."

He sighed. "I guess it would be awkward if I burst a blood vessel while fucking the hell out of you. I mean, if I died on top of you, I might crush you." He sighed again. "But what a way to go."

She shook her head. "So not what you should be saying to convince me."

Then she shrieked as he yanked her to him and shoved her on the bed. "I'm usually better doing, not talking. But I swear I'll be good if you'll just lie with me."

"No sex," she warned, toed off her shoes, then slid under a thin comforter.

"Not right now, no." He joined her, moving slowly. "Let's rest together, okay?" He held her close, and to Jordan, the intimacy was almost better than sex. He muttered something that sounded like her name.

"What?"

He fell asleep with a smile on his face.

Jordan watched him as she drifted into dreams, the scent of Cash giving her peace.

Chapter 12

CASH COULDN'T DIFFERENTIATE THE BLOOD RUSHING through his body as pain or pleasure. His head still throbbed, but not as much as his cock. And the need for Jordan hurt almost as much as it drugged him with desire.

She wore too many clothes. She must have been awake and read his mind because she started pulling off her clothes and didn't protest when he helped her get naked.

His head hurt, but not so much he couldn't process his body's needs. A glance at his phone on the nightstand showed a few hours had passed. Enough of a rest, apparently, because he'd woken with a powerful need.

"Cash?" she whispered, her voice throaty. "Are you okay?"

"Time for some lovin'," he whispered and moved down her body, pushing her thighs wide. He lapped her up, loving her small moans, the way she suddenly clenched at his shoulders yet still took care to stroke around his injury, her small hands so careful as she touched him.

"Wh-what are you doing? Cash, your head…"

"Shh. I need this. I need *you*."

"But Cash…" Jordan moaned, something about him hurting himself.

"I might die from a case of blue balls, but other than that I'm fine," he growled, his desire out of control. He licked the sweet woman with a need that bordered on desperate. What he felt for Jordan went so far beyond lust. He hadn't really known her for very long, yet he felt as if he knew her better than anyone he'd ever met.

"Cash, please," she begged, turning him on even more. "You have to be…careful."

He slid his hands up her slender thighs, taken with the silky smooth muscle, the power in her strength. When he slid a finger inside her, she came, and the heat around him was nothing compared to the heat that burned inside him. Imagining her so hot and wet and tight around his cock was more than he could handle.

He moved too fast, looming over her, and had to fight through the headache piercing his skull.

"You moron," she said through a lot of gratifying panting. "You need to stop. Or at least go slow. Be gentle."

"For you?" Had he moved too fast for her?

She slid out from under him and helped him lie on his back. "No, for you." Then before he could do anything, she laid on top of him and kissed him. Soft lips, a hungry kiss, and then her tongue slid between his lips and she laid claim to every cell in his body.

He groaned, needing her so much. Only with Jordan did he feel a part of something more. He'd lost so much, been alone for even longer despite the connection with his brother. But Reid *had* to love him. Jordan… She might not love him, but she gave more than she took, and Cash latched onto that, greedy for whatever he might get.

When she moved her kisses down his body and stopped to suck his nipples, he nearly lost his mind. "Fuck. Yeah, baby, suck me. Oh, God." He kept grinding against her belly, helpless to stop himself. He was primed and feared going off before he could get inside her.

As if she sensed his frustration, she slowed down even more, licking and nibbling his nipples, running her hot little hands over his chest and abs.

"You're so strong," she whispered then rose over him to whisper in his ear, "so big and hard for me." She licked the shell of his ear, and he felt himself start to spurt against her, holding himself back on prayer alone.

"Wait. Hold on. Too close," he warned, barely able to get it out. She left him then, and he cursed himself for being too honest.

He glanced over at her, taken with the stiff nipples of her pert breasts. Her toned belly had a gentle curve, her ass firm and rounded, the perfect woman. Not afraid to be strong or feminine.

He wanted to tell her that. That he saw the power inside her and respected the fuck out of her for it. Instead what came out was "I'm gonna fuck you so hard."

She grinned at him. "Promises, promises. Condoms?"

"Top drawer." He waved at the nightstand.

She got one out and rejoined him on the bed. The little witch straddled him, balancing on her knees as she ripped open the condom. She moved back and looked down at his ridiculous erection. The thing looked like a damn flag pole, stiff, straight, and bouncing off his belly.

"I'm so hungry." She licked her lips, her hair flowing over her shoulders, her brown eyes dark, wicked.

"You put your mouth on me, I'll come. Make it last."

"You sure?"

"Well, you could always eat me up later, that's if I don't die of an aneurism." A dumb thing to say because she looked horrified and tried to get off. "I'm kidding. I feel fine."

"You're delusional. Cash, I'm worried about you."

"I'm a big boy. Trust me to know what I can handle." He wanted to be deep inside her, without a condom, skin to skin. But even he knew that to say something like that out loud would make her think he really had suffered brain damage. He cleared his throat. "Put it on me."

"Okay, if you're sure."

"Tease."

Jordan scowled. "Ass."

"I'm sorry. You offering something I wasn't aware of? Because I'm game to fill you up anywhere you want."

She blushed. "Such a horn dog."

"You mean a horny devil dog."

She rolled her eyes but didn't dawdle, fitting the condom over him in no time.

Before she could do something else to hurry his orgasm, he gripped her hips and lifted her over him. He grabbed his cock and positioned himself at her entrance. Then she eased down, gloving him in her body.

He had to close his eyes, awash in sensation. Totally focused on the riot of desire flooding his body for Jordan alone.

"Oh, you are so sexy." She leaned down to kiss him, moving him inside her so carefully.

He moaned and kissed her back, taken with her mouth and that tight pussy hugging him so hard.

Jordan rose over him, and he opened his eyes, watching the best fantasy he'd ever had come to life. She rode him, her hands planted on his chest while she moved up and down over the pole between his legs with slow deliberation.

"You feel so good," she moaned. "So deep in me."

"Yes," he urged, watching her breasts rise and fall, her belly and thighs tighten as she moved. "In you, baby. Fuck, I'm gonna come so hard in you."

"Cash," she groaned and did the next best thing he'd ever seen.

"Oh my fucking God. Yes. Touch yourself. Come around me." He couldn't wait, watching her, feeling her. The smell, the taste, her sounds… He shouted as he jetted inside her, felt her tighten like a vise around him and arched up into her, trying to get even deeper while she slammed down around him.

Pure ecstasy blotted out everything but Jordan. They remained connected, his body an intimate part of hers while they both came back to earth.

He stared up at her, dazed and, damn it, beguiled by the beauty smiling down at him. He cupped her breasts, holding her, feeling her heart race and knowing it matched the tempo of his.

"Best damn lay of my life," she told him.

He had to laugh, awash in the endorphins rushing through his system. "Jordan, you are better than any drug. My headache's gone. I swear, it's like I'm high on something."

"So my pussy is like Vicodin?"

"Or Percocet. Definitely better than an ibuprofen though."

"Good to know." She tightened around him, and he trembled with the aftershocks of pleasure.

He tugged her down, and she lay on top of him, still joined together, her head on his chest. He stroked her thick, silky hair. "Hear my heart racing?"

"Yeah." She kissed the spot over his heart, and as

stupid as he knew it to be, he fell hard. Right then, right there, in love.

"Jordan…" *I love you.*

"I have to go."

The bottom dropped out from under him. "Oh, right. Rafi."

"But I'm not leaving until I talk to Reid."

"I…what?"

"You shouldn't have seduced me out of my little nap." She propped herself up on her elbows, staring into his eyes. "You're too sexy for your own good." She harrumphed, and the compliment she'd grudgingly given warmed him. "Until I say otherwise, you're mine. No flirting or sexing up other girls."

His entire world brightened. *Wouldn't be smart to let her see she's gotten the upper hand though.* He blinked at her, pretending innocence. "I'm sorry. What are you saying? You're hooked on me already? Man, I knew it would come to this." He sighed, forcing himself not to laugh when her brows drew together. "Okay. For the sake of your sanity, those mouthwatering breasts, and that tight little ass, sure. I'm okay to be kept."

The smile she'd tried to keep hidden appeared. "Mouthwatering, aren't they?"

"Yes, they are. I want some."

"But I'll have to get off you if you want some titty."

Hearing Jordan say "titty" shocked him.

She laughed as she slithered off him, but when she would have darted off the bed, he caught her. "Easy, doofus. Your brain's still rattled."

"You're telling me." He tugged her under him on the bed and showed her how mouthwatering her "titties" were.

After some time spent kissing and caressing each other, stirring a peculiar, calming build of arousal, she pulled back. He stared down at her, fascinated by the way she watched him as she smoothed his hair back.

"I hate it, but I do have to go."

"I know." He wanted her to stay.

She smirked. "I love how sad you sound saying that."

"What can I say? I'm used to the burr under my saddle that is Jordan Fleming."

"Oh, whatever. I'm no burr. I'm more like a stick of honey you can't get enough of."

He nodded. "So sweet and sticky. I've got some sweet and sticky for you if you want some of mine." He put her hand around his stiffening cock. "And I *love* to keep you well fed."

She gripped him, making him even harder. But when she loosened her hand, he let her go.

"I wish I could stay." He heard the wistful truth in her words.

And knew he was keeping her.

Somehow, someway, he had to fool her into thinking he was more than he seemed. Because, selfish as it was, he wanted Jordan in his life. And maybe, just maybe, if he worked hard at it, he could be the guy she needed.

"I wish you could stay too." He kissed her and sighed. "But you need to get back. Hold on."

He helped her clean up then let her fuss over him but drew the line when she tried to put his shirt on him. "Damn it. I'm not a kid."

"That was never in question." She tucked her hair back, the ragged cut sexy and a little wild. "I was just trying to help."

He shrugged into his T-shirt and walked her to the door. "I'm really okay, you know." He hugged her to him. "I think taking all the blood from the rest of my body and centering it in my dick relieved some cranial pressure."

She shook her head. "There you go surprising me again, using big words like 'cranial.'"

He laughed. "Such a smartass. Go on. Go home."

"Just as soon as you promise to call Reid. Someone should be here to check on you through the night."

"I'd rather it was you," he muttered. He heard Reid's car pull up outside. "Damn."

"So, um, are we 'out'?"

"As in letting everyone know how wild you are for me? Sure. To keep you safe from lechers like Hector, Finley, and that asshole Smith, it's my duty to let them know you're mine."

"Duty, huh?"

He tried to joke it off, but the newness and depth of his feelings made it tough. "Want me to tattoo your name to my forehead?"

"Nah. Enough you know you're taken." She just had to tack on, "For now."

"Oh, you mean until I get bored of all your clinginess and desperation? I'm a total catch, you know." *Great way to keep her, you idiot! Not by insulting her!*

But Jordan being Jordan laughed. "We'll see. I'm pretty sure I have you hooked on my stunning wit and amazing body."

"Don't forget that mouth." He meant that. The woman had skills.

"Yep. Don't forget it. Because if you do, I'm sure someone else out there would be happy to—"

He didn't like "someone else" at all and staked his claim. He kissed her until neither of them could breathe and only stopped when someone cleared his throat.

They broke apart and looked to the open doorway to see Reid staring at them in astonishment.

"Gotta go," she said in a singsong voice. On her way out the door, she added, "And Reid, your brother has a concussion. So make sure to keep waking him up throughout the night. Bye."

———∿∿∿———

Reid stared at his thoroughly bemused brother, taking note of the details. Cash wore casual clothing, not for entertaining a woman, for sure. Though Cash didn't go for more than jeans and a nice T-shirt, Reid didn't think his brother would try to seduce a woman in lounge pants. Cash also seemed…happy. Something he hadn't been in a long time.

"What the hell did I just see? Your tongues down each other's throats?" Reid wanted to be more annoyed that his brother had disregarded the rules concerning Jordan. No fraternizing and no messing around with their employees.

But the gang were like family, and Jordan had seemed more than enamored with Cash. "This isn't just a fuck and run, is it?"

"Hell, no. Besides, any guy who would try to run from Jordan is not only stupid but suicidal. That woman would string up a user by his balls." Cash grinned.

"Ah, okay." Reid sensed something serious between the two but decided to tread carefully, doing his best to mend fences. "I was with Naomi tonight only because

I wanted to give you some space. I mean, I know I'm with her a lot. I would have talked to you except you bailed on me."

Before Cash could respond, Reid plowed on, knowing he needed to get his words in before his brother tuned him out. So far, Cash was listening. "I'm sorry about Mom. I just…I can't get my head around it. Yeah, we had our problems, but she never treated me like I didn't matter." He flushed, knowing Cash had felt that way for a long time. "Dad was always hard on you, but Mom did still know you, Cash. Until the end, she knew me too."

Cash sighed and went around him to the couch, where he sat, crossed his ankles on the coffee table, and put his head back. "Dude, I know. Angela had plenty of issues. But you were a good son, always treated her right."

"I still feel guilty for being away so many years. I used the Marine Corps as an excuse," Reid admitted and sat next to Cash. "I could have visited her more on leave."

"Instead you spent time with me when we caught breaks. You blame me for that?"

Reid stared at his brother's slack face. Though Cash didn't seem to care much about his answer, Reid felt the subtle tension between them. "Hell, no. None of this is your fault. Not any of it. This is about me being a bad son and hating the fact she must have known because she totally cut me out of her will." A hard knot settled in his chest. "I don't care about the house or her stuff. It was never about her things."

Cash settled a hand on his shoulder and turned to face him. "Bro, you're not a pussy if you cry. Go ahead, let those tears fall."

Reid angrily wiped his cheeks.

"Well, maybe a tiny pussy."

Reid couldn't hold in his laughter. "You're an asshole."

"Yeah, I am." Cash sighed and gripped Reid's shoulder. "It's been you and me against the world for a long time, Reid. That Angela for some reason left me everything doesn't change that. She wasn't a good mom, but you've always been a better son than me."

"No, I—"

"Yes, just accept it. I'm good with that." Cash sounded as if he was. "The house, her shit, none of it matters. What matters is you and me."

Reid didn't know why, as Cash had said it all before, but a huge weight seemed to slide off him, unburdening him. "Yeah?"

"Yeah. I love you, Little Brother. I make a lot of mistakes, and you're always bailing me out of trouble. I hate it. I'm trying to do better."

Reid didn't mention that concussion Jordan had told him about, just listened as Cash continued to talk.

"I'm sorry I'm not better about sharing you. Naomi's your girl, and I need to respect that. I *do* respect that. It's just, I guess…" Cash flushed. "I guess I'm worried you'll ditch me for good. I can't compare with her tits and ass."

Reid grinned. "No, you can't. I hate to break it to you, but you're pretty flat-chested."

Cash slapped him on the back of the head, and it felt as if nothing had changed between them, yet everything had.

Reid ducked a second slap to the head. "I know what you're saying. But you have to know you'll always be my brother. My best friend. If you ever needed me, I'd drop everything to come to your side, including Naomi." Realizing how that sounded, he amended, "I mean, not drop her forever. But if you were in danger I'd leave her to—"

"Bro, I get it." Cash smiled. "You still have my back, and I always have yours. And Naomi's a part of you now. You can drag your feet and pretend like she's not it for you, but we both know she is."

Love for Naomi filled the void that Reid hadn't been aware existed, until her. "She is. We're taking any kind of marriage talk slow though. But that doesn't mean there's no room for you in my life—in our life."

"I was acting like a shit, and I know it. This thing with Angela happening now hasn't helped." He gave Reid a pointed look.

"My fault. I agree, I've been avoiding the house and the crap that comes with it. But I want to help you with that mess. And no matter what you say, you're keeping the house. It's yours."

"But—"

"No." He'd talked to Naomi about it, and she supported his decision one hundred percent. "They owe you, Cash. For years of treating you like dirt, for not letting you be a part of our family. Charles and Angela owe you that much." Reid stared into his brother's eyes, willing him to believe it. "You're a great Marine, a great man, and those assholes need to pay for what they did to you." He saw his brother's surprise that he'd refer to their parents in that way. But they both knew the truth.

"Dad tried to make you feel bad about yourself forever, and you still stuck it to him by being a better man than he could ever hope to be. Mom might not have been there, but she knew in the end she loved you."

"She loved you too," Cash said, his voice thick, full of emotion. "Charles was a shit. Angela was just gone from the beginning."

"But we're still here. You and me. And I might have Naomi, but it looked to me like you might have Jordan."

"Nah," Cash was quick to point out. "We're just kind of dating. It's new and probably won't last."

"But you want it to, don't you?"

Cash remained quiet for a moment. "Maybe."

"That's a yes. Now who's being a pussy?" He ignored the finger his brother shot him, relieved to see Cash getting fired up, not so down anymore. "Sure, you get into fights and get yourself in trouble. A lot. Or at least you used to. Let's be honest. You taking down a burglary and saving a boy's life not only was the right thing to do, it's the whole reason our business is booming."

Cash grinned. "Well, not the whole reason."

"And I'm sure whatever happened tonight wasn't just you screwing off."

Cash sighed. "I was trying to help a guy who got jumped by three bigger guys. It wasn't cool. Then they cheated by trying to brain me with a free weight."

Reid snorted. "Only you."

"Hey, it hurt."

"You're always where you need to be, even if you come out with a few scrapes." Reid thought back to Cash's many commendations in the Marine Corps for bravery, for being the guy to do the right thing no matter the cost to himself. "You might be a big idiot, but I'm glad you're my brother."

"Well said, Reid." Cash chuckled. "Now if you're done being a little momma's boy, will you help me clear out the rest of the crap from the house? If I'm gonna keep it, I have to think about whether to sell it or live in it. Since you're moving in with the hot redhead soon."

"Uh, not that soon." Sure, he and Naomi had *talked* about it. A lot, actually.

"Soon." Cash read him clearly, as he always had. "Then I need to figure out what to do. And before you go apologizing again, as much as you like to think I can't live without you, I actually can and have lived on my own." He shook his head. "I'm thirty-six, dickbag. I always knew I'd eventually leave. No living with my sad little bro forever. Fly, little guy, be free."

"Who the hell are you calling a dickbag?" The joy Reid felt, knowing Cash supported and still loved him, overwhelmed him. Cash might not realize it, but Reid knew they'd taken a huge step forward in their relationship. For the first time, Reid realized he didn't need to be his brother's keeper. Just Cash's brother, to love and support him. "You know, Cash, I think you're finally growing up."

"Fuck you."

"But we still need to work on that vocabulary." He grinned at the face Cash made. "Now tell me in detail what happened at the gym. And why do I have a feeling I'll be getting a phone call from Gavin Donnigan again?" This time he'd let Gavin know Cash could fight his own battles but that Reid had no problem playing backup should the Griffiths need to stand tall.

Chapter 13

"HAPPY INDEPENDENCE DAY!" MARIA YOUNGER RAISED her glass and waited for the rest of them to raise their plastic cups as they sat outside at the picnic table in the backyard of the house Jordan had grown up in. "Thank you for your service, Jordan."

Jordan smiled, still cautious, and drank her fruit punch. Next to her, Rafi did the same. Carl, Leanne, her fiancé Troy, and their mother drank a local organic beer, the grownups enjoying a sunny Fourth of July picnic.

The food had been enjoyable if a little bland. The entire picnic was organic, sugar- and gluten-free, and non-GMO. As usual with her parents, no "bad" stuff allowed, even in the food.

Rafi liked being home, she knew, but more than that, he loved being with their parents. No matter what he said or how he tried to act rebellious, he loved them. As he should. It had hurt him, deeply, that the pair had wanted to ship him off to kid boot camp rather than stick it out through the tough times and help him adjust.

Jordan had to squelch her irritation with them, knowing they loved all their children but didn't know how to best help them. Leanne, "La Princesa," smiled her bright-white teeth at Troy, Mr. Wonderful, and toasted him.

"And to my amazing fiancé"—Jordan sipped her punch, having turned the mentions of "fiancé" into a private drinking game—"Troy Fielding, for making partner in his firm!"

They all drank, though Jordan wondered why Leanne had to make a big deal about Troy during the one holiday that celebrated independence. Ironic considering Leanne had never shown all that much independence herself.

And there you go, being bitchy again.

"Not so surprising, Troy," Carl said with a big grin. Of average height but sporting a killer smile and bright-blue eyes, he very well looked the part of Leanne's father despite having no biological tie. Rafi and Jordan, meanwhile, took after their mother's side of the family. Unfortunately, Maria didn't know much about her Brazilian relatives, since her own mother had only ever concentrated on being "American."

The few times Jordan had met her grandmother, Vó Ana had given her treats and spoken in broken English and Portuguese. The woman had passed away when Jordan was six, and all traces of her family's Brazilian heritage had sadly died with her.

Jeff Fleming had, by all accounts, been a good man and loving husband. Jordan remembered his big hugs and smiles and the way he'd been so invested in his family. The accident had hurt them all, but a year later, their mother had found Carl, another good man.

Except Carl let Maria hide from the ugly side of family a little too well. Though Jordan could understand not wanting to deal with angry teenagers, now living with one, she couldn't conceive of washing her hands of her brother. It had been tough enough for her to strike out on her own under the guidance of Army drill sergeants. And she'd been eighteen and of strong mind.

Rafi had problems, issues his family should be helping him resolve.

"Jordan?" Leanne waited.

"I'm sorry. What?"

"How's work going?"

Thinking of Cash, she smiled. "Good. It's not mentally taxing, but I like that."

Her mother sighed. "When are you going to figure out what you're doing with your life?"

Carl warned, "Maria."

"No, Carl. It's a legitimate question. Can you imagine moving boxes when you're sixty years old?" she asked Jordan.

Troy scoffed. "I've told you I can get you a job at my company. They need security people, and you were military police."

The way he said "security people" put Jordan on edge. The man never outright stated his prejudices, but it was clear to her that he thought himself better than everyone else. Except for maybe Leanne.

"I don't want a security job, thanks. I'm using this time to help my brother," she said pointedly to her parents, who didn't so much as blink, "and to figure out my goals. I have the GI Bill to use, and I don't want to make any mistakes and waste credits."

Carl perked up. "See? That's our smart girl. Jordan has always gone her own way, and she's been remarkable."

Jordan liked that he'd stood up for her.

"I know." Leanne gushed. "My sister is tough and a hard worker. I was actually wanting to interview her for a piece we're doing at the magazine."

A stupid e-zine that had over a million subscribers

and put out a corresponding print edition each month. And of course, Leanne was one of its leading contributors and a top editor. It sometimes bothered Jordan that everything her sister touched turned to gold. Then again, if Leanne ever had to deal with adversity, her head would probably explode.

"What a terrific idea, honey." Troy kissed Leanne's cheek. "You're so smart."

Next to her, Rafi whispered, "Barf."

Unfortunately, Maria overheard. "That's the problem, right there. No respect for your family."

"Mom," Jordan said, trying to deflect the negative attention. "Rafi is going to classes and doing his best. And that's not easy." Not when you were a rebellious teenager.

"You should be more like your sister," Carl said.

"Which one?" Rafi gave them an innocent smile. "The hardass Army cop or the blond angel sleeping her way to a Fortune 500 win with Troy? And, dude, are your teeth naturally that white? Because I don't think so. Go easy next time on the bleach."

"*Rafi*." Leanne scowled at him. "Tell Troy you're sorry."

Troy covered her hand. "It's okay, honey. I remember being wild during my teen years." He smiled, and damn if Rafi hadn't nailed it. Those teeth were blinding. "It was all my parents could do to settle me down. I almost attended Berkeley." He laughed. "Imagine not going to Stanford."

Since Carl had also attended that prestigious university, he laughed. "What a disaster."

Jordan made a face her mother saw.

"Problem?"

"Well, yeah. Who cares what college you go to as long as you try your best? And, you know, college isn't for everyone." Jordan knew she sounded defensive, but her argument was on Rafi's behalf, not necessarily her own.

"College actually does serve a purpose, Jordan." Carl sounded apologetic at least. "Sorry, but it's true."

"Only in certain fields," Jordan argued. "I get it if you're in business, becoming a lawyer or doctor."

"And even in the literary and academic worlds." Leanne nodded. "I mean, the fact I went to Princeton was huge in getting me my first job with *The New Yorker* then *Granta*. I was lucky to make connections, which led to this huge step up editing at *Femme Moderne*."

"But that's not for everyone." Cash and Reid hadn't gone to business school, and they were doing well. Maybe not well, but making a decent wage to be proud of. "And, heck, Mom doesn't even work."

"But I did work when you were younger," her mother pointed out. "I went to college and got my degree. The only reason I didn't use it much was because I had you guys to raise."

"And you still have Rafi in high school," Jordan reminded her, wishing she'd kept her mouth shut. The picnic had been going so well. Good food and her parents had been nice. Leanne had been annoying, but Jordan chalked up her own animosity to feelings of jealousy and not liking Troy, not that Leanne had put a foot wrong.

Rafi tensed. "You sick of me? Is this you trying to get rid of me too?"

"What? No." Jordan wrapped an arm around him, waiting for him to squirm free. But he didn't. "I love having you with me. I think you're going to do great, just as soon as we get you through this summer." *Don't do it, Jordan. This isn't the time to confront Mom and Dad.*

Troy opened his fat mouth. "You know, it's common for teenagers to have issues at their age. We all have problems. We just have to muddle through them on our own."

Leanne nodded. "I did. I had a horrible time in AP Chemistry, but I made study friends and got through."

"Jesus, Leanne. This isn't about you or Mr. White Teeth." Hell. Jordan hadn't meant to let that slip.

Troy's eyes narrowed.

Yeah, he must have sensed she didn't like him before because she'd always done her best not to talk to him. But Jordan had been more circumspect about keeping her distance.

"Jordan." Maria gaped. "That's just rude."

Carl glared. "Apologize to Troy." He turned to Troy before she could get a word out. "I'm so sorry, Troy. That was uncalled for."

Leanne leaned against him. "Totally uncalled for. My fiancé has done nothing to provoke this attack but be nice." Her eyes welled.

Terrific. Saint Leanne was upset. But, hey, she'd said "fiancé." The drinking game commenced once more; Jordan took another sip.

Heck, might as well get it all off my chest. "Sorry, Troy. It's not your fault my parents are ignoring their kid." Next to her, Rafi gripped her knee. In support, she hoped, because he hadn't moved out from under her arm. "You guys did the same thing to me when I was younger. I'm not sure why it's acceptable in this family to let young people with problems handle it themselves. I got by. I'm still not sure how. But you would have kicked me out if I hadn't joined the service at eighteen."

Her mother nodded. "And look where you are now. You're independent, smart, and living on your own."

"But Rafi isn't me. He's not Leanne—who you paid for to go to school, I might add."

"She had scholarships too. You weren't interested in college," Carl said, sounding defensive.

"I didn't know what I wanted at eighteen. I only knew I needed a change. Supportive parents would have been nice," she snapped. "Rafi's fifteen. He's having problems in school."

"He's turning into a thug." Carl scowled at Rafi. "Bad grades are one thing. Acting out, cursing at teachers, and skipping school are another."

Rafi spoke up, his voice cracking. "That teacher called me a stupid moron going nowhere in life. And, come on, stupid and moron is redundant anyway."

Jordan didn't dare laugh. Wait. A teacher had called him names? Before she could ask Rafi about it, he blundered on.

"I try, but I'm not smart at some things."

"Which is why we got you tutors," Carl said. "But you wouldn't go to your sessions."

Hmm. Point to the parents on that one.

"Because only the special needs kids go to that tutor, and everyone knows it! I'm not autistic or on some freakin' spectrum. I just don't do well at math."

And see, that there. Jordan would have said *good at math*. Yet Rafi knew when to use *well* or *good*. He could draw like he'd been born with a pencil in hand and could talk about everything from video games to politics. Her little brother had a brain. It just didn't like school.

Troy had the nerve to speak again. "Perhaps another tutor might help?"

Maria sighed. "We've tried other tutors, but when Rafi refuses to go to school, none of that matters."

Rafi stiffened and pulled away from Jordan. "So I guess it's good that I'm out of your hair, living with the only person here who cares." He stood up and went back into the house before Jordan could stop him.

The silence left in his wake seemed to make everyone uncomfortable.

"I hope you're happy," her mother said. "I knew today might be like this, but I'd hoped we could be civil at least."

"Mom, this is ridiculous. Everyone is nice and gets along when you ignore what's really going on."

"Which is what, exactly?" Troy asked.

"One, you are not a part of this family yet, so shut the hell up," Jordan told him, shocking the entire table.

Leanne gasped. "Jordan, you apologize for saying that."

"Two." Jordan turned to her parents. "How can you two call yourselves his parents yet be okay with Rafi going to some military school for kids with disciplinary problems? Rafi's just a kid."

"With disciplinary problems," Carl said drily.

Troy looked as if he'd swallowed a lemon but remained quiet.

"We love him, but I'm sorry," Maria apologized. "I don't understand that kind of behavior. Neither of you two acted out like that." She nodded from Jordan to Leanne.

"Mom, are you deliberately avoiding my entire past?"

Jordan asked, agog. "I skipped school, smoked marijuana, and barely got by with average grades in high school."

"I didn't know that."

"Bull. You totally did because you caught me once in the house with my room all smoky." Not Jordan's brightest moment, but in her defense, she'd thought her parents were gone for the weekend.

By the shock on his face, she saw that Carl hadn't known. "Mom didn't want to rock the boat, so she kept it from you, Dad. I wasn't a bad kid. I was being a teenager. It's normal to want to argue, skip school, act out. We can't all be Leanne who never steps wrong."

"I had problems." Leanne frowned.

"You had good kid problems, like *oh my gosh, I'm getting an A–*." Jordan snorted. "You're also the golden child who can do no wrong." Jordan knew she sounded bitter and probably shouldn't have aired this out in front of everyone at a picnic, but some perverse part of her wanted it on the table. "Rafi needs help. Why not be loving and support him, dealing with a not-so-perfect child? He's a good kid. He just needs to find his way. And believe it or not, he's so smart it's ridiculous. Just because his grades don't show it doesn't mean he's stupid."

"What you're saying is you don't want him at your home anymore." Carl shook his head. "Jordan, we told you he was a handful. He'll get better with supervision away from a too-forgiving family. Rafi needs to deal with the reality of growing up. You call it desertion. We call it tough love."

"Tough love works." Troy challenged her with a thin-lipped smile.

"I am good with Rafi staying with me." Jordan rose,

annoyed with all of them. "But I don't believe that a fifteen-year-old has the capacity to know the reality of growing up. He's allowed to make mistakes, and as the adults in his life, it's up to *us* to make sure he's not making the kind that can screw him up for life. This isn't about money, either. I'm taking care of him just fine." Though the kid was straining her budget with his never-ending appetite. At least she'd fed him at their parents'. "But you'd think you guys would want the best for him."

"We do, which is why this camp, which is not cheap by the way, is the best place for him." Carl put a hand on her wrist to stay her from leaving. "Jordan, we love Rafi."

"Have you even looked into this camp? Because I have. It's for kids with 'behavioral issues,' for God's sake. He's not a criminal, just a kid with bad grades." The thought of Rafi going away and being under guard, around people who could seriously hurt him if they wanted because their motto of "spare the rod, spoil the child" was enforced with physical discipline, scared the hell out of her.

"The camp is for more than that. I know people who've sent their kids there," Carl said. "I *did* research this. I talked to the headmaster too. It's a legitimate alternative."

That Carl's actions seemed to come from a loving place hurt her because he was so wrong and couldn't see it. Her mother, on the other hand, just liked to sweep away problems. Leanne…

"I have to go. Thanks for the picnic." She turned and headed through the house to leave.

Leanne followed her. "Wait, Jordan."

Jordan swallowed a sigh and paused by the front door. Then she turned to face Miss Perfect.

"I never knew you felt that way. That I was the golden child, I mean."

Leanne looked like an angel at that moment. So pretty, so sad for her pathetic younger sister. Jordan wanted to punch her in the face and felt smaller than an ant for her pettiness.

She swallowed. "I'm not sure how you could be so unaware. Growing up, Mom and Dad always favored you. And by Dad, I mean Carl." Because Jeff Fleming had loved his children equally. A pang of sadness speared her. Jeff would never have farmed Rafi out to someone else.

"I—I guess I never realized." Leanne's big blue eyes teared up. "I'm so sorry you felt that way." She reached for Jordan's hand, and Jordan balled said hand into a fist. "I also wish you liked Troy better. He's a nice person, Jordan. If you gave him a chance, you'd see how wonderful he is."

Jordan tugged her hand away. "Seriously? He's a snob. He and Carl get along because they like to make money and both went to Stanford." She said *Stanford* in her snootiest voice. "And I'm sorry for making fun of him, but he has no right to talk about Rafi. He's not family. But you are. How can you not want to help our brother?"

"I am helping, by standing by Mom and Dad." Leanne blinked, and a tear streaked down her cheek. "I love him, I do. But he's out of control. He needs help we can't give him. I wish you could see that."

The problem was Leanne believed what she said. Out

of love for Rafi, she'd let him go off with strangers. "Okay, so you believe that. Have you looked into this camp?"

"Well, no. Mom and Dad said it was okay so—"

"So you look into it. Then you tell me our little brother is better off being run to death or whipped—literally—into shape." Jordan left before she said something she'd regret. Because of course Leanne had to be nice about everything.

Did the woman not realize how bad things could get when the people you should trust worked against you? Putting a vulnerable fifteen-year-old in a situation where he had no power was asking for trouble.

But Leanne loved Rafi and genuinely thought she was helping by not helping.

Gah. Jordan itched to leave. Give her an obnoxious Marine with attitude any day. She texted Rafi for his whereabouts but needn't have bothered. She found him sitting in her car, waiting to escape.

She got in beside him.

He refused to look at her, so still she thought he'd shatter. The poor kid.

In a bland voice, he asked, "Am I moving out or what? It won't take me long to pack."

"Shut up. I'm in no mood to deal with 'sullen teenage boy' after having dealt with 'angelic never-makes-a-mistake girl.'" She started the car. "Now how about a bad-for-you burger and fries while we talk about how much we don't like Troy?"

Rafi's worry faded, and he shared his own bright-white smile. "You're on."

Chapter 14

THE NEXT DAY, THE TEACHER DRONED ON WHILE RAFI doodled in his notebook. He loved his sister even more for standing up for him. She held her own, told people what she thought, and had been a freakin' U.S. Army soldier. And not just a regular soldier but a cop, one who put people in handcuffs and broke up bar fights. Nothing scared his big sister.

While nowadays everything scared him. What would he do with his life if he couldn't even get through tenth grade?

He sighed, a bad move because his teacher called on him to explain something about rational expressions, which was supposed to be dividing fractions... he thought. Maybe. Math made no sense to him and never had. He'd always had a problem understanding it. Though he'd never told his parents, other simple things bothered him. Like telling time, which had been impossible before he'd gotten a digital watch and then a phone. Even money used to confuse him, making the right change a strange and painful undertaking, until he'd found ways to trick his brain into understanding it.

"Mr. Younger," the old windbag started, and the class tittered. The other losers doing summer school had been staying out of trouble, mostly because he, and to an extent Juan, had become Mr. Simpson's bitch. The guy had had a hard-on for Rafi since day one, when Rafi had referred to him as Homer, not realizing the teacher had been in the doorway of the classroom and overheard him. It didn't help that Simpson looked and sounded a lot like the iconic cartoon character.

Unfortunately, Simpson couldn't let things go. Every day he made the already-miserable math and science classes worse, poking fun at students—and Rafi in particular—and droning on about how great the summer would be if they hadn't had to come to class. As if it were Rafi's fault the guy was stuck in a job he clearly loathed.

"Mr. Younger," Simpson repeated. "Frankly, I don't know why you continue to show up to class. You have to be the stupidest student—and I use that term loosely—I've ever had. You understand at the sixth-grade level. You shouldn't even be in this class, let alone the tenth grade."

The silence around them grew unbearable. Simpson had never laid into anybody this badly before. Sure, he'd been mean, but not this level of cruel. Especially because Rafi knew it was true. He blinked back tears of embarrassment and rage. Rafi knew he was stupid. He didn't need some asshole teacher to tell everyone.

"I think it would be best if we assigned you a tutor. Maybe one of the seventh graders down the hall in the gifted classroom." Simpson raised a brow. "How does that sound?"

"Maybe if you were a better teacher, I'd get it."

Simpson didn't flinch. "Maybe if I had any thought that you might graduate and become a functioning member of society, I might try harder. The truth is, all of you are in here because you messed up during the school year. But at least most of you will get beyond this." Simpson gave Rafi a scorching look. "But you, Mr. Younger, are not worth my time. You're dragging everyone down, slowing the curriculum for the others who can do so much more. And let's face it, *if* you graduate, and that's a big *if*, you'll no doubt be living with Mommy and Daddy, unable to get a job, lost in video games and prepubescent fantasies of a life where you never work and always get the girl." Simpson sneered. "Dream on, son. I've seen this all before. You'll be soaking off your parents for the rest of your unworthy life."

Everyone stared at Simpson in shock. Even for him the rant was a bit much. The guy had been on Rafi's ass from the start, but Rafi hadn't wanted to say anything to Jordan because, one, he'd started it and, two, he didn't want to be more of a problem for his sister, who'd already gone out on a limb for him.

"Now why don't you do all of us a favor and drop the class. Retake tenth grade." Simpson sighed. "I suppose I should apologize. Slower students often need special help, and that's something you should be getting. *Out of my class*, that is."

The self-righteous prick. Rafi wanted to punch the asshole for such embarrassment. Everyone watched him, and now everyone knew how stupid he really was. So he fell back on what he knew. "Trouble at home with Marge?"

The class burst into laughter, dispelling the tension. At least, over them. Simpson looked ready to rage.

Rafi refused to stop. "I mean, bald is beautiful. But that beer gut can't be helping things with the missus."

Simpson's eyes widened, and then, in a tone covered with ice, he said, "Get out and don't come back."

"Sure thing, Homer."

More titters, though quieter this time.

"*Get out*," Simpson shouted.

Rafi took his shit and left, knowing he'd screwed up his last chance at avoiding military school. Jordan had the right of it. He'd had his buddy Daniel, video game guru and secret hacker, look into the place. Half the tools who graduated looked like some kind of robot, with short hair, cheesy grins, and the desire to succeed in life. It was like they'd been programmed to conform or something.

Oh man. Now he was good and fucked, thanks to his stupid brain and Simpson.

He wiped his cheeks as he hurried down the stairs and bumped into Juan.

"Whoa, man. You okay?" Juan was a decent guy, sharing his hatred of summer school and a love of the same video games Rafi played. The guy also had friends and seemed to want to bond with a "Brazilian brother." Though Rafi didn't speak Portuguese and had no tie to his roots, he was proud of his Latino blood.

"I'm good. Just sick of Simpson's crap. You missed quite a show."

Juan leaned in with a half chest bump. "I feel you. Simpson's a dick." He paused when someone texted him then whistled. "Shit. Don just told me what he said. That guy is such an asshole. Don't let it sweat you, man." He put an arm around Rafi's shoulders, and the pair walked out of the school.

"You cutting all day?"

Juan had to retake more than a few classes, while Rafi just had math and science, both of which Simpson taught.

"I'm done with school."

"Me too."

Juan smiled. "Awesome. You want to hang?"

"Sure." Not like Rafi had much of anything else to do. What the heck would he tell Jordan? "I'm so fucked."

"Nah. You got friends. I'll hook you up, if you want."

"Yeah? With what?"

"Getting kicked out of school is gonna be a problem for you, right?"

He sighed and nodded.

"So you're needing funds. I got some friends who can help with that."

Rafi didn't know. Juan had a reputation as a go-to guy for illegal stuff, and his family had serious money, so he usually kept out of trouble. Apparently they hadn't been able to buy him good grades, hence summer school. He'd even been rumored to hang out with a gang. Jordan didn't know about any of that, but she'd never liked him. She'd blamed Juan's influence for the bathroom cherry-bomb stunt. Which, actually, had been Juan's idea.

"I will need money." Jordan had been spending more than she could afford for him. He'd overheard her talking on the phone and seen some of her bills, though she'd told him she was okay.

"Perfect. Come on, Rafael. Let's enjoy our summer and get rich while we're at it."

Rafi smiled. "Sounds like a plan."

"Then let's go."

⁓

Cash spent the next few days feeling his way with Jordan. Since Reid had threatened to fire him if he even *thought* about going in to work, Cash sat at home and actually did a lot of resting and sleeping, which helped his head.

She'd kept her distance Wednesday and Thursday night, telling him she needed family time. He had no problem with the distance. Or so he told her. He'd actually missed her like crazy. His only bright spots had been more time with Reid, who'd spent the past two nights with him while Naomi traveled for some business thing, and a phone call from Gavin and Mac. Apparently he hadn't worn out his welcome at the gym.

"Good job kicking ass," Mac, the gym's owner, had told him over the phone. "Those jerks aren't welcome back. Ever. You see them, you save their pounding for me." Since Mac had also done time in the Corps and looked like a linebacker for a pro team, Cash had no problem leaving any ass-beatings to him. The praise had been nice but uncomfortable, made worse because Elliot kept talking about a Cash Appreciation Night at his bakery.

Cash would have refused, except Gavin had called to mention that this get-together would be a good thing for the community. The knowledge that locals protected their own. Cash liked the idea, even if he didn't like being the center of it, and grudgingly agreed to attend if Elliot promised to change the name of the event. Which he *supposedly* had... Now all Cash had to do was milk his recuperation time and hope Elliot had forgotten all about it the next time they crossed paths.

He sat in bed, propped against the headboard, staring at his toes. He wore shorts and a ratty sweatshirt while he waited for Jordan to join him. She'd stepped into the bathroom to get into something more comfortable. He'd surprised her with plans to go bowling...which she had rejected due to his supposed concussion. Cash felt just fine, but when she'd suggested a date indoors, just the two of them, he'd been all for it. Except she insisted they relax and offered a Friday night pajama party. Despite the fact he wasn't a teenage girl, he'd agreed. Sadly, since Jordan didn't sleep naked, he'd offered her something of his to wear. And now Friday Night in Pajamas was a go.

The days away from her had only increased his need for the woman. But at least that hunger went both ways. Seconds after he'd opened the door to her, she'd given him a kiss that had melted his brain.

He sighed. What could he do? He was so into this chick it hurt, yet he noticed she'd been holding herself back. He'd sensed a problem over the phone on Thursday, but she acted like nothing bothered her, and he had to respect her wishes to keep things as casual as she wanted.

But tonight, with Reid shacking up with Naomi and Rafi spending the night with his friend, the one Jordan tolerated, Cash had her all to himself. Time to bombard that emotional blockade of hers. Reid, even Evan, would slyly prod for answers, hurdling obstacles. Not Cash. He believed in annihilating problems head-on.

The niggle of doubt that she'd already had enough of him and wanted to move on but was afraid to tell him had disappeared the moment she'd kissed him.

When Mariah had wanted nothing to do with him, she'd left. No kisses, no passion. And no more bank account, but whatever. Cash had money in the bank again, and Jordan wasn't the type to sleep with a guy for what he could give her. Of that he had no doubt.

She rejoined him, wearing one of his shirts. The thing

came to her knees but molded to her breasts, and he'd never envied a piece of clothing more.

He patted the bed beside him. "Come here."

She sat next to him, her back against the headboard, and crossed her ankles. "Thanks, Conan. I like your taste in clothing."

He grinned. "Anything for you, Ms. Fleming."

"That's Staff Sergeant Fleming to you."

"Fine. You can call me Conan. Or Gunny or Master. Your call."

She rolled her eyes.

He wanted to kiss her, so he did. He pulled away, pleased to see her eyes cloudy with lust. "So tell me. What has your panties in a knot? Because you haven't been yourself since the Fourth. Did you miss me? Is that it? Well, it's all better now, Sugar Lips. I'm here."

She laughed, as he'd hoped she might, and relaxed. "You're still such an ass. Your consistency helps."

He smiled. "And I still have a big dick. You're welcome."

She laughed again then sighed. "I made a mess over July Fourth." She ran through the day then mentioned Rafi not acting right.

"A mess," he agreed. "Makes me glad my mom and dad are dead."

She blinked. "I, ah, I'm sorry?"

"Nah. I told you they weren't good at being parents. You have it bad, but different bad. Your mom and dad actually love you guys, they're just not so good at handling your problems."

She nodded. "I can't believe they can't see how bad military school would be for Rafi."

He played devil's advocate. "But would it be so bad?"

She stared at him with wide eyes. "How can you say that?"

"The military helped me. It helped you. All that structure and discipline."

He could see her anger and braced himself, knowing she'd feel better after she let it out.

"Are you insane? First of all, you *chose* the military. You didn't have anyone choosing it for you. And you joined the Marine Corps—the actual military, not a military school run by wannabe assholes who couldn't hack it in the real world."

"Ouch. You know this for a fact?"

"I did the math." Which wasn't exactly gleaning facts from research, but he let it slide. "I googled the school. The people there take troubled youths and mold them. But molding means they can do whatever the hell they want to these kids. Sounds more like brainwashing and abuse than discipline."

"So Rafi stays with you."

She nodded. "My parents are fine to let him stay with me, but it's all on me. It sucks, I have to tell you. When he's happy and the old Rafi, it's not a problem, well, except that he never stops eating."

Cash's appetite had always been enormous, so he didn't comment.

"But when he's sarcastic and annoying—"

"Like looking into a mirror for you, huh?"

She shot him the finger, which made him laugh. "It's tough to remember he needs my help and not a foot up his ass."

"Which is why you're such a great sister. You're helping him."

"Maybe." She released a huge sigh. "And maybe their idea of having him get in line or deal with the consequences is right. Maybe this military academy would be a good thing and I'm full of worry. I mean, I didn't actually see any accusations of abuse or wrongdoing online about the place. I just don't have a good feeling."

"Hmm. Why not check it out? I could go with you for moral support."

"Thanks, but it's in Pennsylvania."

"Hell. On the East Coast? If he goes and ends up having a problem, he's too far for you or your parents to just drive down there and get him."

"Duh. I know that."

"Okay, smartass." He put her in a headlock, amused with her inability to get free. "So you're still struggling with the whole Rafi deal. But there's something else. Tell me what's really bothering you."

Her muffled "Besides the fact I have your nasty armpit in my face?" made him grin.

"Hey, I'm wearing the Seahawks. Be nice." He let go, and she slapped his chest. "Ow."

"That's what you get."

He laughed.

"I'm a mess, Cash. Lately, I feel so...not me."

"Tell me about it."

She glared.

"Jordan, that's not me being sarcastic. I mean, sincerely, tell me about it."

"Oh." She lost her glare. "I would, but you wouldn't understand."

"Try me."

"You always seem so sure of yourself. Even when

it comes to getting in trouble, you don't hesitate. Guy at the gym is getting a beatdown? You go in and knock some heads around. Smith is an asshole? You go at him, face-to-face, not scared of anything. But not me. I'm so unsure of everything lately." She blinked, and he saw tears.

"Aw, hell. Jordan, talk to me." He pulled her into his lap and rubbed her back while she cried onto his chest. He hadn't thought anything could hurt so much, but feeling her tears pained him worse than being knocked in the head.

"I just feel lost. And stupid."

"You're the least stupid person I know." He kissed the top of her head, wanting her to feel better.

"I don't know what I'm doing with Rafi. He's been secretive and off the past few days. I have no idea why. I was a shit to my perfect sister." She hiccupped. "See? I'm being sarcastic about Leanne. And she's never been anything but nice."

"I hate nice people," he grumbled.

Her laugh hitched and turned into a sob. "I was mean about her snotty fiancé."

"He sounded like a dick."

She clutched him tighter. "He so is. I hate his teeth and his Stanford education."

"Me too." His feelings for Jordan only grew. The woman handled herself at work, did her best by her family, and had helped him more than once, holding her own with him.

"And me. I'm so confused. I like my job with Vets on the Go!, but I know it's not forever."

His heart clenched hearing that.

"I don't want to be sixty and still moving boxes." She cried harder.

He rocked her, telling her everything would be okay, and let her cry it out.

"I just...I don't know anything right now. I should be a retired Sergeant Major in another nine years. Instead I'm starting my life over at twenty-nine. I liked the Army, damn it. It's not fair." She cried some more until her sobs turned to whimpers.

Cash just held her, understanding so much and wishing he could make things better.

But he couldn't, so he gave her what he could. He held her tight, and when her breathing evened and she fell asleep, he laid her gently in bed, pulled over the covers, then joined her, holding her close to protect her from the demons he couldn't see.

When Jordan woke, the room remained dark, and the snuggly heater behind her tightened the hug around her middle.

She blinked, feeling wrung out. Then she recalled crying her eyes out on Cash's chest. *God, how embarrassing.* She had no idea how he'd feel about dealing with a neurotic woman with family issues.

But lying there, she remembered more. How he'd held her tenderly and stroked her hair. How his heartbeat had calmed her and how he'd kept telling her everything would be all right.

He hadn't judged her, hadn't told her what to do. He'd listened and been there—exactly what she'd needed.

She had no idea what to do about these feelings for

him. In addition to her uncertainty came the confusing emotions for a man who could probably do a lot better than an ex-Army MP with nowhere to go.

Sure, she had options, but Jordan couldn't do a whole hell of a lot with Rafi needing her. As much as she wanted to get her degree in…something, she had no time or energy for school, not until her brother was straightened out. Though she had a good fifteen years upon exiting the Army to use her GI Bill, she didn't want to make any mistakes. With a limited reserve of money, she didn't want to hurry into a degree she suddenly found herself not liking after graduation.

Her journey to self-discovery—Miriam notwithstanding, she thought and surprised herself with a grin—seemed on hold. Jordan didn't like not following a specific timetable. She liked order and discipline. She liked having a plan and things making sense.

She put her hand over the strong arm holding her close. Cash she thought she understood. He'd had a crappy home life and had worked ever since to make himself better. He didn't always make the best decisions, but those trials came from a good place, his intent always for the better of others. Giving, affectionate, and brash to hide that loving heart, Cash was a man who valued loyalty and integrity and gave what he got.

She could do so much worse.

And he could do so much better.

Was there a way they could meet in the middle? She'd told him she planned to keep him, blustering through a declaration in hopes she could bluff her way into being the confident, sexy woman she'd once been. And *he'd bought it*. But how long until he realized taking on

Jordan meant taking on Rafi for the next two years as well as all her insecurities?

That she kept thinking long term unnerved her because Cash was a man others coveted. He commanded attention from his sheer size and manner. A natural leader and a natural heartbreaker.

Before last night's meltdown, Jordan had been a woman who didn't need protection. She'd guarded herself and wanted only an equal partner. Now, having exposed her vulnerabilities, part of her felt unworthy of someone so strong. While another wondered how he'd behave now that he'd seen her cry.

Jordan *hated* to cry, almost as much as she hated feeling like a failure. She knew making mistakes only helped prevent future failure, but that didn't make the fall hurt any less. And, yes, she'd fallen. No longer an Army soldier. Now she was a civilian. An employee. A sister. A daughter.

And a lover to one sexy man who could have any woman he wanted. Why, then, did he want her? *And why the hell am I so wussy about life right now?* she asked herself angrily. Jordan didn't mope. She didn't have time for self-doubt, but she could allow that she'd earned a mini-breakdown. She hadn't taken the time to realize all she'd lost after separating from the Army, and she'd been due. If only she hadn't lost it with Cash.

As if he'd heard her thinking about him, he tightened his arm around her. "You okay?" came the gritty question.

She shivered, feeling her every nerve on end. Cash stirred, and he thickened against her bottom.

"I'm good. I think I fell asleep."

"Yep." He snuggled against her and sighed. "With me."

Her heart raced. She wanted to show Cash how much it meant that he'd been there when she needed him. And, hell, she wanted him. She always wanted him. That sexy body did things to her, and adding that to his compassionate nature under the blustery exterior, it made him someone she couldn't get out of her mind.

She reached behind her, angling her hand between them, and found his erection through his shorts. She gripped him then stroked, up and down, feeling him grow harder, hearing his breathing grow shallower.

"You hungry, baby?" he asked, his voice gritty.

"Maybe." She wanted to feel him inside her, just him and her. Protected against pregnancy, though she hadn't mentioned she was safe from babies, Jordan decided she fully trusted Cash, and she wanted all of him.

Just hers, for this night at least.

He kept saying he felt fine, and though she didn't want to cause him any harm with his head injury, he seemed much better. Jordan slowly removed her clothes and tossed them to the floor. She turned and reached for him and found his sweatshirt had gone, so he must have taken it off before joining her in bed. But those shorts had to go. She tugged them and his underwear down his legs, aware Cash did nothing to stop her. Then she turned around, lying naked while he spooned her.

"Fuck, yeah. This is much better." He kissed the back of her neck, that solid part of him insistent against her ass.

Jordan put her leg over his, opening herself, and angled back against him so that the tip of his shaft rested against her entrance. She eased back, and a small part of him inched inside.

Behind her, Cash had frozen, not moving a muscle.

"You sure?" He kissed the back of her neck again, sliding her hair out of the way so he could kiss his way up her neck to her ear. "Want to grab me a condom?"

"No. I want you in me. All of you."

"Jordan, I don't know if I'll stop in time."

Now or never. "You don't have to." Such a huge silence fell between them. "I'm protected, and I trust you."

He gave a long, drawn-out groan. "Man, I hate how perfect you are."

She had no idea what that meant, but then she couldn't think as he slowly slid inside her, the excitement and warmth of her body allowing him an easy though tight passage. With them lying on their sides, he felt huge and thick as he entered her, and the position made it difficult for him to truly move all the way in.

Then he raised her leg higher over his and pushed deeper, and they both gasped, shaken by the feel of him there.

"So fuckin' good," he whispered and began to move.

But he didn't forget her. Cash reached around to her clit. The pressure of his fingers in time with his body inside hers took over every sense. In and out he slid while his skilled fingers played her. He cupped her breast with his other hand, his pelvis rocking against her. Faster, harder.

He rubbed her with increasing pressure as he pinched her nipple, and she cried out as an orgasm overpowered her.

Cash kept rubbing then shoved once more and groaned, shuddering as he filled her.

He murmured something against her shoulder and kissed her, still pumping those hips. And then he lay still.

After a moment, he spoke. "Am I dreaming?"

She smiled, felt him cup her breast, stroking with familiarity, and sighed. "I'm dreaming too. I came so hard."

He groaned. "God, me too. All in you." He withdrew a fraction before easing back into her and cursed. "I want you again. I have to have you."

"No." She pulled away and tried to bodily move him on top of her. When he finally moved where she wanted him, she gripped his slick cock, not surprised he remained half-hard. "*I* have to have *you*."

"You do, huh?" He pushed himself inside her again and lay there, not moving. The moon shifted behind some clouds and allowed a sliver of light into his bedroom. She saw him smile. "I think that can be arranged."

Chapter 15

Cash felt like a new man Saturday afternoon as he and Reid went through their mom's belongings. Nothing bothered him. Even being around Angela's crap did nothing more than mildly annoy him that he wasn't spending his weekend with Jordan.

Being with her last night, so intimately, had changed something between them.

And it wasn't just coming inside her, though remembrances of their time together kept him continually hard and had forced him to wear jeans today. Being able to hold her while she cried, taking care of her, had eased something inside him. He'd been very careful to not treat her any differently when she'd left that morning, having spent the night. Another milestone that thrilled him to no end. Nor had he made a big deal about her being there when Reid popped by to pick him up.

Neither, fortunately for Reid's health, had Reid.

"So."

Here it came.

"You and Jordan together all night, huh?"

Cash groaned. "Do we have to talk about this? How about we play some music and finish putting all this shit outside?" Thanks to Jordan's help, he'd made a few calls and had a donation truck prepared to swing by the next morning to pick up items for a shelter.

"Oh, we have to talk about it." Reid grinned, his gray eyes sparkling. "How often do I get to give my brother the third degree about his love life?"

"At least I've always had one to get interrogated about." A dumb retort, but it was all he had, his thoughts buried in images of Jordan's smile.

And that was another thing. As much as he loved her body, Cash kept dwelling on her laugh. Her smile. How her eyes lit up when something surprised her. Her soft lips would part then thin into a firm line when he inevitably did something to piss her off.

The woman had the sexiest frown, and her growls made his heart race.

"Oh man. Big Brother has it bad for Little Army." Reid snickered.

"Funny. At least my chick could beat yours up without breaking a sweat."

"Oh, so that's what we're judging? Your girlfriend's ability to beat mine up?"

Cash laughed. "Yeah. I'd love to see that. Maybe with some Jell-O or mud in a large ring. And you know, they could be in bikinis. Or topless. I'm open to either option."

Reid stopped packing a moment. "You know, I wouldn't mind that either. But if you think I'd ever suggest it to Naomi, you're crazy. But, hey, why don't you see what Jordan thinks of the idea?"

"I like my nuts attached, thanks." Just another thing he loved about Jordan: her refusal to take any disrespect or to tolerate his nonsense. She wasn't afraid of him. He knew if he upset her, she'd tell him to his face. No passive-aggressive bullshit to sift through.

"Say, I was thinking…"

"Here we go."

"With you and Jordan together, we should make it a point that you're no longer in charge of any hiring/firing decisions. Let's make personnel my bag. But you'll be our image liaison."

"Wait. What?"

"I was talking to Naomi about you."

"Damn it." So much for brotherly good will.

"Now hold on. I know you have a thing for Jordan, and I'm fine with it. But I don't want anyone having a problem with *us*, the company. Right now we're all good. But if someone gets crazy, we don't need a lawsuit."

"Lawsuit? From what?"

"Sexual harassment, dumbass."

Cash frowned. "Jordan isn't going to press charges because I'm sleeping with her." If the woman wanted him gone, she'd tell him.

"I know that. But perception is everything. We'll make a broad announcement that your responsibilities include liaising with interested third parties and scouting the clients' homes, as in you're our lead mover on the ground. Evan is going to handle HR, since he's got a minor in psychology."

"He can do that?"

"It's our company. I can have Finley as our HR guru if I want." They both frowned at that. "So, yes, Evan will be our HR manager. It's good to have a human resources rep anyway because it shows we value our employees."

"So if I make one Air Force joke too many, Funny Rob can complain about it?"

"Exactly."

Cash snorted. "Whatever. Do what you have to do to CYA."

"I just didn't want you to think you were getting a demotion or anything."

"Dude, I'm good just having a steady job I like. I realize I can't do this forever, but it's good now." Jordan mentioning being a mover at sixty had made him think. "And I like it. I like doing physical stuff."

"I know. Plus everyone wants that hunky mover who beats up criminals." Reid laughed at his red face. "Yeah, that's what my last call yesterday was for. The lady also wanted to know if you were single and liked older women."

"How old?" Cash asked just to keep the humor going. No one but Jordan existed for him now.

"Sixty-four. I told her you'd think about it."

"Ass."

"Don't worry. I told her you had a girlfriend." Reid paused. "So you and Jordan are serious, huh?"

"I am. I have no idea what she is, and I'm not pressuring her by asking. So shut the hell up around her."

"Easy." Reid held up his hands. "I'm just making conversation."

"Well, talk less. Pack more. I need to see this place uncluttered."

"You and me both."

Hours later, they'd cleared almost everything but larger pieces of furniture from the home. "What's this?" Reid asked of the boxes by the kitchen wall.

"Those are yours. I think Jordan packed a few because I didn't want to deal. They're for you to go through in addition to the ones you already packed from your room."

Reid nodded. "Sounds good. Now how about you grab Jordan and bring her over to Naomi's tonight for drinks? We can sit around and relax. And, hey, you can bring up the idea of mud wrestling."

"Funny." A double date with Reid and Naomi? That would be his and Jordan's first outing as a couple. "Let me ask her." He texted her, unsure what her response would be.

But she didn't have a problem with it, as long as he picked up dinner. He grinned. "Food included?"

Reid nodded. "I'll make it happen. Chinese okay?"

"Fine. But no chow mein and no telling everyone how I used to think lo mein noodles were really worms. I was a kid, Reid. Let it go."

"A kid? Cash, you were twenty years old and in the Marine Corps."

"Shut up."

Reid just laughed. "Help me carry these boxes to my trunk."

"Watch yourself or you might join them back there."

───※───

Jordan hadn't had a case of nerves this bad since, well, ever. It was important to her that Reid and Naomi like her with Cash. Knowing how close the brothers were, she needed Reid to approve. She had a feeling he already did. He'd always been nice to her at work and had been the first to want to hire her, no matter what Cash said. Reid respected her, but did he respect her going out with his brother?

She could deal with Reid. But Naomi intimidated her. The woman had never been anything but pleasant and professional around Jordan. Naomi was the kind of woman Jordan had never understood, cut from the same mold as her sister Leanne—beautiful, kind, and always perfect.

Already Jordan found herself biased against the woman, which made no sense. She'd met Naomi plenty of times before and respected her. Heck, she loved that Naomi was a take-charge woman running her own company. *How's that for empowering, Miriam?* And knowing Naomi dated Reid put her off-limits with Cash. Even better.

But now that Jordan and Cash were dating, Naomi had the power of veto by proxy—since she dated Reid. It made sense when Jordan thought about it, but when she said it out loud, she sounded like a lovesick moron.

No, not lovesick. *Like*-sick. She couldn't possibly love Cash, not so soon into just knowing him. Of course, it didn't help that she liked everything about him. Even the way he tried bossing her around or acting like he was so superior. She took that as his big-man status. When folks were afraid of you, you didn't have to hurt them to prove a point. And she had a feeling Cash had been proving himself for a very long time.

She stood with him at Naomi's front door, loving the cute cottage in Greenwood. She envied this place, the same way she wished she lived somewhere nicer than that rundown apartment complex in Northwest Seattle. Not that she didn't appreciate the affordable rent, but she'd like to eventually live in a house that looked like the place Cash shared with his brother, with nice furniture and in a decent neighborhood. Maybe in a few years she'd have enough saved up to rent a small cottage like this one, but most likely in a less desirable neighborhood.

"What are you thinking?" Cash tapped her between the eyes. "You have a frown just there."

She smacked his hand away. "Cut it out. I'm trying to focus on being nice."

"Being nice takes focus?" He chuckled. "Oh, sorry. You're serious?"

"Yes. I can be myself around you and the guys. But fancy people think I'm too aggressive. Puts them off."

"Fancy people?" He frowned then nodded. "You mean Naomi. Because even though my brother acts fancy with his tuck-in shirts and khakis, he's like me, only much, much weaker."

She grinned.

"Hey, just stating the facts."

So she was laughing when Naomi opened the door, looking beautiful in jeans and a scoop-neck silk tank. Jeez. Even dressed down the woman looked model-gorgeous. Cash gave Jordan a gentle push inside, and she turned to frown at him.

"Well, move. You're taking up space doing nothing but stalling."

"Jackass," she muttered and gave herself a subtle once-over. Unlike Naomi, Jordan didn't look spiffy in casual attire. She looked…casual. She'd worn her hair down tonight, and the shaggy strands were at best clean. Jordan couldn't afford a hundred-dollar haircut, and if they didn't like it, too damn bad.

Her T-shirt was clean, her shorts not new but decent

enough. And her sandals showed large feet without painted nails.

"I'm so glad you came," Naomi told her and smiled at them both. "Reid's helping with the salad."

"Oh man. Vegetables?" Cash groaned. "What happened to Chinese?"

"My favorite place closed down." Naomi sighed. "Now I have to hunt for a new takeout place. But don't worry. I have something you'll like. I think."

Cash let out a dramatic sigh. "Are we at least having anything that used to walk on its own?"

Jordan swallowed a laugh.

"You and Reid." Naomi shook her head. "Yes, as a matter of fact. We're having burgers and fries with a side salad."

"Sounds good. Thank you for inviting us." Jordan handed Naomi a plate. "Cash told me we didn't need to bring anything, but you're supposed to bring something to dinner," she said more to Cash than Naomi. "So I hope you enjoy dessert. It's a homemade apple strudel."

Reid rushed over. "Oh, wow. Hi guys." He took a look under the aluminum foil protecting dessert. "This smells amazing."

"My woman can cook." Cash wrapped an arm around her waist.

Jordan felt like a prize heifer being appraised. "Thanks for the shout-out, but I can manage." She wiggled her way out from his arm.

Reid slugged Cash in the arm. "*Your woman* seems a little nervous. Relax, Cash."

"She's fine."

"She's right here," Jordan said, feeling less than enthusiastic about the evening as it progressed.

"Ignore them," Naomi said. "Cash is obviously beating his chest, in case we didn't get the fact that you arriving together means you're a couple. And Reid is doing his best to make sure you stay without bolting before we even get to dessert. Apparently he's been through this with Cash before."

Jordan leaned closer to ask, "So Cash makes a habit of bringing women over?"

"No, but he does make a habit of being loud and growly when he comes over to eat. I'm used to that. Wasn't sure you were."

Jordan smiled. "He growls a little. Mostly he's too busy shoving his face full of food to be bothered."

Naomi huffed. "I hear that. Reid had to smack him in the head last time to make sure he saved some food for the rest of us. I didn't mind. But apparently Reid had wanted leftovers to take for lunch the next day."

"He does like to eat." They both turned to see the guys crouched, petting a cat.

"Oh, that's Rex. He kind of owns the place. I just live here."

Jordan went to pet the cat as well, a sucker for furry animals. Reid left them to it, and Jordan took the opportunity to elbow Cash in the gut.

He grunted and gave her a dirty look. "What's that for?"

"Relax. And don't rub in the fact we're dating, okay?"

He stood suddenly, looming over her. "You're embarrassed to be dating me?"

She stood as well, conscious that he continued to loom. "No, nimrod. I'm fine with us dating and everyone knowing it. You don't have to beat them over the head with it is all."

He nodded. "Okay. So, ah, did you tell your brother about us?"

"Not exactly. I'm more concerned with where he's been going lately than sharing my love life with him."

"Is he having more problems at school?"

"I don't know. I left a few messages for the school, but no one's gotten back to me. And I hate to keep bringing it up with him because he shuts down and accuses me of not trusting him."

"You don't trust him. With good reason."

"I know." She sighed. "I wish I was better with him. But, hey, at least he's lost a lot of that attitude he was getting up to with me. Now he's nice all the time, just quiet. When he's home, I mean." Something was off with the kid; she could feel it.

"Okay, enough of that."

"Of what?"

Cash grabbed her hand and gently tugged her toward the kitchen. "No more obsessing over responsibilities. Tonight, be with me and have fun. And apologize."

"Apologize?" She frowned at him.

"For not making *me* one of those apple things before bringing one to Naomi. Come on, Jordan. You're better than that."

She tried not to smile. "Am I though?"

"Sure. You're a genius with a stove, and you know I love your food. But the plain fact of the matter is you're not cooking for me nearly enough."

"Is that right?" She let him lead her into the kitchen, where Naomi and Reid stood watching them.

"Yep. Tell her, Reid."

"That she should cook for you and only you?" Reid leaned against the counter while Naomi finished with the salad. "That your appetite is exceeded only by your ego and fat head?"

"Yeah, that."

Jordan shook her head, more than amused. "I already knew all that."

"Yeah? Well, did you know we once had a pie-eating contest in the Corps, and Cash lost to me?" Reid puffed up. "That's right, Naomi. Your man stuffed more blueberry pie down his—"

"Pie hole," Cash interrupted.

Jordan snickered. "That fits."

"Whatever. I ate more than Cash did." Reid smirked as only a younger brother can.

Jordan felt a pang, missing Rafi, but she refused to feel bad for being out with Cash tonight.

"Oh yeah, Reid. You won all right." Cash smirked right back at him. "He threw up his glorious victory an hour later. Now he can't even look at a blueberry without getting ill. Wuss."

"Oh, er…" Jordan paused for effect. "There are blueberries in the strudel along with the apple."

The horrified look on Reid's face was worth the lie. She laughed her confession, and the others, even Reid, joined her.

"Now I see why you two fit," Reid muttered. "So annoying."

⌁⌁⌁

A half hour after dinner, Jordan felt pleasantly stuffed. Naomi pulled out a board game.

Reid hugged her and set out the board. "Okay, sweetness. It's us against them."

"Trivial what? What the hell kind of game is this?" Cash demanded to know. "I have to think while digesting all that burger?"

"Don't forget the salad." Jordan patted her belly, sated and happy, enjoying the heck out of a double date that felt more like good friends having a great time.

"I hate thinking."

Reid grinned. "Oh, it's on."

The game ended in a draw because Cash answered all of the sports questions correctly. Jordan nailed anything having to do with literature or grammar, and although Naomi and Reid made a great team, they spent too much time laughing at Cash's antics to treat the game seriously.

"Chumps," Cash said under his breath. "So lame."

"I know. Why play if you don't want to win?"

"Exactly."

Unable to leave it at Cash and Jordan winning, Naomi brought out cards for spades while they dug into the strudel. A big mistake considering she had two Marines and a soldier who had spent plenty of deployments with nothing better to do than play cards.

This time Naomi and Jordan teamed up, leaving the brothers to whisper their plans.

"And no table talk," Naomi warned them. She turned to Jordan and in a low voice said, "Use what you got for distractions. I lower my blouse when Reid is up. You wiggle or something when Cash plays."

"Isn't that cheating?" Jordan found herself really liking Naomi. The woman's sharp wit, kindness, and surprising competitive streak were right up Jordan's alley.

"Cheating? Not at all. That's called creative winning. I mean, if they can't focus past breasts or some ass flash, that's on them."

Jordan coughed. "Ass flash?"

"I drop a card and bend over. Reid's ridiculously easy."

When Jordan tried it on Cash, she found him also ridiculously easy. And had the best time ever playing against her lover and his brother.

By the expression on his face, he enjoyed himself as well.

Although his "put up or shut up" should have warned her he'd expect some form of recompense for trouncing them. Too bad for him she had to get home for Rafi.

Or rather, too bad for her. The best ending for this perfect night would be some mind-bending sex with her boyfriend followed by falling asleep in his arms and staying there for good.

Because, damn it, she'd fallen for the big lug and had no idea what to do about it.

Chapter 16

CASH HAD BEEN AMUSED, ENTERTAINED, AND EVEN MORE CONvinced Jordan was the woman he'd been waiting for.

Watching her laugh, seeing her enjoyment in being with his brother and Naomi, and having fun being around her set his fears to rest. Unlike Mariah, Jordan hadn't tried to be the best or brightest in the room. She hadn't vied for his attention, and she'd been pleasant and polite to Naomi, even helping to clean up, though she hadn't had to.

"Good job in there," he said as they left and drove home—well, back to her place.

The hour hadn't yet reached ten since they'd arrived at Naomi's early, but he understood her wanting to be there for her brother.

"Thanks. Glad to know I passed." She shot him a dry look, as if she hadn't cared what the others thought.

The little liar. She'd been so tense, concerned they might not like her. *As if.* She'd been a delight, and Cash never used that word. Ever. He didn't like many people, but Jordan he couldn't do without. She'd charmed Reid without trying, just by being herself. Same with Naomi.

Watching the women together, it would be wrong to say Naomi's natural beauty outshone Jordan's. Because Jordan had a subtle elegance she'd be the first to deny. But it was there regardless. Athletic, feminine, and unique. She didn't have classically beautiful features. Full lips too sensual for traditional beauty. Dark-brown eyes that turned lighter or darker depending upon her mood. And skin a shade between tan and bronze, not creamy white but a rich beige. She had strength of character, an inner toughness guarding a marshmallow of a heart. So, yeah, he saw so much more than the physical with Jordan. But her "physical" stole his breath too. He loved her toned body, her firm, no-more-than-a-handful breasts, that tight ass he could grip just right while sliding inside her.

Most of all he loved her neck, because she fit right where he needed her to when they made love. And he could access it while trailing kisses from her breasts to her ripe lips.

Yep. There went his hard-on, always just a thought away when he was with Jordan.

They turned on the main road toward her apartment, and she put a hand on his arm.

"Slow down, but don't stop."

He followed her orders. "What's wrong?"

"See that boy there?" A lanky teenager stood beside a black SUV with some friends, laughing and smoking as if they had no place to go. The SUV sat outside a nice house and looked like it belonged there. Nothing suspicious about the teenagers hanging out that Cash could see.

Jordan said, "That's Juan, one of Rafi's bad news friends. I'm just glad Rafi's steering clear of him lately."

Except the kid wasn't. Across the street, away from where Jordan was looking, Cash saw Rafi stop, frozen, staring at them in the car. Then he hurried away, hiding behind some bushes. Now, if the kid hadn't been doing anything wrong, why hide? Yep. Busted.

Cash didn't say anything to Jordan, not wanting to ruin her good mood. But he promised himself a talk with the boy later.

He pulled up to her complex and parked then walked her to her door.

"I'm safe enough," she said.

"Humor me."

She rolled her eyes—she did that a lot around him—and they entered.

"So you can see, I'm good."

"I bother you, don't I?"

"What? I—no." She frowned and took off her shoes. He did the same.

"What are you doing? You're not staying."

He ignored her and looked around for Rafi, for her, because he'd already seen the kid. That took all of one minute because the apartment didn't have space. "Nope. He's not here yet."

"He should be home soon though."

"You sound nervous." That excited him. He noticed her keeping an eye on him, saw her continually glance at his crotch, at his chest, his face.

Her nipples were hard points beneath her shirt, and he wanted to make her eyes go dark with passion, to see her lips slick from his kisses.

"I'm not nervous." She gave a nervous laugh. "Now get out."

Her bluntness charmed him. "Make me." He backed her against her front door. "Go ahead. I dare you."

She licked her lips. "Rafi could be home at any minute."

"Guess we'll have to make this fast then." Before she could protest, he kissed her. Hard.

She moaned into his mouth and snaked a hand down his belly.

No surprise she found him thick and aching. She unbuttoned and unzipped him then pushed his pants down. He shoved her pants and panties down as well, then turned her around and pulled her hips back.

"I'm coming in" was all the warning he gave.

Cash shoved inside her, gliding through her cream, and fucked her in earnest. So wet, she made a delicious friction, and he saw her hand move to her front. "Yeah, touch yourself," he whispered, hoping they'd get to finish before her brother returned.

The naughty, rushed aspect of their coupling added to the excitement. As did fucking her without a rubber. "Gonna come in you again, Jordan. Deep in you," he rasped as he took her harder, faster.

"Not before I come first. God, Cash, you feel huge." She moaned, a soft, breathy little sound that turned his world inside out. Then she seized around him, and he couldn't stop himself.

Cash took her like a man possessed and climaxed between one breath and the next. He saw stars, cresting his orgasm and praying for it to never end. Being with Jordan was like having a religious experience. The woman owned him, plain and simple. If he could have, he'd have taken her into her bedroom and fucked her until neither of them could walk then hugged her to him and never let go.

Instead, he waited until he'd started to soften then tucked himself back into his underwear and straightened his clothes. He hurried to get her a paper towel from the kitchen to clean her up.

"Thanks a lot," she grumbled. "You've ruined yet another pair of panties."

"Yeah?" He smiled, feeling damn good about that.

She sighed. "Don't get me wrong. I like you inside me, but condoms made it less messy."

And less fun, he thought but didn't say. "Man, you get to me. I swear, around you it's like my cock is always ready to burst."

"That's an image." She tossed the paper towel in the trash and fixed her clothing. Then she kissed him and opened the door. "Wham bam. Thanks and get out."

He chuckled and put on his shoes. "Glad to be of service, ma'am."

"Shut up." She yanked him back for another kiss then pushed him away. "Stop distracting me. I have a younger brother to berate for not texting me that he wouldn't be home."

"See you at work?" He and Reid had a bit more packing to do at their mother's the next day.

"Yep. At work, where you will not rip Smith's lips off when he tries to rile you. And where you'll ignore anyone flirting with or teasing me. Like *you promised*." A good point. They hadn't yet been together at work while a couple. The past few days he'd been home due to his head.

"I'd say scout's honor, but I was never a scout." He nodded. "It won't be weird. Just…don't ignore me and act like I don't exist, okay?" He'd spent a childhood with a woman who'd treated him that way, had almost married another who'd acted no better. It would kill him for Jordan to treat him like he didn't matter, even in pretend.

"I won't. And don't ignore *me* the next time I warn you some loose chick wants in your pants."

He blanked then blushed recalling the incident from a few weeks ago. "Come on. That woman was old enough to have been my mother. And it wasn't my fault. I was trying to catch her falling from a ladder."

"That fall conveniently happened right when you passed by. Her hand landed in your lap."

He grimaced. "The guys razzed me about it for days. You weren't much better." He couldn't help laughing because that woman's move had actually worked. "But, really, can you blame her? I'm me."

"The 'I'm me' excuse is pathetic. Although if you're saying it's okay for you to mess around, that means it's okay for me to mess around, right? You know, just in fun." She gave him an overdone wink. "Maybe I shouldn't be so quick to ignore the guys asking me out."

"I was kidding, and you know it." The thought of Jordan with anyone else enraged him. More, it hurt. "That lady really was an accident. I swear."

She grinned. "I know. I just like giving you shit."

"Jackass." He laughed when she blew him a kiss and flipped him off, then slammed the door in his face.

Sunday went well with Reid. Cash finally had his mother's house cleared of everything but the furniture he still debated keeping. The donations truck had picked up the many items he'd left outside. Reid had taken a few more boxes back to their house for a later inspection. Now Cash had to figure out what to do with the place. Emptied of almost everything, it didn't feel like the hell he'd grown up in. Could he live here?

Should he keep it? Sell it? Maybe even rent it? Jordan

was no help with ideas, deferring to him on everything. Annoying, but she had a point. The house was his burden to handle.

The week passed swiftly. By Thursday, Cash had done his best to treat Jordan like everyone else at work. It helped that Reid had made two formal statements explaining Vets on the Go!'s new hierarchy because Cash still had a problem being Jordan's "boss" *and* lover. But now, with Evan heading up a new human resources department and Cash having nothing to do with personnel management anymore, work wouldn't stand in the way of their relationship.

The others didn't seem to care either way and teased him about being "the common man." Then Jordan had reiterated that by calling him an asshole and daring him to fire her.

Which of course he hadn't. Finley and Funny Rob had taunted him and didn't stop until he put Finley in a headlock, threatening to drag all their sorry asses to HR for the constant harassment. All in all, it had been a decent week, and he'd managed to mostly ignore Smith and his many sneers.

Now known as the company's PR liaison when not working regular moves, Cash had a fancy title and no idea what they meant him to do with it. Wasn't PR what they paid Naomi, owner of Starr PR, to do?

Despite her and Reid being a thing, Naomi had first come to them as a public relations expert. She still worked for them, and they paid her. Reid and Naomi did well separating business from pleasure.

If they did it, so could Cash and Jordan.

He thought about her all the time, and he knew her

brother's distance and odd mood continued to bother her. He decided it was past time to have a talk with Rafi. So after work Thursday, he cleaned up then drove over to Jordan's. He planned to offer to take Rafi to dinner for some guy-to-guy bonding, knowing Jordan wouldn't mind. For some reason she considered him a kind of mentor for the kid, and he had no desire to disabuse her of the notion. Plus he wanted to help the boy.

He had a feeling she had no idea Rafi and that Juan kid were hanging out.

He parked and headed to her apartment. But as he walked down the outer hallway, he slowed, hearing an unfamiliar male through her front door.

"I'm sorry," the man said, not sounding sorry at all. Cash recognized smug when he heard it. "But if you don't have the money, you'll have to leave."

"But Mrs. Alvarez was fine with what I was paying before," Jordan said. "I have a contract to prove it."

The smug jerk continued, "The contract is only valid if Mrs. Alvarez owns the property. She's dead, and it's mine now. Like I told you, I'm her son. I inherited the building." A pause. "But I'm sure we could come to some kind of agreement."

That suggestive tone told him all he needed to hear. Cash saw red.

Behind him, he heard footsteps and turned.

Rafi barreled toward him, a frown on his face. "What—?"

Cash shushed him then motioned to the door. His first inclination had been to bust in and kick the new landlord's ass. But he figured it was Jordan's play, so he'd wait it out.

Rafi still frowned but crept closer, keeping quiet, and listened.

"Are you kidding me?" Jordan barked an angry laugh. "Let me get this straight. If I sleep with you, you'll let me keep my apartment?"

Oh man. Cash couldn't wait to see what she did to the guy.

"To keep it at the rate you have now. It's not free." The man chuckled. "Although if you're as good with that mouth as you look, we could negotiate the price. Why don't we find out?"

Rafi looked to intervene, and Cash held him back. He took the key Rafi had in hand and quietly put it in the lock then turned the deadbolt.

"*Motherfucker*." Jordan's rage sounded fierce.

Cash pushed the door open and held Rafi back when the boy made to rush inside.

They watched as Jordan not only disabled the fool, she nailed him in the stomach with a right cross he hadn't expected before manhandling him to the floor. In seconds, she had removed his belt, turned the guy belly down, and tied the belt around his wrists behind him. Her knee rammed into his back while the dickhead wheezed, still trying to catch his breath.

Jordan had yet to stop cursing.

Love rocked Cash from head to toe. Damn, but she could *move*. He beamed. "Just…wow."

She blinked up at him and slowly stood. "Cash?"

Rafi looked stunned.

"See, man? Your sister had it all under control." He lost his smile when he noticed how much larger the new super was.

"You'll regret this, you bitch," the guy threatened in between panting. "Get out. And get ready for the police to drag your ass to jail for assault."

Cash toed the guy in the ribs, not hard but enough to introduce himself. "Shut the fuck up, asshole." The guy glanced up at him and paled. Cash smiled down at him. "Hey, Jordan. Why don't you and Rafi grab some stuff and pack up your car? I'll watch your new landlord for you."

"Don't hurt him," she ordered. "I mean it."

"Nah. I know he's the type to sue first, ask questions later." He glared down at the dead man walking. "Don't worry. I know how to handle his type."

She gave Cash a suspicious look. "Come on, Rafi. Help me pack some clothes." They darted to her bedroom, leaving him alone with rapey Casanova.

Cash leaned down and released the belt. The landlord hurried to his feet and moved back from Cash then tried to run around him for the door.

Cash stepped in front of him, causing contact. The man bounced off him, but the brush was good enough for Cash. He clenched his hand into a fist. "Now you're assaulting *me*?"

"What? No."

Before the man could move, Cash slammed him against the wall so hard his teeth rattled. "Look, fuckhead, you did something to my girl I'm not happy about. So this is what you're going to do. You're going to wait until she packs up all her stuff and leaves. You're going to wait until I tell you she's done. Tomorrow, in a week, whatever she needs to get out of here. Understand?"

"What? No, this is my—"

Cash punched him in the gut, right where Jordan had socked him. He didn't use too much force, not wanting to cause major damage, just enough to get the dick's attention. And it had the loser gasping in pain.

"I *said* I'll tell you when you can have the unit back. She's out of her lease as of right now. And you're going to leave her the fuck alone or you'll deal with me." He leaned closer. "I don't give a shit about the law. In fact, I like dancing all over it. So you want to play, keep pushing."

"Wh-what can you do?"

Cash smiled. "You've got balls, I'll give you that. But guess what I have. An unregistered Beretta. Oh, and about a dozen ways to kill a man without leaving a mark. Us combat Marine types like to challenge ourselves. I bet I could make this look like a B&E. Wipe away all the prints and have the cops scratching their heads for leads. Or, hell, maybe we could make it look like you had a heart attack. I know a guy who has the drugs to make it happen. Then again, I could just beat you to death. More fun for me that way."

The asshole looked white enough to pass out, his eyes wide with fear. "No, no. We're good. It's okay. She's free to leave whenever."

"That's right. And I'm going to talk to every other tenant here. You try any sleazy shit with any of them, I'll be back. Just me and my Ka-Bar." He gave the guy his best mean smile.

The man looked about ready to piss himself and held up his hands in surrender. "No, no. I won't. It's all good. Everything's good, buddy."

"I ain't your friend, dickhead." He finished by

grabbing the guy's wallet and making a big production out of saying his name and address out loud. "Okay, Ricky Alvarez. You and me, we don't want to meet again, do we?" Then, because he didn't like the guy, he kneed him in the balls and watched him fall to the floor in tears. "Do we, Ricky?"

"No. God, no." Ricky, the shithead, was crying. Cash wouldn't have thought less of him for crying the pain away, but he had a feeling the tears came from fear. So pathetic and typical of a bully. Stand up to them, and they crumbled.

He glanced up and froze. Jordan and Rafi stared at him with wide eyes.

Shit. "What? He tripped into my knee."

Rafi swallowed audibly, took a wide step around Cash, and darted outside with his duffel bag.

Jordan groaned. "This is going to come back on me. Thanks a lot."

Cash squatted down and forced Alvarez to meet his gaze. "Is it, Ricky? Is this going to come back on my girlfriend?"

"N-no. Not at all." He blubbered and moaned, cupping his crotch. "S-sorry you have to leave. I'll pay your deposit back, no problem."

Jordan frowned. "But I didn't—"

"You do that," Cash interrupted. "Or I'll be back." Then he dragged the fucker outside into the hallway and left him there. "Lock up, Jordan."

"Don't tell me what to do," she snapped as she locked up, a full sea bag over her shoulder.

He didn't dare offer to take it from her, warned away by the glint in her eyes. He followed in silence as she stomped through the hall and down the stairwell. He only stopped when she did, next to her car.

Seeing her anger and pain poleaxed him all over again. "Damn, Jordan. I'm so sorry."

"Oh, you asshole." She smacked him in the chest.

"Uh, Jordan, I think we should go," Rafi said from the other side of the car. He gave Cash a tremulous look before hurriedly looking away. "Now would be good before that guy calls the cops."

"He won't be calling anyone." Cash ignored the need to go back and finish the son of a bitch. "Seriously, you guys are free."

"To go where?" Jordan shouted. "This is my home."

"It was your home." Cash ignored her protests and squirming and hugged her to him. "I'm so proud of you for taking him out. You are so awesome."

She relaxed at once. "What am I going to do?" she asked, her face muffled against his chest.

"You're going to follow me home. Reid spends all his time at Naomi's anyway, so I doubt he'll be there. Then you guys are going to settle in until you find a new place to live, okay?"

Rafi didn't speak, just stared at his sister for guidance.

She pulled back and looked up at Cash. "You saw me take him down, huh?"

"Like a calf at a rodeo. It was beautiful." He caressed her cheek.

She narrowed her gaze on him, full of threat and anger and affection. "Well, I can do the same to you. You've been warned."

Man, I love you. He cleared his throat. "Um, okay. So do you want to come back to my place now?"

"I guess."

He laughed. "It's not a gulag, you know. We actually have cable. And beer."

Rafi gave a tentative smile. "Beer would be good."

"Dream on," he and Jordan said at the same time.

Jordan finally gave Cash the smile he'd been waiting for. "Oh hell. Let's go. But I'm paying you rent."

He pulled her closer and whispered, "I'm sure we can work something out."

She shoved him away but couldn't hide her smile. "You wish."

"Always."

Chapter 17

Jordan lay on the couch while Rafi took over Reid's room. She'd refused to take Cash's bed, and as much as she wanted to, she couldn't sleep with him with her brother right next door.

What the hell am I going to do?

She'd been happy to be in the apartment complex while figuring out her future. Then Rafi had come, and it had become a godsend. The rent, for Seattle, was cheap. The location couldn't have been better, just minutes from work and from a bus stop Rafi used to get to school. And she hadn't had to put down a deposit.

Which reminded her, Cash had insisted Alvarez pay her back for something he didn't owe her. The guy was a dick, but she didn't want to be guilty of extortion.

She thought about what Cash had said and done to Alvarez. Had she not known him, she'd have been scared out of her mind. As it was, she'd taken Rafi aside earlier and explained Cash hadn't meant any of that, that he'd just been trying to scare the guy. She didn't know if Rafi believed her. Hell, she didn't know if she believed herself. Cash had been in the infantry in the Marine Corps. She knew that much. But she didn't know what all he had been into during his time served. From what she'd seen and knew of him, it wouldn't surprise her to learn he'd been in a special unit overseas doing classified things.

But she did know he'd never hurt her. No matter

how violent or crazy he might act, he'd never, ever been cruel or vicious toward her. And he'd been nothing but nice with Rafi…who now slept in Cash's brother's bed because they had no home.

Jesus, I'm homeless.

After waiting for the panic to lessen, she let herself accept the worry and let it go. Not having a home was temporary. She had savings and a job as well as the drive to succeed. Cash's place was fine short term, but it would take time to find an affordable apartment in the city, especially one with a location that fit both her and her brother.

She sighed. Just one more cog in the wheel of progress.

A door opened and closed, and then a body walked toward her. Expecting her brother to want to talk, she sat up in the dark, propped against the couch, and adjusted the lightweight blanket over her. "Rafi? Over here."

"It's me." Cash looked like a mountain of dark as he hovered by her. "I can't sleep. Want something hot to drink?"

"Sure." She followed him into the kitchen, dressed in ratty shorts and a top that looked decent enough. If only Cash would stop staring at her breasts. She couldn't see him, exactly, but she felt his stare like a physical caress. "Stop looking at my chest."

He chuckled. "Good guess." He flicked on a light, and they blinked. "You have pretty good night vision."

"Obviously you do too." She crossed her arms over her chest and refused to give in to her grin at his sigh of disappointment. "Thanks for helping us tonight."

He shrugged it off. "No problem."

"What were you doing there anyway?" She waited

while he put the water on and set two mugs and tea bags on the table. "And what's your thing with tea?"

"It's all we have. I drank the last of the cocoa months ago, and I can't do coffee at night. As for what I was doing at your place, I'd hoped to take Rafi to dinner. You know, for a man-to-man meal where we talked away from big sis. Thought maybe he'd open up without you there."

"Oh." She owed him again. "That was a nice gesture." "I thought so." He leaned against the counter, wearing a T-shirt and shorts and looked like a god doing nothing but breathing. "I'm just… When I heard you with that dickhead, I wanted to rip his head off. But I waited to see how you'd handle it."

"And?"

He glanced around before saying in a low voice, "I have never seen anything more beautiful in my life than you taking down that shithead. Well, except watching you come. Because that is just unforgettable."

Her cheeks felt hot, and her pleasure at his compliment made her even warmer. "I didn't scare you?" She'd intimidated a few exes with her moves, but she'd rationalized they hadn't been able to handle the real her, so it hadn't hurt when they'd split up.

"*Scare* me? I'm dying to spar with you at my gym. You want in?"

That was such a Cash response. "Sure."

"Awesome. I can't wait." He smiled.

Her belly fluttered, and that floating sensation, as if she'd been lost for so long and now found something real, centered her in the now.

"You okay?" He took a step forward. "I really am

sorry you had to handle with that guy. I would have come in to handle him, but I knew you could deal."

"How long were you outside the door?" She hadn't realized he'd been out there. She figured he would have busted down the door the moment he'd heard her in trouble. That he hadn't…

"Long enough," he growled. "That fucking asshole."

"But you let me handle it." So not the way Cash normally did business. He bashed heads in then tried to settle things down after.

He shrugged. "You were an MP. You know your shit."

She'd always wanted to be treated like an equal yet still like a woman. In the Army, her peers had treated her more like a platonic pal, so she'd made do being seen as one of the guys instead of as Jordan, a woman who happened to be military police. She'd known plenty of female soldiers who took advantage of those wanting to protect them. Or given the slim ratio of women to men, built a stud farm, taking their pick of all the hottest guys around.

Not Jordan. She wanted to be seen for her strengths. As a woman, yes, but one who could kick ass. Cash, by giving her the time to fight her own battle, had given her so much more than a chance at a victory. He'd given her trust both in herself and in him.

"What did I do now?" He groaned. "You look like you want to kick my ass."

He tensed when she rounded the counter toward him, and she would have laughed at the big tough Marine afraid of "Little Army." But she felt so much for him she couldn't speak.

So she hugged him tightly and planted a kiss right over his heart.

He let out a ragged breath and caged her, protectively, in his big arms. She couldn't be sure, but she thought she heard him whisper against her hair, "I am so gone for you." Then he kissed her, and they stood together, no words needed.

———

Rafi watched them, bemused to see his sister so... content at being held by a Neanderthal. Rafi didn't know that much about Cash, but there was no mistaking the goofy look on the guy's face. He'd never seen anyone move with such brutality when Cash had kicked Alvarez's ass. Well, except for watching his sister nail the prick.

He couldn't believe Jordan had been so exact, so lethal when taking a bigger man down. She hadn't been cruel, just firm. But Cash... He'd been ruthless. Those hands like weapons as he'd punched Alvarez before nailing the guy in the nads.

So totally cool. And terrifying.

And now the guy cuddled his tough sister in his arms as if she meant the world to him.

Would he have made a move if he hadn't looked up and seen Rafi standing there?

"Tea?" Cash asked.

Rafi shook his head and tiptoed back out of the room, overhearing his sister say, "Yeah, let's have that tea now."

He went back to bed, wondering what to do. How much had Cash seen earlier when his car had slowed near Juan's crew? How much did he know? And would he end up using those fists against Rafi when he realized just what Rafi had done?

———

The next morning, Rafi hustled off "to school." He'd had his hacker buddy circumvent the emails and change Rafi's emergency point of contact to intercept a few phone calls—Daniel was an evil teen genius—so his sister still had no idea he'd been kicked out. Unfortunately, leaving with Juan last week had been a disaster. He'd almost rather be back with Dickhead Simpson than be messing around with the stuff Juan was into.

Though Juan wasn't all that important in the scheme of things, he knew bad people, the kind who had ties to the West Side Wolves. WSW was a bad news gang. And Juan worked for them, or, more specifically, he worked for Paul Lasko, a bully with an addiction to heroin and his switchblade, and who'd gotten kicked out of school last year. Everyone at school had heard about the guy.

Unfortunately, Lasko had ties to WSW and a cache of drugs. The police had supposedly raided the gang a few times. It had been on the news, but the court dates were taking a while, and Toto, their leader, was out on bail. Unconcerned, according to Juan, because Toto "knew people."

Rafi about lost his mind when he'd seen the baggie of drugs Juan flashed around, crap Juan was selling at school. Crap he wanted Rafi to start moving for him.

This was so beyond Rafi's comfort level it wasn't funny. Bad stuff like this happened on television to idiots who didn't know better. Rafi did, and he'd never done drugs. Sure, he'd had a beer now and then, had cut school, even dumped that cherry bomb down a school toilet, but that was the extent of his illegal extracurricular activities.

Until he'd made the mistake of joining Juan for a ride. He'd seen things he couldn't unsee. And now Lasko knew his name because stupid Juan had called and told him.

Rafi wiped tears from his eyes, helpless and hopeless.

All Rafi had wanted was to get through tenth grade and move back home. He couldn't keep leeching off his sister, and now that his high school career had ended, that East Coast military academy would be his future unless he could make a better one. But selling drugs?

He huddled in an alley on the other side of town, careful to keep his hoodie up and his face down. He had to make some big decisions. If he didn't start selling the stash Juan had given him, Rafi would get in trouble with Juan's posse. Or worse—as Juan had threatened—with Lasko and his switchblade.

It wasn't as if Rafi hadn't tried to leave. When he'd first seen that baggie and heard Juan's proposal, he'd been set to bolt. But the guys had all been around, and Juan had called him a pussy. Rafi hadn't wanted to seem weak. So he'd gone to a WSW club, hung out and drank and laughed with the guys. And when Juan had put that baggie of pills in his hand in front of the others, Rafi'd had to say yes or face down half a dozen kids who thought themselves part of WSW. In reality, they were a bunch of rich banger-wannabes trying to act big and bad. But Lasko was the real deal, and Juan knew him.

Juan also knew where Rafi lived and what Jordan looked like. Rafi wanted so badly to tell, but a rat wouldn't be worth shit at school or on the street, and neither would the rat's sister.

He wiped his nose on his sleeve, feeling small and

frightened and…lost. At least he and Jordan no longer lived in the apartment complex. Maybe Juan wouldn't be able to find them. Especially if Rafi kept out of sight. And Cash would protect Jordan if the gang got wind of them.

Maybe. Except Jordan had been seen on TV with that Vets on the Go! job. Everyone knew where that crew was headquartered.

He slid to the ground, hugged his knees, and spent the next hours killing time, waiting until he could go home and pretend everything was okay. For a little bit, at least. He'd take what he could get until he worked up the stones to run away. Then, and only then, he might be able to turn this mess around.

Jordan hadn't wanted to leave Rafi alone, but Cash had stayed behind at his place because he said he was too tired to hang out with the guys after a long week at work. Personally, she thought he just wanted to keep an eye on her brother for her so she could go out. And Lord, she needed it. Friday night at Ringo's was just what the doctor ordered.

Around her, the Vets on the Go! crew laughed and teased. The bar started to get crowded. In the corner, a group of older men swore as they pointed and yelled at a baseball game on TV.

Jordan glanced at her friends, aware no one paid her too much attention. A good thing or a bad thing?

She and Cash had worked well together all day, no strangeness after crashing on Cash's couch last night. They'd driven in separately to work. No one had teased her about Cash or made any suggestive comments, so she didn't think the guys knew about her and Cash being an item. Staying the night with him—sadly in separate rooms—had given her a great night's sleep. She didn't know what Rafi thought about their temporary quarters. He'd been quiet before he'd darted off to school in the morning. But he'd been polite to her and Cash, so who knew?

She stared at the scarred table, lost in thought.

"You look like you're gonna cry, Jordan." Lafayette pushed a beer her way. "Upset because your best girlfriends Hector and Cash aren't here to lean on?"

She snorted. "I'm upset because Simon isn't here. I could do with a little eye candy." She gave him a disdainful once-over that had the others laughing.

Funny Rob, Stan, Finley, and Lafayette had shown up tonight, along with the surprise additions of Evan and Reid. Evan planned to start dropping by work the following week, and he wanted to get to know the group better, so, according to Reid, he'd forced Reid to bring him by.

"You want eye candy?" Finley batted his eyelashes. "I'm right here, Jordan."

She grinned. Truth to tell, the guys were all good-looking in their own way. Finley was prettier than the rest, though Evan and Reid had that sophisticated-sexy thing going on. Lafayette was no joke with that build and that smile. Lucky, lucky Simon. Rob and Stan were about even, both cute ex–Air Force nerds who made her laugh.

But Cash…he by far outshone everyone. And her hottie had stayed home to look after her brother because he knew she worried. As pretty on the inside as he was on the outside. She had a feeling he'd die of embarrassment if she ever told him that, which made her smile. "Anyway," she said, pointedly ignoring Finley, which made him laugh, "I thought this week went pretty well."

Reid nodded. "It did. You guys are killing it. We have no shortage of jobs, and Evan's run our numbers to show—"

"A numbers guy. Nice." Funny Rob waggled his brows. "Do you like to cook too? As in, the books?"

Evan sighed. "This is like a bad—really bad—gangster movie. I'm an accountant. I do the books *legally* for the company."

"Oh. Not so exciting then." Rob looked disappointed.

"Nope. But where I come from, boring is good. That means stability, from which you generate income to start new growth. From growth can stem upward mobility or too little cash flow because you grew too soon, and debts pile up. But we're not there yet. So right now, boring is good." He grinned.

Handsome, lighthearted, and happy when not complaining about being overworked by a she-demon or nearly falling asleep for being too tired, Evan would have been perfect for the Leannes and Naomis of the world. He was a nice version of Troy.

And totally not her type.

However, he *was* the new guy on the team. She should properly welcome him to Vets on the Go! "It's nice to have you with us, Evan." She gave him a wide smile. Lafayette frowned, no doubt knowing her too well. Because that smile said shit was about to start. She ignored him and projected an air of innocent acceptance. "Say, Evan. Have you met everyone?"

"I think so. I met Heidi before she left for training. Tim and Martin checked in on their way to a new job a few days ago. Tim doesn't say much, does he?"

The quiet pair worked well together and didn't mingle with others, but Jordan liked them. Martin, small and scrappy, filled the silences Big Tim left in his wake. The guy was as tall as Cash but not as forceful a personality.

"He's pretty quiet," she agreed. "I was wondering… Have you met Miriam yet?"

The guys went still and zeroed in on her.

"No, why? Is she new?"

When Reid would have answered, Jordan cut him off. "No. She works down the hall from Vets on the Go! at that clothing shop. I was just thinking, since you're our human resources guy and much more easygoing than half the people around here, you should talk to her. I don't think she likes us."

Funny Rob was the first to jump in, playing it cool. "Yeah. She always gives me dirty looks. I don't think she likes Asians."

"I don't think she likes you giving her that *look*," Stan corrected. "You know, the one that says you wonder what she looks like naked?"

Evan groaned. "It's like I'm dealing with Cash but in bigger numbers."

No one said anything. So far so good.

"Miriam's annoyed with us, is that what you're saying?" He turned to Reid. "Have you talked to her? I'd think you'd want to play nice with the other businesses in the building."

Behind Evan's back, Jordan motioned for Reid to play along. He coughed to hide the smile she saw peeking through. "Uh, I, yeah. I've talked to her a few times. She's a nice woman, but you know how Cash is. And, Rob, didn't I talk to you about that?"

Rob shrugged. "Finley did it first."

"And that makes it all right," Jordan said in a huff. "Evan, look, you're not like the guys. You're good-looking."

"Hey!"

"I'm hot!"

"Sophisticated," she continued, "and you know how to talk to people. I think if you charmed Miriam, she'd stop threatening to file a complaint with the landlord."

Evan swiveled to glare at Reid. "You never told me you had problems with the other tenants. This is why you wanted me to fill the HR role, isn't it? Not just for our people but to deal with the other businesses in the building. Because you hate PR, don't you?"

"Of course not."

"Isn't it *your* job to smooth things over, Reid? You should handle this."

"Ah, yeah, it is. Jordan, why didn't you tell me about this before?"

She sighed. "I did, Reid. Remember two days ago? I mentioned it, but you were on hold on the phone or something." *Sooo many lies.*

"Oh, right. Now I remember." He clapped Evan on the back, an invisible "kick me" sign the rest of them could see.

She and the others did their best to hide their grins.

"Look, man, we're so busy lately some things got pushed aside. Can you talk to her for me? Like Jordan said, you're good with people. I bet Miriam will take to you, and maybe you can convince her we're not that bad. I'll talk to Cash about leaving her alone. And that goes for the rest of you."

"Got it, boss." Lafayette saluted.

"That salute sucked." Reid rolled his eyes. "It's so hard working with non-Marines, Evan. But you eventually get used to it."

That started the trash talk about Navy squids, Army pukes, Air Force dweebs, and knuckle-dragging Marines. Jordan was laughing and having a blast. The beer flowed. Nachos and wings joined the table. The guys told hilarious war stories and even wittier moving stories, culminating in Funny Rob's encounter with a crazy man who wanted him to move a houseful of mannequins he'd swear were alive.

"I'm not kidding. I think one of them waved at me. Ask Finley."

"I wouldn't be surprised." Finley shuddered. "I was too busy trying to figure out what to do with all the dummy body parts. And a few of those supposed mannequins looked like sex dolls. Seriously, that dude was weird."

"Totally weird," Rob agreed.

"Speaking of weird," Lafayette muttered as Smith ambled to the table. "Well, well, Smith. Who thought you'd join the fun?"

Jordan didn't know why Smith acted so hot and cold with the team. She'd worked with him more often than the others, and Smith pulled more than his fair share. He'd teased her a few times, but he'd never been anything but professional or quiet when working. She liked being around him, though she'd never admit that to Cash. Oddly enough—or maybe not so oddly, since

Smith and Cash looked enough alike to be brothers—
she felt safe with Smith.

"Hey, Smith. Pull up a chair." She kicked out the one
next to her, and he sat down with his beer.

"Smith." Reid nodded at him.

Smith nodded back and raised a brow at Evan.
"Slumming?"

Evan shot him a bright grin. "I am now."

The guys guffawed. Even Smith cracked a smile at
that. Then he gave another subtle glance. "You guys are
missing some familiar faces. Where are the twins?"

"Right here. I'm not that dark I blend into the walls,
am I?" Lafayette asked with a raised brow. "Although
Simon says I'm gorgeous, so smooth and dark like
chocolate, he wants nothing more than to lick me up."

Funny Rob choked on his beer.

Jordan grinned. "You know, Simon has a point.
You're beautiful, and you know it."

"I do." No small amount of bashfulness on that killer
grin.

"I *meant* Hector and Cash," Smith said in his trade-
mark sardonic voice. "Half the time I expect to see
one of them buried up the other's ass. And, hey, why
aren't they here kissing *your* ass, Jordan? Trouble
in paradise?"

It bothered her that Smith had the same green eyes
as Cash. Same color, same shape. And he had the same
bad attitude, unfortunately. "You know, it was a real
party before you arrived. What's wrong? Did girlfriend
number four hundred and twelve dump your ass?" A
glance around the table showed the mood was considerably cooler.

Reid shook his head. "Do you ever just relax and let go, Smith? I mean, it's Friday. Chill, man."

"Hard to do that with that stick up his ass," Finley muttered.

Stan and Rob choked on laughter.

"Say that a little louder, squid."

Jordan rolled her eyes. "We went over our insults like twenty minutes ago. Squid isn't even that original. Where were you then?"

Smith didn't seem to want to let go of his bad mood. "So you and Cash aren't fuck buddies anymore? I mean, I get it. Who would want to be with a guy that stupid? I doubt he knows what to do in bed. With a woman, I mean."

Lafayette leaned forward. "You got a problem with gays, Smith?"

"Nah. But a guy like Cash would freak the fuck out if you even mentioned he might be gay. And that's who you're sticking up for? A homophobic prick with nothing more than swagger going for him."

"Smith, I think you need to leave." Reid started to say more, but Jordan beat him to it.

"What exactly is your problem with Cash?" she wanted to know. "He's a hell of a great guy. He helps everyone. He's nice, deep down."

"Way deep down," Finley said.

"Shut it, Finley. And he always has your back. Even yours, taking crappy shifts so you could have that time off you needed. And you treat him like dirt. Cash is a stand-up guy."

"And he's hot, don't forget that," Lafayette added with a wink, taking the tension from the group.

Funny Rob cracked up. "Totally hot."

Smith studied her, then smirked. "I knew you were sleeping with him." He sat back and crossed his arms over that broad chest, looking smug. "What's wrong? Too embarrassed to admit it?"

She felt herself blushing and couldn't look at Reid, who knew. Oh hell. Why not admit it? It's not like she was doing anything wrong.

"So what if I am?" Lots of rumbling from the table, and money changed hands. "What are you guys doing?"

"Sorry," Lafayette apologized. "I thought it would be sooner."

"Told you." Finley waved at Stan. "Pay up."

"Shit." Stan forked over a few bills.

Smith frowned. "How can you stand him? He's a prick."

"And you're not?" she shot back.

"Hey, I'll give you a better ride than he will. Wanna go?" He reached to take her by the hand, and she'd had enough. In one motion, Jordan stood and grabbed him. Twisting his wrist, she had him out of the chair and down on one knee, his arm locked at his wrist. "You done insulting me and Cash yet? Or are you still craving more negative attention?"

Around them, the bar quieted.

To her consternation, Smith started laughing. "You win, Little Army."

"Oh, fuck you." She tossed his hand away and straightened to a standing ovation from the table. "And fuck you too." But she couldn't help grinning at them. "You morons."

Smith didn't apologize for insulting Cash, but he did settle down. He didn't say much for the rest of the night, but no one asked him to leave. Reid studied him often, an odd expression on his face. He murmured something to Evan, who looked over at Smith, his eyes narrowed.

Then the pair stood. "More work to do early tomorrow. See you guys later. Oh, and the tab's on us." Reid smiled then flipped Smith off, shocking everyone. Reid rarely used bad language or did anything crude. "Don't be an ass if you can help it, Smith."

Smith tipped a beer his way. "But I can't help it." He paused, his gaze on Reid. "It's in the genes."

They stared at each other in silence before Finley whistled and whispered, "Draw your weapons on the count of ten…"

Smith snorted. "Asshole."

The whole party broke up soon after. As Jordan turned to get in her car, Smith stopped her.

"What do you want now?"

He shoved his hands in his pockets and stared at her with a hooded gaze. "Sorry if I was out of line."

"*If?*"

"Fuck. I'm sorry, okay?" he snarled and stomped away.

She answered to the wind, "Apology accepted."

Chapter 18

WHILE JORDAN TOOK A MUCH-NEEDED BREAK AT RINGO'S Bar with the guys, Cash stayed home, ready to have his talk with the kid.

He didn't need to know Rafi to realize something bothered Jordan's brother. If Cash so much as breathed too loud, the kid twitched. At first he'd wondered if Rafi was scared of him from that incident with the landlord the other night. But whenever Cash neared Reid's room, where Rafi was sleeping, the boy fidgeted something fierce.

Time to quit all the secrets.

"Rafi, it's over. I know what this is about."

Rafi's eyes grew huge. "Y-you do?"

I have no idea. Cash narrowed his gaze and recalled a few interrogation techniques he'd witnessed years ago. It was all about head games.

Silence could be a supremely effective tool.

Several seconds passed.

Rafi turned from worried to irritated. "You don't know shit because there's nothing to know."

Cash remained quiet.

Rafi squirmed. "Quit looking at me like that."

"Like what?"

"Like you're going to do to me what you did to Alvarez," Rafi said, not with fear but with a hint of challenge.

Rafi reminded Cash a lot of Jordan. He smiled at the thought. Rafi cringed.

Fine. Time for some honest talk. "Rafi, why have you been pissing your pants since the minute your sister left?"

"Um, because I watched you beat up some guy twice my size?"

"Nope. You've been on edge since before the thing with the landlord. Look, your sister isn't here now. It's just you and me. What's going on?"

"Nothing."

Stubborn son of a bitch. "You know, I was once like you."

Rafi snorted. "I doubt it."

"I was skinny and mouthed off all the time. But I wasn't that smart, and I didn't have people to help me out. Hell, I was living on my own at sixteen. Barely graduated high school. Nobody but the Marines would have me. Got into more fights than I can remember and still do."

"Great. You're big and bad, and my sister likes you. You're awesome. Now can you leave me alone?" Rafi stood, to leave the house or go back into his room, Cash didn't know.

He did know he'd gone through Reid's room earlier today, and he'd noticed the kid tried to hide a backpack way back in Reid's closet. Though Cash had wanted to look inside, he hadn't because he didn't want to violate the kid's trust.

But maybe Cash could bluff his way past Rafi's defenses. Before the teenager could walk away, he asked, "Is it about what's in the bag?"

Bingo. Rafi froze and turned to face him, horrified. He whispered, "Did you look inside?"

Cash gave him a mean look. "What the hell do you think? Better yet, don't tell me. Let's wait for Jordan to get back and see what she thinks."

The kid crumpled. He sank down into the couch and burst into tears. Heavy, heartfelt sobbing that tore Cash right up.

"Aw man. Don't freak out." Should he join Rafi on the couch? Give him a hug? A manly pat on the shoulder? Or would that stress him out even more? Instead, Cash remained seated in his chair and watched Rafi wipe his face.

Cash left to grab a box of tissues from the bathroom then tossed it to him. "Here."

After Rafi blew his nose a few times, he settled into uneven sobs. "You can't tell Jordan. Promise."

"I don't lie to your sister. She deserves better than that."

"Yeah." Rafi cried harder. "I just…I don't know how it happened."

"Start at the beginning."

"I should just go, and this would all be over."

"Look. I'm not letting you leave. I'm willing to keep this between us…*if* you give me a good enough reason to." Cash wasn't sure what he was dealing with, but it couldn't be good if Rafi fell apart over it.

The hope on the kid's face made Cash feel terrible for maybe lying. "I-I got kicked out of school." Rafi waited for Cash to react.

Cash showed no expression. "Go on."

"And I was hanging around th-this guy. Juan. He was in my class."

"This the guy your sister doesn't like?"

"Yeah." Rafi sighed, blew his nose again, and continued. "He's nice. Or at least, he was. But he's into some bad stuff. I didn't know. And then it was too late. I had to say I'd do it, or he'd hurt me and Jordan. He knows where I live."

"He knows you're here?"

"No. I meant at the apartment." Rafi looked like a little kid all tucked in on himself. He rocked as he spoke, and Cash felt bad for him. Fifteen years old and having to deal with his sister's and his safety, with no one to confide in who might understand. Jordan, for all her love for Rafi, had been a cop. She lived in black and white. "Juan sells drugs at school."

Hell. "What kind of drugs? For who?"

"I don't know. The pills in my bag, some weed, sometimes heroin, I think. I saw rocks in his stash. And he's selling them for WSW."

"Shit."

"I thought he was talking smack. I mean, he likes to brag a lot. I don't care. I'm not into drugs or anything." Rafi wiped his cheeks. "I don't want to sell drugs."

"No, you don't." A hell of a mess. "So you couldn't tell Jordan about getting kicked out of school, and you couldn't tell her about selling drugs."

"Yeah."

"Right. But back up. What happened at school that you got kicked out?"

Rafi looked down and seemed to grow smaller, were that possible. "I'm not smart. At all. I mean, yeah, I can do writing and stuff. I like to draw. And I like to read, but don't tell anyone. Reading is for nerds."

"Yeah." Cash chuckled. "I'm kidding."

Rafi relaxed a little. "I can't do math. At all. It's confusing all the time. And I hate being so dumb. I really tried. But this year my friends didn't help. The tutor my parents paid for was a pervy old guy. I didn't like him."

Pervy? Angered at the idea of some teacher getting gropey with his students, Cash growled, "He mess with you?"

"Nah, but I didn't like the way he looked at me sometimes." Rafi paused. "Like he knew I was stupid and hated me."

Cash knew all about feeling stupid. "Summer school didn't work either."

"No. Simpson is a dick. He was always making fun of the kids, me especially." Rafi explained the Homer joke, and Cash couldn't help laughing.

"Okay, that's funny."

"I thought so." Rafi's smile faded. "But last week, he was all over me. Like, on me in front of *everyone*. He told me I was a loser and stupid and should drop out. Like, that even the middle school kids were smarter than me."

"Wait. A teacher told you that? In front of the class?"

"I wouldn't be surprised if someone recorded it and posted it all over the place. It was really embarrassing."

"What an asshole." Teachers should never berate a kid for trying. "You weren't screwing off or anything? Didn't provoke the guy? Not that that makes it right, what he said. I'm just trying to get the picture here."

"No, I was actually trying to learn. I think he must have been having a bad day or something. But after he went off, I said something about him not giving it to Marge enough. You know, Marge, Homer?"

Cash covered his grin. "I get it."

"Then he kicked me out, and I took off. Juan was outside in the stairway, and he hates Simpson. So when I told him what happened, he offered me a ride." Rafi paused. "We, uh, went to a bar to hang out. It was cool."

"And illegal, which makes it that much cooler."

Rafi flushed. "Yeah. I had a beer, was talking trash with the guys. He's got five or six friends he hangs with. Some go to our school, some go to a school near us. All are seniors, I think. Anyway, he just whips out this bag of *heroin* and hands it to his friend to sell. They're all watching me while the guy takes it. Then Juan hands out more baggies. He starts bragging about how he's friends with Paul Lasko, and everyone knows Lasko works for WSW and Toto."

Cash knew those names. Unfortunately, West Side Wolves had been on the news nightly since a big drug bust a few weeks ago.

"Then Juan's telling the guys I'm cool, no snitch. I'm with him. I kind of had to take the baggie. I mean, they were talking about some guy who'd bailed on them before and how Lasko took care of him. Like, *took care* of him."

Cash nodded. "I get you. So now you're out of school. If you don't sell drugs, he'll gut you. And he'll hurt Jordan?"

Rafi nodded. "I tried to get out of it, later, when it was just Juan and me. But he said if I didn't, I was a fool and a narc. And nobody turns on WSW. Then he said he knew about my pretty sister and it would be sad if something happened to her." Rafi scowled, looking more angry than scared. "I mean, he threatened my sister."

"But this Juan kid, he's not actually a gang member."

"I don't think so. But, hell, I thought he was just always talking a big game. I didn't know he really knew Lasko or had drugs and stuff. It's just… None of it seems real."

"Man, you're in a shit sandwich for sure." The cops in the city were cracking down on drugs and gangs, hard, lately. "What's the plan?"

"Plan? There is no plan." Rafi sat up, clenching a tissue. "Maybe if I run away, they'll leave Jordan alone."

"And maybe they won't." Cash wanted to do the right thing. "So we could call the cops." As much as he wanted to get the law involved, he didn't want Jordan's brother dragged down with Juan's group, and he had no doubt Juan would be shitty enough to try to drag Rafi under the bus with him.

"No cops. No."

"Because that will get you a target on your back. No cops." Cash didn't want Rafi having to fear Toto. "You never met Lasko or Toto? Just Juan and his flunkies?"

"Yeah. A bunch of rich kids pretending to be tough. That's all I thought they were."

"And maybe that's all they really are." Though Juan had to be getting drugs from someone. "Go get me your baggie."

Rafi sighed and left, returning with the bag in question. Cash studied it. "I'm no expert, but I think this is heroin."

"Yeah." Rafi paced, hugging his arms to his chest. "Heroin. Jesus, I have a bag of H in my house." Rafi paused. "Your house."

"Hey, it's a rental. Doesn't count." Cash stared at the

baggie, wondering what the hell to do. "I should tell Jordan," he thought out loud.

"Are you *crazy?*" Rafi stared at him. "My sister will march to Juan's house and think she can make him do the right thing. But she can't. Juan's parents are rich. Like, serious moneybags. They don't care what he does. And Juan gets away with everything. I think the only reason he was even at summer school was to deal drugs."

"Makes sense." And, yeah, Cash could see Jordan on her soapbox, the ex-Army MP taking a stand on doing the right thing and putting away a drug dealer with ties to WSW for good.

Cash would rather leave that shit to the police. Let them deal with gangs and drugs. Only Rafi and this mess with the potential to hurt Jordan concerned him.

"Okay, this is what you're doing to do. When I tell you to, you're going to call Juan. You'll tell him you want to see him at his club. That you can't deal drugs for him, but you're happy to hand them back in person."

"I can't do that."

"You can, and you will." Cash stood, towering over Rafi. "Because I'm gonna go have a chat with your friend."

"They might have guns." Rafi looked worried.

"Did you see any?" But Cash would be prepared.

"No, but that doesn't mean anything."

"This bar. You know for sure it's a WSW hangout?"

"Well, no. But that's what Juan said."

"Where is it? What's the bar's name?"

Rafi told him, and Cash wrote it down. He had a friend he could call, a buddy he'd worked with on the first security job he'd found upon returning to the States. Though Cash hadn't lasted at the job, he'd made some contacts.

"Now, as for the rest of it, you're going to tell Jordan about school and about this shit-for-brains teacher. You let her handle that. Because what that guy said is wrong."

"But it's not." Rafi teared up again. "Man, you don't get it. My brain is just wrong. I can't do math or fractions or multiplying. None of it! It took me forever just to understand how to deal with money because the dollars and cents part gets confusing. I'm fifteen, and I still can't tell time unless it's digital! Adding and subtracting, word problems, it's all a mess."

Cash frowned. "What do your parents say?"

"I can't tell them. I don't want them thinking I'm a moron. I deal. But now I can't hide it anymore. It's so hard to do anything at school, and I hate it."

"Okay, settle down." The kid was getting all riled up. "First things first. You trust your sister with the school nonsense. This teacher should *not* be around kids. If I have to go in there, I might hurt him."

Rafi blinked.

"I'll handle Juan. Don't worry. I know what I'm doing. But you have to promise me you won't run away and you won't lie to Jordan. Not anymore."

"I-I won't." Rafi looked at him with a spark of hope. "But if she knows about Juan, I won't be able to stop her from going to the cops. She's big on no drugs."

"I know. Maybe you can keep that part about Juan out of it. Just stick with the school crap. I'll handle Juan. He won't be a problem to you anymore. I swear."

"Okay."

"Promise. Because if Jordan finds out about Juan, you'll be getting me in trouble too."

"I swear." He held out a pinkie, and Cash stared at it. "Shake. Pinkie promise, man. You never break that."

Cash shook his head. "Yeah, okay. Pinkie promise. Now watch TV or something while I make a few calls. Don't do anything, no calling Juan or leaving the house, until I tell you."

"I'll stay. I promise."

"Good. I'll order us a couple of pizzas in the meantime." Cash went into his bedroom and shut the door. After ordering food, he scrolled through his phone and found the number he wanted.

Ritter picked up on the second ring. "What?"

"Yo, Ritter. It's Cash Griffith."

"Cash. How are you, man?" Ritter was a decent guy. Tall and built like a tank, he'd been a heavyweight fighter in his younger days and had segued into security work. Like Cash, he had a low tolerance for assholes.

They'd bonded over beer and a loathing for their boss then quit that bank security job around the same time. Right before said bank had been cited for fraud, embezzlement, and a host of other problems Cash hadn't needed to be around.

"I'm good. Working with my brother now."

"Yeah, saw your ugly face on TV a few weeks ago. Nice moves."

"Whatever. Helps get chicks though."

Ritter laughed. "So what's up?"

"I figured you were still doing security. That's your thing, right?"

"Yeah. It suits me."

"I'll bet. Do you think you could help me dig up some

info on a kid I think is pretending to have connections to WSW?"

Ritter whistled. "That shit's hot right now. Federal and local law enforcement are all over that."

"I know. But what I'm hearing from some teenage banger-wannabe isn't fitting." He explained the situation to Ritter.

"I'm actually at work now. Gimme twenty minutes, and I'll get back to you."

"Thanks. I wanted to meet this kid and take care of the problem. Just need to know what I'm really dealing with." Should he bring just his fists or some harder ammo? "I might need the name of a cop you trust too. Someone who could bust a guy for drugs and not take down any innocent parties with him."

"I know a guy."

"Thought you might. I'll owe you, man."

"Yeah, you will."

"Talk to you soon." Cash hung up and waited.

He went back to the living room and saw Rafi lounging on the sofa watching TV. The boy bolted up when he saw Cash.

"Relax. I'm waiting on a callback."

Rafi stood. "I, ah, thanks. For helping."

"Sure."

The boy followed Cash into the kitchen. "Don't suppose the pizza came yet."

"Nope."

Cash opened a cupboard and saw his stash of Oreos gone. He glanced over his shoulder.

Rafi flushed. "Sorry. I was hungry, and all our food is at the apartment."

"Not a problem. We'll get more."

Rafi watched him.

"Just say it, whatever's on that teenage mind."

As he'd hoped, Rafi smiled back. "Are you being nice to me because you're doing my sister?"

"Nope."

Rafi frowned. "Nope, you're not just being nice to me, or nope, you're not doing my sister?"

"Nosy little bastard, aren't you?"

"It's just, Jordan is the only one who's stood by me through all this."

"I know. She's cool."

"Yeah. So if you're trying to use her or something, don't. She's the best person I know. And I'm not just saying that because she's my sister and she stuck by me. She's good. She always does what's right, no matter what."

"I know. Trust me, your sister tells me how great she is all the time at work."

Rafi chuckled. "That's her way of flirting."

"Interesting technique."

"She was always weird around guys. She's not like Leanne. Our older sister looks like a living Barbie doll and acts all helpless. Not Jordan."

"A Barbie doll?" Because Rafi and Jordan looked anything but nice, plastic, or pretty. The pair were more like dark-haired, good-looking, pain-in-the-ass bookends.

"Yeah. Leanne's always been Mom and Dad's favorite. We all know it. But Leanne's also really nice a lot. So it's hard to be mad at her."

"Jordan doesn't like Leanne's fiancé." As soon as he said it, he hoped he wasn't talking out of turn, but Jordan seemed close to her brother.

"He's an ass. But he's rich and nice around our parents, so they love him. It's so strange. My parents are usually pretty cool. I know they love me, but they are so warped about dealing with stuff they can't understand. Like, everything has to be right in their world or they fall apart. Leanne was super smart and funny and got great grades. Never drank or did drugs. Always listened to Mom and Dad. So they gave her everything. Until me, Jordan was the family rebel.

"She told me she used to get in trouble a lot when she was in school. But she made it through and kicked butt in the Army. Now she's back, and she's helping me out when she could be making a real life for herself. I don't want to hold her back. And I want her to go to college or be whatever she wants to be."

Cash kept it casual while wanting to interrogate the kid. "She wants to go to college?"

Rafi nodded. "She has all these brochures she goes through at night when she thinks I'm sleeping. I think it's the GI Bill or something. But it's a way for her to go to college. Except she can't with me in the way." He sighed.

"Look. I don't know your parents, but let me tell you what I think. They're idiots."

Rafi frowned.

"I call 'em like I see 'em. Your older sister might be super nice, but I don't see her standing up for you. Life is all about dealing with conflict. I should know. I deal with it all damn day. And I know you don't turn a blind eye and run when it gets tough. You don't cut out the ugly when it's staring you in the face. You deal with the bad and make it good."

"That's not what my family does."

"That's on them, not you. I bet if you told your sister about your problems, she'd find a way to help you." He paused. "I had a buddy in the Marine Corps. Smart guy, smartass too." Rafi grinned with him. "Joe was hell on wheels with a weapon. Expert marksman and could quote you specs on anything. Knew all about politics and who was outmaneuvering who all the time. But he'd spent years growing up thinking he was dumb. Because he couldn't read. Turned out he had dyslexia, but no one figured it out until he almost lost it. As in, committed suicide."

"That sucks."

"It does. But Joe fixed it and moved on. Now he's got a wife and two ex-wives and is living it up in Hawaii."

"Two ex-wives?"

"Well, he's book smart but an idiot about women."

"Oh." Rafi cleared his throat. "So, ah, you think maybe I have dyslexia?"

"I don't know. I think dyslexia is when you confuse your letters. But maybe there's a kind of dyslexia about math. Hasn't anyone ever had you tested or anything?"

"No. But I didn't want anyone to know. I got through until now with my friends helping. I guess it was cheating, kind of." He blushed. "I count on my fingers when no one is watching."

"So what? That's why we're born with fingers *and* toes. So you can at least hit twenty." Cash grinned. "I hated school, so I'm not the best person to talk about it being so amazing." He grimaced. "I just wanted to graduate so I could join the Corps."

"Me too."

"You want to join the military?" Cash brightened.

"Well, I've thought about it. You get to go places

and fire weapons and stuff. Jordan says I should join the Army."

Cash winced. "Dude, just…no. The Army is mediocre at best." Damn if Rafi didn't raise one brow the same way Jordan did. "And, yeah, your sister is hot shit, but only because she was always hot shit. The Army didn't make her great. She's been great all on her own. Now, the Marine Corps helped shape me. I was a total assface before I joined. And no comments that I'm an assface now, got it?"

Rafi cleared his throat. "Right."

"They really do turn the worst of us around." Mostly. It wasn't the Corps's fault they'd had so little to work with. Feeling like the worst imposter, Cash kept talking up the service, sharing a few stories about pranking his buddies and making Rafi laugh.

Then the doorbell rang.

"Pizza!"

"Settle down, mini-Jordan. I'll get the door."

Cash grabbed the pizza, tipped the guy, then placed the boxes on the counter.

"Two pies?" Rafi took down plates.

"I'm not that hungry." The phone rang. "Help yourself. I gotta get this."

It was Ritter. And he told Cash everything Cash needed to know.

Chapter 19

Jordan and Cash had the following day off and spent their Saturday as a couple. Now that she'd let the proverbial cat out of the bag about them dating, Cash told her he wanted them doing couple-y things. So they held hands, walked in the park, and went shopping.

"I really hate grocery shopping," Jordan growled.

Cash squeezed her hand and grinned. "I love it."

"That's because you do nothing but eat. You couldn't have saved me a slice of pepperoni last night?"

He tossed four bags of chips into the cart. She had a feeling that would last through Monday. Maybe.

"Hey, you were eating wings and drinking beer without me. Fair's fair." He hugged her to his side and planted a kiss on her head. As if she was a three-year-old he'd decided to humor.

Just to yank his chain, she told him, "Smith was there."

His smile thinned. "Oh?"

"Yes, oh. The bastard goaded me into telling everyone we're dating. Then I put him in a wristlock and took him down."

He stopped walking. "You did? Please tell me someone got that on film."

"I don't think so."

"Damn it."

A woman with her toddler walked by and frowned at him.

"Five bucks says that kid's next word is *damn*," Jordan murmured.

He groaned. "What are you, the language police?"

"Once a cop, always a cop." She added some fruit to the cart, and he made a face. "Oh please. You like bananas. I saw a bunch in your kitchen."

"I like banana-flavored pudding."

"How can you be so fit when you eat so much crap?"

"Good genes, I guess," he said, with no small amount of sarcasm.

That he'd echoed what Smith had said struck her. They looked so much alike, almost more than Cash and Reid did. It was uncanny. But no. They'd know if they were related, wouldn't they? She wanted to ask, but knowing how much Cash disliked Smith, she kept her thoughts to herself.

"Have you figured out what you're doing with your mom's house yet?"

"I think so." He kept walking.

She followed him with the cart. She guided him past the caramels by the apples and handed him a bag of apples instead.

"Jordan, you're sucking all the joy out of shopping."

"Welcome to my world."

He laughed and hugged her close as they walked, pushing the cart together, and she felt a happiness like no other. She wasn't unaware of the many side glances they received. So many women eyeballing Jordan's boyfriend. How could they not? When smiling, he outshone every man she'd ever dated, seen, or fantasized about.

"It's kind of annoying how good-looking you are," she said.

He nodded. "I know. My beauty is a curse."

"I mean it." She saw him try to shrug away the compliment. Cash did that a lot. He was the first to tell everyone how great he was. But if anyone agreed with him, he turned the praise into a joke or ignored it.

"You're prettier than I am," he pointed out.

"Well, yes. I'm a girl. I wouldn't call you pretty."

"Stick with magnificent. That works."

Again with the humor. Before she could say something about his habit of twisting praise, he asked about dinner. She let him change the conversation, resolving to get back to it later.

"Yes, yes. Stop whining. I'll cook you some steaks tonight."

"Finally. I thought I'd have to get ugly and start begging." He winked.

A tall, beautiful redhead brushed by him and gave him a second glance. One he ignored, fortunately for him.

"See," Jordan said loudly enough to be heard by the woman who didn't move far enough away. "Women think you're available. But I bet if they knew we were together and how skilled I am with a pistol, they'd all leave you alone. No matter how magnificent you might be."

The redhead *moved*.

"You are so badass." Cash's smile blinded her. "How about we drop the food and go home so I can show you how much I appreciate a badass? Rafi's at Daniel's today, right?"

She let him have one kiss then pushed him away. "Stop." She laughed. "Yes, he's out. You want to leave? Fine. But we're buying all this before we go. No way am I coming back to grocery shop again with you."

"Aw, honey. You're no fun."

They purchased the groceries and headed back.

A question had been nagging her. "You never did tell me about your plans for your mom's house."

He tapped the steering wheel, and she wondered what he had to be nervous about. Because that tapping was one of his tells.

"Cash? Are you okay?"

"I need you to hear me out on something. It's important."

"Okay."

He put on his emotionless mask, the one that normally meant something had upset him.

She put a hand on his thigh, and he tensed. "You can talk to me."

He glanced at her before focusing once more on the road. "It's… Wait. Did you talk to Rafi yet?"

"Rafi? I saw him this morning, when I made us all breakfast. You were there." She frowned. "What am I missing?"

"Nothing. Never mind."

"You told me last night went fine. That I had nothing to worry about with my brother."

"Well, he's a teenager. And he's a boy. Of course you have stuff to worry about. Just not super bad stuff. I don't think he's murdered anyone. Yet."

"Cash."

"Jordan, Rafi is a nice kid. You're a terrific big sister, and he knows it." A significant pause. "You're putting your life on hold for him. He told me about your college plans."

She groaned. "I'm not waiting to go because of him.

Well, not exactly. I just want to take my time before I go back to school. I want to pick a major I can live with."

"Good." He coughed, sounding nervous. "So, well, uh, you need money for college. For books. I hear they're expensive."

"Yeah, they are." She studied him. "What the hell is wrong with you? Are you okay?"

"I'm fine, damn it. Thanks for asking." He tapped the steering wheel some more. "I was just thinking that if we lived together, you could save on rent."

She hadn't expected *that* bombshell. "Say that again?"

He gripped the steering wheel so hard his knuckles turned white. "I've been thinking about moving into my mom's. It would become my house. New paint, no tacky rose wallpaper, and no more hoarding."

"Right. No more hoarding." Her heart raced. *Living together?* What, as roommates? Lovers? Something more?

"It's in a nice neighborhood. The mortgage is paid, so it's just utilities really. That and my food bill," he tacked on, trying to sound lighthearted and failing. "I have a ton of room in there. So, uh, if you felt pressured to be with me to stay there, you wouldn't have to. You don't have to fuck me to live there or anything. I mean, I *want* to fuck you. All the damn time. But I know you need space for Rafi and that it weirds you out if we're together and he's around.

"I just think it makes sense. That way I can save money by moving out of my current place when Reid leaves. And you can move in with me. Like, we can be together. With Rafi. And, well, in the house."

She stared at him, having never heard him speak so fast for so long.

After a moment, he groaned. "You are killing me. Did I just mess everything up or what?"

"I'm confused. You want me to move in as your roommate? But no more sex?"

"*What?* No." He finally arrived at his house and pulled into the driveway, parked the car, and turned to face her. "I want you in my bed, in my life, and in my house. With me. You need a place to stay. I need you. Seems like an easy thing to fix."

"I..." She had never thought he might ask, and not so soon.

"Look, think about it, okay? You don't have to make up your mind now. You're fine staying with me here as long as you want. I can always rent out my mom's place and we could live here." He blew out a breath. "What I'm saying is, you could live here with me until you find a place to rent. If you wanted to go, I mean."

She hated that he felt so nervous he kept repeating himself. But, dang, he was so cute. He wanted her with him. To move in with him. "Is this because you feel sorry for me?"

"Huh? *No.* You put Smith in a wristlock. I think I love you." After a *very* awkward silence in which she feared his face would burst into flame, his cheeks had turned so red, he corrected himself. "I love you for hurting Smith. Not for...I don't... Well, I do have...feelings I..." He leaned his head back and closed his eyes. "Shoot me now."

"Oh, no. This is the most fascinating conversation I've ever had with you." She laughed, unable to help herself. She lowered her voice to mimic his. "I mean... Feelings...I...well... Bananas."

"Shut up." He lifted his head and glared. "My blood sugar is low. That's my excuse. What's yours?" He slammed his way out of the car, his face still beet-red, and grabbed a bunch of grocery bags.

She followed, taking the last two, and joined him inside. "My excuse? For what?"

"For being obnoxious," he snarled as he slammed things into cabinets and shoved items in the refrigerator.

She trailed him down the hallway toward the bathroom, where he tossed a bundle of toilet paper. Before he could leave, she blocked his way. "So huffy."

"So huffy? You're such a jerk sometimes, Jordan."

Not so amused, she stared him down. "What is your problem? We had a great day, lots of fun, laughs, then you got weird in the car, and now you're acting like an ass."

"*My problem?* My problem, Jordan, is that I love you. And I don't want to scare you away, and you're such a pain in my ass." He ran his hands through his hair. "*Fuck.* You know the last woman I told that to? She cheated on me, stole from me, and nearly had me arrested for trumped-up claims of abuse. And the first woman I ever loved hated my guts for no apparent reason. So excuse the fuck out of me for being weird in the fucking car!"

He picked her up, set her down behind him, and stormed from the bathroom.

It took her a moment to process because she kept hearing "I love you" in Cash's snarly, grumbly voice. This from the crass, less-than-sophisticated brute who hadn't wanted to hire a woman in the first place. The soft teddy bear of a guy who would do anything not to have a woman cry on him, who pretty much supported her through everything she'd ever told him, loved her.

Giddy and thrilled, she darted out of the bathroom and found him closeted in his bedroom, the door locked shut.

Bull. Shit.

She spotted the spare key over the doorway and had to use a chair to reach it. Then she fit the key in the door and pushed her way inside.

"It was locked for a reason," he growled, looking miserable as he stood by the window, staring outside.

"Cash. Look at me."

He refused to move. Refused to glance her way. So she decided to get his attention.

Jordan walked to him and tugged him by the waist to turn. He opened his mouth, but she put a finger over his lips. She tugged his shirt over his head, aware he let her. Then she tapped his shoes with her toes, signaling for them to go. He slipped them off, following with his socks.

Neither of them spoke, but Jordan guided him to disrobe piece by piece until he stood before her naked and aroused.

She kissed her way down his chest, stroking him everywhere she could reach. He felt so soft yet hard, so warm and coarse. The breathy sighs he made, the grunts and groans, had her wet and willing. But she wanted to do this for him. And, hell, because seeing him come turned her on.

"Jordan," he whispered as she kissed her way down his body. His cock was thick and slick at the tip. His balls hard, heavy. She took them in hand and blew over his cockhead.

He jerked, his breathing loud in the otherwise quiet room.

She put her mouth over him, licking him clean, and he gripped her shoulders.

He pushed deeper, and she took more of him inside. Then she eased her way over him, relaxing to take him impossibly deep.

He swore, trembling, but made no move to push.

Jordan pulled her mouth back, sliding over him. She let him fall to her lips before taking him to the back of her throat once more. And as she did, she fondled him, stroking his thighs, his balls, cupping the hard knots and rubbing them while he whispered her name and clenched his ass tight, as if to keep control.

The sweet torment aroused her to no end, and she loved knowing she could make him so lost to her touch.

"Oh fuck, Jordan. Honey, I'm gonna come. I'm so close."

She bore down, sucking harder while she rubbed his balls.

Cash gripped her shoulders tight and shattered, coming down her throat while he pumped in her mouth.

"Shit. Oh fuck. Jordan. Baby, yes. Oh God, yes."

When he'd finally finished, she eased off him, her jaw sore. He pulled her to her feet and hugged her, his body like a furnace.

She glanced up and saw his eyes suspiciously shiny. But she didn't mention it, and neither did he. "You have too many clothes on."

She let him strip her naked then obeyed his command to lie down on the bed, her knees up, her legs spread wide. Cash lay down between her legs and rested his chin on her belly.

"Jordan, you mean everything to me." He watched her, laying everything on the line.

She wanted to say it back, to tell him she loved him too. But he didn't let her. Because his mouth settled over her sex, stealing her breath. Then his tongue went to work.

He licked and kissed and plunged his tongue inside her. His large hands stroked her thighs, her ass, then slid up her body to play with her nipples.

She writhed beneath him, but he refused to budge, giving no quarter as he brought her so close to orgasm... then left her on the edge. Only to build her up again. And again.

He constantly had her teetering on the edge of bliss before pulling back.

"Cash, please. I need you inside me."

Only then did he rise over her, his mouth slick, his green eyes dark.

"You need me. Say it again." He settled over her, staring at her mouth.

"I need you. I need *you*," she emphasized, in case he didn't get it the first time. "I lo—"

She didn't get the rest out because he fastened his mouth to hers and shoved his thick cock inside her at the same time.

She screamed into his mouth as he rode her with a fierceness that prolonged her orgasm.

He pulled his lips away, hammering inside her while her body clamped down tight, wanting nothing more than to feel him spill inside her.

She moaned as he tensed, coming with her at last.

They lay together, spent but not done. Jordan and her man. It had been the most intense experience of her life.

Still inside her, Cash had to lean up to stare down at her and wiped tears from her cheeks.

"Was I crying?" Surprised but too sated to care, she saw him nod. "Oh. I don't think I can move. I don't think I can think."

He grinned, his beauty as much from his joy as his dark good looks. She just stared at him, not sure how this man could be hers.

"What are you thinking now?" He toyed with her hair. He started to withdraw from her then surged deeper, their connection so much more than physical.

They both sighed.

Jordan loved him. Cash Griffith, a man who gave his everything to those who mattered. And miracle of miracles, she mattered to him. Yet he could be skittish. She had to be smart about how she interacted with him. Twice she'd tried to tell him how she felt, but he'd shut her down. Why?

"What am I thinking?" she asked, trying to figure him out.

"Yeah." He stared down at her, as if looking into her soul.

So she told him the truth. Rather, she told him *a* truth she knew he could handle. "Cash..."

"Yeah?"

"I think we left the ice cream out."

—◦◦◦—

Cash stared down at the woman he'd confessed to loving, seeing in her a future he could only pray he'd have a shot at keeping. Then her words sank in.

"*Shit*. Not the cookies 'n' cream!" He dashed out of the bedroom and found the mushy container by the fridge. He stuffed it in the freezer and returned to find Jordan in the shower.

Hmm. Shower sex. Okay.

Despite having bared his heart, he wasn't as out of sorts as he'd expected he might be. Though the fallout from Mariah's deception had gutted him, Cash had done his best to put her in the past. His few Marine buddies hadn't liked her much. And Reid had never cared for her. She'd ended up being a user and a liar.

Jordan was nothing like her. Smart and funny, she held her ground. She had integrity, and she was loyal to those she loved. More importantly, his friends all liked her, as did Reid. So maybe he hadn't chosen wrongly this time around. Chosen? More like he'd been lucky enough to find a woman like her to put up with him.

She pulled back the curtain when he opened the bathroom door. "Well? Get in here."

He stepped in the tub and let her move him out of the spray so he wouldn't block her from the warm water. The spray jetted over her dark hair and clung to her golden skin, making her shine.

"Oh yeah. I do love you wet."

She grinned. "Blowing you made me really wet."

"Well, it made me really hard, so I guess we're even."

"Maybe." She stood there, her hair slicked back, a golden mermaid…with a side of teeth. "Cash, I—"

"No. I don't want to hear it. Not yet."

"But I—"

"No. Think about it, Jordan. Don't feel you have to say it back. And don't feel pressured about anything."

"But—"

"The love stuff slipped out. Pretend I didn't say it, okay?"

She gave him a puzzled look. "Pretend?"

"Did I stutter?"

She frowned. "Fine. But I'm just going to say this once."

"If you must." His heart hammered, not ready to hear her rejection. Not yet. He'd fucked up and admitted to things too soon, he knew. But if they stepped back from all the emotional bullshit, maybe he could keep her a little longer.

"I hate your shampoo."

He blinked at her. "What?"

"You heard me. I'll buy the shampoo and soap for all of us from now on. So don't bring any of this to the new house, okay?" At his obvious confusion, she said more slowly, "Your mom's place that's now yours, where we'll be living? You did say we could live with you there."

"Ah, yeah. Uh-huh. Right." His heart raced. *Jesus, she'd said yes?*

"And that's final. Now wash my back like a good boyfriend."

She turned and tilted her head down, holding her hair off her graceful neck.

Where we'll be living, she'd said. With him.

"Um, okay." Dazed, he grabbed the soap and washed her, mesmerized by her sleek lines. So full of love, he let the warmth fill him, and then, because he couldn't help it, his hands traced more of her, encouraged by her pleas.

And Cash learned something important. He really did love Jordan wet.

Chapter 20

SUNDAY, WHILE CASH WENT WITH REID TO HIS MOTHER'S house to do some final cleaning, Rafi had asked to spend the day with Jordan. Pleased and surprised her brother finally consented to spending time with her, and of his own free will, she took him to one of his favorite breakfast places in Green Lake. He loved Sofa's Bakery for their ham and gruyere croissants. She loved their asswidening pastries.

Her stomach protested, loudly, that she needed to eat. By the time they reached the front of the line, she didn't see any croissants left. She did, however, see the guy Cash had saved from a beating. What was his name again?

"Well, well." The handsome guy gave her a big grin. "You're Jordan, Cash's main squeeze, right?"

Conscious of her brother listening with a fascinated look on his face, she nodded. "Um, yeah. This is my brother, Rafi. Rafi, this is —"

"Elliot Liberato. I own the joint." He looked around him. "Impressive, huh?"

From behind him, a tall woman with dark hair and toned arms, wearing a sleeveless Sofa's shirt, scoffed. "I'm sorry. *Who* owns the place?"

"It's family run," he said smoothly, leaned closer, and added, "But I'm really the brains behind everything." Elliot cleared his throat. "What can I get you — on the house?"

"No, no." Jordan tapped her wallet. "I'll pay for—"

"You'll pay *nothing*." Elliot swept his hands in front of him. He seemed to have a tendency toward drama, and his voice rose and fell with an actor's grace. "I'm still alive because of your boyfriend's heroic sacrifice."

"Elliot. You've met Cash. He likes to fight."

"He saved *my life*." Elliot wiped at his eyes. "Those are imaginary tears, at the thought, the *travesty*, of me being dead. And what a crime that would be."

Rafi snickered.

"Elliot, for God's sake," growled the tall woman behind him. "We have a line, and I'm pretty sure your savior wants to order."

"Thanks," Jordan told her.

"No problem." She cuffed Elliot in the head. "Little brothers are such a pain."

He turned and glared at his sister before facing Jordan once more, this time wearing a sweet smile. "What can I get you two?"

"I'll take a small vanilla latte and something like that." Rafi pointed to the sign on an empty tray behind the glass case. "I wanted a ham and gruyere croissant too, but I think you're out."

"Not for you, handsome." Elliot called over his shoulder, "Sadie! Chop chop. Get the young man an H&G, stat. And add a donut and a cowboy cookie. He needs to eat." To Jordan, he asked, "And you, pretty lady?"

She laughed. "I'll have a coffee and that Danish right there." She pointed to the one she wanted in the glass case.

"By your command." Elliot bowed and grabbed her an extra pastry as well.

She had to admit she liked him. She made a last

attempt to reach into her wallet, saw his glare, and refrained. He had their order ready to go in no time.

"Thanks, Elliot." She smiled.

"Anytime. Oh, there's an empty table behind you. Hurry or you'll miss it."

They snagged the lone available table. Before they could sit, Sadie hurriedly wiped it clean. She eyed them both, her gaze flat, untrusting, before giving them a grunt and half smile. Then she ordered them to sit, eat, and enjoy before she left.

"Well, *she's* happy to be here," Rafi murmured.

"No kidding." They grinned at each other then dug into breakfast.

Rafi polished off his croissant and an old-fashioned donut before starting a weird conversation about their terrific weather.

Curious to know why he'd wanted to come with her, Jordan remained quiet, letting him take the lead.

He fiddled with the lid of his coffee cup. Then he started talking about the various shades of blue and green in the park, which he associated with the summer blooms and clear sky.

Jordan let him ramble while she took her time appreciating the delicate raspberry filling of her light and flaky Danish. *God, how are Elliot and Sadie not four hundred pounds?* She could never work in the food industry, she decided. Not if she wanted to keep her fighting weight.

"Jordan, I have to tell you something."

Please do. And if it's about the shade of my Danish, I might brain you. She took a sip of coffee, felt human, and sighed. "I'm listening. I have food and coffee. The weather is fantastic, as you've said fifty times." He blushed. She finished with "Life is good."

"I got kicked out of school," he blurted.

She froze then put her coffee back down. "You *what?*"

He looked so sad, so downcast, that she forced herself to remain patient.

"Rafi, tell me what happened."

He fidgeted while explaining in detail an outlandish altercation between himself and his teacher. "I'm sorry. I shouldn't have mouthed off, I know. But he was really mean."

"Wait. That really happened?" Her brother was a lot of things, and, yeah, he occasionally lied. But she didn't think he was lying about this. He looked too ashamed, for one, and he'd never been a bad student. Not until this year.

"I swear it did. I bet one of the kids recorded it on their phone. Jordan, he went off on me. He's done that before to other kids during the school year. But I never had him until summer school."

"He was a jerk." She wanted to smash Mr. Simpson's face in. "And I'm going to fix this tomorrow."

"No, wait."

"No one talks to you that way. I mean *no one*."

Rafi stared at her then slowly smiled. "Thanks, Jordan." The smile brought back the boy she'd grown up loving. Unfortunately, it faded as fast as it had appeared. "But he wasn't all wrong."

"What?"

"I'm not smart, and I never have been. I'm just good at faking it." Rafi explained how he'd had help, pretending an understanding of math for the longest time. By the time he'd finished, Jordan wanted to cry for him.

"Why didn't you tell anyone?"

He blinked back tears, his voice gruff. "It's embarrassing. I can't do what sixth graders can. I really am stupid."

"You are not," she snapped. "I don't want to hear you talk that way. You've been reading at an advanced level since you hit elementary school. Mom still brags about you. And none of us can draw like you can. So you're not good at math?"

"Or science, really."

"Or science. No one's good at everything." But his details about his difficulties made her think something else might be at work. "You need to see a specialist. Someone who can help you specifically with word problems and multiplication. What was wrong with that tutor Mom and Dad got you a while ago?"

Rafi shrugged. "I don't think he liked me. He knew I had problems. I didn't want to stay."

"Looks like I'll be talking to him too. Jesus. If you hate kids and don't want to be a teacher, don't teach!" She gnawed on her last pastry, needing to tear through something. "You haven't had the best luck with the other tutors I tried to get for you. But I understand now. So if we take care of all this, do you think you can stop bombing toilets and harassing your teachers?"

"Jordan."

"I get it, Rafi. You hate school. I'd hate it too if my teachers were jerky to me, I didn't understand stuff, and no one helped me. You're there to learn, you know. Not just to put a check in the block that you attended class."

"Tell that to Simpson."

"Oh, I will. Trust me."

They talked for a bit longer.

"I have to use the restroom. I'll be right back." Rafi left the table.

Jordan took the time to text her mom. Pleased to see her folks would be home for a few more hours before heading to a garden show, she set up a meeting. It was time to talk truth with her parents, and time to get Rafi back with the family that should have supported him from the get-go.

———— ⁓ ————

An hour later, Rafi sat in the living room at his parents' house, staring at his mom and dad. He hated having to tell them he wasn't smart. Knowing you were an idiot and having to admit it to those who believed in you hurt.

Jordan had accepted him even when he'd been a troublemaker. And she didn't seem to mind he was a moron. He still had a tough time believing it, but Cash had been right. Finally confiding in her had been the right thing to do. Telling her about the drugs? Heck no. But in this, the school stuff, he'd done something right.

He just wished his parents, especially his dad, didn't have to know about his lack of brainpower. They just stared at him. He'd told them everything about his problems learning, including Simpson losing it with him in front of the class. And still they didn't speak.

Dad finally responded. He frowned. "All this time and you still can't figure out what the big and little hands on a clock mean?"

"No, Dad." Rafi glanced away, unable to look his father in the eye.

Having been in business forever, his father lived and

breathed numbers. How disappointing it must be to have a son who didn't.

"Hell." His father swore again. "Rafi, if we'd known you didn't understand, we'd have helped. I know Jordan's got you brainwashed that we're ogres."

Jordan flushed. "Dad."

"But your mom and I love you, Son. You were so full of anger and bravado that we didn't know what we could do for you. Despite Jordan and you thinking we were just shipping you off to any old military school, I have friends whose children have attended, and those boys came back better than fine. It's a safe place and still an option if you'd like."

"No."

"Okay. Like I said, it's just an option."

His mom squeezed herself between him and Jordan on the couch and drew him close for a hug. "Oh sweetie. We love you and miss you. We just want the best for you."

"So do I," Jordan was quick to point out.

"But your methods aren't ours." Mom smiled. "The Army worked for you, Jordan, for a while at least. So we thought it could help you too, Rafi. But now we can see that's not what you need. Although someone to kick you in the tail and get you to behave wouldn't be such a bad thing."

Rafi smiled. "Well, I don't know that I'd join the Army anyway, Mom. Cash thinks the Marines are much better."

"Cash?" His mother frowned. "Who's Cash? A school friend?"

As expected, his sister went off. "Marines? Please. You need a magnifying glass to detect Marine brains."

"I'm telling Cash you said that."

"Go ahead. We all know the Army rules."

"Jordan." Their dad shook his head. "Rafi, you can come home whenever you want. We promise not to ship you off to Pennsylvania…unless you *want* to go. Once you see their brochures, you might change your mind. They have archery there."

"Really?" He'd always wanted to try that.

Jordan shook her head. "Dad."

Their father grinned. "Hey, I can try, can't I?" He studied Jordan. "I think if you're honest with yourself, honey, part of why you were so against Rafi going away to school is due to what you went through. You trusted your superiors, and they turned on you and your friend. What's to prevent someone from taking advantage of Rafi?"

"True." She frowned. "But my biggest problem was you guys dumping him. He needs help."

"We know that now," Carl said. "But, honey, sometimes tough love works wonders. It did with me."

"It did?" Rafi had never heard that story.

His dad cleared his throat. "I was too smart for everything when I was your age. I thought I knew best. I never listened to my parents. They were dirt poor and lived out in the country. So what did they know? But they did me the biggest favor they could have when they kicked me out of the house. It made me grow up and learn to be a man, enough that when I came back to school, I gave it my all.

"Yes, I attended Stanford. And I have never worked so hard to get somewhere in my life. I've never been handed anything. I've had to work for it. That's why we wanted you to go out and learn, the way I did. The way

Jordan did." He turned to her. "Say what you want. But it worked for you too."

"We're not all you, Dad," Jordan said, but Rafi could see her thinking about what their father had said.

"I don't know why you thought we wanted him to fail," Mom said. "We love Rafi and you."

"Not like you love Leanne," Jordan muttered.

Mom blushed. "I swear, you are so competitive with your sister."

"Please, Mom." Rafi had to defend Jordan this time. "We both know you guys favor Leanne. It's clear any time we're all together. You treat her like she's better than all of us. The rest of us might as well not exist."

He was surprised to see his parents look discomfited.

"It's just…" His dad trailed off. "We don't mean to. She's just so easy. Leanne did well in school and never gave us any problems, so of course we supported her." His gaze narrowed on Rafi then Jordan. "Which we would have done for you two, but you had to be stubborn about things."

Jordan gave him a rueful smile. "I guess you have a point. But you can't deny you guys like her better. I could see that if she was your kid, but geez, Dad, she's your stepdaughter. Rafi's your own blood, and you treat Leanne better."

Rafi loved that she said what he'd been dying to for years. "Yeah. Why is that? Is it because she's blond, like you? And we look too Brazilian or something?"

Jordan tilted her head. "A good question. Are we too dark for the Youngers?"

"That's *nonsense*," their mother cut in. "You look just like me. You're beautiful. Carl didn't have to marry me, you know. He did it because he loves me, including the way I look."

Their dad huffed. "I can't believe you guys think like this. *Of course* I love all of you. Yes, you guys favor your mother. And you're lucky you do. She's gorgeous. I'm sorry if it seems we love Leanne more. We don't. We love all of you equally."

Jordan scoffed.

Dad pointed at her. "*That's* why it's easier to deal with Leanne. She never argues with us, never tells us we're wrong about anything."

"Even when we are." Mom sighed. "I can see your point, kids. We're sorry. We do love you all. And we'll try to do better at showing it. If we seem like we like your sister more, it's just because she's on her own now and happy, in love. No matter how you feel about Troy," she said, staring at Jordan this time, "he loves Leanne and takes care of her."

Dad looked down. "She is easy to handle. But you shouldn't feel less because of it. I'm so sorry, Son, Jordan. And Rafi, you should never feel like you can't come to us with problems. That's what we're here for." He turned to Jordan. "Before you step in with some remark about military school, we had no idea he had a problem learning or we'd have treated this differently. Defacing school property and mouthing off to teachers isn't because of that though, is it, Rafi?"

"No." He sighed. "You're right. But I did some of that because I was frustrated I wasn't smart."

"You *are* smart." Jordan, once again, refused to let him belittle himself. Man, he loved her. "You're just not learning math at a level you should be. Now stop being a dork and let Mom and Dad get you a tutor you like. I'll talk to the guy or lady and make sure they aren't an asswipe."

"Jordan." Their mother pinched the bridge of her nose. "Language?"

"Sorry, Mom." But she wasn't because Rafi saw Jordan's grin.

Mom laughed. "What am I going to do with you?"

They all sat around smiling at each other, and Rafi felt better about life than he had in a long time. "Now can we stop talking about me and instead talk about Jordan and her new boyfriend?"

His sister punched him in the arm. "Ow."

"Who?" Mom straightened in her seat.

"Cash." Rafi felt smug, glad not to be in the hot seat for once.

"Your school friend?" Dad's eyes grew wide.

Jordan blushed. "No. Geez, Dad. That's gross. And illegal."

Rafi laughed. "No, Cash is Jordan's boyfriend. They work together, and he's a Marine." Yeah, he'd thrown Jordan under. But he didn't feel bad about it. He had a feeling Cash would be coming to family dinners soon enough. And maybe Rafi liked seeing his sister the center of his parents' attention. Time for the good daughter to stand in the spotlight.

Now if he could just forget about Juan and the drug problem. He tried hard to have faith that Cash would sort it all out. But in Rafi's experience, bad news had a tendency to circle back and bite a guy in the tail. He looked at his family, smiling and laughing with each other, and treasured the moment. Knowing it wouldn't last.

Chapter 21

CASH COULDN'T BELIEVE THE CHANGE IN REID. BEFORE, HE'D had to beg his brother to help him with the house. This time Reid arrived with a box of donuts and coffee, a smile on his face.

Cash grunted, not pleased to be up and moving on a Sunday morning before ten. "Must have gotten laid last night, eh?"

Reid smiled. "Apparently you didn't. Guess Jordan wised up about you."

Cash smirked. "Oh, I'm a happy man. I just hate mornings."

"Too bad. I like Jordan. Thought she was smarter than that."

"Ha ha." Cash could see his brother was yanking his chain. Reid liked Jordan. "So, ah, we're gonna move in together. Here. Her, me, and her brother."

Reid paused in the act of biting into a sugar bomb. "Moving in together?"

Cash hated the tension he could feel growing. "Well, I mean, I know you and Naomi are moving in together soon. You're just waiting to pull the plug on our place because of me."

"That's not exactly true." Reid bit into his donut, studying Cash, and took his time chewing.

"Oh, for fuck's sake, spit it out."

"The donut?" Reid said with his mouth full.

"No, asshole, why you're not ready to move out."

Reid finished chewing and swallowed. "Well, part of it was keeping the place for you. With two of us paying rent at Chris's low rate, it's a steal." Their buddy Chris had kept the rent low, helping out two old Marine buddies. "But Naomi and I have been talking, and we want to be smart about our relationship. I mean, Bro, we just started dating not long ago. I love her like crazy, but slowing down a little is working for us. I hadn't realized she was as nervous as I was about this. We still want to live together, but we're not rushing it."

"But you're over there all the time." Cash never would have guessed Reid to be anxious about moving in with the woman he loved.

Reid sipped his coffee. "Frankly, I'm surprised Jordan said yes to moving in with you. Wow." Reid paused. "Is she desperate?"

"Ass. Yes, she is." Cash sighed. "I maybe rushed her, 'cause I can't stop thinking about her. And it's the answer to all our problems. I figured you'd be moving out soon. I have this place, free and clear. And Jordan needs a place to stay." He'd already explained to Reid about the landlord situation.

"I still can't believe she beat him up then you beat him up. It's like you're the perfect couple to both attract lawsuits and do jail time together." Reid shook his head. "I was hoping she'd be a *good* influence on you."

"Hey. That fucker put his hands on her. She was defending herself."

"Relax. I'm teasing. Well, kind of. She did the right thing. You, on the other hand, had better hope Alvarez is so scared he doesn't realize he can press charges."

"I think we're good. Besides, I had witnesses."

"Jordan and her brother. Oh great. Because they're impartial."

"You know, I'm sensing some sarcasm."

Reid's eyes narrowed. "You're sensing a lot of it, yes. But you know what? Who can blame you? If it was me, and some douche tried to hurt Naomi, I'd have been all over him. Not you. You let Jordan kick his ass then you finished."

"Hey, he was breathing and unbroken when I left him."

"Well, there's that." Reid shrugged, rubbed his hands together, then nodded to the living room. "So tell me what you're thinking of doing to fix all this."

Feeling a strange sense of enthusiasm for the project—he'd never been a house-and-home kind of guy—Cash walked his brother through the place, putting his own stamp on things. "I think the structure's sound, but it wouldn't hurt to have a professional take a look. Other than that, paint and maybe some new appliances, and the house is solid."

"You need furniture. Factor that in." Reid followed him into Angela's bedroom. "What do you call this color? Puke green?"

"I'd go with puke. Or maybe pea soup or sour lime." Cash hated the damn color, especially because it matched that shitty rose wallpaper in the hall. "I was kind of thinking Jordan could help me pick out furniture. You know, get a woman's touch."

"What does her place look like?"

Cash frowned. "I got the feeling she just kind of moved in not long ago. It's small, and the furniture was kind of like Angela's."

"Older and crappy?"

"Yeah." Maybe not the best idea to get Jordan's help after all.

"She could be renting it furnished. Or she has shitty taste." Reid shrugged. "You could always just walk around a furniture place and test her on what she likes. Then if you agree with her taste, you let her help."

"Good point." Cash glanced around, bemused he didn't feel awkward about making this house his own anymore. "This is the biggest room in the house. I should probably keep it as the master, right?"

"I would." Reid didn't hesitate. "The bed is old but in good condition."

The sleigh bed had a high headboard and low foot-board. It was a dark cherry wood and actually hand-some. And it was the same bed his father and mother had shared. "Nope. That's got to go."

"Good call. I'd do the same. But the dresser and mirror are keepers. So are the bookcases."

"Maybe." Cash could see how he felt, and how Jordan felt, about keeping them. "But I'll definitely need a new bed and mattress."

Reid opened the nightstand drawers, saw them empty, and peered under the bed. "You got everything out of here. Good job." He stood and looked around. "You know, once you paint over all this and give it a good cleaning, it'll be your house. It's big too."

"Yeah. At first I figured Jordan could move into the rental with me, but with Rafi so close, I'd never get any action."

"See? And you call yourself stupid. Nah, my broth-er's a thinker." Reid laughed at him. "Smart move.

Bigger house, more chance of getting lucky with her little brother far down the hall. Especially with these thin walls." Reid tapped the wall above the headboard and frowned. He tapped another section of the wall.

"Is it me, or is that section there hollow?"

"Yeah, it sounds like." Reid looked closer. "See the faint lines here?"

Cash leaned in. "They're obvious now that you point them out. How did we never notice that before?"

Reid studied the wall and pointed to a small hole. "See that? I think she had a picture over it."

Reid and Cash moved the bed back so they could easily access the wall.

Reid tapped again, then pushed, and a section of the wall opened. "Shit. I know what this is. Dad built a wall safe, only it wasn't a safe, just a hidden pushout he built into the wall. It was years ago. He had some cash and a gun he kept in here. Oh wow. I'd totally forgotten about all that."

"Seriously? Wonder what's in there now."

Reid stepped back. "It's your house. You do the honors."

"Thanks so much." Cash pulled the square of wall out and exposed a small cache of his mother's riches. A tattered copy of a favorite romance. A few videos he had no intention of watching. Especially if the *General Hospital* labels were to cover up some naughty-mom movies. Gross. He spotted a bundle of cash and brightened. He pulled it out, only to flip through so many ones.

"Yeah, that's Mom. A big spender." Reid laughed. "Hey, man, you're loaded!"

"Shut up."

"And just think, you can copy and sell her homemade porn tapes. Because you know that woman did not keep her soap operas locked up."

"That's disgusting."

"Disgusting and funny." Reid shoved Cash aside and reached in to take the tapes. "I'm going to have Naomi watch them for me. If they're sex tapes, I'm trashing them."

"And if they're old soaps?"

"I'm still trashing them. But I have to know."

"You're an idiot."

Reid grinned. "Yeah, I am." Then he frowned. "What's back there?"

"Huh?"

Reid nodded. "It's dark and blends with the dark wood of the back, but it looks like a journal."

"Oh hell. It's probably her diary."

"You know what? You keep the tapes. I'll take that."

"Nope. I'm going through this."

"Well?" Reid waited.

Cash sat with him on the bed and opened it up. Their mother's perfect handwriting, in a cursive that looked like scripted font, detailed events dated back to when Cash and Reid had been in elementary school.

"God, that's old." Reid leaned closer, and Cash shoved his head out of the way. "Hey."

"Hold on." Cash read through his mother's thoughts, hearing her as a real person. A young woman with thoughts and dreams. "Damn. She sounds half normal. She's bitching about Dad ignoring her. He worked too hard. She was lonely. And apparently he didn't hold a candle—her words—to her soap operas and books. He was no romance novel hero."

"Huh. Never would have thought." Reid gestured for Cash to hand him the book.

Cash did and stood to look through the rest of her hidey-hole. "I never did understand why she thought Charles would be more than he was. He was a simple guy who loved his wife and his son."

"Sons," Reid murmured.

"Sons, until something went wrong." Cash sighed and pulled out the rest of Angela's prized possessions, sad to see what they amounted to. Some old photos of him and Reid as babies. A few photos of her parents he recognized from seeing them a long time ago. A few trinkets and figurines he couldn't care less about. He counted out the stack of money, surprised to find a fifty buried in every few one dollar bills. All said, he counted out five hundred bucks. "Not bad. We'll split this, okay?"

"Oh my God."

Cash glanced up.

Reid looked pale. "Cash, uh, this I think explains things."

"What? What does it say?"

Reid started to hand him the book, but Cash shook his head. "You read it."

Reid blew out a breath. "Okay, fine. But remember, you and I are brothers, family, no matter what. Say it."

Shit. Cash could feel what was coming, had known it for years but never wanted to acknowledge that truth.

"We're brothers," Cash agreed. "You and me. The only family we got."

"Remember that." Reid clenched the journal tight. "Okay, this is from Mom over twenty years ago. *'I just dropped Reid and Cash off at school. Cash started third grade today, and Reid started first. So cute, my little boys. Charles left early, too busy building a new home to give today the importance it deserved. But why am I surprised? The man works, comes home expecting his dinner and his wife at his beck and call.*

"*'We made love last night, but it was over too fast.'*"

He paused.

Cash wiped a hand over his face. "Can you skip that part?"

"No. I read it, you have to hear it." Reid cleared his throat. "Ahem. *'He never takes time for me. Just a few grunts and it's over. But it's hard to blame him. He is his father's son. I hated Jonas so much. He treated Barbara terribly. At least Charles loves me, in his own way. I just wish it was enough. But it's not so hard anymore, not when he's coming for me.'*"

"He?" Cash's heart raced. "He who?"

Reid continued, "*'Our meeting was fated. Destiny. My one and only. It doesn't matter that he's married, that I have Charles. Allen has always been the great love of my life.'*"

"Jesus Christ. Allen?"

Reid nodded, his gaze somber. "Sounds a lot like *all-in*, doesn't it?"

My little all-in, what his mother had called Cash in private. "Oh my God."

"It gets better, or worse, depending on how you look at it. *'Allen arrived at noon. I had missed him so much. We made sweet love, and it was like being born again.*

*When we're together, it's as if nothing else matters. He
asked me about Cash again, but I told him we can't go
back and redo our lives. Charles can never know that
Cash is not his son. He loves them both so much. It took
all I could do to convince him that Cash was his in the
first place.*

   "*'When Charles first learned about my affair, he
cried. I've never seen a man cry like that. But he forgave
me, and he forgot, and he never knew Cash wasn't his.
Then we had Reid. Our little family was perfect.'*"

   Cash was reeling. "God, I'm really not his."

   "We kind of figured that, Cash. This isn't a big revelation." Reid watched him with care. "You want me to
keep going?"

   "Yeah. A little more, I guess." Cash had always wondered about his father. And now it made sense. Charles
must have found out that Cash wasn't his. No matter
that the older he'd grown, the more he'd resembled his
father's size and stature. His biological father must have
been a big guy too.

   Finding it hard to breathe, he sat down.

   Reid continued. "*'I can't leave Charles. Allen can't
leave his wife. It's so sad, our pure love that can never
be allowed. The yearning for my dearest burns me so.
That we must keep our deepest feelings a dark secret.
Will our true love ever be known to the world?'*" Reid
scowled. "That's awful. It's like she was trying to write
a romance novel using her own life as material. And it's
just...bad."

   "Yeah." Cash swallowed around a dry throat. "So
Charles knew. But he never said. I don't get it. He hated
me. Why not tell me the truth?"

"I don't know. Maybe when I read further into this?" Reid paused. "I think you should do it."

Cash's hand shook as he took the volume from Reid.

"Hey, it's getting late. I'm going to grab us some sandwiches. You stay here and read that, okay? I'll be back."

Cash nodded, poring over his mother's book. It was like hearing her speak, all that bad dialogue and romantic fiction so much bullshit. She'd been a spoiled, selfish woman caught up in her own ideals of love and romance. While Charles had been no prince, he'd put food on the table and a roof over her head. He'd provided for his family and watched over Reid and Cash as much as he'd been able.

Cash remembered camping with his dad. Playing sports, learning how to build things, to fix an engine. Tons of stuff a boy should learn from his old man. But none of it had been enough for Angela. He read:

> *It's Cash's seventh birthday. I don't know if I can do this anymore. Pretending to lose my baby boy four years ago has eaten at me. So much I couldn't write during that dark period. Only Allen kept me sane. That and my little All-in. Cash is so dear to me and favors his father so much. I wish I could show him how much I love him. Those beautiful green eyes are so soft, so loving. My little All-in, I call him, in remembrance of my truest love.*

> *Charles has no idea, and it's best I keep it that way. If he knew Allen's name, who Allen really was, I fear he'd kill my love.*

But my baby boy, my little Riley. So special. I miss him every day, but at least he's in good hands with Meg. I miss my sister. I miss my son.

And it happened. As I'd feared, I made a mistake. Charles heard Cash talking about what should have been our little secret, my private nickname for my boy. Charles came to me and demanded to know why I'd called him that. And it all came spilling out. How much I missed Allen. How Cash reminded me of his father.

Charles hit me that day. Only once. A slap across my face.

And then he cried. My big, strong husband cried like he'd only cried that one time before. And I knew then I should never think to leave him. Not when my love meant so much to him. I saw the depth of Charles's pain, and it moved me so.

I swore I'd never see Allen again. And from that day forward, I meant it. Allen was heartbroken. But Charles. He glowed with joy, that I'd chosen him over my true love.

I tried to hold onto that joy. But so lost without Allen, I turned inward. And found happiness in the words of others.

Cash couldn't catch his breath. He set the book down and put his head between his knees, feeling ill.

Riley? Fuck me. She had another kid, and she gave him away?

He caught his breath and read through the passage again, realizing what must have happened. After having him and keeping him a secret, Angela kept fucking around with her lover—Allen, his father—and had gotten knocked up after Charles's vasectomy. No way she could try to pass off another kid as his. How the hell she'd hidden that pregnancy Cash had no idea. Then he recalled his mother going to visit her family for a few months when her sister had fallen ill, back when he'd been little. He remembered because Charles had made him and Reid grilled cheese sandwiches and watched football with them on TV. They'd shared late-night treats and time with Daddy—Charles.

According to the journal, Angela had barely shown with him or with Reid. She must have been small enough to fool everyone into thinking she'd just gained a little weight then hidden out at her sister's for the last months of her pregnancy. She'd returned home the same old mom. At least, Cash had no recollection of his mother having another child.

So he wasn't Reid's full brother. They shared a mother. And Cash had a full younger brother somewhere.

"Somewhere? Who the hell am I kidding? There's a six foot four shithead at work who looks just like me," he said out loud. Hearing it, he felt totally drained, shocked, saddened, and so fucking angry he wanted to hit something.

Could Smith be his brother? But she'd called the boy Riley. Smith—that arrogant piece of crap—couldn't possibly be his brother, could he? Had he known all this time? Was that the reason for his attitude? Or was Cash reaching, delusional just because some idiot at work happened to look like him?

He lay staring at the ceiling, knowing he needed to read the rest of her journal but was unable to muster the strength to learn more secrets.

He heard the front door open and close.

"Cash?"

Reid had returned. He entered the bedroom, took a good look at Cash, and grabbed the journal. "I'll read the rest. I can guess at some of it already."

Cash just lay there, wrung out, unsure about everything.

Reid remained quiet and sat by his side.

"You know the worst part about losing Mariah?" Cash said out of the blue.

"What?"

"Knowing she agreed with Angela. When she called me nothing, said I was too dumb to realize she'd been cheating or stealing, that I didn't have an emotional core and couldn't connect, I believed her. When she told me I was heartless and never saw to her needs, it was like I'd taken a page from the Charles Griffith school of relationships. But even that was a lie."

"Don't do this to yourself, Cash."

So numb yet still feeling a blurred pain in his chest, Cash rubbed his breastbone. "Man, I don't even know why I'm upset. I mean, Charles was a dick. You and I used to talk about him hating me because I wasn't his kid. But he never mentioned it."

Reid sighed. "Maybe he couldn't admit it out loud. He did love Mom."

"He did. She says he did at least." Cash kept staring at that ugly popcorn ceiling. "You and I are half brothers."

"Which we'd also guessed before. So what?"

"So what?" Cash repeated, feeling out of sorts, and sat up.

"Do you think I love you any less because you have a different dad?"

"No. Yes. No. I don't know." Cash hated that the numbness started wearing off, that he felt so sad and angry. "She fucked us all up."

"Yes, she did."

"I'm not even good enough to be hated by my own father. Allen fucking left."

"Yeah, well, Charles hated you enough for the both of them," Reid said wryly.

A hard knot of laughter stuck in his throat. "At least I get why now." Another thought penetrated, and he hated that it pierced like an arrow through his heart. Corny and trite but real all the same. "She was never calling out to me. I was her tie to Allen. All-in my ass."

Reid said nothing, no doubt having figured it out before Cash.

"Even there at the end, it was all about her ex-lover. Not her son." And that bothered Cash far more than it should have. "Angela was dead to me for so long. But I thought she kind of loved me. But no. I was just an echo of Allen. Shit, Reid. I never had anybody." And that hurt, so fucking much. What was wrong with him that his supposed father, mother, and real father didn't like or want him?

"Shit. It's not you, it's them." Reid vaulted to his feet and crossed to block the bedroom door before Cash could leave. "They don't matter. We had the same shitty mother, Cash. And yeah, different deadbeat daddies."

Reid clutched his shoulders and shook him. "But you have me. I love you, Cash. And I see you. I always have." Reid's eyes glittered. "You're everything to me. I looked up to you growing up. I still look up to you. When everyone else shit all over you, you stood strong. You never gave up. I joined the Corps because of you, and, man, it was the best thing I ever did. If I didn't have you, I'd be lost."

"You don't have to say that." *So empty inside…*

Reid shocked him into awareness with a punch to his gut that had him bending over to catch his breath. "Stop it right now. You get out of that everyone-hates-me mentality. Because I need you. The guys at work need you. Jordan needs you. *You*—not Charles's, Allen's, or Angela's son. They don't matter. *You* matter. Now quit being a pussy and hit me back."

Reid, that idiot, stood over him, shaking, ready to take a punch.

Cash felt the rage in him, the need to lash out at someone to make the pain go away. But not Reid. "I'd kill you with my mighty fists," he said, trying to sound lighthearted. Except his voice sounded gravelly, and that last part broke on a sob.

So he reached for Reid and gave him a bear hug, needing that support, that honest acceptance from someone who knew him and yet loved him anyway.

"Yep, you're a big pussy," Reid said, clutching him back as tightly. "My big brother. I love you, Cash. You're all I've got. Evan and Aunt Jane don't count. They're too nice."

After some time, they gradually broke apart. Both of them had tears, and Cash felt shaky and light-headed.

"Fuck. Is she even my aunt?"

"What? Who?"

"Aunt Jane was married to Charles's brother. Technically, I'm not related to him or Evan. And, hell, I like Evan."

"Shut up." Reid gave him a watery smile. "Evan is a smart guy. He and I have talked about you for a long time. He looks up to you too, you know."

"Wait. Talked about me?" Cash wiped his eyes, still shaky but now bolstered knowing he still had Reid.

"He's smarter than you and me combined. And you know, there's something about the new guy at work that reminds us of you."

Cash groaned.

"I know, I know. But Friday night, Smith showed up. And, Brother, he really does look an awful lot like you. And he's angry at the world." Reid paused. "That could be you if you didn't have me."

"Shit. You think he's Allen's son too, huh?"

"Maybe. Maybe not. Although we just read about someone named Meg being Mom's sister, and a woman named Margaret was Mom's only friend before she died. You know the name Meg is short for Margaret."

"Damn."

Reid nodded. "And it's too huge a coincidence that your angrier twin just happens to hate us and works at Vets on the Go!"

"Is that why you hired him?"

"Partly. And partly because he's a big strong Marine and we needed people. He works hard. Jordan likes him." At Cash's scowl, Reid said, "But not that much. She did put him down when he insulted you. She put him down hard."

Cash nodded. "She did, didn't she?"

"Yeah. Cash, you love her, right?"

"I guess." What would she think if she knew he was some bastard's love child? Wait. No. He was a bastard and his mother's love child.

"Does she love you?"

It was on the tip of Cash's tongue to ask, "How could she?" But that would be selling Jordan short. One thing he'd learned about the woman. She knew her own mind. "I don't know. I hope so."

"I like her. She's solid and cute, and she says the funniest things. Like how great the Army is." Reid grinned, and Cash found himself smiling with him. "Talk to Jordan. She's not a part of our fucked-up family. See what she thinks about this whole mess. And, Brother, whatever you do, don't screw up your future because Angela screwed up your past."

Chapter 22

HOURS LATER, CASH KEPT THINKING ABOUT WHAT REID had said as he waited at a seedy bar downtown for the punk, Juan, to show up. He hadn't answered Jordan's texts except to tell her not to expect him back until later.

He wanted to talk to her, yet he didn't. For the same reason he refused to allow her to tell him how she felt about him. If she told him she loved him, he'd talk himself out of believing her. Because how could a woman as amazing as Jordan love a loser like him? What did that say about her?

And if she didn't love him, that would just break him.

So, yeah, he was mental and unable to deal with much more than hurting someone. This meeting with Juan could not have come at a better time.

He held the baggie of drugs in his pocket. He hadn't brought his pistol, though he'd thought about it. The gun would only provide a temptation to use it. More of a mess he didn't need.

Since Ritter's info had insisted Juan Williams had no connection to WSW, Cash figured the kid either wanted to get noticed and invited to join the gang, or he'd been talking out his ass to impress his buddies at school. Either way, pressuring Rafi to join him wasn't happening.

A glance around the bar, also not a WSW hangout, showed some older guys, four around Cash's age and a half dozen more much older, keeping to themselves.

Some of them played pool, while three of them sat at the bar, flirting with the tough chick behind the bar and the barfly who looked like she needed a shower, stat.

But her sly smiles and slight belly exposed by her barely there top didn't seem to bother the guys ogling her. Hell, if her skirt was any shorter, they'd call it a thong.

He shuddered, wanting out of this place. He needed to feel clean, to see Jordan's smirk and hear her laughter, grounding him. Instead, he sat at a booth in the corner and toyed with his beer, his eyes scoping the place for danger.

Three of the guys near the pool tables kept him in their sights, so he subtly did the same.

A cocky little bastard having Juan's description strutted into the bar with four friends, all looking like rich high school dropouts. Cash recognized the pricey haircuts and shoes. He knew all about wearing hand-me-downs. He also knew castoffs never looked that good, so the used-looking clothes these kids wore no doubt came from some designer trying to make a statement.

Cash stood and met the kid and his friends halfway. "You Juan Williams?"

"Yeah." Juan sneered at him. "Who wants to know?"

After a cautious glance around, which showed him pretty much the bar pretending not to pay them any attention, Cash held out the baggie to Juan. "These are yours. Rafael Younger belongs to me."

Juan raised his brows. "Oh? You muscling in on the West Side Wolves, fuckhead?"

A few guys near the back turned their full attention to them.

Cash bit back a sigh. "Try again, you little punk. First

of all, no one here is messing with WSW. You're not a player, and you're sad trying to be one. My advice to you is to leave before the Wolves hear you're using their name to sell product. Rafi is out. He never wanted in, and if your buddies were smart, they'd get the hell out too. From what I hear, Toto and crew are no one to mess with."

The big guys by the back settled down at that. Cash would have to tell Ritter that his intel might not be the best. Seemed like WSW had ears in a lot of places.

"I never said I was WSW," Juan said quickly, glancing around. "I'm not dumb enough to deal with them. I know Lasko's brother. I'm just helping Rafi out."

"By trying to force him to sell drugs? Kid, go back to school, take that payout from your rich mommy and daddy, and stick your nose in a book. Selling drugs is asking for trouble. And you sure as shit don't want to get into a gang. Watch the news. The cops are all over those guys. It's only a matter of time before WSW gets dragged to jail or shot by a rival gang. It's too high for your pay grade, son. So take your fancy stash and blow."

"Fuck you." Juan nodded to his friends. "I'm friends with WSW. And you just made a big mistake."

Before his closest buddy could bring out the item from behind him, Cash pounced. He had the kid jacked up and the kid's gun in hand in seconds. So not what he'd intended by trying to get Rafi out of trouble.

"Look, Juan. Guns are trouble." He shoved the boy he'd taken the gun from, ejected the magazine, and emptied the chambered round in seconds. Then he tossed the gun to the floor. "With one punch I can dislocate your jaw before your second boy there grabs his gun. And when he tries to shoot me, I'll be using you as a shield, so he'll end up shooting through you first. Dead is dead. Don't be stupid. Get lost and quit selling drugs. It's not often in life you get a second chance."

Three of the boys with Juan bolted for the door. No one stopped them. But the boy he'd disarmed backed up with Juan, who pulled a gun of his own. His arm shook as he sighted in on Cash.

But the little bastard hadn't released the safety.

Cash walked right up to him as the kid kept trying to shoot, aware that they now had everyone's attention. The kid next to him tried to punch him, but Cash deflected the punch easily and shoved the boy away. He grabbed the gun out of Juan's hand. Then he bitch-slapped him.

"That's for pulling the trigger." He looked to the bartender. "I don't suppose you could call the cops on these little assholes?"

She popped her gum. "Nope."

Cash sighed. "Fine. I'll do it."

"Uh, not a great idea," she said and nodded to the group by the pool table, who looked tense and not at all happy at the idea of police.

"Fuck. Okay. No cops." Everyone settled down. "I don't suppose you could refuse the kids service if they showed up again?"

She nodded. "Oh, that we can do. We don't like guns in the bar, you little assholes. That brings trouble." A large bald man appeared from a room behind the bartender. "Lane will show you out."

Cash frowned. "He's not gonna hurt them, is he? I mean, they're stupid, but they're teenagers."

She sighed. "Lane, don't hurt them. But we will be

keeping the guns and the baggie as collateral, should you idiots ever come here again."

Cash couldn't be sure she wasn't including him in her warning. "I'm leaving too, no worries."

She winked at him. "Nah, you can stay, sweetheart. I like 'em big."

The guys at the bar laughed. The barfly whistled. "Me too."

Lane hauled the kids by their collars outside. Someone collected the guns. And then the bar returned to normal.

Before Cash could leave, one of the big guys from the pool tables neared him. Just great.

"Hey, we want to talk to you in the alley."

"Why?"

"Please." The man who smiled showed a gold tooth.

Cash realized he wouldn't be leaving without a fight. But not wanting to involve more people than he had to, he sighed and reached into his pocket. He'd left his phone ready should he need help. And it looked like he'd be needing that after all. He hit a button before turning his phone silent, alerting Ritter to send help, ASAP.

"Fine." Cash followed Gold Tooth, aware the guy's two large friends walked at his back. They pushed through the doorway, and he found himself shoved up against the wall getting patted down. They turned him around, each thug pinning one of his arms to the brick wall. A workingman's crucifixion, he thought with ill humor.

At least he'd been smart enough not to bring his wallet. But he had his phone. Or he'd *had* his phone.

Now Gold Tooth tried to scroll through it but got stuck at the authentication.

"Hey, what's your password?"

The other two men had height and muscle, but nothing Cash couldn't handle unless they turned out to be ninjas or MMA types. One was bald and wore a red shirt. The other had a cap of dirty brown hair and wore blue.

The alley was empty and dark, barely lit by an overhead streetlight. There was a dumpster to the right, and trash littered the tarmac; the scent of stale beer and vomit made the place altogether unpleasant.

"What is this about?"

Gold Tooth scowled. "I said I need your password."

"No. I'm not a cop. Not gang-affiliated. I just came to deliver a message to some wannabes. So what's the problem?"

Gold Tooth shook his head. "The problem, cowboy, is that this is our bar. And we like WSW. We didn't like what you said about them being in jail or shot up. We want you to say you're sorry." He smiled.

Red Shirt. "Yeah, say you're sorry."

He had horrible breath. Cash cringed, and Blue Shirt laughed as well. "Scared?"

"Of his breath," Cash muttered, to which Blue Shirt laughed again.

"I like this guy."

"I don't." Red Shirt frowned.

Blue Shirt hit Cash in the gut. A love tap. "Better, Jim?"

"A little." Jim—Red Shirt—grinned.

"Look, I'm sorry." Cash sighed. "There. We good now?"

The thugs holding him froze and looked back at Gold Tooth, apparently not having expected him to cooperate.

Gold Tooth blinked. "What? Oh, ah, yeah. That's right, you're sorry. Fucker."

Cash was really tired of all this. His mother's revelation, worries about Jordan, Rafi, now this? He'd had too much to handle all day. And he needed the fight. "You know what? I *am* sorry. Sorry Jim here smells he like blew a zombie and swallowed some bad jizz. Sorry that gold tooth in your watermelon-sized head is fucking with the tiny signals trying to get to your brain. Sorry that Blue Shirt can't hit worth a damn. No doubt he can't swing more than that tiny dick—"

Cash lunged out of their holds before a metal pipe made contact with his head. *Jesus.* He didn't think his brain could take another bashing so soon. Gold Tooth swung again and managed to hit Jim in the back.

It would have been comical if he'd seen Blue Shirt's punch to his ribs. Or if he could have avoided that kick to his knee...

After his visit to the bar Sunday evening, Cash realized his arm had to be broken, the pain super intense and not getting any better. So Monday he'd spent several hours at the hospital getting his arm taken care of—the splint and sling were such a bitch—then hung out at Ritter's place after debriefing the guy.

By noon Tuesday, Cash knew he'd put it off as long as he could. He'd already texted an apology to Jordan, explaining he'd gotten some bad news at his mom's and was trying to deal with it. He'd also texted Reid because his little brother could be such a pain in the ass with all the worrying.

And then he'd texted Evan because with Cash's injuries, he'd be out a few weeks and wouldn't be able to help anyone move anything—according to the doctor. But Cash figured after a few days managing the pain and finally getting a damn cast, he'd get back to packing and moving small boxes at least.

He'd intended to avoid work, but Reid had threatened to sic Naomi, Aunt Jane, and Evan on him if Cash didn't show his face sooner than later. That little fink Rafi had told Reid a few things he should have kept to himself.

Cash knew the crew would be mostly out on the job, but he still did his best to scout around before parking his car and entering the Vets on the Go! building. It probably hadn't been too smart to arrive at noon, during lunch, but most of the gang ate when working, so he figured lunch to be as safe as it could get. With any luck, Reid would be out too and Cash could leave a message with Dan, face to face. Then Dan could tell Reid that Cash had nothing more than a busted arm, softening the news before Cash delivered it in person.

At the top of the stairs, he took a moment, as his bruised ribs protested. He held his left arm closer to his body, hating the necessary immobility, and walked quietly down the hallway.

Unfortunately, one of the geeky computer repair guys standing outside his repair shop saw Cash and gasped. "Hell, man. What truck ran you over?"

"Yeah, right? Can you believe it was a fight over an apology? Some women don't like it unless you're on your knees then unconscious."

The guy's eyes widened. "A *woman* did that to you?"

"You know the short, pretty one with the dark hair who works with us?"

The guy nodded, still gaping at Cash's cast and black eye.

"Well, I still love her, but I won't ever piss her off again. All I'm saying."

The guy nodded. "Good idea." He swallowed loudly then darted back into his shop.

His mood restored, Cash continued to the end of the hallway. Inside the office, he found it empty except for Dan working the front desk. Fortunately, Cash wouldn't be upsetting any customers with his injuries.

"Damn, son. What the hell ran you over?" Gunny Dan Thompson, their octogenarian admin expert, who they couldn't do without, shook his head. "Marines, always in the thick of things. Don't suppose we'll be seeing more calls because of this, will we?"

The last time Cash had been in a violent altercation, he'd been filmed saving a kid from a burglary. The business had gotten substantial PR from it, and they'd been busy ever since. Although, come to think of it, Cash had beaten a few assholes since then. Namely, a few guys at Jameson's Gym, right before he'd gone at it with Reid. And then, sure, Elliot's assholes. Hmm. Maybe he did have a tendency to fight a lot…

"And a head wound? You're not answering me." Dan sighed. "Your brother's gonna have a field day with you."

Cash grinned. "I'm sure."

"You want something to eat, kid? I just ordered some sandwiches for us. I can add one for you."

"Could you? Some meat would be good."

"I have you covered."

"Thanks, Gunny."

Dan smiled. He loved when the guys called him Gunny. Like Cash and Reid, he'd cherished his time in the service and missed it since he retired. But around everyone at Vets on the Go!, it felt like a special branch of the military still existed. A bunch of veterans who loved their country and their respective services. It felt like…home.

Cash paused before going through the door to Reid's office, hoping he wouldn't soon be home*less*.

Taking a breath, but not too deep to cause more pain, he opened the door and went inside. And froze when he saw Jordan, Naomi, Reid, and Evan in deep discussion.

Jordan stared at Cash in shock. She'd been ready to read him the riot act since Rafi had confessed everything to her last night.

Talk about not having one of her better days. Between busting his teacher's balls, getting the guy suspended, having a last-minute panic attack because she'd committed herself to moving in with her boyfriend, and then learning Rafi had been involved with drugs, she was entitled to be a little nutty.

And Cash—nowhere to be found.

So she'd been ready to chew him up and spit him out, only to have Reid sit her down and explain a few things.

Now, though still angry, she also wanted to protect and offer comfort to the man she loved, who had to be hurting. Hurting a lot, she saw, staring in shock.

"What the fuck happened to you?" she barked.

Evan blinked. "Ah, now I understand about filling in. Cash, sit down." Evan left his seat and gently guided Cash to it.

Cash did his best not to complain, but Jordan saw his wince and felt the rage bubble up. She'd crush whoever did this to Cash. Then she'd tear into him... Oh screw it. She'd hit Cash first.

Verbally. "This came from the drugs, didn't it?"

She should have thought that through first because after the room silenced to a funereal hush, everyone started talking at the same time.

"Cash, not again." Reid scowled. "What did we say about being smart? What all did you break?"

"Oh my God!" That was Naomi. "You poor thing. Who did that to you? Do you need some ice?"

"That's gotta hurt." Evan leaned against the wall. "I'm so glad I'm not you."

Jordan glared at her lover. Her boyfriend. The asshole who'd stolen her heart. "You lied to me, and we promised to be honest with each other." That got everyone quiet.

"It's not my fault." Cash refused to meet her gaze, with his good eye at least. The other was still swollen and purple.

"It's never your fault," she snapped. "I've been talking to Reid. I know all about you, buddy."

That must have been the wrong thing to say because he whipped his head up and glared back at her with his good eye. "Oh yeah? What do you know?"

"Jordan, maybe—" Naomi tried.

But Jordan cut her off, too worried and mad to be cautious. "I trusted you. And then you went behind my back and got involved with my brother?"

"I was helping him. Just like you asked me to."

Jordan hated that Cash had been hurt, as much as she hated that he hadn't trusted her to handle her brother's mess on her own. "How are you helping him? By nearly getting killed?"

"No, damn it." He tried to stand and sank back down, his expression agitated.

"What if you'd taken Rafi with you? He'd be looking like you right now."

"Seriously? You think I'd take a kid into a dangerous situation?" As soon as he said it, he looked around at everyone staring at him. "I mean—"

Everyone talked at once again, this time yelling at Cash.

He motioned for Evan, who helped him up while chastising him.

"Shut up!" Cash yelled.

But Jordan refused to be cowed. "You could have been killed!"

"You have no idea what happened, so don't tell me shit."

She didn't like his attitude. "Well, genius, tell us. Did you walk into a door or what?"

He snarled at her. "I went in place of Rafi because I thought it might get rough. And I was right!" Then he pointed at Reid. "And you, don't even think of blaming me for this. I didn't try to get my ass handed to me because I wanted to play mind games with you. I got jumped by three guys in an alley, okay?"

Reid held up his hands. "Hey, I'm concerned about you. Don't blame me for being worried."

Jordan poked him in the chest, and he gasped at the pain. "*I* blame you! You should have come to me. Instead I had to hear this from my brother after the fact!" She couldn't help the tears in her eyes. "You want us to live together and tell me you love me, and you do something like this. We're either a team or we're not!" She was so angry she feared poking him again, so she stormed out of Reid's office. But before she could leave the Vets on the Go! space, Cash yanked her back into the lobby.

Dimly aware of the others fanning into the space around them, she had to endure Cash's death glare all on her own. "Trust you? Love you? Of course I do. I also know you. And the first thing you'd have done if you found out about Juan and Rafi and that baggie of drugs is go to the police. Then you'd be dealing with Rafi on charges of possession. And the kid's got enough to worry about without a record."

"No, I—"

"I told him I'd help him. I did."

"You should have trusted me to help!" It hurt so much he hadn't.

"Bullshit. If you by some stretch didn't call the cops, you'd have wanted to go with me."

"Oh, and I can't handle my little girlie self? Please. I can handle—"

"You'd have distracted me and given them a target." He scowled. "I disarmed Juan's friend, and I disarmed Juan when the little shit tried to shoot me. But guess what, Jordan? The bar didn't call in the cops. Because places like that don't. Not everyone sees things in black and white, baby. Deal with it."

She drew in a breath and didn't know what to say or do, she was so mad.

"And then some assholes with ties to a gang wanted me outside. So I went, and I handed them their asses.

The only reason I have this"—he motioned to his splinted arm—"is because one of them blindsided me with a lead pipe to the arm. I have this habit of not seeing the danger until it's on top of me." He loomed over her. "Like you. What? I made a mistake, and now you don't want me anymore?"

The anger and hurt in his voice shook her. Where had he gotten the notion she no longer wanted him?

"Well, fuck you. I still love you, and it's worse than this damn broken arm because it's probably never gonna heal right!"

He had the nerve to walk away from her and everyone with an "I'm on a break!" shouted over his shoulder.

She followed him down the hall and dragged him to a stop. "No, uh-uh. You don't get to just walk away. I'm not done."

"Whatever, say your piece." He turned and watched her with a sneer that looked right at home on his face. Or on Smith's.

What Reid had confirmed still floored her. The question she'd been dying to ask, about Smith's resemblance to Cash and his animosity being a little too off, might have some roots in the family drama Reid wasn't ready to discuss yet, but he'd welcomed her to ask Cash about it.

A tale of family secrets right up there with the best dramas on TV.

"You know why you're an asshole? Because you didn't trust me enough to talk to me first."

"Rafi knew as well as I did that—"

"Rafi is fifteen years old! What's your excuse?"

He didn't like hearing that. She poked him again, not even sorry seeing his wince.

"I would never jump into danger without talking to you. And I wouldn't do something that involved your family without talking to you first."

"What family?"

"Reid, you jackass." She poked him again, lighter this time, but to make a point. "I know about your mom and dad. I know you had a shitty life. But don't even try putting this on me."

"Please." He snorted. "You've never even told me how you feel."

"Are you serious?" She threw her hands up in the air and let out an angry laugh.

Across the hall, the door opened. A computer repair guy, Tom, she thought, poked his head out, saw her, and quickly closed the door.

"I never told you how I feel because any time I *try*, you stop me and tell me to think about it. To wait. Because you can't hear the truth? Or because you don't want it? Look, I'm sorry your mom was so crazy, that your dad isn't your dad, that you have family drama coming out the ass." She was pulling no punches. "I love you, you asshole. And for you to think I'd just walk away because you made a mistake? What the hell is that?"

He blinked at her, his glare fading.

"I trusted you with my fears. With my family. I love you, and you treat me like shit."

"What? I, no, I—"

"I deserve to be a man's equal partner. We're lovers in every way that matters or we're not at all. In case it's escaped your notice, King of the Ass..." A lame insult but she was so angry she had a tough time coming up with words. "…*I* still love *you*. But I'm so mad at you now *I* need a break!"

She left him standing there and was nearly to the stairwell when she heard a meek voice say, "Don't worry, man. We called the cops. She can't hurt you and get away with it. Not on our watch."

Men. They were all insane.

Chapter 23

CASH HAD ROYALLY FUCKED UP. BUT HE WAS SO DAMN happy Jordan hadn't broken things off he felt giddy. *She loves me.*

"Easy, guy. Come on back with me." Evan put a shoulder under his good arm and walked him back to Reid's office.

Naomi waited until he sat then pecked Cash on the cheek with a chaste kiss. "Get well, sweetie. Maybe your painkillers can help with all the male stupidity." She waved at Reid and Evan then left.

Cash sat staring at his brother and cousin. "Did Jordan say she loves me?"

"Yep, he's an idiot. Definitely your brother." Evan shook his head and sighed. "Cash, what happened to you?"

Cash slowly explained the whole of it, ending with, "So I wasn't trying to be a superhero. One of the assholes nailed me with a pipe before Ritter and his cop buddy showed. I just wanted to save Rafi some hassle. The poor kid has been through a lot."

Reid nodded. "Jordan told us. But why didn't you ask one of us to back you up?"

Cash looked from Reid to Evan and laughed until he had to stop from rib pain. "Sorry. That's like taking a virgin into dragon territory. They'd have roasted you alive. Besides, Evan looks like a cop."

Evan perked up. "I do?"

"Evan." Reid shook his head. "It's like trouble just finds you, Cash."

"I know." Cash eased into his seat. "Think she'll forgive me?"

"I don't know if I forgive you for not having me there to help, but you can pay it out in trade." He cleared his throat. "Naomi and I are going to live at her place starting in September. So I need your rent until the end of August."

"Wow. That's only two more months."

"I know." Reid groaned. "I have to tell Chris we're moving out. I don't know if I can do it yet. Moving in with Naomi... That's a big step."

"One Cash already decided to make with Jordan, apparently," Evan commented. "And then he questioned her commitment by not telling her about the situation her brother was in. Interesting way to show her how much you care, Cash."

Cash swore and asked the question a second time, "Think she'll forgive me?"

Evan nodded. "But it'll involve a lot of groveling."

"I don't know." Reid looked pensive, and Cash tensed. "She was really mad. Worse, she was hurt. She thinks you didn't trust her about something that involved her own family. And sometimes women don't forgive stuff like that."

"Fuck. Really?" Cash had figured he'd try charming her out of her anger. Maybe let her pick out their new dining room table or something. That's if she still wanted to move in together.

"Look, the woman agreed to live with you," Reid said. "She tolerates you on your worst days. You guys have worked well together from the first, and anytime anyone tries to talk bad about you, Jordan is there defending you."

Evan agreed. "You should have seen her handle Smith after he insulted you. It was awesome."

"Then you take her family problems and decide to handle them yourself because you don't think she'll handle them the right way." Reid emphasized, "*Her* way."

"Yeah, but—"

"But nothing. It's her brother, her family. How would you feel if she'd seen Mom's journal, read it, then decided to make peace between you and Smith because that's how she thinks you should handle it?"

Cash's gaze darted to Evan.

"Cash, I've suspected the whole 'other dad' thing for a long time. I don't care either way." Evan grinned. "But, man, can you not see how alike you and Smith are? It's weird."

Reid shrugged. "I see it, but it could also be a big coincidence."

"Take off the blinders, Reid." Evan shook his head.

Cash dreaded the idea of Smith as a brother. He didn't like the guy. "Damn. You think he knows?" Even worse. "Does Jordan know?"

Reid answered, "When I told her you'd had some unsettling information over the weekend concerning our mom, she asked me about Smith. I think she sensed a connection there. But she never said anything because she knew it bothered you." Reid paused then twisted the knife. "Apparently she thinks you should handle your personal business. She stayed out of it."

Cash groaned. "Hell. I know I fucked up."

"Yep." Evan crossed his arms over his chest. "So fix it. That woman is amazing. You know it; we know it. She puts Mariah to shame, and she's nice. We like her."

"Huh?"

"Yeah." Reid smiled. "Evan and I like her. We're cool with her becoming family."

"Wait. Family?" Cash glanced at Evan again, a pang of depression that Evan no longer belonged to him.

"Oh stop." Evan sighed. "Cash, you're so obvious. I've always considered you more like a brother than a cousin. I still do. And when Mom hears about this, she'll be thrilled. She never liked Uncle Charles. And to be honest, neither did Dad, and Charles was his brother."

"Ha. I wondered." Reid grinned. "Good old Aunt Jane."

"She used to talk about trying to adopt you guys all the time. She mentioned it to your mom once. That was the only time your mom put her foot down. Aunt Angela said you were her kids and for my mom to butt out of your lives."

"She did?" Reid frowned. "That's surprising."

"Yeah." Evan paused and said to Cash, "You know, I can ask my mom if you want. But I don't think she ever knew for sure you weren't Uncle Charles's. Like I said, she and I don't care either way. You're family. As pathetic as you and Reid are—"

"Hey." Reid frowned.

"You're family." Evan turned to Reid. "So him being broken moves up my timeline. I'll give my notice immediately, do some work from home, and I can help fill in for the hardhead for a while."

Reid looked relieved. "I have a few standbys we can

use until Cash is back too. But with you filling in, we shouldn't be hurting. I can pull some time as well to cover moves. My wrist is just about healed up." From a break not too long ago. Reid's cast had come off just last week.

Evan shook his head. "Sure it is, hard head. I'll do it. You save your hands for typing and answering phones."

Cash realized what his cousin had said. "Wait. So you're seriously quitting your job? For me?"

"Well, quitting *earlier* for you. But I'm actually quitting for me. I'm done with the accounting firm. I want to be my own boss for a while." Evan smiled, looking pleased. "Just saying that makes me happy."

"Just remember to pay yourself for your time. It's not much, but you'll earn it," Reid insisted.

"Seeing as I'm our bookkeeper, I know exactly how much we can afford," Evan reminded him then laughed. "I'm giving myself a raise."

"Ha ha." Cash's mind was on Jordan and how to make things right. "Ah, since I'm no use here, I think I should go home, think, and rest."

"Or just rest. Thinking doesn't seem to be your strong suit lately," Evan not-so-helpfully pointed out.

Cash shot him the finger. "How's that for thinking?"

Evan laughed.

Dan knocked on the doorway. "Sorry to interrupt, but there's a cop out here waiting to take a statement about some kind of domestic dispute? Something about a woman abusing one of ours?"

Cash groaned. "Oh, for fuck's sake. I was kidding."

"Huh?" Dan pushed back his ball cap to scratch his head. "Oh, and you owe me twenty bucks for the sandwiches. And three for the Tums. You guys are giving me ulcers."

-------◆-------

Once Cash had dealt with the officer, who took his "misinterpreted" story about an "abusive" Jordan in good humor and left, Cash went home. With Reid for real moving in with Naomi soon, Cash needed to get the mess of his life together. And first on that list was talking to Jordan… Just as soon as he took a nap because he could barely hold two thoughts together.

He woke to feel someone watching him. Praying it was Jordan, he slowly opened his eyes, thinking carefully about what to say.

Except when he opened his eyes, he saw Rafi standing in the corner of his room.

Cash focused. Light streamed through the window, so it couldn't have been too late. He tried to rise too quickly, forgetting how much his ribs ached, and groaned.

Rafi looked upset. "Need help?"

Cash shook his head. "Nah. I need to get used to this." Slowly, he rolled to his good side, sat up to put the sling back on, and somehow managed to land on his feet after pushing off the bed. Once standing, it took him a minute to get his bearings. After fighting off dizziness, he took a few steps toward the doorway.

"Want some tea?" Rafi asked.

"Tea? No thanks."

Rafi shrugged. "You seem to like tea a lot, so I thought I'd ask. Can I get you something else? You're supposed to be relaxing."

"I guess I could eat."

Rafi smiled. "Okay. Go sit on the couch, and I'll get you a sandwich."

Oddly comforted by the kid's presence, because Jordan couldn't be *too* mad at him if she let her brother hang around, Cash sank into the couch and rested his arm on a bolster. It helped to elevate it. He turned on the TV and flipped through the channels before settling on some B-horror movie while wondering how next to deal with Jordan.

Rafi appeared with two plates. He set one in front of Cash and kept the other for himself.

"Peanut butter?" Cash asked.

"And jelly. With a side of chips."

The boy had made two sandwiches for him, Cash was happy to see. "Sounds good." They ate in silence until Rafi asked if he wanted anything to drink.

"You don't have to wait on me."

"You're an invalid. Besides, I owe you."

"Well now. You're damn right you do."

The boy flinched. "I'm sorry. I didn't know you'd get hurt."

"You narced me out to my brother *and* your sister. After you pinkie promised!"

"They broke your arm. I—"

"Hey, Rafi. Pay attention. The injuries are nothing. But Jordan is really pissed at me."

Rafi paused. "You're not mad about getting beat up?"

Cash grimaced. "It was one against three, and for the record, *I* beat *their* asses. Plus this didn't happen because of Juan. It happened because three assholes who should have minded their own business didn't." Four assholes including him, but whatever. "So yeah, you owe me because your sister thinks I don't trust her. Where is she, anyway?"

"She's at Mom and Dad's. She's staying there." Rafi swallowed. "I told her I'd watch out for you."

"What the hell, man? I thought you didn't narc."

Rafi sighed. "I'm sorry I told her about Juan. But after hearing you got hurt, I felt terrible. I need to fight my own battles. The ones I can win at least." He gave a shy smile. "I did what you said and told Jordan about that teacher. She went to school yesterday and ripped him a new asshole."

Cash grunted. "Damn straight. Your sister doesn't play around."

"It was awesome. She tried to talk to him in private outside the classroom. But he saw me and tried to act like a big man in front of all the students. Then Jordan showed him up, let him have it, curse words included." Rafi's smile blinded him, and Cash wished he'd been there to see it shake down. "She told him he was a poor excuse for a teacher and threatened to report him for it. When he tried to pretend it never happened, one kid told us he'd recorded it and sent Jordan the file. She went straight to Simpson's boss. His ass is out on suspension."

Cash held up his good hand and contained a wince when Rafi high-fived it, shifting Cash's ribcage. "Awesome, man."

"It was so great. Some of the kids told me they felt bad for me and missed me. I guess I thought I was the only loser there, but a lot of them hated Simpson too. Nobody wants to be in summer school." He chuckled. "Plus they liked I had the balls to call him Homer to his face."

"That was funny. But you'd better not dis your teachers again or your sister will crush you under her little Army boots."

Rafi nodded.

"What's the deal with you moving back home?"

"After she and I talked, we went to see my mom and dad." He told Cash all about the talk he'd had with Jordan and his folks. "It turned out okay. They do love me, but I'm still not going to that military camp."

"Your sister is so badass." Cash loved her more with every story. She stood up for those she loved, never backing down. To have someone like that in his corner... To know that a woman of value could feel like that for a guy like him? It meant everything.

"Yeah. She, um, she's not happy with you." Rafi groaned. "I know, I should have kept my big mouth shut. But I overheard her talking to Mom."

"And?"

"She was talking to Mom about you. And she's into you, man. Or at least, she was." Rafi winced. "I think you hurt her feelings."

"Not more talk about trust. Jesus. I wanted to keep her safe." He frowned. "And, okay, I should have told her about you and Juan. I was wrong." Man, had that hurt to say.

"Maybe you could apologize? I'm moving back home, so it's just you and Jordan in your new big house. I'm pretty sure she still thinks you're hot shit, even if you are a Marine."

"Funny."

"I know. But seriously. She was asking Mom a lot of questions. And some of that was about living with someone who doesn't value you and if, like, a guy really respects you as a woman if he walks all over you. It didn't sound too good."

"Shit."

"I think you need to make a big apology. Trust me, my sister loves hearing the words 'I'm sorry.'"

"I was thinking I'd make a big production out of a date. I'll grovel and beg her to take me back. I look pretty pathetic. I think I can work with that."

"You do look weak." Rafi looked him over. "Pretty lame."

"Smartass."

The kid smirked. "Hold on." He left and came back with a piece of paper. "See if you can do this again."

Cash glanced at the paper and stared in awe. "What the hell?"

"I drew that of you guys after that night I saw you hugging. Remember? You asked if I wanted tea."

Cash stared. The picture appeared almost lifelike, done in pencil. A rendition of him holding Jordan in his arms and looking down at her like he loved her. "You're fucking incredible."

"Ah, that's just a rough draft." The boy blushed. "I can do better."

"No. I like this. You gonna let me have it?"

"Sure. But I really can do better. That lovesick look on your face was pretty unforgettable though." Rafi watched him with deep-brown eyes just like his sister's. "You have a crush on Jordan, don't you?"

"Nope. I love her. That's much different than a crush." Each time he admitted his feelings out loud, they became more real, the ache in his heart heavier.

"Oh man. I knew it. But at least if you come to family dinners, they'll be more fun than dealing with Troy."

"Mr. Teeth?"

Rafi chuckled. "That's him."

"So help me out with Jordan. You know what she likes. I was thinking flowers and chocolates. You know, girlie stuff. But I'll romance it up. And, no, you don't need all the details."

"No, I really don't. Though looking at you, if you can manage to kiss her without falling down, it'll be a miracle."

"You know, even with one arm, I'm pretty sure I can kick your ass."

"If you're kicking ass with one arm, that's probably how you're losing your fights."

Cash laughed until he groaned. "You are *so* like your sister."

"Thanks."

"You're welcome."

───※───

Jordan hadn't said so, but work Wednesday felt odd without Cash there. Rumor had it Evan would be stepping in for the next few weeks. Apparently the walking wounded needed time to recover. *Yeah, time to put his brains back in and think before he speaks.*

She wanted to sock him in the mouth then kiss the sting better. So many conflicting feelings about the Marine. She loved him; she wanted to kick him. She missed him; she wanted to keep her distance and figure out her feelings.

Next to her, Smith worked like an automaton. She couldn't help herself and had cornered him earlier in the morning to ask if he was in fact related to Cash by blood.

His blunt "Yes, and it's none of your business," uttered so quietly and with so much bottled-up pain, had made her drop the subject then and there.

Hours later, she still couldn't help thinking about Cash's strained family ties.

Now, knowing what she did about the relationship, she too clearly saw the similarities. Both big, brawny men. They had similar facial features and coloring, and those killer dark-green eyes under slashing brows. Also, despite Smith's grumpy nature, he'd never done anything to make her feel unsafe. Even when he'd grabbed her in the bar, he hadn't done more than annoy her. Just like Cash, making her feel protected.

"Quit staring at me," he grumbled as he stacked another box. "It's creepy."

"Such a lovely manner you have. Did they teach you that in the Marine Corps?"

He bared his teeth in his semblance of a grin.

Next to her, Hector shook his head. "Something definitely crawled into his brain, ate the meat, and left a shit of an attitude."

She cringed. "Terrific image for me to take to lunch, Hector. Thanks so much."

He tapped her on the arm. "No problem, Little Army. Now quit flirting with Smith and get back to work."

"This is why no one likes you, Hector."

He smiled. "You know you love me."

The rest of the afternoon passed in a weird lull, with sporadic humor by the team and occasional derision from Smith. But it was as if everyone missed something. Or someone. Without Cash, the party seemed less than it should be.

Her phone rang at the end of the day. "Hey, Rafi. How are you?"

"Good." He lowered his voice. "Jordan, I think something's really wrong with Cash. I called Reid, and he came over, but Cash pretends around his brother, and Reid doesn't see it."

"He's a big boy. He can handle himself." He needed her.

But does he really? Needed her to…what? To accept him running her life because she was too stupid to make her own decisions?

Anger flared.

"Jordan, please." Rafi sounded desperate. "I'm afraid. And he's hurt because of me. I think he might not be right in the head."

She snorted with amusement.

"I'm serious," Rafi snapped, unlike his recent pleasant self. "I know you're having some problems with him. I get it. But, Jordan, what if he has some kind of head injury and dies? How are you going to feel about him then?"

Rafi disconnected and turned to the head case watching him. "She told me she'd be over in an hour."

"How'd she take it? The head injury and dying part was a nice touch."

Rafi nodded. "I thought so. Playing on her sympathy didn't work, but guilt did. Good luck tonight. You're gonna need it." Rafi grabbed his jacket and paused by the door when his phone pinged. Reid was waiting for him outside in his car. He read the text and grinned.

"Reid said to crawl to her on your knees. Because if you blow this, he's disowning you. Something about moving in with…Smith?"

"Fuck." Cash growled to himself then pointed at Rafi. "And don't you be saying 'fuck.' Don't swear in front of your sister."

"Got it. No fucks around Jordan."

"Right."

Rafi rolled his eyes. Cash wasn't paying attention to him anyway, no doubt nervous about dealing with Jordan. Rafi could relate. "I'll pray for you, Cash. Just… if you have to, cry. Nothing freaks out my sister more than some tears."

Cash blinked then gave him a wicked grin. "Thanks, kid. You're all right after all. Now get lost before you ruin my night."

Rafi left the house. How Cash thought he was going to seduce Jordan into a yes looking like death was anyone's guess. Then again, Jordan seemed to like them big and heroic, so maybe Cash's war wounds would win him a few prizes.

He met Reid's gaze and gave him a thumbs-up before getting in the car.

"Has he got a prayer?" Reid asked as he backed up.

"Only if my sister is desperate. But the good news is she's been hopeless for years. So maybe the big guy has a shot."

"That's positive thinking for you." Reid grinned.

Chapter 24

JORDAN KNOCKED AND WAITED THEN WALKED INSIDE WHEN she didn't hear anything. The door to Cash's home was unlocked, which wasn't like Cash.

Her brother had left for their parents' half an hour ago, needing to be home to talk to the educational therapist they'd arranged for him. They were still working with a specialist to diagnose his learning disorder. But now knowing of Rafi's issues, the therapist could figure out how to help him.

It still amazed her how much better Rafi acted after that big conversation with her and the family. So much tension from keeping secrets.

To her parents' credit, they'd done better the past two days about communicating. And her mother hadn't once, in any of their conversations, bugged her about her job.

"Cash? Hello?" Jordan continued into the house and stopped when she saw the kitchen island occupied by a bottle of wine and two glasses. A vase of red roses sat beside it with a card made out to *Jordan* propped against it.

She looked around. Still not seeing Cash, she opened the envelope.

I'M SORRY.

She liked the apology. And the roses and the wine.

In the living room, she saw a box of chocolates on

the table and another card next to a small, wrapped box. I'M SO SORRY.

Hmm. She liked this even better. After unwrapping the box, she found a coupon book of vouchers. One for a backrub. A few apologies on bended knee. Some groveling too. Oh, and of course, a bunch of sex coupons, courtesy of Cash Griffith. The big idiot. Behind all that, at the back and embossed in gold, there was a marriage proposal written in Cash's bold hand.

FOR WHEN YOU'RE READY, TURN IN FOR AN I DO.

Her heart stopped.

Okay, the rest had been nice. Appropriate and even funny. But a marriage proposal *in a voucher?* And so soon? "Cash," she yelled, not so amused by this game anymore.

She found him finally in his bedroom, noticing the neatness and lit candles. And the still body lying on the bed.

Worry set in. "Cash?" She moved toward him with dread, not seeing his chest rising or falling. Hell. What had Rafi said about a brain injury? "Cash, wake up!" she yelled as she reached him and felt for a pulse.

The speed with which he grabbed her wrist surprised her, and she tried to twist out of his hold, yanking him with her so that she fell over his body.

He groaned but didn't release her and said, his voice groggy, "Jordan?"

She peered into his eyes, now open and glazed with pain. "Oh shit. I'm all over you." She would have moved back, but he groaned again.

"Don't move, please."

She stayed still.

"Sorry. I was sleeping. I meant to be awake when you

came, but I think your sneaky brother drugged me with a pain pill to make me drowsy."

"Oh." She stayed still but knew she had to be hurting him, lying against his ribs. "Should I get up?"

"Slowly, okay?"

She gradually slid off him, taking care not to jostle his splint, and sat next to him on the bed, looking down. The swelling around his eye had lessened, but the color had deepened. His bruises had to hurt, and she knew his ribs and arm pained him.

And he'd gotten hurt trying to help her brother.

"I'm sorry," he whispered before she could berate him for getting himself injured again. "I respect you, okay? And if you had pulled some kind of interfering shit on me, I'd be pissed as hell."

"Well, okay." She had to admit, she liked him knowing he'd done wrong. "Will you do it again?"

"Yes and no. I'd help you or Rafi again, no question. But I'd tell you about it first."

She sighed. "You mean you'd *ask* if I wanted the help?"

"Huh? Oh, yeah. Ask. I'd definitely *ask* you."

She laughed. "I'm still angry with you."

"I deserve it. Damn, Jordan. I fucked up. But let me apologize, okay? Don't…" He cleared his throat. "Don't leave me."

She wanted to yell at him for thinking so little of her that she'd ditch him at the first sign of trouble between them. But hadn't he told her about his mother and another woman he'd loved? "Cash, I hate to break it to you, but you said I could have a cheap place to live. And that's worth its weight in gold."

"Oh. Yeah." He brightened. "Good."

"And I love you, you moron. Why would I leave you over your inability to make sound decisions? Because I'm pretty sure you'll keep messing up. If I leave you every time that happens, we'll be worse than Latoya and Roger." From his silly reality TV show.

His wide grin made her so damn happy. "Yeah, that's a good point." He looked her over as if memorizing her features. "I'm sorry I was an ass. I promise to communicate better."

"O-kay." Who was this Cash? "It's the brain injury making you sound different—sane—isn't it?"

He chuckled. "Probably. Why don't you kiss it better?"

She leaned close and kissed his cheek with a tenderness she felt deep inside, only for this man. Then she continued to kiss every bump and bruise she could see, and there were many.

"I feel better already."

"Liar." She lay down with him, careful not to hurt him. "But I accept your apology."

"Was it the 'I'm sorries,' the vouchers, or the flowers? The candy?"

"How about all of the above? And does it really matter?"

"Hell no. I'm just making sure I have the answer right now for when I screw up again." He kissed the top of her head. "Jordan, I missed you. When I thought you might leave, it about crushed me."

"You're an idiot."

"Yes, but I'm your idiot. You have to keep me. No one else will."

That he believed that nonsense bothered the heck out of her. "You're gorgeous, strong, and smart, and you protect people. Women are always eyeballing you, and everyone at work is in mourning because you're not there bossing them around."

"Yeah?"

She smiled against his chest. "Don't sound so happy about it. Even Smith was more mopey today than usual."

"God, don't mention him."

"You have to deal with him sometime."

"Yes, but not today."

She nodded. "Okay. Today is just for us."

"Help me up, would you?"

She got them both into a sitting position. When he patted his lap, she straddled his thighs and sat carefully so she could look into his eyes when she set the rules.

"Now, you shush and listen to me." She stared him down, waiting for him to nod. "I love you. Period. That means the good parts and the bad parts. And you said you loved me back."

"I—"

"Save all questions 'til the end, Marine."

He smiled and remained quiet.

"I'm not immature, irresponsible, or unintelligent. I make up my own mind, and I'm decisive. I've decided I want you. No one else. So this is what happens. We start living together. We make choices together. We talk, and when we argue—and with us, it'll be a lot—we always go to bed happy, no arguments between us. Good?"

He nodded. "Yes. I think—"

"Shut up." She bit her lip to contain her smile, especially when he frowned. "Swear to God, talk about failure to follow simple instructions."

He rolled his eyes, and she snickered.

"Now, as I was saying. This relationship is about respect. We've had this conversation, so I'm going to drop it. I say what I mean. No passive-aggressive crap is allowed in our relationship."

"Thank God."

"I'll allow that." She gave him a look, and he quieted but remained smiling. "I want us to be equals. That means we share money, we share chores, and we share bodies. I like fucking you."

He gave her the goofiest grin.

"I like loving you too. So no more talking down about yourself. If I can get over being unsure of myself for the first time in forever, then you can get over feeling like a loser. I don't date losers. And I sure as hell won't marry one."

"Yes, ma'am."

"Still talking. Friggin' Marine."

He ran his hand over her thigh.

"Stop that. You're in no condition for nookie."

He looked so sad she had to laugh. "No BJs either, not until you take a few days to heal. Then I'll blow your mind, okay?"

"How about cuddling?"

"Fine. Now shut up. I'm almost done."

He nodded.

"Cash, I love you. We both have issues, and together, we'll work them out. We will fight. We will make up. But we have to be open to screwing up. Note I'm tell this as much to myself as I am to you. It's tough not being the best right now. I'm a sucky civilian. But I can be a better one. I gave up my dream of retiring from the Army when I left. Now I need to figure out what I'm going to do with the rest of my life. But whatever I do, I want to do it next to you."

"Okay, Ms. Bossy. I'm done shutting up."

"Must have killed you to be quiet for all of four seconds," she muttered, thoroughly in love with her Marine.

"You love me. I love you. But you need to know what you're getting. I'll never cheat on you. I'll never betray you. I'll try really hard not to lie. Rafi made up the part about me having some kind of brain bleed. I'm fine."

"He's such a punk."

"I like the kid." He gripped her thigh. "Jordan, I love everything about you, and I never want you to change. I'll be with you every step of the way, no matter what. But you have to know. I'm not some snooty college guy and never will be. I'm blue collar and happy about it. Heck, I might be moving couches when I'm sixty. You gonna be okay with that? Because I doubt I'm ever going to be rich."

"If I decide to be rich, maybe I'll be the one making the money."

"Outstanding." He crooked his finger, so she leaned close. He kissed her. "I never want to go to bed mad either. I've still got a mess to sort out with Smith and my supposed real dad. My family is Reid—and soon Naomi—Evan and Aunt Jane. And you, of course. That's it."

"You'll meet my parents. You already know my lying, drug-pushing brother. And you'll end up meeting the perfect Leanne and Mr. Teeth."

"I can't wait. Sugar Boots, we'll take it slow. You and me, we have time. Let's get to know each other better. Live together, make love all over that damn house. Oh, and you have to help me with the furniture. Because we have none."

"Sounds fun. Just one thing."

"Whatever you want, it's yours."

"If I said your soul?" She arched a brow.

"Take it."

"So easy." She gave a fake cackle. "But seriously, that last voucher. You try proposing on paper or via text, it's over."

He nodded. "Got it. I just thought I'd put it in there so you know where I'm heading with all the flowers and chocolates. I'm seducing you into keeping me."

"Done."

"Man, and you said I was easy." He smiled.

Jordan felt as if she'd won the lottery.

Sometime later, as they watched Cash's favorite reality TV show while she fed him chocolates and a decadent lasagna he'd purchased to impress her, he brought up the topic she'd been expecting.

"So Smith admitted it? He's actually my brother?"

She nodded.

He was quiet for a moment before a slow smile crept over his face. "But more importantly, the entire crew misses me, eh?"

She snorted on laughter. "Yes, but I'm sure with Evan we'll make do." Which reminded her… "Did I tell you I've conned Evan into dealing with Miriam, our latest 'work problem'?" she ended in quotes. She explained the situation then gasped when he planted a kiss on her.

"Man, and you wonder why I love you. Just promise me you'll wait until I'm there to see it unfold."

"Of course I know why you love me. I'm Little Army, and I conquered Mount Griffith."

"You did indeed, my drama queen. Now shut up and watch. I think Michele's back for revenge."

She reached across him for the popcorn. "Oh, I can't wait."

———~~~———

Evan hadn't waited to give his notice. To his surprise, Vanessa had been nice about him leaving.

"We'll definitely miss you, Evan, but I understand. I'm taking weekends and early Fridays starting next week. I miss my baby girl and Cam." Her husband.

He'd stared in shock, and she'd laughed.

"What? I am human, you know. Call me if you need a reference, and don't be surprised if we shoot some clients your way. You're too good not to continue in the job."

"Thanks, Vanessa." They'd shaken hands a week ago, sealing the deal. Evan and the dragon lady, who'd realized what he had—that life could pass you by if you didn't stop and smell the...

"What is that smell?" he asked his cousin as he exited Reid's office. Someone must have had big plans for the evening. It smelled like the cologne counter at a department store.

Before Reid could answer, Cash entered the lobby, the crew waiting to welcome him back before they turned in for the day. Cash looked a lot better than the last time Evan had seen the guy. The shiner had faded, and only a light purple bruise underscored his eye. His arm was now in a cast and would be that way for the next eight weeks, but it was the way Cash walked, with purpose, not in pain, that showed he was on the mend. The light in his eyes as he rejoined his friends, and Jordan, was telling.

Here stood a guy who had everything. Evan envied him, but he knew Cash had more than earned it. Such a great man, one Evan was proud to call family.

As one, the group ignored the mostly sullen Smith, who lingered by the wall. Though Smith hadn't been hostile to Evan yesterday, during Evan's first move with Vets on the Go!, he hadn't been friendly either. Evan had no idea how Jordan got along with the guy, but then, she got along with everyone. He loved working with her because she was up front about procedures and didn't let anyone screw with the "new guy."

"Um, Evan?"

He glanced up to see everyone looking his way. "What?"

Hector sighed. "Reid, he has to. I saw the landlord talking to her yesterday. The guy glared at me in my Vets on the Go! shirt. I told you she hasn't forgiven or forgotten the situation."

Reid groaned.

Ah, yes. The Miriam's Modiste issue. Evan shook his head. "Are you serious? You told me you were going to handle it while I finished up at work last week."

"I'm sorry. I meant to." Reid ran a hand through his hair. "She sent me an email via her lawyer earlier. Hector's right. Can you go talk to her? I, ah, kind of told her I'd be sending someone to handle the situation."

Evan shook his head. "Show me the email."

Then Cash swaggered past. "I'll talk to her. I don't need a stupid email to make things right."

"Hell." Evan hustled past him and stopped Cash with a hand to his chest. "I got this. Go back into the office. All of you." He didn't turn to see if they obeyed. Instead he walked to Miriam's Modiste and pushed through the door.

"Hi. We're open and just getting ready to start in the back. Oh, hello, handsome. And what can I do for you?" asked a middle-aged woman in a diaphanous jade-green dress.

Evan blinked, feeling distinctly out of place, especially when he saw two women in bathrobes lie down on blankets in the back room. Distracted by what appeared to be a settee in the middle of the room, surrounded by those blankets, Evan murmured, "Reid sent me to solve your problem."

"Ah. I see." She smiled at him, and Evan had a feeling he'd stepped into something he shouldn't have.

Jordan and Cash exchanged a grin. The rest of the group joined them as they tiptoed down the hallway toward the still-open door of Miriam's.

Cash could see a hint of a gauzy green dress and Evan's pant leg. It was all he could do to suppress a laugh.

"Shh. Quiet, guys," Jordan told the group. "What's he saying?"

Cash put his ear closer to the slowly closing door and managed to hear Evan's surprise.

"Um, Miriam? Are you sure we should go into the back? I—Is that woman *naked* back there?"

Silence, some scuffling as the pair moved away. Then

Evan again. "Holy shit. Is this legal?" A pause. "What? No, I'm not taking my clothes off!"

Cash turned to Jordan and planted a big, wet kiss on her mouth. "I really, really love you."

Jordan laughed. "I know."

"Quick, he's coming out hot. Let's fly!"

—⁓—

They disappeared back down the hallway toward the office. But not before Evan caught sight of them. He sighed, both amused and annoyed he'd fallen like an easy mark.

"Damn. I guess I really am the FNG." The fucking new guy.

Someone reached around the door to the office and taped a piece of paper to the door.

WELCOME TO *VETS ON THE GO!*, NEWBIE!

Evan laughed. Ah well. Time to act the part.

And get even.

*Keep reading for a sneak peek at the next book in
Marie Harte's Veteran Movers series!*

Chapter 1

THE SIGHT THAT MET EVAN'S EYES HAD HIM STARING,
unsure of what to do. Though he owned part of his and
his cousins' local moving company, he'd only been
doing the grunt work of actually moving people for the
past two weeks. With one of his cousins temporarily out
due to an injury, Evan had willingly stepped in to take
up the slack.

At first, being able to get out from behind a desk,
away from a past life of accounting, had seemed a bless-
ing. Sure, he was still sore, taxing his muscles on a daily
basis doing manual labor, but he considered the physical
exertion to be just the thing to kick-start his new life.

No one had mentioned what to do when the client got
into a free-for-all in the middle of the living room.

The client, Rachel Kim, a petite Korean woman with

a soft demeanor and a cute dimple, was wrapped around a tall, statuesque black woman. Rachel had her in a headlock, clinging to her like a koala on a tree.

"I'm taking it!" she shrieked and refused to let go. "It's a memory, and it's mine!"

"Idiot, it's not yours," the other woman managed, gripping at the forearm across her neck. "It's *ours*! Ask Kenzie. Rachel, get off!" She swung around, and the two did an odd dance as the poor woman tried to shake her human burr. "Besides, you don't deserve it! Leaving me for a man? Way to idolize a penis, love slave."

O-kay. That was more than he wanted to hear. Evan had been hired to move Rachel's things, not involve himself in her private life.

"Shut up, Lila. You're just jealous! Backstabbing *bitch*." Rachel started going off in what sounded like Korean.

Lila choked, and Evan stepped forward. Then he realized she was laughing. Well, as much as one could laugh while gasping for oxygen. She continued to struggle for freedom to no avail.

Evan decided he should probably get involved before Lila passed out. But just as he took a step to separate the two women, sunlight beamed through the front windows, illuminating the avenging angel who stormed through the front door, her brown eyes blazing.

His world stopped. As if the woman had been bathed in radiance, she made everything around her pale in comparison. He found it difficult to breathe.

Long, light-brown hair floated around her shoulders, framing an attractive face full of life and emotion. She looked to be about his age, and she moved with grace and energy. "You two are being ridiculous," she huffed as she tried to pull Rachel and Lila apart. Dressed in ripped khaki shorts, a *Drink Local* T-shirt, and flip-flops, she shouldn't have appeared so impressive. But she did.

Evan just stood there, staring, trying to figure out what the hell was happening as his heart raced, his focus narrowed to this one incredibly arresting woman.

"Well?" the angel snapped at him. "You going to help me with these two or what?"

He started. "Oh, right." But he hadn't taken a breath before Rachel shifted to the new arrival, latching onto her and including her in the weird three-person tango.

"Nooo," Rachel moaned. "Everything is changing too fast."

Evan blinked, and the three women dissolved into tears, crumpled to the floor, and hugged one another. No one made any sense as emotions and a jumble of words, everyone talking over everyone, filled the air.

"Ah, you guys need help?"

They continued to wail, ignoring him, so he left them to their emotional crisis while he tried to figure out why he'd…panicked? Frozen? Lost his mind?

He'd once done the Heimlich on a choking man in a crowded restaurant while everyone else watched in shock. He'd prevented a young lance corporal from shooting his instructor at the rifle range during training back in his Marine Corps days. And he'd more than once talked down his oldest cousin from a fight, saving him from jail time and accompanying fines. Evan didn't panic, and he *always* knew what to do.

So why the hell had the sight of that woman frazzled him?

He walked out to the moving van, grabbed his water, and guzzled it. August in Seattle typically proved to be hot, but temps had been higher than normal, and the current heat wave had his shirt plastered to his back. The sun continued to blaze overhead, spotlighting the charming home he'd parked in front of. A small Craftsman-style cottage with a surprisingly wide doorway, thank God. Getting furniture through some of the older homes in the city took real work, and Evan always wondered how the people had gotten their furniture in to begin with because not everything came in pieces from IKEA.

He held the cold bottle against the back of his neck and studied the front walkway. The front door remained open, and he could see and hear the three women crying, laughing, and talking together.

Talk about weird.

"Yeah, they can be a bit much to take."

Evan spun around to see a lanky teenager approach. "Huh?"

The boy nodded to the home. "Chicks. Can't live with 'em, can't live without 'em."

"Wise words from one so young." Evan grinned.

The boy smiled back. "I live down the block, but this area is usually pretty loud. I think the women who live here had some kind of party pad. Lots of guys coming over to both places." The boy nodded to the home next door as well. "My mom told me to steer clear, but maybe now that the crazy lady is moving soon too, I can swing by more."

"Crazy lady?"

"Yeah." The boy peered at the doorway. "See that

woman with the long brown hair? Not Lila, the African
goddess—she makes everyone call her that. She's kind
of mean. I'm talking about the crazy one."

"Rachel?"

"Nah, she's just hyper. The other one is batshit nuts."

His angel. "Ah. How crazy, exactly?"

The boy sighed. "I'm not supposed to tell anyone
because my mom says it's bad to spread gossip, but
I'd be careful if I were you. She tried to stab some guy
who broke up with her a month ago. At least I saw
her screaming and waving a knife at some dude. Then
another guy calmed her down, and her wacko friends
stepped in." He shrugged. "I don't know, but it was a
mess. Had the cops down here."

Considering what Evan had just witnessed, the scene
didn't seem so far-fetched. "Thanks."

"Sure. Just like to help." The boy looked at the truck.
"Vets on the Go!? You some kind of animal doctor or
the military kind of vet?"

"Military kind. Our company employs veterans to
help people move."

The boy glanced around. "Just you?"

"Yeah. I'm just helping one of the ladies move out.
And she mostly only has smaller stuff. Though I'm supposed to have some help on the larger furniture. But her
boyfriend hasn't arrived yet."

"Well, if you need help, let me know. Got a phone?"

Evan frowned, wondering if this was part of a scam
to steal cell phones, which had become a citywide problem recently.

"Whoa." The boy raised his hands, appearing harmless. "Easy. I'm not gonna take it or anything. I'm just

gonna give you my number. You can text me if the boy-friend doesn't show."

Not that Evan would. He could just see the boy getting hurt and the company being liable for a lawsuit. "I'm good, kid. But thanks anyway."

"Your loss." The boy smiled to take the sting out of his words. More shouting from inside the house turned them both in that direction once more. "Well, I'd better leave. If my mom catches me around here, she'll ground me." The boy turned and tripped, and Evan caught him before he hit the pavement.

The kid quickly righted himself, a flush on his cheeks. "Nice catch."

"Thanks."

"Well, if you change your mind, I'm the red two-story four houses down. Good luck with the crazy ladies." The boy waved goodbye.

Evan waved then turned to the job at hand. He'd given the women enough time to get it together. He had a schedule to keep, and this house had to be moved *today*. Time to load the rest of the boxes from the bedroom.

Skirting the drama in the living room, he emptied what remained into the truck, leaving room for a few larger pieces, like an armoire, desk, chair, and bed. Rachel didn't actually have that much to move, so she'd only requested one mover and a smaller van.

He stared at the armoire and frowned, wondering how he might heft it out himself. Even with the dolly, it would take some doing. Fortunately, Rachel's boyfriend arrived, and they muscled it and the other big pieces into the truck. The women had vanished.

Though Evan would have liked to have seen the "bat-shit nuts" looker again, he thought it for the best that he didn't.

"Thanks, man." Will, Rachel's boyfriend, tried to tip him as he locked up the back of the truck.

"Nah. This is such a small move. It's no biggie." It wasn't as if Evan needed the money. And Will had been a big help; he had a good amount of strength behind those wide shoulders.

"Take it," Will insisted, and Evan reluctantly pocketed twenty bucks. "Trust me. You doing this saved me a lot of hassle." Will wiped a hand over his face and asked in a lower voice after glancing around, "Did she freak out?"

"Uh, yeah. You could say that. Wrapped herself around her friend Lila like a boa constrictor and was choking her over something she insisted on taking with her. Apparently they disagreed over the thing."

Will sighed. "That stupid trophy."

"I don't know what the fight was about. I just know it got a little ugly. Then some other woman arrived, got sucked into the group brawl, and they collapsed into tears. Then laughter, then tears again. It was scary."

Will laughed. "Better you than me."

Evan wanted to ask about the sexy kook, but he stopped himself. "I'd better get going. Got to get this unloaded before traffic gets too bad." Traffic was always bad in the city, but there were degrees of road rage Evan could handle.

"Gotcha. My brother's waiting for you at my place, and you can just unload it all into my garage. He'll help with the bigger things."

"Great." Evan reached into his back pocket to verify the address on his phone. And found it empty. "Shit." He double-checked the vehicle to make sure he hadn't left it inside. Nope. Not there either.

"What's up?"

"My phone's missing." The same phone he'd had in his back pocket when he'd helped the boy who'd tripped over his own feet.

That freakin' kid.

"What color is it? I'll check the house."

"It's a red iPhone." Evan went with him. Nothing turned up.

"Man. That sucks." Will shook his head.

Evan would strangle the boy when he found him. "You ever see a tall teenager hanging around here? Light-brown hair, brown—maybe hazel—eyes?" He frowned. "Good-looking kid, seems friendly. Lives a few blocks down in a red house."

Will shook his head. "Red house? Never seen him."

"Well, he apparently knows all about the crazy lady who lives next door."

"Kenzie?"

"I don't know, but I need my phone. My life is on that thing." At least he'd password-protected it.

"I know what you mean." Will shrugged. "Might as well see."

They walked next door and knocked at the back entrance. Will shouted to be heard over raised voices, "Yo, Kenzie. I got a problem."

The door opened, and Evan's angel opened the door…holding a knife.

Evan gaped. "Holy shit. The kid wasn't kidding."

She stared from them to the knife in her hand and blushed. "I was just making a salad. Cutting vegetables."

"With a *butcher knife*?" Evan had a tough time believing that. Then he met her striking gaze, that color in her eyes an intriguing mix of green and brown that seemed to change as he watched her. All thought left his mind.

Her blush intensified. "All the other knives are dirty..." She threw over her shoulder, "Since someone hasn't done the dishes like he was supposed to!"

No one answered, though Evan heard Rachel and Lila talking in another room.

Kenzie stepped back. "Come on in."

Evan knew it wasn't smart, but drawn to Kenzie and needing his phone, he followed her into the kitchen, Will behind him. Rachel and Lila joined them.

"Hey, babe." Rachel gave Will a kiss, the petite woman comfortably enfolded by the larger man hugging her so tightly.

"Lunatic." Will grinned. "Oh, and Lila. Didn't see you there, Lunatic Junior."

Lila flipped him off.

"What's going on?" Kenzie asked Will while studying Evan with an odd look on her face. He couldn't tell if it was fear, disdain, or curiosity because the expressions flashed by so fast and she refused to meet his gaze. Probably a good thing, considering a smart guy shouldn't want to be on this woman's radar. No matter how fine she might be.

He couldn't help noticing her long, slender legs or the curves under the thin cotton of her T-shirt. Or that she must be reacting to the cool breeze that suddenly blew through the room because her nipples had turned to hard little points.

Forcing himself to glance away before he embarrassed himself by leering, Evan noticed a surprisingly neat and orderly kitchen, something he wouldn't have considered of the emotionally unstable woman.

Will explained, "Someone took Evan's cell phone. Some teenager who lives a few doors down in the red house."

Rachel frowned. "Red house? That's Tom McCall's place, and he's eighty-four. His grandkids live in Vegas, and they're in their thirties."

Kenzie's eyes widened. "He did not."

Lila blew out a breath. "Oh boy."

"What's going on?" Evan had a schedule these people were destroying minute by minute. Though it was no hardship to covertly take in Kenzie's appeal, he had a job to do. "Look, I really have to get going. And I need my phone. So if you have any idea where this kid is, I'd appreciate you telling me."

Kenzie gripped the knife in her hand even tighter, Evan noticed. "Ah, maybe you should put down the weapon, Kenzie." Saying her name gave him an odd thrill, and he chalked it up to adrenaline.

"Knife? What?" She looked confused.

Lila answered, "I think he means the potential murder weapon in your hand. Put it down before you stab someone."

Will took a step back, and Rachel planted herself in front of him. "Not the face, Kenzie. You can stab him anywhere else, but I like my men pretty."

"Jesus, Rachel, it was one time and an accident," Kenzie snapped.

"That I'll never forget." Will showed Evan his fore-arm, where a large scar bisected his arm. "Almost took my arm off."

Lila and Rachel erupted into laughter.

"If you could see your face." Will grinned. "Kidding, man. This is from a car accident years ago. Kenzie only stabbed me with a paring knife when I got too close to her cucumbers."

Kenzie chimed in, looking furious, "That I was in the middle of cutting. *Daniel*," she shouted. "Get your ass down here!"

"We can never be truly sure it was an accident," Rachel added in a loud whisper.

Will nodded. "I still have the emotional scars."

Evan felt as if he'd fallen down the rabbit hole. "You people are giving me a headache. Do you or do you not know where my phone is?" He stared at the knife still clutched in Kenzie's hand.

She dropped it in the sink and stomped into the living room.

Everyone followed her, so Evan did as well. He couldn't help noticing a fairly neat and eclectically deco-rated house full of color. Rich hardwoods and handcrafted moldings gave the house an upscale feel, but the furniture appeared worn and comfortable. No sign of clutter except for some gaming magazines, a pair of large sneakers by the couch, and an opened bag of chips on the coffee table.

They continued up the stairs and passed two bed-rooms and a bathroom then paused at the doorway to the last bedroom down the hall.

"He's not here," Kenzie fumed. She spun around and moved so quickly she knocked into Evan.

He gripped her shoulders to stop her from moving *through* him. The contact startled him, once more shocking him into immobility.

Kenzie stared back, her lips full, rosy, and begging for a kiss.

Someone cleared her throat.

Evan immediately dropped his hands and stepped back. "Sorry." *Shit*. His voice sounded thick, gravelly.

"S-sure. I just… It's my…"

"Mom! I'm home," a familiar voice called from downstairs.

Evan stared into Kenzie's face, putting the pieces of the puzzle together. Now that he thought about it, the boy did look a lot like his mother. Yet their ages seemed a little close for her to be a mom. Unless she'd had him as a teenager herself.

Her eyes darkened. "*Mom?*" She stormed past Evan.

He noted the caution on the others' faces. "This can't be good."

Rachel sighed. "You got that right."

Then he followed the group once more, aware he was losing time, his focus, his phone…and wondered when crazy had become contagious.

Chapter 2

KENZIE SYKES RUSHED DOWNSTAIRS TO SEE HER "SON" smiling like an angel.

Ha. More like the devil in disguise. She must have been very bad in a past life to be saddled with such a little punk. One not so little anymore. The boy had surpassed her own five-seven frame years ago and now took great delight in looking down on her. Literally.

"What's up, Mom?"

"Look, bozo, we're not doing this again. Give him back his phone."

"What? Whose phone?"

"And quit calling me Mom." Her cheeks blazed, and she wondered why today of all days she had to meet Evan—Adonis personified.

When she'd spied the hottie moving Rachel's things, she'd peered through the window, catching every glimpse she could. Tall, muscular, great cheekbones. And that ass... She sighed.

So *of course* Daniel had to ruin it for her. Because no way sexy mover guy would want to go out with a woman surrounded by so much nuttiness. Not that she'd ask him out or anything, but a girl could dream.

First, he'd seen her break down with her best friends. Then her thief of a brother had stolen his cell phone. And Daniel had been doing so well lately.

Mr. Not-So-Innocent blinked. "Why are you so mad?"

She knew that look, the one that said Daniel had done *exactly* what he'd been accused of.

"Buddy, where's my phone?" Evan's deep voice sounded calm, but she knew he had to be furious.

"Buddy?" Daniel raised a brow and in a lofty tone added, "My name is—"

"Daniel. Thomas. Sykes," she answered for him in precise, clipped words. "You give the man his phone back *right now*."

"But Mom…"

"And quit calling me Mom!"

Behind her, Rachel snickered. Will coughed to stifle a laugh.

"It's not funny."

"It kind of is," Lila muttered.

"Hey, I don't have his phone. Frisk me." Daniel held up his hands.

Evan sighed. "I'm so behind." She noticed him glancing at the clock on the wall. "Look, kid, I have a job to do. Just give me the phone, and I'll let this go."

Daniel shrugged. "I saw it on the ground, so I picked it up and put it on the hood of your truck. If it's not there now, it's not my fault."

Evan stormed out the door, and Kenzie rushed past her brother with the others. She saw Evan reach for a phone on the hood of his truck.

Suddenly she felt bad, that she might have accused her brother of something he for once hadn't done.

"Told you," Daniel said.

Evan glared at him. "Neat trick. Especially because it was in my back pocket until you bumped into me. But whatever." He turned, speared Kenzie with a frustrated expression—*how is this my fault?*—then got into the truck and left.

"Well, that's a potential love slave down the drain," Lila said. "Too bad. He had a nice ass."

"True." Rachel and Lila bumped knuckles.

Will rolled his eyes.

Daniel gagged.

Kenzie turned and yanked her brother into the house. She didn't yell at him, just stared, giving him her guilt-heavy "I'm so disappointed" look because she knew how much he hated it.

He tried to outlast her, but as usual, he failed. "I hate my life!" He rushed away, heading upstairs. A door slammed.

She turned to see her friends pitying her. "Oh, screw off."

They started laughing, and she couldn't help a sigh. "That was terrible, wasn't it? That guy is never going to help any of us move ever again." Sad, but since a relationship didn't seem to be in the cards for her anyway, losing the moving god before she'd had a chance to screw up their relationship could only be expected.

"That poor guy. A twenty-buck tip wasn't enough." Will shook his head. "Daniel is such an ass." He chuckled. "I love that kid."

"Shh. Don't let him hear you," Rachel admonished and in a lower voice added, "not in front of Kenzie."

She wished her friends would discourage her brother from his illegal antics. But since Daniel had been banished from anything computer-related for the next few weeks until school, he'd taken to "acquiring" electronic devices from friends to reach the internet. Now, how to make him stop behaving like a jackass and turn back into the responsible teenager he'd once been, back before the evil entity called puberty had entered his body and turned him into a conniving monster?

"Still, too bad you didn't get a shot at being Moving Man's love slave," Lila said. "Because he was giving you the eye. We all saw it."

"I did," Will agreed.

"And he was sex-ee. With three e's." Trust Lila not to let it go.

"So *you* date him." Kenzie shrugged, pretending the potential loss didn't annoy her. Which told her she'd better start putting in overtime at the job. If she had time to think about dating, she had enough time to take on that pain-in-the-ass client she'd told herself not to take.

"I'm not into white guys." Lila grinned, lying through her teeth.

Even Rachel snorted at that.

Lila frowned. "And you, hush. You got your own white guy."

"I'm a quarter Hispanic, actually," Will cut in. "And my uncle is—"

"Besides, Moving Man wasn't looking at me like he wanted to do me. Which is too bad because I could teach him some things—"

Kenzie groaned. "Can we please not talk about him anymore? Why don't we focus on what's really bothering all of us?"

"The fact that no one has commented about how fine *I* am?" Will asked. "Because I'm much better looking than Evan."

Rachel nodded solemnly and patted Will on the arm.

"No, what's really bothering us is the fact that you're stealing Rachel," Lila answered. "I mean, I know you're not. Not really. You're all in love and stuff, but I'm going to miss my roomie." Lila teared up.

Damn it. Kenzie thought she'd expended enough tears for the day. "I'm going to miss you too."

"I feel it, right here." Rachel put a hand over her heart. "But we'll always be sisters from other misters."

"Oh my God." Will let out a loud breath. "We're just moving eight blocks over. You still work together all the time, and we're within walking distance."

"I feel it," Rachel repeated. "Not the same."

Will groaned. "I need a drink. I'll talk to you drama queens later." He gave Rachel a peck on the lips. "I've gotta get back to work. See you soon, Meryl Streep."

They watched him leave.

"Yep. Thrown over for a penis." Lila shook her head.

Daniel froze behind her, having come into the kitchen. He turned around and stomped back the way he'd come, throwing over his shoulder, "Have I mentioned how much I hate my life?"

COMING AUGUST 2019!

Acknowledgments

Thanks to the great folks at Sourcebooks for making this book possible. I couldn't do it without you!

About the Author

Caffeine addict, boy referee, and romance aficionado, *New York Times* and *USA Today* bestseller Marie Harte is a confessed bibliophile and devotee of action movies. Whether biking around town, hiking, or hanging at the local tea shop, she's constantly plotting to give everyone a happily ever after. Visit marieharte.com and fall in love.

BODY SHOP BAD BOYS

These rough-and-tumble mechanics
live fast and love hard.

**By Marie Harte, *New York Times* and
USA Today Bestselling Author**

Test Drive
Johnny Devlin's had his eye on
bartender Lara Valley for ages,
but she's rejected him more than
once. What will it take for him to
prove he's worth a second look?

Roadside Assistance
Foley Sanders might look like a
bad idea, but underneath, he's
all gentleman. What's a bad boy
to do when the goddess of his
dreams won't give him the time
of day?

Zero to Sixty

When the puppy who's stolen Sam Hamilton's heart runs into blond, beautiful Ivy Stephens, he can't help hoping she'll take in one more stray—him—for good.

Collision Course

Joey Reeves is determined to stay away from Lou Cortez, the ace mechanic with a reputation for irresistible charm. The last thing she needs is to tangle with the hottest guy in town...

"The chemistry sizzles from every page."

—Night Owl Reviews Top Pick for Test Drive

For more info about Sourcebooks's books and authors, visit:
sourcebooks.com

BAD BACHELOR

First in the Bad Bachelors series

If one more person mentions Bad Bachelors to Reed McMahon, someone's gonna get hurt. Reed is known as an "image fixer" but his womanizing ways have caught up with him. What he needs is a PR miracle of his own.

When Reed strolls into Darcy Greer's workplace offering to help save the struggling library, she isn't buying it. But as she reluctantly works with Reed, she realizes there's more to a man than his reputation. Maybe, just maybe, Bad Bachelor #1 is THE one for her.

"Sizzling, sexy, and so much fun!"

**—Sarah Morgan, *USA Today*
Bestselling Author**

For more Stefanie London, visit:
sourcebooks.com

PUPPY LOVE

No matter the job—no matter the need—these service dogs in training will always fall in love at first bark.

When Sophie Vasquez and her sisters dreamed up Puppy Promise—their service puppy training school—it was supposed to be her chance to bring some good into the world. But how can she expect to do anything when no one will take her seriously?

Enter Harrison Parks, a rough, gruff, take-no-bull wildlife firefighter in need of a diabetic alert service dog. He couldn't be a more unlikely fit for Sophie or Bubbles—the sweet Pomeranian she knows will be his perfect partner—but when Sophie insists he give them both a shot, something unexpected happens: he listens.

As it turns out, they all have more than enough room in their hearts for a little puppy love.

For more info about Sourcebooks's books and authors, visit:
sourcebooks.com

Also by Marie Harte